Praise for

New York Times and *USA Today* Bestselling Author

Diane Capri

"Full of thrills and tension, but smart and human, too. Kim Otto is a great, great character. I love her."
Lee Child, *#1 World Wide Bestselling Author of Jack Reacher Thrillers*

"[A] welcome surprise… [W]orks from the first page to 'The End'."
Larry King

"Swift pacing and ongoing suspense are always present… [L]ikable protagonist who uses her political connections for a good cause…Readers should eagerly anticipate the next [book]."
Top Pick, Romantic Times

"…offers tense legal drama with courtroom overtones, twisty plot, and loads of Florida atmosphere. Recommended."
Library Journal

"[A] fast-paced legal thriller…energetic prose…an appealing heroine…clever and capable supporting cast…[that will] keep readers waiting for the next [book]."
Publishers Weekly

"Expertise shines on every page."
Margaret Maron, Edgar, Anthony, Agatha and Macavity Award-Winning MWA Grand Master

DEAD LOCK

by DIANE CAPRI

Published by: AugustBooks
http://www.AugustBooks.com

ISBN: 978-1-962769-70-9

Original cover design by: Cory Clubb

Dead Lock is a work of fiction. Names, characters, places, and incidents either are the product of the author's imagination or are used fictitiously, and any resemblance to actual persons, living or dead, business establishments, events, or locales is entirely coincidental.

Published in the United States of America.

Visit the author website:
http://www.DianeCapri.com

ALSO BY DIANE CAPRI

The Hunt for Jack Reacher Series

(in publication order with Lee Child source books in parentheses)

Don't Know Jack • (The Killing Floor)

Jack in a Box (*novella*)

Jack and Kill (*novella*)

Get Back Jack • (Bad Luck & Trouble)

Jack in the Green (*novella*)

Jack and Joe • (The Enemy)

Deep Cover Jack • (Persuader)

Jack the Reaper • (The Hard Way)

Black Jack • (Running Blind/The Visitor)

Ten Two Jack • (The Midnight Line)

Jack of Spades • (Past Tense)

Prepper Jack • (Die Trying)

Full Metal Jack • (The Affair)

Jack Frost • (61 Hours)

Jack of Hearts • (Worth Dying For)

Straight Jack • (A Wanted Man)

Jack Knife • (Never Go Back)

Lone Star Jack • (Echo Burning)

Bulletproof Jack • (Make Me)

Bet On Jack • (Nothing to Lose)

Jack on a Wire • (Tripwire)

Tracking Jack • (Gone Tomorrow)

Jack Rabbit • (Night School)

Shadow Jack • (Blue Moon)

The Michael Flint Series:

Blood Trails

Trace Evidence

Ground Truth

Hard Money

Dead Lock

Cold Impact

The Jess Kimball Thrillers Series
Fatal Distraction
Fatal Demand
Fatal Error
Fatal Fall
Fatal Game
Fatal Bond
Fatal Enemy (*novella*)
Fatal Edge (*novella*)
Fatal Past (*novella*)
Fatal Dawn
Fatal Shot

The Hunt for Justice Series
Due Justice
Twisted Justice
Secret Justice
Wasted Justice
Raw Justice
Mistaken Justice (*novella*)
Cold Justice (*novella*)
False Justice (*novella*)
Fair Justice (*novella*)
True Justice (*novella*)
Night Justice

The Park Hotel Mysteries Series
Reservation with Death
Early Check Out
Room with a Clue
Late Arrival

Short Reads Collections
Hit the Road Jack
Justice Is Served
Fatal Action

CAST OF CHARACTERS

Michael Flint
Kathryn (Katie) Scarlett
Alonzo Drake
Madeline (Maddy) Scarlett
Carlos Gaspar
Harry Fisher
Vivian Fisher
Jason Fisher
Bruce Fisher
Dylan Michael Fisher
Kevin William Fisher
Maureen Laura Fisher
Elizabeth (Lizzy) Pace
Devon Cole
Frankie Tantanella
Pauline Craig
Ralph Milliken
and
Kim Otto

For the readers who have supported me and enjoyed my books and asked for more.

I couldn't do this without you.

Thank you.

DEAD
LOCK

"It is easier to forgive an enemy than to forgive a friend."

— *William Blake*

CHAPTER 1

Off the coast of New Zealand

EVENTS UNFOLDED PRECISELY AS Michael Flint had planned.

The South Pacific Ocean's sliver of new moon was barely visible through the heavy clouds. The line between sky and sea lay beyond his vision, and without the tiny red glow from his altitude and direction indicator Flint might have lost track of which way was up.

A third of a mile from his target, he eased back the throttle on his dinghy and killed the engine. In normal circumstances, he would never think of traveling so far in such a small craft at night, but his circumstances never seemed to be normal.

In the darkness, the red and white navigation lights on the superyacht were plainly visible.

"We should paddle the rest of the way in," Craig said.

Flint's client had once been the chef aboard *Insatiable*. Tall, sturdy, and competent Cynthia Craig was no stranger to hard work.

They sat on either side of the boat, silently easing the paddles in and out of the water, rowing in unison. Flint had every confidence in her abilities. And her determination.

Two years earlier, her father-in-law, billionaire Rupert Tulane, died. He'd lived a life overflowing with every luxury and died quietly in his sleep on board his beloved superyacht, *Insatiable*. Two hundred and forty feet, six decks, and twelve cabins impressed even those who traveled in his extremely wealthy, powerful circle.

A congenial man who liked his food, Tulane had teased Craig that one day she would own *Insatiable*. It had been a standing joke between them.

"Not long now," he would say with a grin.

Or, "Mine yet?" she would ask with a wink.

When he passed away, Rupert's son, Leo, had immediately sacked Craig. She wasn't surprised. Her replacement looked good in a skimpy bikini, and Leo worked hard at his party-boy image.

Six months afterward, she'd received an anonymous email claiming she'd been included in Rupert's will. Eight more months later, her lawyer finally uncovered the truth.

Rupert Tulane had indeed bequeathed *Insatiable* to her.

She couldn't afford to operate the yacht, but a $150 million gift was nothing to walk away from.

A year later, Leo Tulane's lawyers were still stalling. Which was when she searched for alternatives to collect what was rightfully hers. She found Flint.

It took Flint less than twenty-four hours to locate *Insatiable* and another two weeks to unravel the problem. Leo had been left a fortune, of course. But it was a tiny fraction of his father's total wealth. So Leo had simply taken off in the yacht and left his lawyers to handle the fallout.

Leo kept the ship in international waters off New Zealand to avoid trouble with the authorities over his wild, often drug-fueled, parties. Which also made taking possession of the yacht a difficult proposition.

Flint was comfortable with impossible odds. Even if it meant rowing a small boat in the cold dark ocean miles from the shore.

Around three hundred yards from the yacht, they stopped rowing.

Craig spoke into a short-range radio aimed to reach her contact on *Insatiable*. "Hey, Stranger."

They waited for a reply. The tiny boat rocked on a gentle swell. With a storm approaching from the east, the ocean would be rougher tomorrow. *Insatiable* remained rock steady, stabilized by the latest technology. Which Flint planned to put to good use.

After exactly sixty seconds, Craig repeated the radio message. This time a reply came immediately.

"Let's party," a man replied.

Flint grinned in the dark. The contact on the boat had two possible replies. One phrase if they needed to abort. But "Let's party" meant they were clear to board.

A moment later, the rear navigation lights on *Insatiable*'s port side blinked out. Flint and Craig resumed silent paddling.

Insatiable's hull towered above the dinghy as a deep blackness against the faint reflective clouds. They stopped paddling a few feet from the ship. Directly above their position, a tiny flashlight blinked twice.

A moment later, a rope descended. Flint ran his hand along the first few feet of the rope to confirm it had been knotted at two-foot intervals to make climbing easier. Satisfied, he held the rope out to Craig.

"Ready?" he whispered.

She took the rope. "Positive. Board now. Dump everyone off tomorrow. Just be back here as planned."

"Ten a.m. On the dot," Flint replied.

She gripped the rope and started to climb. He worried about letting her go alone. He would have chosen another plan, but there was no time. It might be months before *Insatiable* would present itself in a suitable location again.

He lost sight of Craig as she climbed the rope. A few moments later the flashlight blinked again. He tied the rope around the handle of a large plastic container. A hundred pounds of dead weight was hard to lift, but Craig's work with the rope took up the slack and it ascended smoothly. He caught sight of the container go up and over the gunwale.

The flashlight blinked one last time, and Flint turned away from the yacht and paddled. Smooth strokes. Carefully. Quietly. Tomorrow, when he returned to *Insatiable*, stealth wouldn't be required.

Six hours later, Flint stood at the wheel of *Sand Dollar*, a fifty-foot charter sport fishing boat with a large open deck large enough for thirty people or more behind the wheelhouse. He navigated over the white caps that rocked the boat left and right.

The weather had turned at sunrise. The approaching storm threatened to engulf everything in its path. Flint had been lucky last night. These five-foot rolling swells would have aborted their earlier approach to *Insatiable*.

Sand Dollar's engine note rose and fell with a repetitive cadence in response to the swells. If he'd had options, Flint would have turned into the waves to blunt the rolling, but he had no better choices.

He'd departed idyllic Russell on the long narrow peninsula in the Bay of Islands a couple of hours earlier. Running due west, he spotted *Insatiable* at about three miles. This time he made no attempt to hide his intention, keeping the prow of his boat aimed at the boarding steps on the port side.

Insatiable was drifting free, not underway. Despite the waves, the rear swim deck had been lowered. A group of people had gathered on the main deck around the boarding steps. Using binoculars, Flint identified Leo in the center of a group of bikini-clad girls.

More importantly, two large men stood to the right of the group, Saul and Chad, Leo's personal security. Both had muscles bulging under tight T-shirts and rap sheets dating back decades. One spoke into a handheld radio, and the other had binoculars trained on Flint.

Flint smiled. Partly to irritate the thug, but mainly because he was getting all the attention he hoped for.

Two hundred feet from *Insatiable*, Flint launched a small drone. Purchased two days earlier, he'd sprayed it with paint aptly named sky blue. Steering the device to three hundred feet in the air, he pressed a button on the remote control to lock the camera on Leo.

The loud buzz of the drone's four propellors would be audible on the yacht.

From Flint's research, Leo's security were muscle men not known for brains or marksmanship. Which meant the drone should survive the next fifteen minutes and that was all he needed.

Flint motored the final distance up to the yacht, stopping thirty feet from the hull, the prow of his boat pointed at the boarding steps. Someone activated a switch, and the boarding steps rose to the horizontal and recessed themselves into the superstructure.

Leo leaned against the deck's railing, twenty-five feet above Flint, sneering down.

One of the guards produced an automatic weapon. The cluster of girls drew back a step.

Leo said something inaudible, and they returned, closer to him. He wrapped an arm around a dark-haired girl's waist with the sneer still firmly fixed on his face.

Flint picked up a bullhorn. "Leo Tulane."

Leo kept up his sneer, silent.

"Are you Leo Tulane?" Flint repeated, raising the volume on his bullhorn.

One of the guards handed Leo a bullhorn. The yacht rocked as a monstrous wave passed through and Leo grabbed hold of the girl to avoid falling while the boat rolled.

Which was when Flint realized Leo was under the influence of alcohol or drugs. Leo pulled the girl back and held her tight against him as he leaned forward to speak through the bullhorn. "Who's asking?"

"It's a simple enough question," Flint replied. "Seems to be taxing you, though."

Leo laughed. The gaggle of girls laughed with him. Then he released the brunette and leaned over the railing. Flint resisted the temptation to grin as the man struggled to coordinate pressing the talk button on his bullhorn while shouting obscenities.

One of the girls stepped away from the group and headed toward the ship's enormous main deck lounge. Not what Flint wanted, he needed as many people in one place as he could muster.

"Your audience doesn't care what you think either," Flint pointed to the departing girl.

Leo barked instructions in the girl's direction. She turned, swaying for a moment before forcing a smile and stumbling back to the group.

Flint held up a two-foot-long cardboard tube sealed on both ends. "Consider yourself served."

He hurled the tube high over the yacht's railings. The tube bounced twice on the polished wood deck before rolling to a stop. One of the guards handed it to Leo.

Leo laughed as he waved the canister in front of the girls. He turned to Flint as he held the tube over the railings intending to drop it into the ocean.

"You see that?" Flint gestured toward the drone. "Real-time streaming video delivered to a server in the US. Remarkably clear video and audio."

Leo waved the tube in the air as if performing for the camera. "Here's what Leo Tulane thinks of your papers."

He let go and the canister hit the water with a small splash. It bobbed along the waves.

"Oh look. Now's your chance." Leo mimed swimming. "Dive in. Grab your precious papers."

The waves pushed the tube against *Insatiable's* hull before drifting aft. Leo pointed to the tube.

"Come on! Let's see hero man rush to save his precious papers." Laughter broke out among his entourage. One of the guards pulled a large gun and unleashed a storm of shots at the tube. One went through the center, pushing the tube along the waves as it sank.

Leo placed his hands over his heart, pretending to be hurt as the tube disappeared.

Flint kept a straight face, even though he wanted to smile. Never before had yesterday's newspaper drawn such attention. Leo would likely have been confused if he had opened the cylinder. His guards, however, should have recognized the tube for what it was. A decoy. A distraction. A prop in an elaborate con.

On the edge of his peripheral vision, Flint saw Craig wave. She held up both hands, fists clenched. A simple yet unmistakable symbol. In a matter of minutes, *Insatiable* would be hers.

"What's that?" Flint pointed to wisps of smoke emerging from the doorway of the main deck lounge.

Leo scoffed without turning around. "How stupid do you think I am?"

"Dim as a broken bulb but take a look." Flint shook his hand, still pointing to the main deck lounge.

"Yeah, yeah."

"Suit yourself."

CHAPTER 2

SMOKE FLOATED THROUGH THE open door. Moments later, it positively poured from a deck hatchway behind Leo and his entourage.

Perhaps they smelled smoke or maybe someone saw it, but however the group realized, they turned as one. Screams and shouts sounded. The guards ran into the main deck lounge, returning moments later with inadequate fire extinguishers.

The rest of the group shuffled along the railing away from the superstructure and toward the back of the ship.

An alarm sounded, followed by an artificial voice bellowing loudly from the intercom. "Danger. Danger. Engine room fire. Engine room fire."

Flames burst from a hatchway along the walking path outside the main lounge. Flint knew another such staged conflagration had also been started on the far side of the boat, constraining Leo and his friends to the rear of the ship.

Chad and Saul jumped into action. They emptied fire extinguishers into the smoke and hurled them down the hatchway and into the staged flames.

Several below deck workers appeared wearing dirty jeans and T-shirts. In moments, they dragged a firehose from a storage container.

The yacht lurched. The port side dropped six inches in one swift movement when the port side ballast filled as fast as possible. Flint grinned. Craig had briefed the below deck crew well.

Leo and his entourage stumbled forward, coughing and grabbing for the railings. In the rush, a brunette, toppled over the edge and dangled above the water while clinging to the railing. Two of her friends grabbed her wrists while she screamed.

The port side of the ship continued to inch down. In moments, the deck sloped at least twelve degrees. A plume of thick black smoke burst from the lounge and the flames from the deck hatchway continued unabated.

The tilt of the ship meant the girl's feet no longer contacted the sloping hull. She kicked wildly, as her screams moved up a notch.

Flint eased his boat alongside *Insatiable*. Waves bumped the small craft against the big ship's hull, but Flint kept close and under the dangling girl. He wouldn't let her drown and if she went in the water, the height of the waves would complicate her rescue.

Flint abandoned the helm to help the girl. He hurried across the craft to stand under her, arms out.

"Jump!"

She continued to scream.

"Jump! Jump!"

The girl glanced down and her screams momentarily halted.

Flint waved his arms, indicating he would catch her. "Jump!"

Waves pounded the two boats together, the bumpers causing them to bounce apart a couple of feet each time. Flint debated returning to the helm to reposition, but the girl finally half swung, half pushed herself from the yacht and let go.

Her long hair trailed behind her as she fell. Flint leaned out, arms at full stretch and caught the girl in the crook of his elbows and pulled her close. He swung her over the boat and deposited her on her feet. She clung to his arms, shaking. Her mouth hung open and her glazed eyes didn't blink.

Flint's boat rocked as waves pounded it against the bigger ship's hull.

"Sit," he said, wriggling from the girl's grasp and placing her hands on the back of a seat. She looked shocked as he returned to the helm and powered *Sand Dollar* away from danger. After a moment, she sank onto the seat, still dazed.

Smoke poured from *Insatiable's* doorways. Flames around the deck hatch continued unabated.

The yacht had developed a considerable lean, more than ten degrees. Hopefully, the below deck crew would cease filling the port ballast tank.

The slope bunched the passengers up at the railings, pushing against each other. Crew members struggled to move across the sloping deck, grabbing one handhold after another. Judging by their cries, they had not been able to activate the fire hoses. The captain shouted orders with a thick Scottish accent through a Tannoy system, but the crew didn't seem to take much notice.

Waves rocked *Insatiable*. Leo clung to the railing, as did many of his passengers. The big ship shuddered with each rise and fall, as if the gyro stabilization had ceased to function, which Flint knew was perfectly true. Life aboard the big ship would feel seriously uncomfortable at this point.

Now they were in the danger zone. Flint was no murderer. The rate the ship had developed a list meant they only had minutes before the lean would be uncontrollable, and the ship would capsize.

With the bullhorn, he shouted to the passengers to move to the rear.

"You did this!" Leo yelled back through his bullhorn.

"Who, me?" said Flint, gesturing to *Sand Dollar* as if the idea were preposterous.

"You're going to pay for this!"

The rescued brunette shouted for Emma to jump off *Insatiable*. One girl in the entourage, presumably Emma, climbed the railings, looked down and shook her head.

The brunette pleaded with her to jump, but Emma stepped down and joined the rest of Leo's guests staggering along the deck toward the rear.

Saul stumbled around the group and caught up with Leo. The pair talked a moment before Leo gestured to Flint. *Insatiable* rolled with the waves, the entourage on deck squealing as they clung on for dear life. Saul pushed away from the group and pulled out what looked like an H&K MP5, a compact, lightweight, and highly reliable submachine gun. In close combat, it could be devastating.

Flint slammed the throttle lever forward and *Sand Dollar*'s engine roared. The rear of the boat dug in as the bow lifted. The big engine shoved the craft forward as if hit by a tsunami. The brunette screamed, falling backward in the boat.

The H&K bucked in Saul's hands, the sound of its shots lost under the engine roar. The only saving grace Flint could see was that the gun was the short barrel variety, not as good for shooting a moving target.

Flint curved *Sand Dollar* around in a wide arc. Saul stopped firing. It seemed unlikely he would be out of ammunition, so Flint kept at least a couple of hundred feet away and reduced the engine power to keep the boat a more difficult target moving over the waves.

Insatiable listed badly. The lower deck portholes were submerged, and spray from the waves broke over the main deck. The crew appeared to be struggling to launch a small bright yellow boat from the rear swim deck. Leo and his entourage arrived at the stern, staggering down the steps from the main deck. Saul abandoned his attack and made his way aft, regularly looking sideways at Flint.

Flint drove *Sand Dollar* around the front of *Insatiable* and approached the rear on the starboard side. Tilted upward, it made it more difficult for anyone to take pot shots at him.

Using his bullhorn, Flint hailed Leo. "Your ship is sinking. I have enough space for your passengers and crew. Tell your goons to knock it off."

Leo gesticulated and shouted something inaudible over the noise of sea and engines, his bullhorn apparently lost.

One of the crew slipped off the swim deck. The remaining crew members frantically threw ropes and a life preserver ring at the man in the water. He disappeared in and out of view in the four- to five-foot waves.

Flint blipped the throttle to move his boat closer, careful not to run over the crewman. The man's face appeared over a wave. He swam hard for *Sand Dollar*. Without leaving the helm, Flint threw the man a life preserver attached to a rope. Once the man had it in his hands, Flint pulled him back in. He climbed into the boat, panting. He wriggled out of the ring and looked up, relief written all over his face.

Leo shook one of the crew, a stocky, muscular man with a buzz cut, and shoved him back toward the yellow boat. The man finished untying the boat and slid it over the edge of the swim deck. Leo shoved him aside and crouched as if preparing to jump ship. The boat lurched on a wave and the side caught under the swim deck. A second wave rolled the yellow boat. The strain ripped the mooring rope from a bollard, and the yellow boat curled away from *Insatiable*.

Leo leaned forward but didn't jump. He turned and swung a broad roundhouse punch at the crewman's head. The man twisted, deflecting the blow with his shoulder, and grabbed Leo's forearm. With one push he shoved him to the side. Leo stumbled back and fell overboard.

As Leo screamed and thrashed, the waves pushed him away from *Insatiable*. In moments, he was closer to *Sand Dollar* than *Insatiable*. Flint lobbed the life preserver in his direction. Leo caught it on the first throw, but Flint only pulled it in until Leo reached the hull. Flint tied the rope around a cleat as Leo struggled unsuccessfully to pull himself up over the side.

"Tell your goons to drop their weapons!" yelled Flint.

Leo continued to struggle. Flint blipped the throttle, lurching the boat forward, dragging Leo and no doubt straining his muscles to the limit. Leo screamed. Flint repeated his demand.

Leo shouted something unintelligible, and Saul and Chad made a show of laying down their machine pistols. Probably not their only weapons, but better than nothing. Flint pulled Leo onto the boat and left him heaving and coughing on the floor.

Navigating a large circle, Flint approached the swim deck with *Sand Dollar*'s prow into the waves. It didn't stop the rocking and rolling, but it was better than nothing.

The crewman he'd rescued threw a rope to his colleagues, who looped it around a bollard. They pulled *Sand Dollar* alongside *Insatiable*, the hulls rubbing and grinding as the waves rocked the pair.

A blonde from the entourage stood on the edge of the swim deck, head bobbing up and down with the waves, apparently timing her jump. One of the people behind pushed her and in one stumbling step she landed on *Sand Dollar*. Spurred by her success, the rest of the group rushed over. Flint used the bullhorn to tell them to spread out. The last thing he needed was the boat unevenly loaded.

The crew followed the guests. Eight of them. Not the entire crew for a ship of *Insatiable*'s size, but enough to satisfy any questions that might arise in Leo's feeble mind. The last to step onto *Sand Dollar* were Saul and Chad. Flint had the feeling it was nothing to do with chivalry.

Weighed down, occasional waves sloshed over *Sand Dollar*'s gunwale. Several of the deck hands got busy with a couple of buckets.

At Flint's urging, the first crew member he'd rescued took the helm. Flint pushed his way through the crowd to Saul at the rear. "Anymore?"

"Don't care." Saul pulled an MP5 from his Hawaiian shirt. "Just go."

Flint pointed upward. His drone still hung in the air, camera staring down. "You're going to shoot me? On livestream?"

The entourage shuffled back, silent.

Saul adjusted his grip on the weapon.

Leo pushed his way through the entourage. "We're in charge now, pal." He looked at Saul. "Throw him overboard. Make it look like an accident."

Saul laughed, raised his gun and turned toward the drone. "Or we could do this." He fired, the gun bucking and hot shells falling to the floor.

Flint slammed a punch into Saul's kidneys while reaching for the gun. Saul curled sideways, groaning. Flint kicked the back of his knee, and the man went down as Flint pried the gun free.

Chad leaped forward, his weapon ready.

"Don't even," said Flint, whipping Saul's gun toward Leo.

No one spoke.

Chad shuffled.

Leo's wide eyes took in the automatic weapon in his face.

"Drop it," Flint said to Chad.

Chad didn't move.

Flint punched the barrel of the gun against Leo's forehead. Leo took a half step back, blubbering.

"Even if your pet thug thinks he could get a shot off, you won't survive," Flint advised.

CHAPTER 3

LEO PANTED, CLOSE TO hyperventilating. It seemed to take an eternity for him to get himself under control and say, "Drop it. Drop it now."

Chad moved slowly. Reluctant. He lowered his gun, placing it on a tackle box. Flint gestured for him to step back and he did.

Saul rolled onto his knees.

Flint waved his gun at Leo. "Take him up front."

The pair moved away, Leo warily glancing backward at the gun. Flint waited until he had a clear space around him to release the rope tying *Sand Dollar* to *Insatiable*.

Keeping his gun on Leo, Flint looped the rope around his forearm. With his free hand, he lifted a small hatch, roughly cut in the molded shell of the boat's rear seats. The crewman at the helm stared backward. Flint reached into the hatch opening, his fingers finding a plastic handle.

Chad leaped forward.

Flint pulled on the handle. Below deck, two wedges dropped into place, locking the rudder mechanism in the straight-ahead position. An electromagnetic device jammed the throttle levers on full power. The engine roared, and the boat lurched forward, the rear digging in as the propellor gained traction.

Chad found his gun.

As the rope around Flint's arm reached its full length, he put one foot on the rear seat.

Chad raised the weapon.

Flint flew from the back of the boat. His grip had remained secure on the rope tied to *Insatiable*, and *Sand Dollar* whipped away from under him. He descended into the water as gunfire rang out.

With swift strokes, he pushed himself below the waves and under the rear of *Insatiable*. Occasional lines of white bubbles traced the path of bullets in a wild arc around him.

It only took moments for the beat and throb of *Sand Dollar's* propeller to fade, along with the frothy path it churned. He clicked the MP5's selector to safe and, on the count of sixty, rose to the surface.

The waves tossed him back and forth. He looped the MP5's strap over his head and swam hard for the rear of the ship. Craig knelt on the swim deck, one arm wrapped around a bollard to stop her sliding with the tilt of the ship, and the other stretched out to him. He timed his grab for her hand with a rising wave that practically lifted him onto the swim deck.

Behind her on the main deck, two crew members extinguished the fire in the hatchway with a hose, the same hose that had previously been non-functional.

"The crew agreed to the plan?" said Flint.

Craig nodded. "Leo gets zero points for popularity."

"Excellent."

Flint felt a low throb from the engines and the propellor churned the sea behind the boat. They were moving. Slowly.

"Captain chose five people to run the ship. The rest of the crew boarded your boat to make sure the passengers left," she said.

"Any more of Leo's thugs?"

"Just the two."

Thick smoke still poured from the main lounge, the result of the smoke bombs they had smuggled aboard the previous night. The ship rocked on a wave. "The ballast?" he said.

"There's some problem with the electrics."

"We have to get the ship back upright."

"They're on it. Three men. Manually pumping the tanks. But it's slow, and we don't have long."

Flint frowned.

She pointed out to sea. Flint exhaled at the sight of *Sand Dollar*, sideways on. "Turning," he said. "Must have unlocked the rudder."

"We can move," she said. "But the captain doesn't want to steer until the ship's balanced, and the electrics are back. One wrong wave and the ship could roll."

"Slow is better than nothing, I guess."

Flint levered himself onto his feet. *Sand Dollar* was mid-turn. He watched it a moment until he realized Saul was leaning over the side, a rope trailing in the water. "They're using a bucket for drag. It'll turn them around eventually. Where's the helm?"

Craig pointed forward and up.

"Let's go."

She led the way up the main deck and past the hatch where the fire had been set. The expensive looking wooden planks were charred. In the hatchway, the steps were gone, and the metal handrail was scorched. Bending down, he could see the conflagration had been confined close to the hatch, the rest of the corridor was untouched by the flames. A good trick by the crew.

They skirted around the main lounge, up a level to the bridge deck, through an exercise room and onto the bridge.

A lone man sat at the helm, the glass panel displays around him dark. He stared out the windshield, not breaking his vigil when Flint entered the room.

"Flyin' damn close to tha' wind, we are," he said, with a thick Scottish accent. "No steerin' and twelve degrees o' list in a swell like this." To prove his point, a wave struck the boat at an angle, sending water and spray up over the port side deck. The ship rocked. "Be gettin' worse, too," he muttered, tapping a mechanical barometer on the wall beside him. "Storm'll be here in an hour."

"Can you point the nose into the waves?" said Flint.

"Tha' be the prow, an' nay, can't be steerin' till we get the electrics back."

"Leo is on his way back."

The captain turned to show his name, Peabody, visible on the breast pocket of his jacket. "Is he now," he said.

"Anything to repel pirates?"

"Shotgun, pistol, an' two automatics." Peabody jerked a thumb toward a cabinet on the wall. "Leo's men took 'em a while ago."

Flint held up his gun. "I believe I have got one of them back."

The captain grunted.

Flint checked the magazine. Out of thirty rounds, it only had seven shots left. Saul had used the rest in his futile attempt to shoot down the drone.

"Firehose be the only thing now," said the captain.

"Spear gun?" said Flint, not exactly sure how he'd used it when he didn't want to injure bystanders.

"Ah dinnae ken."

Flint frowned at the man's language.

"He doesn't know," Craig translated.

Peabody grunted his agreement.

Flint crossed the width of the ship to look from the port window. *Sand Dollar* had turned ahead of *Insatiable*. That allowed them a good chance of an intercept. Perhaps Leo's men weren't entirely dumb after all. The small boat pounded over the waves, creating giant plumes of spray. The people on board must have been holding on for dear life.

"Going fast," Peabody, arriving beside Flint.

"I wedged the throttle wide open."

"So tha' lass said."

"They're steering using drag."

The captain produced a set of binoculars, adjusted them for focus and followed the boat a moment. "An' they have me automatics."

"I have one."

"Well they've found another."

"MP5s?"

"Aye. An' they be on a direct path." The captain handed over the binoculars. "Two minutes. At tha' most."

Flint studied the approaching boat. Saul had indeed found another gun. That probably meant they had plenty of ammunition as well. Flint's seven shots weren't going to be a lot of use. Especially as he didn't want to hurt any of the rest of the entourage.

"They're aiming for where the ship will be," he said.

"Aye. Figured out we're movin'."

"We need to go faster."

"Nae. We're pushing the limit now."

Flint raised his eyebrows. "Another knot?"

The captain muttered something then walked back to the helm and inched the throttle forward. Whatever difference it made to the noise from the engine was muted long before it reached its well-heeled owners, but Flint sensed a tiny acceleration.

"The galley," Flint said to Craig.

Her eyebrows squeezed down, a look of shock on her face. "Food?"

"Soap."

She broke out of her trance and led him down three floors, sliding down ladders between each floor in a direct route from the rear of the bridge. She landed on each floor with an easy gait, knees bending to absorb the impact and moving for the next ladder without a pause. The engine noise grew louder. Voices could be heard shouting.

Two corridors later, they entered a storeroom with rows of shelves stacked with provisions. A metal railing kept the contents from falling off in rough seas. Craig found the cleaning products on the first try.

Flint said, "The swim deck is the only place for them to board, right?"

She nodded. "Dockside gangplank is on the main deck, and the boarding steps are pulled up."

"Good. Find a bucket."

She frowned a moment before running off. Flint unscrewed the tops from a half dozen industrial-size bottles of washing up liquid before she returned with two five-gallon buckets. They filled both buckets, squeezing the plastic bottles to transfer the liquid as fast as possible.

She led him back through the ship, up one floor, and out of a door on the port side to the rear of the main lounge. *Sand Dollar* was a hundred yards away, closing fast. The increase in *Insatiable*'s speed hadn't been enough. Leo would intercept them at the rear of *Insatiable*. The swim deck. Exactly what Flint didn't want.

He dropped to the deck as Saul started firing. Craig did the same. The shots went wild.

"Get back inside," he said, reaching for her bucket.

"No," she said. "They stole this from me, and I'll be damned if they're going to get it back." Bent double, she hustled for the safety of the garaging superstructure where jet skis were stored.

Flint followed on her heels. The gunfire stopped. He hefted his bucket and scrabbled around the garage.

The noise of *Sand Dollar*'s engine grew rapidly. Saul and Chad were on the gunwale, the boat only fifty feet away, readying to jump.

Flint briefly considered using the H&K, but with the bulk of the entourage behind the thugs, there was no clear shot that wouldn't endanger innocent lives.

The rope he'd used to pull him from *Sand Dollar* trailed in *Insatiable*'s wake, twisting and flipping in some wild snake dance. He watched and waited for it to buck up, closer.

One of the thugs fired. The sharp noise grabbed Flint's attention even though the bullet passed harmlessly overhead.

The far end of the rope whipped onto the swim deck. He grabbed it. The fibers stung as they slapped his hands and burned as he gripped tight to tame its energy and pull it in. It trailed across the rear swim deck, from the bollard on the port side to him on the starboard.

Leo had used drag to turn *Sand Dollar* around, but he wasn't the only who could use that trick.

Flint threw the liquid soap across the swim deck, hitting the transom and steps. Bubbles burst into life in the ship's wake. He repeated his throws, coating the entire rear of the ship in the clear liquid.

More shots sounded. One bounced off the ship to his left, leaving a long dark scar on the brilliant white plastic. *Sand Dollar* was twenty feet away. He rolled back, gripping the end of the rope tight as he slid down the superstructure to Craig.

He pointed to the steps on either side of the garage, the only pathways from the swim deck to the rest of the ship. While she emptied her soap over each side, he looped the rope around the handle of his bucket, tucking the free end under itself for a clove hitch, and pulled tight.

She dived to safety just as *Sand Dollar* hit the rear of *Insatiable*. It was a glancing impact, scraping the hulls together. Screams and shouts filled the air. The entourage no doubt traumatized by the switch from party to open combat. But there was one word that stood out, one word he was waiting to hear. "Go!" Saul shouted.

Shouts turned to gasps from the entourage.

Flint felt more than heard the thump of boots on the swim deck, followed by scrabbling. Shouts and curses filled the air.

Sand Dollar barreled past. The entourage huddled midships and Leo on the closest edge, shouting and gesticulating. To Flint's relief, neither Saul nor Chad had remained aboard, they were on *Insatiable*'s swim deck behind the superstructure, slipping and sliding.

Several shots sounded. Flint couldn't see either of the attackers, so they were firing blind, maybe accidentally as they struggled to stay upright.

Sand Dollar continued on its way, leaving the sea behind clear. He pulled the rope tight, from the bollard on the port side to him on the starboard before throwing the bucket, underarm, a looping shot. It cleared the superstructure and the railings to fall into the foaming sea behind *Insatiable*.

The bucket filled with water in an instant, scooping everything in its path. It stayed still while *Insatiable* continued on its way. The motion snapped the rope tight before sweeping it across the swim deck at knee height. Saul and Chad cried out. Flint peered around the garage in time to see them slap face down on the swim deck and slither overboard, guns lost and splashing in the foamy wake.

Flint threw two life preservers. The men swam hard for them. Once back in the bridge, he'd inform the coast guard. And the police.

Craig stood and stared at the two men. "An irresistible force and slippery objects."

She turned her stare to Flint. "You know what I'm going to say, don't you?"

Flint shook his head.

"You sure clean up good," she said with a grin.

Flint groaned.

In the distance, *Sand Dollar* slowed and turned. The crew would head back to the harbor. They'd be given tickets and re-board *Insatiable* at the port. They'd no doubt receive a significant bonus from Pauline Craig.

Leo would fare less well, but Flint wasn't about to lose sleep over that.

Slowly, the undamaged lights came on all over *Insatiable*. Electrical systems buzzed and thrummed back to life. The ballast tanks began to slowly right the ship.

He followed Craig back up to the bridge, confident in the knowledge he'd righted a wrong, too.

CHAPTER 4

Two weeks later
March 15
Houston

MICHAEL FLINT WAS REVIEWING case files in his Houston office when one of his secure laptops chimed with an incoming call. He clicked the answer button.

Banks of monitors, server racks, and the perpetual glow of screens that never went dark provided the background, and Carlos Gaspar's familiar face filled the screen.

"I've been asked to pass this along," Gaspar said without preamble from his Miami tech cave.

"Asked by whom?"

"One of my favorite ghosts. Can't say more."

Gaspar had retired from the FBI after a long and successful career. Meaning he was exceptionally well connected.

His network of intelligence contacts included sources in every agency from Langley to Fort Meade, along with a few that didn't officially exist. Gaspar's information was always solid, even when he couldn't reveal sources, means, or methods.

Flint's government service was murkier than Gaspar's, but intel from confidential classified sources came with limits they both respected.

He poured himself coffee from the perpetually brewing pot on his credenza. "Right. What's the message?"

"Guy you'd want to meet wants to see you."

"Why?"

"Didn't ask. Couldn't tell you if I had."

Flint scowled at the screen, which caused Gaspar to grin. Their relationship had developed its own rhythm.

Gaspar handled tech surveillance, databases, digital forensics, and more from his Miami base.

Flint worked both the office and the field. He'd built an exceptionally lucrative business finding people and things other investigators couldn't find, usually for clients who could afford to pay handsomely for success and discretion.

"What's the message?"

"Check your front door. Package just delivered."

"Hang on." Flint walked through his house to the entrance where he found a padded envelope on the doorstep. He picked it up and opened it on his way back to the office.

Inside was a burner phone with a text message showing on the screen: *Tonight. Oak Hotel lobby bar. 8 o'clock. Come alone.*

Flint read the message twice as he settled back in front of the laptop. "Not much of a message. Why should I care?"

"My contact didn't say. But he's reliable." Gaspar's sources had never steered them wrong.

"The Oak. Gotta have serious money to walk through the door there."

"Figured you'd appreciate that," Gaspar deadpanned.

"Okay. Thanks." Flint disconnected and pocketed the phone.

Six hours later, Flint pulled his Range Rover into the parking structure beneath The Oak Hotel and found a spot on the third level near the elevator and the emergency stairs, just in case.

The Oak's lobby was all understated luxury and quiet money, the kind of place where billionaires conducted business over twenty-thousand-dollar bottles of wine. The bar occupied one corner, dimly lit and designed for conversations that weren't meant to be overheard.

He spotted the man immediately. Tall, thin, late thirties. Sharp suit that probably cost ten grand. Sitting alone at a corner table with his back to the wall and clear sightlines to all entrances. Preoccupied. Detached.

He looked up as Flint approached. Pale blue eyes that seemed to take in everything and give away nothing. Flint had seen that look before. In mirrors, mostly.

Jason Fisher. One of the wealthiest men on the planet. Owner of Onyx, the tech conglomerate. Famously high-functioning autistic. Not as wealthy as Elon Musk, but much wealthier than the King of England.

What the hell was he doing here?

"Michael Flint," Fisher said with a quick nod. Not a question.

"Jason Fisher," Flint replied, taking the seat across from him without waiting for an invitation. "Your message was pretty light on details."

"Security." Fisher gave him a brief grin. "What are you drinking?"

"Not sure how long I'll be here," Flint replied by way of rejecting the offer. "What do you want?"

"Authorities claim my siblings died more than twenty years ago. I have reason to believe otherwise," Fisher said. "I need to know the truth."

"Twenty years is a long time. Memory fades. Evidence disappears. Witnesses die."

"The official reports at the time say they died in a house fire. Accidental electrical fault." Fisher's voice was steady, but Flint caught the tension underneath. "No bodies were ever recovered."

"Fires burn hot enough to vaporize bodies all the time," Flint replied.

"Hot enough to consume three children and their babysitter without leaving so much as a tooth fragment? Not likely." Fisher's replies were characteristically cold and rigid.

Flint studied Fisher's face. Flint had seen him on magazine covers and financial news programs. In person, he exuded a coiled intensity, like a spring under pressure. Not a man to cross.

"Why me?" Flint asked.

"Maybe you're the wrong guy, if you're asking that question."

"Humor me," Flint said flatly. He was long past the point where he needed to take every case that came along. Even if the potential client was the mercurial Jason Fisher.

"Because you find people who don't want to be found. You don't give up." Fisher stated without emotion as he cocked his head and leveled a flat stare toward Flint to finish with the most important point he wanted to make here. "And you don't ask questions about things that aren't your business."

"What makes you think your siblings don't want to be found?"

Fisher reached into his jacket and withdrew a small tablet. He turned it toward Flint. The screen showed a grainy security camera image. A man at an ATM machine, face partially visible in profile.

"This was taken six weeks ago," Fisher said. "The man in the photo is twenty-seven years old. He should be dead."

Flint looked at the image. The resolution was poor, but he could make out enough details. Average height, dark hair, lean build. Unremarkable.

"Could be anyone."

"Could be. Except for this." Fisher swiped to the next image.

A side-by-side comparison. The ATM photo next to what looked like a pre-school picture of a young boy. Maybe three or four years old. Same nose. Same jawline. Same way of holding his head slightly tilted to the left.

"One of my brothers," Fisher said as if he were discussing strangers. "Identical twins. Dylan and Kevin Fisher. Three years old when they died. I can't determine from this image which brother this is, but both of them would look like this today."

Flint picked up the tablet and examined the comparison more closely. The similarities were striking, but facial recognition software could be fooled or results faked. Especially with low-quality surveillance footage like the sample Fisher had collected.

"You run this through any databases?"

"Several. No matches. But that doesn't mean anything. If someone wanted to disappear, really disappear, they could do it. New identity, new background, new life."

"Or it could be coincidence. Guy who looks like your brothers. Human appearance is fairly generic in most respects."

Fisher swiped to another image. Two birth certificates. *Dylan Michael Fisher and Kevin William Fisher.*

Then the Social Security death records. *Dylan Michael Fisher and Kevin William Fisher. Deceased.*

"Officially, my brothers are dead. Have been for twenty-four years. Which suggests only three options." Fisher said. He held up one finger at a time as he ticked off the possibilities. "Either a mistake was made by the arson investigators. Or my brothers have doppelgangers. Or at least one of them is still alive."

Fisher had his attention now. The case was a challenge with impossible odds. Just the kind Flint appreciated, and Fisher probably knew as much. Which was okay. It meant Fisher had done his homework.

Flint took one more look at the images on the tablet and then settled back in his chair. He nodded toward the bartender, an old friend.

He poured a healthy three fingers of his best whiskey and handed it off to the waitress who delivered the glass to Flint with a smile.

"What aren't you telling me?" Flint sipped the whiskey. He raised the glass toward the bartender with appreciation.

Fisher took that in before he replied, "About what?"

"You've got enough money to hire dozens of private investigation firms. But you're sitting in a hotel bar with me. Why?"

Fisher was quiet for a long moment before he spoke softly, as if he were sharing state secrets. "There are people who wouldn't want certain questions asked. People who benefited from my siblings staying dead."

"What kind of people?"

"The kind who burn down houses with children inside."

Ambient noises from the bar filled the space between them. Conversations, laughter, glasses clinking against the tabletops.

"You think someone killed your family deliberately."

"I think they wanted my father to stay quiet. And when he wouldn't, they sent a message."

"What kind of message?"

"The kind written in fire."

"My prices are outrageous."

Fisher reached into his jacket and withdrew a check, sliding it across the table. "To get started. Plus a heavy bonus if you find them alive."

Flint glanced at the check. Seven figures. Pocket change to a man as rich as Fisher, but a sum Flint wouldn't normally ignore. Which Fisher must have already known. Another indication that he'd done his homework.

"And if they're dead?"

"Then I want the people who killed them. All of them."

"That's not what I do."

"You find them. I'll handle what happens next."

Flint studied Fisher's face. He wasn't lying about wanting his brothers found. But he wasn't telling the whole truth either. There were layers here. Layers meant complications.

But the photos nagged at him. What if Fisher was right? If his siblings survived the fire, didn't he deserve to know?

"I'll need everything you have collected so far," Flint said. "Police reports, fire department records, witness statements, insurance claims. Everything from the fire and all subsequent investigations."

"Already compiled." Fisher slid a key card across the table. "Room 1247. Everything I could find is waiting for you."

Flint didn't touch the key card. "Presumptuous, don't you think?"

"I was confident you'd want to find the truth."

Flint pocketed the key card, collected his whiskey glass, and stood. "I'll be in touch."

"Mr. Flint." Fisher's voice stopped him before he could turn away. "Time is a factor here. If my siblings are alive, they may not stay that way. Certain parties have a vested interest in keeping the past buried."

"What parties?"

"Find them," Fisher said simply as he dropped a couple hundred dollars on the table to pay for the drinks and buy silence from the staff. "Before someone else does."

Flint watched Fisher until he cleared the exit and then looked down at the key card in his hand.

Room 1247.

A substantial retainer.

Four dead, three children and the babysitter, who might not be dead at all.

Flint finished his beer and headed for the elevators. The smart thing would be to walk away. But Fisher was right about him, too. He wanted to know the truth.

Besides, the check was already in his pocket.

CHAPTER 5

March 16

Houston

FLINT PULLED INTO THE private airfield in the darkness. The sky was still black overhead, only the faintest hint of gray beginning to show in the east. The Gulfstream sat on the tarmac, gleaming white under the lights. Drake was already there, conducting his pre-flight inspection.

"Morning," Drake called out as Flint approached, not looking up from the engine housing he was examining. "Coffee's in the cockpit. You look like you could use a gallon or two."

"You got that right." Flint climbed the steps into the cabin carrying a leather briefcase stuffed with files.

The interior was configured for work. Two facing seats with a table between them, plus a small galley and communications setup. He set the briefcase on the table next to a thermal carafe of strong black coffee.

Drake finished the inspection and joined Flint a few minutes later, settling into the pilot's seat. "Kentucky? Mind telling me why we're flying to the armpit of America before the sun comes up?"

"Client meeting last night. Jason Fisher."

Drake's hands paused over the instrument panel. "Jason Fisher as in Onyx? The tech guy?"

"That's the one."

"Christ, Flint. What'd you do, cure his mother's cancer?"

Flint didn't have the energy to laugh after he'd stayed up most of the night. "Fisher's siblings died twenty-some years ago. He thinks they're still alive and wants me to find them."

Drake finished the pre-flight checklist and started the engines. The Gulfstream's twin turbofans spooled up with a familiar whine.

"Ground, this is November-Seven-Four-Delta-Fox requesting taxi for departure," Drake said into his headset. He listened for a moment, then nodded. "Roger, ground. Taxi to runway two-seven via Alpha."

The aircraft began moving toward the runway. A few minutes later, Drake switched frequencies.

"Tower, November-Seven-Four-Delta-Fox ready for departure on two-seven."

Another pause as he listened to the controller.

"Roger, tower. Four-Delta-Fox cleared for takeoff."

Flint opened his briefcase and pulled out the first folder from Fisher's collection.

"All those years," Drake said to Flint over the headsets once they were airborne and climbing. "That's a long time to wait for justice."

"He was seventeen when it happened. Probably took him this long to get rich enough to afford answers."

Drake nodded. "Or to get powerful enough to survive after asking the wrong questions."

Flint looked up from the police report he was reading. Drake had a point. Flint's clients only came to him after they had exhausted other options. Or when they needed an expendable asset.

"Tell me about the case," Drake said.

Flint leaned back in his seat. "Rural Kentucky. House fire destroyed the Fisher family home. Three children and their babysitter presumed dead. No bodies recovered."

"No bone fragments or dental remains? Nothing at all?"

Flint shook his head. "Fire department said the heat was intense enough to destroy everything."

"Bullshit," Drake replied. "We've seen lots of forensic evidence from all kinds of fires. Something always survives, even after a fire that burns hot and uncontained for hours. Certainly not a normal fire."

"That was my reaction too." Flint stretched his neck, which had kinked during his all-nighter studying Fisher's files. "If there were actually no remains, this fire was arson. Some accelerants will burn hotter and destroy most evidence."

"Yeah, but even cremated bodies, which are burned at very high temperatures under well controlled circumstances, don't actually turn to unidentifiable ash," Drake replied.

"Can't argue with that," Flint said while covering his mouth to yawn. He swallowed the last of the coffee in his cup and poured another.

Drake checked the flight pattern as the autopilot banked the aircraft to the right, following the flight path toward Kentucky. "Who were the victims?"

Flint consulted his notes. "Dylan and Kevin Fisher, three-year-old twins. Maureen Fisher, eight months old. Elizabeth Pace, sixteen years old. The babysitter."

"That's tough," Drake said, shaking his head. "What about the rest of the family?"

"Parents Harry and Vivian Fisher. Two older sons, Bruce and Jason. They were at a basketball game in town when the fire started."

"Conveniently out of danger, or was that also planned?" Drake asked. "Were they establishing an alibi?"

"The parents and older boys were already gone when the fire started." Flint leaned his head back and closed his eyes. "The younger kids and babysitter weren't supposed to be there either, but the twins had colds, so the parents wanted them to stay home. Last-minute change of plans."

Drake was quiet for several minutes. Through the cockpit windows, the sun was beginning to rise, painting the clouds below them in shades of orange and pink.

"What's the family situation now?" Drake asked.

"Father died ten years ago. Natural causes, according to the records. Mother still lives in Kentucky. Same property. Rebuilt the house exactly as it was."

"Because that's not morbid at all," Drake said sardonically.

"One surviving brother, Bruce Fisher, lives in California. Software engineer. Keeps to himself." Flint yawned again. "Our client, Jason, became absurdly rich. Tech, defense contracts, AI development. Forbes says he's the number two wealthiest man in the world, behind Elon Musk. Hundreds of billions."

Drake whistled softly.

Flint returned to discussing the police report. "The investigation was perfunctory at best. Fire department arrived seven hours after the blaze started. No arson investigation to speak of. No follow-up on the missing bodies. Case closed within a week."

"Wow," Drake said, as if he couldn't come up with anything better.

"Look at these." Flint held up two photographs. The ATM surveillance image Fisher had shown him and the altered childhood photo.

"That's the same person."

"One of the twins. Dylan or Kevin Fisher," Flint said. "This surveillance photo was taken six weeks ago."

"Which means either the fire investigation was completely wrong, or someone's been living under a false identity all these years."

"Or both."

Below them, the landscape was shifting from Texas plains to the rolling hills of Arkansas.

"What do you know about the babysitter?" Drake asked.

Flint opened another folder. "Elizabeth Pace. Lizzy. Junior at the local high school. Average student. No behavioral problems. Worked part-time at her uncle's gas station."

"Boyfriend?"

"Nothing in the files. She was quiet. Unremarkable. The kind of kid who slips through the cracks."

"Which she literally did."

"Exactly." Flint nodded. "Her disappearance was barely investigated. Parents filed a missing person report, but law enforcement across the country was overwhelmed. Locals assumed she died in the fire with the Fisher kids. Mostly because, by all accounts, she was a great babysitter. They figured Lizzy would never have left the kids alone."

Drake was quiet for a long moment. "If three kids and a teenager survived that fire, where have they been all these years?"

"That's what we're being paid to find out."

"And if they didn't survive? Or if someone used the fire as a distraction and simply grabbed them up?"

Flint had been thinking the same thing. "Then Jason Fisher is paying us to find the four bodies *and* the people who put them in the ground."

"Either way, we're walking into something that's been buried for two decades. Who has enough power and wherewithal to cover up four deaths and make them stay covered?"

"That's a good place to start."

"The kind of people who kill to keep secrets don't usually develop a conscience after more than twenty years," Drake said dryly.

"Agreed."

Drake checked their position on the GPS display. "ETA Keeneland Regional Airport in thirty minutes. After we land, where do we start?"

Flint looked out the window at the Kentucky hills beginning to appear below them. "The crime scene. Always start with the facts."

"The house literally burned to ashes and the kids are long gone. What evidence could possibly still be there?"

"We won't find much at the house, I'm sure," Flint agreed. "We need to get a firm understanding of the setting, at least. After that, someone knows what happened that night. Someone always knows."

Drake began their descent toward Keeneland, just outside of Lexington, Kentucky. The morning sun was fully up now, burning off the mist that clung to the rolling pastures dotted with rolling hills and white fences, as far as the eye could see.

As they dropped below the clouds headed for landing, Drake asked, "Why now? Jason Fisher's had money for years. Why hire you now instead of five years ago?"

"He says he just found the video. And he's developed a new facial recognition software capable of matching the video to the old photos," Flint replied.

"You believe that?"

The Gulfstream's wheels touched down on the Kentucky runway with a gentle bump. They were here. In the heart of Bluegrass country, where old money and older secrets ran as deep as the limestone caves beneath the rolling pastures.

Flint shrugged. "Until we have contrary intel, we'll work with what we've got."

CHAPTER 6

March 16
Rural Kentucky

THE REBUILT FISHER HOME sat on the same footprint where the original house had burned years earlier, nestled in a valley between two rolling hills about fifty miles southeast of Lexington. Drake parked the Toyota Land Cruiser at the end of the gravel driveway and Flint studied the structure through the windshield.

Three stories, red brick construction, Georgian colonial architecture with symmetrical windows and white trim.

Drake emerged from the driver's seat, adjusting his sunglasses against the midday glare. "Creepy as hell, rebuilding it exactly the same."

"Grief makes people do strange things."

They walked up the gravel path toward the front door. The property was isolated, woods stretching behind the house and the nearest neighbor at least five miles away through the rolling hills. Perfect place to make something happen without witnesses.

Flint knocked on the front door. Shuffling slow footsteps approached from inside, as if she were afraid to pick up her feet. Vivian Fisher, Jason's mother, opened the door. A tired woman in her early seventies with graying hair pulled back in a simple ponytail and no makeup.

"Mrs. Fisher? I'm Michael Flint. Your son Jason hired me."

Her pale blue eyes, the same color as Jason's, studied Flint's face for a long moment. She glanced at Drake, then back to Flint.

"He said you might come by." Her voice was soft, with the faint accent of someone who'd lived in Kentucky her entire life. "Come in."

The interior was as unsettling as the exterior. Traditional furniture, family photographs on the mantelpiece, everything arranged with the careful precision of a museum exhibit. Or a shrine.

Vivian led them to a sitting room with two sofas facing each other across a coffee table. She took the chair by the window. The afternoon light caught the lines around her eyes, deeper than they should have been for her age.

"Jason thinks his siblings are alive," she said without preamble.

"Do you?" Flint asked.

"I lost my children years ago. I've mourned them every day since." Her hands were folded in her lap, but Flint caught the slight tremor in her fingers. "I can't hope they're alive. When that hope is destroyed, it would kill me."

Flint leaned forward. "Mrs. Fisher, please tell us about the night of the fire. We need to understand what happened."

Vivian's face went distant. "October twenty-third. Bruce had a basketball tournament at the high school. We went. Harry, myself, Jason, and Bruce. We left at six-thirty."

She paused, her fingers working at the hem of her sleeve.

"The twins both had colds. Coughs and runny noses, like kids do. I almost brought them anyway, but Harry said the gymnasium would be drafty and might make them worse. Maureen was teething and fussy, too. In the end, we decided to leave all three with Lizzy."

"Elizabeth Pace," Flint said, leading her along.

"That's right. Sweet girl. She'd been babysitting for us since she was fourteen. The children loved her." Vivian's voice caught slightly, and tears filled her eyes. "She would never have left them alone. Never."

Flint changed the subject before she could spiral into sobs. "What time did you get home?"

"Ten forty-seven." Her precise answer suggested she'd relived this moment thousands of times, looking for answers she never found. "The house and everything in it was gone. Just the foundation and some smoldering timber. The fire department was here, but there was nothing left to save."

"No remains were found?" Drake asked.

Vivian shook her head. "Fire chief said the fire burned too hot for too long. Old wiring, I guess."

"Did you believe that?"

She paused a good long while before she replied, "Harry didn't."

"What did your husband believe had happened?" Flint asked.

"Harry had made some bad business investments a few years earlier." Vivian's voice became careful, choosing each word. "Pain management clinics. He thought he was helping bring healthcare to rural communities. He didn't know his business partners were involved in illegal activities."

Flint noted the diplomatic phrasing. Jason had mentioned his father staying quiet when he should have spoken up. Was this what he meant?

"What kind of illegal activities?" Drake asked.

"Pills. Prescription drugs. Smuggled in. Stolen and sold illegally. Several things like that," she said in a whispery tone. "When Harry found out, he tried to get out of the business, but it was complicated. The DEA got involved and..."

"You think the DEA was at fault for the fire and the death of your children?" Drake asked incredulously.

"Harry cooperated with them. Gave them what information he could. They stopped hounding him." She stood and walked to the window. "He thought it was over."

"But it wasn't," Flint said.

"Harry's contact at the DEA stopped returning his calls two weeks before the fire. We found out later the man had been found dead in a Louisville hotel. They said suicide."

Flint felt pieces of the puzzle beginning to connect. A DEA informant. A house fire that destroyed evidence. Missing or dead children.

"Who else knew about Harry's cooperation with the DEA?" he asked.

"Harry never told me the details. Said it was safer if I didn't know." She returned to her chair, suddenly looking every one of her seventy-three years. "After the fire, he never spoke of it again. Not until the day he died."

"What did he say then?"

"That he was sorry. That he'd failed them." Tears started down her cheeks and her voice caught. "That he should have brought all the children to the game that night. We mourned the house, of course. It had been in my family for more than a hundred years. But the children…"

Drake pulled out a small notebook. "Mrs. Fisher, do you remember anything unusual happening that week? Anyone who came by the house? Phone calls? Anything out of the ordinary?"

Vivian was quiet for a long moment. "There had been some strange calls before. Harry would answer and whoever was on the other end would hang up. That went on for about two weeks before the fire."

"Anyone come to the house?" Flint asked.

"A few days before, someone called asking about buying one of our horses. Harry told them we weren't selling, but they wanted to come look anyway. Harry said no."

"Did they come anyway?" Drake wanted to know.

"I saw a white van parked at the end of our drive one afternoon. Just sitting there. When I looked again an hour later, it was gone."

Flint made a mental note. Surveillance, most likely.

"Mrs. Fisher," Flint said carefully, "Jason showed me surveillance footage of a man who looks like one of your sons. Taken six weeks ago."

Her hands gripped the arms of her chair. "Don't."

"If there's a chance they survived."

"I said don't." Her voice was steel now. "I can't go through that again. I've built a life around accepting they're gone. If you tear that down..."

She stood abruptly and walked to the mantelpiece, picking up a framed photograph. Three small children playing in a yard. The twins and baby Maureen.

"Find the truth if you must. But don't ask me to hope. I've used up all my hope. I can't be disappointed again," she said in a whisper. "It would kill me."

Flint and Drake left a few minutes later. As they walked back to the Land Cruiser, Drake said, "She knows more than she's telling us."

"Probably knows more than she wants to admit to herself," Flint agreed. "Someone was definitely watching the family. Getting ready."

Drake started the engine. "Ready for what? Arson or kidnapping?"

"Seems like both."

They drove in silence for several miles through the rolling hills dotted with horse farms and pastures before Drake spoke again. "If Harry Fisher was a DEA informant and someone wanted him silenced, why not just kill him? Why the elaborate fire? Why take the children?"

"Send a message. Eliminate witnesses." Flint had been wondering the same thing since Jason first approached him. "Or the children might have been insurance. Guarantee Harry's continued silence."

Drake popped his eyebrows north. "For twenty-four years?"

"Harry's been dead for ten. If the children were taken as leverage against him, what happened to them after he died?" Flint mused aloud. He didn't have the answer. But he intended to find out.

Drake guided the Land Cruiser through the winding country roads. They needed to examine the property more thoroughly, check the woods behind the house where someone might have waited. Sometimes the land held clues that buildings couldn't hide.

Flint's experience led him to believe he was only beginning to scratch the surface of whatever had happened on that October night.

Odds were that the children and their babysitter had died tragically in the fire.

But if the Fisher kids were missing or hidden, someone had gone to extraordinary lengths to keep them that way.

Flint studied the side mirror as Drake guided the Land Cruiser down the long and winding gravel drive away from the Fisher house. A black SUV sat parked on the shoulder of the main road, positioned with clear sightlines to the property entrance.

"Company," Flint said.

Drake checked his rearview mirror. "How long?"

"Wasn't there when we arrived."

CHAPTER 7

March 16

Rural Kentucky

DRAKE PAUSED THE LAND Cruiser at the end of the gravel drive and glanced in both directions down the empty two-lane country road as if he were worried about the non-existent traffic.

The black SUV's engine started.

"Competent surveillance," Drake said as he looked away. "Government plates?"

Flint used the passenger mirror to get a better angle. "Can't tell from here. But they're not trying to hide."

Drake turned right, heading back toward Lexington. The black SUV pulled onto the road behind them, maintaining a careful distance of about two hundred yards.

"Could be protection," Drake suggested. "Jason Fisher looking out for his investment."

"Could be."

But the positioning was wrong. Protective surveillance stayed closer and used multiple vehicles for better coverage. This felt different. Predatory.

The road wound through a valley between two hills covered in dense woodland. No houses visible, no side roads for the next five miles. Perfect place for an ambush if someone wanted privacy.

Flint checked the weapon holstered under his jacket and confirmed the backup magazine in his pocket. "How's our fuel?"

"Tank's three-quarters full." Drake's hands remained relaxed on the steering wheel, but Flint caught the slight tension in his shoulders. "You thinking what I'm thinking?"

"That we're about to find out who doesn't want questions asked about the Fisher family."

A second black SUV appeared ahead of them, cresting the hill and approaching fast. It slowed as it drew closer, then pulled into the oncoming lane and stopped sideways across both lanes of the narrow road.

Roadblock.

Drake slowed the Land Cruiser. "Military or law enforcement experience likely."

The SUV behind them accelerated, closing the distance rapidly. In seconds, they'd be boxed in with nowhere to go except into the trees.

Flint readied his weapon. "How's the suspension on this thing?"

"Built for off-road." Drake downshifted and pressed the accelerator. "Hang on."

The Land Cruiser surged forward, engine roaring. The roadblock was a hundred yards ahead. The pursuing SUV was fifty yards behind and gaining fast.

Drake aimed the Land Cruiser directly at the left front corner of the blocking vehicle. At sixty miles per hour, the Toyota's reinforced front end would punch through the lighter SUV's quarter panel and spin it out of the way. Basic physics and superior engineering.

Muzzle flashes erupted from the roadblock. Automatic weapons fire stitched across the Land Cruiser's windshield. The glass spider-webbed but held because it was designed to stop small arms fire.

"Armor?" Flint asked.

"Factory security package. Won't stop rifle rounds, but it'll handle pistol caliber."

More gunfire from behind. The rear window exploded inward, showering them with safety glass. The pursuing SUV had pulled alongside, and passengers were firing through open windows.

Drake yanked the wheel hard left, then right, weaving to spoil their aim. The Land Cruiser's heavy suspension kept them stable while the shooters struggled to maintain accuracy from their moving platform.

Fifty yards to the roadblock.

The blocking SUV's doors opened. Four men in tactical gear took positions behind the vehicle, assault rifles trained on the approaching Land Cruiser. Qualified shooters. Expensive equipment.

"Who has this kind of manpower?" Drake shouted over the gunfire.

"Someone with serious money and federal connections." Thirty yards.

Flint aimed through his side window and put one round into the roadblock SUV's front tire. The tire deflated rapidly, dropping the front end and tilting the vehicle toward the drainage ditch.

Twenty yards.

The shooters behind the roadblock adjusted their aim, concentrating fire on the Land Cruiser's engine block. Steam began pouring from under the hood. Temperature gauge spiked into the red zone.

Ten yards.

Drake held course, aiming for the SUV's damaged front corner. Impact in seconds.

The Land Cruiser hit the roadblock fast. The Toyota's reinforced bumper and frame rails transferred the energy directly into the SUV's weakened front end. Metal screamed. Glass exploded. The blocking vehicle spun sideways and flipped, rolling down the embankment into the trees.

The Land Cruiser bounced over the debris and kept moving, but its engine was dying. Steam poured through the bullet holes in the hood. Temperature gauge buried in the red.

"How far to the next town?" Flint asked.

"Five miles. Maybe six." Drake coaxed more speed from the failing engine. "We're not going to make it."

In the rearview mirror, the pursuing SUV had stopped at the crash site. Men getting out to check on their teammates. Well disciplined. No one left behind.

But they'd be mobile again in minutes.

"There." Flint pointed to a dirt road that led up into the hills toward a cluster of farm buildings. "We go to ground."

He turned onto the dirt track. The Land Cruiser labored up the steep grade, engine knocking and grinding. Half a mile up the hill, the motor seized completely.

They coasted to a stop beside a weathered barn surrounded by rusted farm equipment and overgrown pastures. The place looked abandoned. No vehicles, no lights, no signs of recent habitation.

Flint grabbed his go-bag from the back seat. Communications gear, extra ammunition, medical supplies, cash. Standard field kit for situations exactly like this.

Drake checked his sidearm and shouldered his own pack. "Not long before they find us."

"Ten minutes if they're good. Five if they have air support."

They moved toward the barn. The main doors were chained shut, but a side entrance stood slightly ajar. Inside, sunlight filtered through gaps in the old wooden siding, illuminating bales of moldy hay and farm machinery that hadn't run for decades.

Flint found a position near a window with clear views down the hill. Drake took the opposite side, covering different approaches.

"Motion sensor cameras would help," Drake said as he moved into position.

Flint pulled out his satellite phone and speed-dialed Gaspar in Miami.

"You're supposed to be investigating a cold case," Gaspar answered on the first ring. "Not starting a war."

"Someone just tried to kill us. Coordinated assault, federal-level resources."

"How federal?"

"Black SUVs, tactical gear, disciplined fire teams. Either government or someone with government connections."

Gaspar was quiet for a moment. "I'll make some calls. See who's been asking questions about you lately."

"Do it fast. We're pinned down in rural Kentucky with limited ammunition and no backup."

"GPS coordinates?"

Flint read them from his phone.

"I'll see what I can do," Gaspar said. "But it'll take time to get help to your location."

"How much time?"

"Dunno. Not minutes."

The sound of vehicles approaching drifted up from the valley. Multiple engines. They'd found the abandoned Land Cruiser.

"Gotta go," Flint said.

He pocketed the phone and checked his ammunition. Three magazines for the Glock. Forty-five rounds total. Drake would have similar loadout.

Not enough for a sustained firefight against a competent, well-trained team.

"Options?" Drake asked.

Flint studied the terrain through the barn window. Dense woods covered the hillside above them. Old bridle trails visible through the trees. If they could reach the high ground, they'd have better defensive positions and multiple escape routes.

"We go up."

"On foot?"

"Unless you've got a helicopter hidden somewhere."

Drake grinned despite their situation. "Fresh out, I'm afraid."

They gathered their gear and moved toward the barn's rear exit. Outside, Flint's ears noted approaching vehicles. Experienced drivers, taking their time, setting up a proper perimeter before moving in.

These weren't random thugs or local muscle. Someone had deployed serious assets to stop their investigation.

Which meant they were asking the right questions.

Flint just hoped they'd live long enough to find the answers.

The rear door of the barn opened onto a steep hillside covered in second-growth timber. They could hear the vehicles clearly now, at least three of them. Engines shut down near the abandoned Land Cruiser.

"Move," Flint said.

They sprinted up the hill toward the tree line, boots slipping on loose shale and dead leaves. Behind them, voices called out tactical commands.

Definitely military or ex-military, Flint noted.

They reached the woods as the first shots rang out from below. Live rounds snapped into the branches nearby, accurate enough to be dangerous but not close enough.

Warning shots. They wanted Flint and Drake alive for questioning.

That was useful intel. These guys wanted information, not two dead men who couldn't confess what they'd learned about the Fisher case.

They pushed deeper into the forest, following what looked like an old deer trail up the ridge. The trees provided concealment but wouldn't stop rifle bullets. They needed distance and elevation.

"How's your cardio?" Flint asked, breathing hard from the climb.

"Better than yours, old man."

"We'll see about that."

They climbed for seven minutes before pausing again to listen. Voices below, closer than expected. Their pursuers were experienced trackers, moving fast and quiet through the woods.

Flint checked his phone. Still had a signal, barely. He sent a quick text to Gaspar: "Thermal imaging likely. Need extraction ASAP."

The reply came back immediately: "Working on it. Stay alive."

Sound advice.

They continued climbing, using the terrain to cover their trail and confuse pursuit. But thermal imaging would make hiding difficult. Body heat stood out clearly against the cool March air.

Near the ridge top, they found what they were looking for. A clearing. Thirty feet of elevation and clear sightlines in all directions.

"High ground," Drake said.

"Best we're going to get."

They climbed quickly to the clearing. Flint quickly located pursuers moving up through the trees. Six men in tactical gear, spread out in a proper search formation. Qualified hunters.

But elevation was a force multiplier. Two experienced shooters with good position could hold off a much larger force, at least temporarily.

Flint's phone buzzed. Text message: "Help en route. Hold position."

He read the message to Drake, who nodded.

"How long?" Drake asked.

"Didn't say."

"Then we'd better make ourselves comfortable."

The first hunter broke cover at the bottom of the hill, moving carefully but steadily upward. They knew where Flint and Drake had gone. Just a matter of time before they reached the clearing.

Flint waited. When the situation seemed hopeless, he made it expensive for the other side and hoped for a miracle.

In his experience, miracles usually came in the form of superior firepower and good timing.

The lead man was fifty yards away and closing when Flint heard the distinctive whop-whop-whop of helicopter rotors approaching from the east.

Gaspar sent the cavalry.

The tactical team below heard it too. They went to ground, taking cover behind trees and rocks, probably unsure if the approaching aircraft was friendly or hostile.

The Black Hawk helicopter crested the ridge. It circled the clearing once and then settled into a hover just above the platform.

A door gunner leaned out, scanning the woods below with a mounted machine gun.

A voice called through a bullhorn. "Weapons down. Move away from the area."

The tactical team below ignored the command. They melted back into the forest, recognizing superior firepower when they saw it.

A rope dropped from the Black Hawk's door.

"Time to go," Drake said.

They clipped their gear to the rope and winched up to the helicopter's cabin. Strong hands pulled them inside as the aircraft lifted away from the ridge.

"Michael Flint?" The co-pilot had to shout over the engine noise.

Flint nodded.

"Compliments of your friend in Miami. He said you needed a ride."

The Black Hawk banked south toward Lexington, leaving the tactical team stranded in the Kentucky hills. Through the cabin window, Flint could see them emerging from the trees, watching the helicopter disappear.

Soldiers once. Probably paramilitary now. Well-equipped. Well-trained. Well-funded.

Someone with serious resources wanted the Fisher investigation stopped.

Which meant they were closer to the truth.

How close could they get before the opposition stopped playing games and decided that Flint was too dangerous to live?

CHAPTER 8

March 16
Kentucky

THE BLACK HAWK'S ROTORS chopped air as it set down fifty yards from the Gulfstream. No parting words with the flight crew. Courtesy worked both ways. Some favors were better left unacknowledged.

Flint flashed the pilot a thumbs-up before he ducked low and ran. Drake stayed close behind. The helicopter lifted off the second they cleared the downdraft.

Drake headed straight for the Gulfstream. They had to get airborne before whoever deployed the tactical team decided to escalate.

The encrypted satellite phone in Flint's jacket vibrated. He checked the display. Texas area code. Mount Warren.

Finally.

Flint walked toward the maintenance hangar. He found a quiet spot away from airport personnel and security cameras. The phone kept buzzing.

On the fourth ring, he answered. "This is Flint."

"Sheriff Matt Milliken, Mount Warren Police Department. You left a message about an old case."

"Thanks for calling back, Sheriff. I'm working on genealogy research. We're seeking family connections in your area from the 1990s." Flint delivered the cover story like it was gospel truth. "Marilyn Baker's name came up in our database. We need to clarify some potential familial links."

The ruse was solid. Genealogy research was booming. Police departments fielded calls from researchers all the time. Even small-town sheriffs like Milliken were approached by heir hunters and investigators regularly as more and better DNA techniques had been developed.

"Marilyn Baker." Milliken repeated the name like he hadn't heard it in years. Long pause. Decision made. "I remember the case. What kind of familial connections are you looking for?"

Flint heard the caution. Cops didn't like private investigators poking around their cases. Even stone-cold ones.

"Our client is looking for family members. There's a potential inheritance involved." Flint chuckled. Friendly. Warming him up. "Where there's a will, there's a war, you know?"

"True that." Milliken's tone softened slightly.

"DNA matches suggest Ms. Baker, or someone related to her, is connected to our client. But her case file has gaps we can't fill from public records." Flint sounded eager to share everything he knew. Standard interrogation technique. Give to get. "Background information, mostly. Who she was. What her life was like. Who might have known her well enough to provide family details. The murder investigation isn't our focus. Understanding her social connections helps us build the genealogy profile."

"I see," Milliken replied. "Which firm did you say you're working for?"

Cops were inherently skeptical, and Milliken was no exception.

Flint had anticipated the question. "Heritage Family Research in Dallas. We specialize in cases where official records are incomplete. Sometimes we need to broaden our scope."

Heritage Family Research was a real business and large enough to handle this kind of work. Flint worked with them occasionally. If Milliken called to verify, he'd get the right answers.

Milliken didn't mention he'd been first deputy on scene when Marilyn Baker's body was found. His first homicide case, but not the last. He'd spent twenty-four years as a deputy before his predecessor died on the job, which promoted Milliken to top cop. Now, he'd served as Mount Warren's sheriff for the past eight years.

The sheriff's tone shifted. "That case has stayed with me. We never got the answers her family deserved."

"I understand the murder remains unsolved." Flint kept it simple. Let Milliken fill the silences.

"Officially, yes. We had a suspect. James Preston. Could never make the charges stick." Milliken paused. "Preston was later convicted for killing another young woman in a different county. He was executed, but he denied killing Marilyn Baker and we can't prove that he did."

Flint already knew all about Preston, but he let Milliken tell it anyway. "So you believe Preston killed Ms. Baker?"

"Preston was our best lead. But I always had questions. Small town, limited resources. We probably focused on Preston as the obvious suspect more than we should have."

Exactly what Flint hoped to find. A cop with a conscience who understood the limitations of the original investigation.

"What kind of questions were left open?"

Milliken went quiet. Flint covered one ear to reduce the airport noise. Trucks starting up. Distant whine of jet engines. Crews shouting over the racket.

"Flint, I'll be honest with you. I'd like to see Marilyn Baker's case properly resolved. If your genealogy work can uncover information that might help, I'm game." Sheriff Milliken said. "You come to Mount Warren. We can sit down and go through what we know. I'll share the case files. Introduce you to people who knew Marilyn. Maybe your fresh eyes will see something we missed."

Flint allowed a bit of enthusiasm to color his tone. "When would it be convenient for us to meet?"

"Next week should work. Call my desk clerk and set it up."

"I appreciate that, Sheriff. Will do."

"One more thing," Milliken said sternly. "Marilyn Baker was a good person. Devoted teacher. Devout Catholic. Loved by everyone who knew her. She deserved better than dying alone, face down in mucky canal runoff. If you can help us finally give her, her family, and our community justice, you'll have my full cooperation."

"Understood. Thank you. I'll be in touch." Flint ended the call and pocketed the phone. Exactly what he'd hoped. A lawman who wanted justice, even if it took years to get there.

Flint scanned the airport. No black SUVs. No tactical teams. That didn't mean they weren't being watched.

He made his way to the Gulfstream and climbed the jet stairs. He pulled the stairs up and sealed the door before taking the co-pilot seat and fastening his harness. "Any word from Gaspar about who tried to kill us?"

"He's working on it. Preliminary guess is private military contractors, not government agents. Whoever hired them has serious money and connections." Drake was completing the pre-flight checks, eager to get airborne before anything else went wrong.

"Gaspar say that?"

Drake shook his head. "Didn't need to. It's obvious."

Flint nodded. "Right."

Drake gave him a quick grin. "What's the plan? Do we keep pushing on the Fisher case, or do we take a strategic pause to figure out who wants us dead today?"

Flint considered the options. Back at the Fisher home, the tactical team had been methodical but not lethal. They'd wanted information, not bodies.

Which meant the Fisher investigation was getting close.

But close to what?

"We keep pushing. Carefully. No more solo trips to interview witnesses. We assume everything we do is being monitored."

"And if they escalate?"

"Then we push back. We didn't survive three tours to be intimidated by corporate thugs."

Flint's thoughts shifted between the two investigations.

Fisher's powerful enemies were willing to deploy fully equipped tactical teams, armed to kill. The Baker case offered a cooperative sheriff carrying thirty-two years of frustration.

Two cases involving official investigations that had missed the truth. Two families who deserved answers.

Both were equally important to him right now although one case was strictly business and the other was personal to Flint.

The Gulfstream's engines spooled up. Through the windshield, Flint saw the Kentucky hills where they'd nearly been killed an hour ago.

The aircraft lifted off and banked south toward Houston. Flint began planning his next moves.

The Fisher investigation would continue to take the front row seat.

But he'd be returning to Mount Warren sooner than he'd told Sheriff Milliken.

Much sooner.

CHAPTER 9

March 16
Houston

BACK AT HOME, FLINT'S house felt impossibly quiet after the chaos in Kentucky. No helicopter rotors. No gunfire. No tactical teams melting into the forest like ghosts. The Black Hawk had set them down forty minutes ago, but Flint could still hear the chaos in his head as he headed for the shower.

He'd changed into comfortable clothes, poured a glass of whiskey, and settled into his home office before Drake arrived. He'd stopped off somewhere to shower, too. He dropped his gear bag by the front door and walked straight to the kitchen. Ice clinked into a fresh glass. Bourbon followed.

"They weren't weekend warriors," Drake said when he joined Flint in the office. They clicked glasses of the good stuff and swallowed, waiting for the warmth to spread and relax them. "Military contractors. Maybe former Delta or Rangers."

"Agreed." Flint nodded

"We're moving in the right direction."

"Or we're about to get ourselves killed." Drake raised his glass.

They drank and burned away some of the Kentucky dust.

Flint walked to the sliding door that opened onto his back patio and stared at the gently undulating water. The pool lights were on. Peaceful. Normal. Same as when he left home this morning.

"If we take Vivian's word at face value, Harry Fisher was a DEA informant for three years," he said without turning around. "Why did the dealers wait that long to eliminate him?"

"Maybe they didn't know he was the leak." Drake settled into one of the leather chairs. "Three years is a long time to feed information to the feds. He must have been cautious enough to avoid drawing the wrong kind of attention to his actions."

"Or maybe they found out back then and decided to send a message." Flint turned back to face the room. "Burn his house. Kill his children. What if it was a demonstration? To make sure other potential informants understood the consequences."

Drake's eyebrows climbed toward his hairline. "Or maybe the kids were insurance? If they were kept alive, held hostage, maybe to force Harry's silence?"

"Doesn't make sense. If Harry knew the kids were alive, why wouldn't he tell his DEA handler and try to get them back?" Flint swallowed more whiskey. "I'm thinking they believed they did kill the kids, and the babysitter. They probably threatened the wife and the teens, too. So Harry stays silent for ten years because nothing could bring them back to life. Eventually dies of natural causes. No more leverage needed."

"What about the ATM photo of one of the boys?" Drake asked.

"Lots of room for error there." Flint shrugged. "Fisher believes in his new software, but age progression and facial recognition combined to establish a positive ID seems like a stretch."

Drake was quiet for a moment as if the wheels were turning in his head.

"We need to get into Harry's business at the molecular level," Flint said finally. "Find out exactly what he invested in. Who his partners were. How the DEA approached him."

Jason Fisher's files contained Harry's financial records going back several years before the fire. Business incorporation documents. Partnership agreements. Tax records.

They spent the next hour spread across Flint's dining room table with papers arranged in chronological order. A timeline of Harry Fisher's descent into the opioid distribution network.

"Look at this," Drake said, holding up incorporation papers. "Appalachian Healthcare Partners. Incorporated in Nevada. Harry Fisher, primary investor."

Flint found the corresponding financial records. "Initial capital investment of $3.2 million. Source listed as sale of thoroughbred stallion."

"Horse breeding profits?"

"Old Kentucky money," Flint said, shaking his head. "Vivian said the house had been in her family for over a hundred years. Thoroughbreds were her family's business before Harry got involved."

Drake studied the partnership structure and summarized. "Harry Fisher put up the money. Three other partners handled operations. Pain management clinics popped up across eastern Kentucky."

"Looks like it was a legitimate operation at first," Flint said, reading the early financial reports. "Everything looks clean for the first couple of years. Standard medical practice income and expenses."

"Then what changed?"

Flint found the answer in a series of bank transfers starting three years before the fire. Large cash deposits that didn't match the clinic's patient volume. Payments to pharmaceutical distributors that exceeded logical prescription needs.

"After a year or so, someone started diverting pills. Thousands of them." He showed Drake the financial anomalies. "OxyContin launched, and two years later,

Kentucky was becoming the epicenter of prescription opioid abuse."

Drake whistled softly. "Harry walks into the perfect storm. Thinks he's funding rural healthcare when he's actually bankrolling pill mills. It must have freaked him out when kids and neighbors began dying of opioid overdoses."

"The crisis takes hold and begins to escalate. DEA finds Harry's name on everything. Bank accounts. Leases. Corporate filings." Flint could visualize how it played out. "They investigate, arrest him, give him a choice. Cooperate or face prosecution for murder and running a criminal enterprise."

Drake drained his bourbon and poured a second glass. Flint declined. He wanted a clear head.

"So Harry becomes an informant," Drake said, resettling into his favorite chair. "Feeds information to his DEA handler for three years. Patient lists. Pill counts. Meeting schedules. Anything that helps the feds build a case."

"Until someone in the pill ring figures out they have a leak," Flint said.

The story ended when the house fire on that October night destroyed everything Harry held dear. Three children and a babysitter gone without a trace.

Flint leaned back in his chair. "We need to find out who Harry was reporting to. His DEA handler died two weeks before the fire. Supposed suicide."

"Convenient timing."

"Yeah." Flint pulled out his phone. "I've got a contact at DEA. Specialized in informant protection protocols during the opioid crisis."

"I know someone too." Drake nodded. "He can access old case files without triggering security alerts."

They agreed to split up the investigation. Drake would work his contact to identify Harry's dead handler and research the specifics of the DEA operation. He'd also continue investigating the tactical team that had ambushed them.

Flint would handle follow-up interviews with locals who might remember details about the Fisher family that hadn't come out in the original investigation.

"Where will you start?" Drake asked.

"Small towns have long memories. Someone saw something that night." Flint gathered the financial records into a neat stack. "I'll work the neighbors. People who knew the family."

"Better you than me. I hate small-town politics." Drake grinned. "Meanwhile, I promised Scarlett I'd stop by and walk Whiskers. She and Maddy are at the movies."

Flint grinned. He had given Scarlett's daughter, Maddy, a Schnauzer puppy for her seventh birthday. Scarlett pretended to be annoyed about the gift, but Flint could tell she was warming up to the little dog. In truth, Whiskers was a stinking cute bundle of joy for Maddy. Which made the gift a big success as far as Flint was concerned.

Scarlett would have to forgive him. Eventually.

After Drake left, Flint sat alone in his study reviewing what they'd learned.

Harry Fisher had been an unwilling participant in an illegal opioid distribution network. The DEA had leveraged his exposure to turn him into an informant.

The criminal distribution ring had discovered Harry's betrayal and decided to send a message that would resonate throughout the regional opioid trade.

Which meant that the fire that destroyed Harry's home and killed his family was a calculated business decision.

Flint shook his head. "Cold-hearted bastards."

All of that history would normally have been forgotten more than twenty years later. But someone still considered the truth dangerous enough to deploy military contractors to kill Flint and Drake.

Which meant the conspiracy had grown. Expanded. Still worth killing to protect.

None of which could have happened by wishful thinking. There was a powerful force behind the evolution. Who or what was it?

Flint's encrypted phone buzzed with a text message. He recognized the number.

He'd sent a message to Sheriff Milliken two hours ago. *Available to meet tomorrow afternoon?*

Milliken had typed back: *Yes.*

Flint asked, *What time works for you?*

The response came quickly: *2 p.m. Mount Warren Sheriff's Department.*

Flint replied *Okay* and then deleted both messages before he turned off the phone.

Flint was juggling two investigations now. Both were cold cases with no immediate urgency. But Jason Fisher's case took priority because he was a paying client and because Flint had agreed to take on the matter.

His mother's murder was less urgent. He was still ambivalent about taking it on anyway.

Both cases involved official investigations that had failed.

Both families deserved better.

Tomorrow he'd drive to Mount Warren and begin asking questions that should have been asked thirty-two years ago. Whoever killed Marilyn Baker got away with murder.

Time to change that.

But Jason Fisher's siblings could still be alive, if Flint could find them first.

He checked his weapon and travel gear. After the ambush in Kentucky, he wasn't taking any chances.

Mount Warren was a seven-hour drive. Plenty of time to think about how to approach a cold case murder without revealing that the victim was his mother.

He glanced outside where Houston's city lights stretched toward the horizon.

Somewhere out there, tactical teams were reporting to their employers. Whoever was pulling the strings would know the Kentucky operation had failed.

They'd try again. Different approach. Better planning.

Let them come.

He set his phone alarm for 6 a.m. and fell into bed.

CHAPTER 10

March 17

Houston

FLINT'S ALARM BUZZED FIFTEEN minutes early. He'd slept fitfully and lain awake for the past hour anyway. Staring at the ceiling and thinking about tactical teams and tactical mistakes had not fully metabolized the adrenaline that flooded his system in Kentucky.

The pre-dawn darkness pressed against his bedroom windows. Occasional headlights swept across from the street below. Houston's humid air clung to the glass, a hazy barrier between his quiet sanctuary and the awakening city.

He rolled out of bed and headed for the kitchen. Coffee first. Then a shower and the seven-hour drive to Mount Warren.

Flint's encrypted phone sat on the kitchen counter where he'd left it. Two missed calls from Gaspar in Miami. Both logged at 3 a.m.

Which wasn't all that unusual.

Gaspar rarely slept, anyway. He'd been shot in the line of duty back when he was still FBI and there had been only so much the doctors could do. He never complained or let the pain interfere with his work. But he popped Tylenol like candy when he thought no one would notice.

Steam rose from the coffee maker. The rich aroma filled the small kitchen. The granite countertops reflected the under-cabinet lighting. Light and shadow created sharp angles across the room's clean surfaces.

Flint poured coffee and hit the call back button.

"You're up early," Gaspar said when he answered on the first ring.

"Couldn't sleep. You called?"

"Found something. Thought you'd want to know before you left for Mount Warren."

Flint checked his watch. He needed to be on the road soon to make the meeting with Sheriff Milliken. But Gaspar wouldn't have called unless it was important.

"What did you find?" Flint asked.

"I ran those database searches you wanted. Missing children, homeless shelters, social services records."

Flint scratched his befuddled head. "I didn't ask you to run any searches."

Gaspar was quiet for a moment. "Drake called me around midnight. Said you wanted systematic searches for displaced children. Three kids and a teenage female."

Flint smiled despite himself. Drake had anticipated the need.

"Drake give you any parameters?"

"Geographic focus on states near Kentucky. Children aged approximately three years and an infant. Teenage female, sixteen to eighteen," Gaspar replied. "Emergency housing situations most likely to yield results."

That sounded like Drake. Thorough. Methodical. He'd probably been thinking about the search criteria during the flight back to Houston.

"What did you find?"

"Illinois homeless shelter in Ravenswood. Late October. A young woman with three children arrived without warning seeking emergency housing."

Flint grabbed a pen from the drawer. The ballpoint clicked when he pulled it from its holder. "Names?"

"Lisa Peterson. Children listed as Melvin, Dennis, and Carolyn Peterson."

"Ages?"

"Melvin and Dennis were reportedly four years old. Carolyn was nine months."

The ages were close enough to the Fisher children. The twins, Dylan and Kevin, would have been three at the time of the fire. Maureen would have been eight months old.

"The woman's age?"

"Eighteen. Claimed to be fleeing an abusive family situation. Said the children were hers and she needed protection."

Smart cover story. Lizzy Pace would have been sixteen back then, but claiming she was eighteen gave her adult legal status. Which meant she had total legal authority over herself and her children.

Old enough to make decisions for all four of them without requiring permission and protection from child protective services.

"How did you track this down?" Flint asked.

"Started with the Department of Children and Family Services databases in states surrounding Kentucky. Cross-referenced emergency placements by date range and family composition. This case pinged in Ravenswood, Illinois, because the family had no prior records. No birth certificates. No medical histories. Nothing but the clothes on their backs, actually."

Flint said, cocking his head as he poured a steaming cup of coffee. "Did they check DNA back then?"

The early morning light filtered through the kitchen window. Long shadows stretched across the hardwood floor. Traffic sounds from the street below grew more frequent as Houston came to life.

"No DNA. But the social worker noted several red flags. Lisa Peterson was evasive about her family background," Gaspar's keyboard clicked as he pulled up more files. "The children seemed frightened but not malnourished or abused. The biggest red flag was the medical examinations."

"Why?"

"Recent smoke inhalation damage to their lungs. All four of them showed damage to both lungs."

"Sounds like a promising lead, doesn't it?"

"Possibly." Gaspar sipped and swallowed before he continued, "The smoke inhalation was documented during the intake physicals. Consistent with exposure to house fire, according to the records."

Flint nodded, clicking the pieces into place. Lizzy must have grabbed them from the nursery and hustled them out of the burning house.

She might have seen the arsonist. The boys might have seen him, too.

But then what?

CHAPTER 11

March 17
Houston

"HOW LONG DID THEY stay at the shelter?" Flint asked.

"Initial placement was approved for thirty days. They were gone before the term ended. But there are follow-up records." Gaspar summarized aloud while reading from one of his screens. "Lisa Peterson got a job at a convenience store. Rented an apartment. Enrolled the children in daycare."

Flint asked, "How long did they stay in the Ravenswood area?"

"Fifteen or sixteen months," Gaspar summed up the reports. "She was a good tenant. Paid rent on time. Neighbors described her as quiet, devoted to the kids. Worked double shifts to support them."

"Any social services involvement after she left the shelter?" Flint asked.

"Minimal. The kids were healthy. Well-fed. Peterson attended parenting classes voluntarily. Took them to the public library for story time," Gaspar scanned faster through the reports. "Everything you'd expect from a young mother trying to do right."

"Any photos in the files at all?" Flint asked.

"Not so far, but I'll keep digging."

Lizzy Pace had been sixteen years old when she fled that burning house with three children. She'd somehow managed to create new identities and build a stable life for them.

Flint wagged his head slowly as if he couldn't quite believe it. Not many sixteen-year-old babysitters would have been so resourceful. Lizzy Pace was a remarkable girl.

"Then what happened to them?"

"Another tragedy, unfortunately," Gaspar replied. "Lisa Peterson was diagnosed with pancreatic cancer a couple of months before she died. Stage four. Terminal."

Flint felt a physical pain in his chest. Lizzy Pace had saved those children. Hidden them. Protected them with a false identity. Then cancer had destroyed her and taken what little security the kids still had.

"She died," Gaspar continued quietly. "Stepped in front of a bus."

Flint felt his eyes pop open almost without his volition. "Intentionally?"

"Coroner ruled it accidental."

"You think otherwise?" Flint asked.

"Dunno. Nothing about her behavior screams suicide risk. But she was weak from chemotherapy. Maybe not thinking clearly. She could have stumbled off the sidewalk at the wrong time," Gaspar said while skimming the accident reports. "The bus driver was devastated. Retired from his job the same day and left the state."

Flint processed the timeline. Lizzy Pace had been sick for two months. Dying. Worried about what would happen to the Fisher children when she was gone.

She was probably overwhelmed and could see no other way out. People had certainly killed themselves for less.

"What happened to the children?" Flint asked.

"The state took them into emergency custody when she didn't return to pick them up from daycare and there was no other option." Gaspar paused. "Foster care placement initially."

Flint nodded. It made sense. Three traumatized children. False identities. No verifiable family history. Social services would have had no choice but to place them in the system.

"Were the siblings kept together in the same facilities?"

"Negative. Separated. Three different families. Three different cities across Illinois," Gaspar murmured as he read. "Eventually, all three families moved out of state. It'll take a while to track them down."

"Do you have the placement records? Photos in the later files?"

"I'm working on it. Foster care databases are more restricted. But I can access them, with a bit of effort."

Flint glanced at the clock. "I've got to get on the road. What can you tell me at this point?"

Gaspar's keyboard clicked faster. The sound came through the phone like distant rain on a tin roof. "Preliminary records show Melvin Peterson was placed with a family in Peoria. Dennis Peterson went to Springfield. Carolyn Peterson was placed in Chicago."

"Adoption records?"

"That's where it gets even more complicated. All three children were eventually adopted, but their files were sealed. Closed adoptions. New names. New identities."

"New identities? Why?" Flint asked.

"Buried deep in the original file was a medical history. Lisa, the young mother, told her initial case workers that she'd run away with her children because she'd been impregnated by her father. She said he'd also threatened to kill them rather than let that knowledge go public," Gaspar said with a low whistle. "No one would want to return those kids to a man like that, even if they could have found the non-existent dude."

"Right. Lizzy Pace might have been sixteen, but she was a very brave and brilliant girl, wasn't she?" Flint checked his watch again. "Send me everything you have. Names, addresses, placement histories. We can talk more later."

"Already in your secure email. Along with copies of the original shelter intake forms."

"Anything else?"

"One more thing," Gaspar said. "The convenience store where Lisa Peterson worked. It's still there. Same owner. Guy named Ahmad Patel. He might remember her."

Flint wrote down the address. Ravenswood, Illinois was a sixteen-hour drive from Houston. Doable as a day trip, possibly, but only if he postponed the Mount Warren meeting.

Which wasn't feasible. Sheriff Milliken had been waiting thirty-two years for someone to care about Marilyn Baker's murder. Flint wouldn't make him wait any longer.

"I need to call Drake," Flint said. "Coordinate next steps."

"He's probably still asleep." Gaspar put a grin in his voice. "Like normal people."

"Drake's not normal people." Flint joked as he ended the call and headed to the shower.

Twenty minutes later, he was dressed and preparing to leave. He dialed Drake.

"Morning. Been up since five. Couldn't sleep either. Too much excitement yesterday," Drake said with his usual good humor. "Gaspar find anything useful?"

"Possibly."

The sky had lightened from deep black to charcoal gray. Streetlamps still glowed along the residential street. They created pools of yellow light that would soon be overwhelmed by the rising sun.

Flint brought Drake up to speed on Gaspar's initial search results. Drake listened without interrupting.

"So the kids are alive," Drake said finally. "Lizzy Pace saved them."

"And may have died protecting them."

Drake sounded troubled. "Which means Jason Fisher is about to learn his siblings survived the fire but lost their protector to cancer."

Flint had also considered the emotional impact such news would have. Jason Fisher had hired him to investigate whether his siblings might be alive. Learning that they'd all survived, but then suffered more trauma, wouldn't be easy news to deliver or receive.

Didn't establish exactly what happened to the children after Lizzy Pace died, either.

"When do we tell him?" Drake asked.

"Not until we have more concrete information. Adoption records. Current identities. Maybe contact information."

"He's paying us to find answers. This is a pretty big answer we found."

Flint understood Drake's point. But partial information could be worse than no information. Jason Fisher would want to contact his siblings immediately. Which could be disastrous for everyone involved.

CHAPTER 12

March 17
Houston

"WE'LL DO THIS ONCE and do it right, okay?" Flint said. "Develop the complete information first. Then present it to Fisher in the best way possible."

"Agreed. What's the plan?"

"Go to Illinois. Track down the adoption records. Get current identities and location information. I'll handle a few loose ends today and reconnect with you tonight."

"You sure about splitting up? Those tactical teams are still out there," Drake cautioned.

Flint had been thinking about security all morning. Military contractors didn't give up after one failed operation. They'd regroup. Better planning. Different approach.

"If they're monitoring us, they'll expect me to stay local and continue the Fisher investigation."

And if he were being watched, going in the opposite direction might cause enough confusion to buy them some time.

"Maybe," Drake said dubiously.

His concerns were valid. Mount Warren was a small town. Which meant limited law enforcement and fewer witnesses. If the Kentucky tactical team wanted a second shot, rural Texas would be ideal hunting ground.

"Don't worry. I'll take precautions," Flint said.

"What kind of precautions?"

"Same ones you'll be taking." Flint walked to his gun safe. "Backup weapon. Extra ammunition. Encrypted communications via secure satellite phone. GPS tracker."

The safe was built into the wall of his home office. It was concealed behind a framed photograph of the Houston skyline. He entered the combination and the steel door swung open. He scanned his collection of weapons and tactical gear. Everything was organized exactly as he'd placed it.

He pulled out his backup pistol and a spare magazine.

"Body armor?"

Flint grinned. "That's a bit extreme for the job. But sure. Why not? Concealed vest. Light enough for comfort. Effective against small arms fire."

"What about the truck?" Drake asked.

Flint's Ram 1500 wasn't armored, but it was reliable and fast. More importantly, it wasn't the vehicle the tactical team had seen in Kentucky. Still, he didn't want them targeting his personal vehicle, either.

"I'll take a rental. Something anonymous. Pay cash."

"Good thinking. I'll do the same. What about communications?"

"Check in every two hours. If you don't hear from me, assume something's wrong."

Drake was quiet for a moment. "Maybe we should stick together."

"We need you to work the Illinois angle. This job is already difficult enough. We can't let the trail get any colder," Flint replied. "And we don't want them to find the kids before we do."

"True. But if those guys grab you, the kids won't be helped either."

Flint understood Drake's concern. He wasn't wrong. There absolutely was danger ahead. For both of them. For half a moment, he considered changing his plan.

Marilyn Baker's murder had been unsolved for thirty-two years. Would a few more weeks really matter?

He shook his head quickly to reject the suggestion. He'd found a cooperative law enforcement officer who'd been first on the scene where Marilyn Baker died. Which meant Sheriff Milliken was Flint's best chance to solve his mother's murder.

Milliken was willing to talk now, but he could change his mind. Or be ordered to let the case languish while pressing matters took priority.

No. Flint would forge ahead. Some opportunities didn't come twice.

Flint said, "Engage well-placed paranoia. Trust no one. Assume everyone's watching."

"Roger that. I'll work with Gaspar until I hear from you," Drake replied. "We may need additional resources."

"Jason Fisher will be more than happy to pay for whatever we need, trust me," Flint said. "Get whatever you need, and I'll worry about the cost later."

Drake paused. "You realize what this means?"

"Lizzy Pace was a hero. She saved three children and died protecting them," Flint said. "What more do we need to know?"

"Twenty-four years ago, someone ordered the Fisher house torched intending to kill everyone inside. Most likely an arsonist. The conspiracy had serious resources and a very long reach," Drake replied. "The family thought the kids and Lizzy were dead. Why'd they let it go?"

Flint had been thinking the same thing. Yesterday's Kentucky ambush proved someone was still actively protecting those secrets. Which suggested the original conspiracy was still operational.

"Whoever ordered the fire might still be alive. Still powerful. Still dangerous," Drake said. "And now they may know we're close to finding the Fisher children."

"They failed and they're likely to escalate. When we find one of the missing kids, we'll need to move fast," Flint said. "Before the opposition can regroup to stop us."

"Or eliminate us completely."

"That too," Flint checked his watch. Houston's traffic patterns would have shifted from early commuters to a steady flow of rush hour. "I'll call you from the road. Keep Gaspar working. And watch your back."

Drake said, "Copy that. You, too."

Flint hung up. Three names, written in Lizzy Pace's handwriting, on shelter intake forms.

The Fisher children survived the fire. Lizzy Pace had saved them and protected them until cancer, and a heavy bus, finished the job the arsonist started.

Now someone was willing to deploy military contractors to keep the kids concealed.

But the Fishers were out there somewhere. Foster families. Adoptive parents. New names and new lives.

Jason Fisher deserved to know his siblings had survived.

Lizzy Pace deserved a medal for saving them.

Outside, Houston was waking up. Early commuters heading to work. Normal people living normal lives.

The sky had shifted from gray to pale blue. It was streaked with thin clouds that caught the early light. Traffic sounds grew steadier. The city shook off sleep and prepared for another day. Somewhere in the distance a dog barked, and a garbage truck rumbled down a parallel street.

Somewhere out there, tactical teams were planning their next move. Corporate resources being reallocated. Better equipment. Better planning.

Let them come.

The truth was surely worth the risk.

CHAPTER 13

March 17
Houston

FLINT HAD PACKED LIGHT. A small black duffel bag containing concealed body armor, backup Glock, three spare magazines, and basic medical supplies. Everything else he might need was already in his head.

He locked the house and walked four blocks through the quiet residential neighborhood to the taxi stand on Westheimer. The morning air was cool and humid, typical for Houston in March. A yellow cab idled at the corner. The driver read a newspaper folded to the sports section.

"Where to?" the driver asked as Flint slid into the back seat.

"Thornton's Body Shop," Flint replied. "Do you know it?"

"Yeah," the driver said as he started the meter and rolled into traffic.

The twenty-minute ride took them through downtown Houston and into the industrial district. Thornton's specialized in customized vehicles for clients who valued discretion and durability over flashy rides.

The shop owner, Big Jim Thornton, was waiting with keys to an armored black Ford Expedition. From the outside, it looked like any other suburban family hauler. Inside, it featured ballistic panels in the doors, run-flat tires, and a reinforced frame. The frame itself was designed to punch through roadblocks.

"Same as always," Thornton said, handing over the keys. "Bring it back in one piece."

"That's the plan."

Flint loaded his gear and pulled onto the Interstate headed north. For the first fifty miles, he maintained steady highway speed. He checked his mirrors for surveillance. Three different vehicles had followed him for varying distances. All eventually exited or changed lanes in patterns consistent with normal traffic.

Which didn't mean he was totally clean, but it was mildly reassuring.

He left the interstate and picked up the state highway west toward Mount Warren. A two-lane road cut through the rolling Texas countryside dotted with pine forests and cattle ranches. Light traffic. Good visibility. Perfect conditions for spotting trouble.

Twenty miles from Mount Warren, the road curved through a dense stand of loblolly pines. Flint rounded the bend and saw the problem immediately.

A white panel van sat sideways across both lanes blocking the road completely. Only an instant glance was required to size things up.

No skid marks. No accident damage. Deliberate placement to block the road.

Flint's foot moved to the brake pedal. His eyes swept the tree line on both sides of the road.

Brief movement in the shadows was followed by muzzle flashes erupting from concealed positions.

Automatic weapons fire stitched across the Expedition's windshield.

The reinforced glass spider-webbed and held.

Rounds sparked off the armored door panels.

In his rearview mirror, a second vehicle appeared around the curve behind him. Black Suburban. Accelerating fast.

More shooters.

Flint was boxed in.

Nowhere to go except through the trees.

He floored the accelerator and yanked the wheel hard right. He aimed the Expedition's reinforced front end at the thickest part of the pine forest. The heavy SUV crashed through the undergrowth. It snapped saplings and bounced over fallen logs.

Branches scraped against the armored glass. He fought to control the vehicle on uneven terrain.

Behind him, the Suburban tried to follow and got hung up on a stump twenty yards into the woods.

More gunfire erupted from his left. The tactical team had repositioned. They tried to bracket him between multiple firing positions.

This team was better equipped and better trained than the Kentucky crew.

Flint's encrypted phone buzzed with an incoming call. He crashed deeper into the forest as he glanced briefly at the caller ID.

Drake's number.

He answered the phone as he steered around a massive oak tree.

"Little busy right now," Flint said.

"Flint, listen to me," Drake said urgently. "Change of plans. Don't go to Mount Warren."

A high-velocity round punched through the Expedition's rear window. Flint ducked instinctively but managed to maintain his grip on the steering wheel.

"Too late for that," Flint said.

"What's happening?"

Flint processed the tactical situation as he navigated between two massive pine trunks. "Roadblock. Coordinated assault. Pros. For sure."

The Expedition's engine roared. Flint pushed it up a steep incline covered in loose pine needles.

His pursuers were on foot now. They followed his tire tracks through the forest.

"Get to Illinois," Flint said. "Work the adoption angle. Don't let them slow you down."

"What about you?"

Another burst of automatic weapons fire echoed through the trees behind him. Closer than before. They were gaining ground.

"I'm currently discussing strategy with some very unfriendly people in a pine forest outside Mount Warren."

"Flint—"

The encrypted satellite phone went dead.

Electronic jamming.

Flint focused on driving. The trees were thinning ahead. They gave way to open pastureland. He could see a farmhouse in the distance. Maybe a quarter mile away.

If he could reach it, he'd have better cover. Possibly a landline to call for backup.

He pressed the accelerator and his SUV burst from the tree line into bright sunlight.

Behind him, the tactical team emerged from the forest on foot. They spread into a skirmish line and advanced across the open ground.

Flint counted at least six shooters. Full tactical gear. Advanced optics. Coordinated movement patterns revealed extensive military training.

He floored the accelerator toward the farmhouse. The SUV's engine began to sputter. Steam poured from under the hood. At least one round had found the radiator.

The SUV was dying.

Three hundred yards to the farmhouse.

Two hundred.

One hundred.

The engine seized with a grinding metallic shriek. The SUV coasted to a stop fifty yards short of the farmhouse.

Which, Flint could now see, was abandoned. Boarded windows. Collapsed front porch. No help there.

In his mirrors, the tactical team closed fast.

Flint grabbed his gear and rolled out of the disabled vehicle. He used it for cover while he quickly evaluated his options.

The abandoned farmhouse offered concealment. No escape routes.

The open pasture provided no cover at all.

But there was something else.

He spied an old storm cellar built into a low hill behind the farmhouse. Stone construction that would stop rifle rounds. Single entrance that he could defend.

If he could reach it.

Flint slung the duffel bag over his shoulder and sprinted toward the cellar. The first shots rang out behind him. Rounds snapped through the air around him. They kicked up dirt clods from the pasture.

He dove behind the storm cellar's entrance. A burst of automatic fire chewed into the stone wall where his head had been.

The heavy wooden door was secured with an old padlock. The wood around the hasp was rotten. Flint kicked it twice and the door swung open.

Inside, concrete steps descended into darkness.

He tumbled down the steps. More gunfire erupted outside. The cellar was maybe eight feet square. It was carved out of limestone bedrock. No windows. No back door.

Perfect defensive position. Or the perfect trap. Could go either way.

Flint pulled on the body armor and checked his weapons. The backup pistol held fifteen rounds. Three spare magazines gave him sixty total.

Against multiple expert shooters with automatic weapons.

Not great odds.

Footsteps approached the cellar entrance. He heard voices calling crisp tactical commands.

Flint found a defensive position and waited.

The first shadow appeared in the doorway.

CHAPTER 14

March 17
Texas

FLINT PRESSED HIS BACK against the rough-hewn wall and assessed the situation as rapidly as possible. His nose wrinkled when he caught a whiff of limestone that smelled like damp earth as the cold seeped through his jacket.

Tool marks scarred the stone walls as if picks and chisels had carved the space from bedrock. Moisture beaded on the limestone surface and water dripped steadily into puddles on the uneven floor.

"You've been in worse spots. All you gotta do is survive the next sixty seconds," he murmured aloud. But it wasn't so simple, and he knew it.

Angular shadows fell across the concrete steps in the pale afternoon light, and he flattened himself against the wall.

Every sound echoed in the confined space like whispers in a cathedral. Which meant to stay undiscovered he barely moved.

A shadow appeared in the doorway, backlit against the daylight streaming down from above. Flint noted the man's gear and his rifle aimed and ready.

Before he could see the attacker's head, Flint aimed and squeezed the trigger.

The shot echoed through the limestone chamber like a cannon blast bouncing off the stone walls. It hammered his eardrums. Smoke burned his nostrils.

The point man dropped instantly.

His rifle clattered down the concrete steps.

The harsh metallic ringing seemed to go on forever in Flint's ears, making sounds difficult to discern.

Shouts erupted outside. Heavy boots scrambled across gravel.

The wounded man groaned.

"Man down!" one of his cronies called out. "Medic! I need a medic over here!"

The injured man struggled to wiggle out of his vest and slapped both hands over his bleeding wound. His voice was weak and barely audible. "Tom, I'm hit bad."

Flint stayed in position with his pistol aimed at the entrance. He waited for the next attempt. His breathing came fast and shallow in the confined space while sweat stung his eyes despite the cool underground air.

More voices. Tactical commands barked in crisp language. A communication style Flint appreciated in combat.

"Flank left around the building," the team leader ordered. "Cover that entrance."

A moment later, someone dragged the wounded man back from the entrance. His boots scraped against concrete. They pulled him clear, but he'd died in the process.

The sounds above faded to whispers, then silence.

The man's rifle lay on the floor near the stairs. A modified AR-15. Flint could barely see the grip and stock from his position in the dim light. He made out black polymer furniture. Extended magazine. Optics mounted on the rail system.

Flint moved fast. Three quick steps. The limestone walls seemed to press close on either side. He grabbed the rifle and the vest, solid, familiar, and reassuring in his hands.

He scrambled back to his defensive position before the outside team reacted.

"Movement in the target area," one of them called out. *Much better odds now.*

The cellar felt smaller with the rifle in his hands. The barrel length forced him to keep even closer to the wall, but the firepower advantage was worth suffering the cramped conditions.

"We know you're in there." The team leader again. Calm but pointed. His words echoed down through the entrance. "Let's discuss this like adults."

Flint said nothing. No point in conversation with people trying to kill him. His breath misted in the cool air. The stone walls absorbed sound from outside and amplified every noise.

The leader continued. "Nobody else needs to get hurt today. We just want to talk."

Long pause.

He made out radio chatter too quiet to hear clearly or understand.

Flint surmised the team was regrouping to plan their next move, which was worrisome. He scanned his position again.

The storm cellar had been built to last. Limestone blocks fitted together with minimal mortar. The ceiling was low enough that he could reach up and touch the wooden beams that supported the entrance.

"Your call," the team leader warned Flint after losing patience with his powers of persuasion. "Easy way or hard way. What's it going to be?"

Flint checked the rifle. Thirty-round magazine. Three spares from the vest. Full automatic capability. Standard military loadout. The weapon had been well-maintained. Clean action. No visible wear.

As satisfied as possible with his position, Flint readied himself and waited.

The second assault came swiftly.

"All units, fire on three," the leader threatened Flint and commanded his team simultaneously. "One... two... execute!"

Instantly, fire flew toward the entrance from multiple positions. Muzzle flashes were visible through the entrance like strobe lights.

Flint detected the sharp rifle cracks mixed with the deeper noise of shots from automatic weapons. Once they began, Flint assessed capabilities and fighting strength.

Not as good as he'd expected. Which was more than okay.

Rounds that actually managed to enter through the open space sparked off limestone walls. White chips flew like shrapnel. The stone absorbed most of the impact while fragments stung his face and hands.

A second man rushed the entrance as four men provided cover fire. He stood a moment too long in the open.

Flint put two rounds center mass this time because the man was standing and well lit, which gave him two clear shots.

The shooter's body armor absorbed some impact but the hydrostatic shock from the pressure wave assured that he'd never move again. His body tumbled down the steps, coming to a full stop at the bottom and blocking the small walkway.

"Man down!"

The gunfire stopped abruptly.

The sudden silence was almost as jarring as the gunfire.

More shouting. Angry voices fueled by adrenaline and astonishment. The practiced calm was cracking. Flint grinned.

They'd lost two men already. How many were they willing to sacrifice?

"This was supposed to be a simple extraction," one of the team complained loudly in the strange silence.

"Nothing's simple with this guy," another replied.

"What's the plan now, boss?"

Flint settled in to wait. His defensive position was nearly perfect. Single point of entry. Stone walls thick enough to stop rifle rounds. Clear field of fire at anyone else foolish enough to try those steps.

The only weakness in his current position was that he had no escape route. He shrugged. Nothing he could do about that now.

He'd counted six voices earlier. Now, two were permanently silenced. Four more.

The air inside the cellar grew thicker with gun smoke and stone dust. Every breath tasted like limestone grit and burned powder. Sweat soaked his shirt despite the underground chill.

"Won't be long now," he murmured.

He'd barely muttered the words when he heard them discussing gas canisters. Tear gas or some kind of crowd control agent, no doubt.

Metal clinked against metal. They were preparing weapons. What kind?

"Deploy on my signal," the leader said loudly, and then issued quiet final instructions too low to understand.

A man with canisters rushed forward and appeared briefly at the entrance.

Flint shot him before he could deploy the weapons.

Three rounds slammed the man high in the chest. He fell back and dropped the canisters. All three clanged on the steps as they rolled and bounced down.

They came to rest against the body at the bottom but didn't activate.

The voices outside grew heated. Flint caught fragments of an argument.

Panic. Excellent.

"Three men down," one said. "This is bullshit."

"Shut up and do your job," the leader snapped harshly.

Professionalism predictably gave way to anger and impatience when the team wasn't as well trained as expected. Flint allowed himself a quick smirk.

"Two-man entry," the leader called. "Continuous fire until we're in position."

Thanks for the warning, pal.

A moment later, two men rushed forward from different angles. One high. One low. Both moved fast and shot continuously.

Muzzle flashes lit the entrance like flash lightning.

Stone chips flew from the steps where bullets struck.

Flint waited for the right moment and took the high man first. Two quick shots. He fell backward, away from the entrance.

Then Flint shifted to the low man who was scrambling for cover.

He fell backward up the steps, firing as he went.

Flint seized the moment to take him out. He fell, blocking the entrance.

Both targets were done before they'd made it anywhere close to his position.

Five down. Flint grinned.

Even the wind had died to nothing. The only sounds were Flint's breathing and the steady drip of water somewhere in the darkness behind him.

He'd been careful with his ammunition. Twenty-three rounds left in the current magazine. Three full spares. Enough for a sustained fight if necessary.

But the fight seemed to be over. Dust motes danced in the shaft of light from above.

Still, he waited. Flint excelled when patience was required.

Was the field clear?

Could be a trap or total withdrawal.

Either way, the cellar had kept him alive. No point in getting careless now.

He waited a full twenty minutes of complete silence.

He heard no human activity anywhere nearby.

Even the insects had gone quiet. The afternoon light from above grew softer. Clouds passed across the light he could see from the entrance.

Time to find out what was going on. He couldn't stay in the limestone cave forever.

Flint moved to the entrance. He listened carefully. Nothing.

The stone steps felt solid under his boots as he climbed around the fallen.

Rifle ready, he scanned for threats.

Each step moved him closer to the surface and whatever waited above.

When his head cleared the entrance, he scanned quickly and then thoroughly.

The farmhouse yard was once again vacant. Five bodies were scattered in the area around the cellar's entrance.

No movement anywhere else.

Blood soaked into the hard-packed earth.

Gear lay abandoned where the men had fallen.

Flint moved carefully, using the ruined farmhouse for cover.

Broken boards and shattered glass crunched under his feet.

He found tire tracks in the dirt near the north corner of the farmhouse. Two vehicles. Deep tread marks in the soft earth. Both gone.

He'd counted six voices initially. Five were dead. Only one man left, the leader.

Had one abandoned the field at the outset and the leader before he finished the job?

They'd been poorly trained, but well-equipped fighters. Flint's instinct said the leader, at least, would not have retreated to return and report such a colossal mission failure.

He studied the tree line until he found it.

Dense woods maybe a hundred yards from the farmhouse. Perfect overwatch position for a sniper with a long-range rifle.

The shadows under the trees were deep enough to hide a dozen men, if that many were involved. Too much cover for his comfort.

A gunshot came from the overwatch position exactly where he'd expected.

He saw a bright muzzle flash in the shadows.

The high-velocity round zinged past his head.

Close enough to feel the pressure wave.

Flint dove behind a concrete foundation wall to avoid the next shots. Rough cement scraped his palms and his face when he hit the ground.

"Sorry. Missed," a voice called from the woods. "Won't happen again."

Probably the leader and the one who reported to the boss. He'd stayed behind to finish the job after Flint took out his team. Which meant failure was not an option.

"You killed five of my men, Flint," the sniper called out. "As a professional courtesy, I'll make this quick."

So they knew his name.

What else did they know?

And why did they want him dead?

No time to figure that out at the moment, but the questions bumped up a few rungs on his mental priority list.

Flint low-crawled along the farmhouse foundation. Concrete blocks provided decent cover. They were old and weathered and thick enough to stop rifle rounds.

He worked his way toward the woods gradually closing the distance. Gravel bit into his knees and elbows, but he moved carefully and didn't rush.

The sniper fired twice more. Both shots hit the wall close enough to shower Flint with debris.

Flint registered the marksmanship, which was not quite good enough.

More sniper bullets followed and sent shock waves through the foundation blocks.

"You're making this harder than it needs to be," the sniper called out.

Flint said nothing. He reached the tree line and moved into better cover.

Pine needles carpeted the forest floor and muffled his footsteps. The canopy overhead blocked most of the remaining daylight.

All of which was more than okay. Flint was now invisible to the rifle scope.

The predictable sniper would relocate or risk being flanked.

Flint caught a glimpse of his gear as the sniper moved deeper into the forest. He was no more than a shadow among shadows now, but not quite silent enough.

The cat and mouse chase through dense timber lasted several minutes.

Flint followed broken branches and disturbed ground. Boot prints in soft earth. Scuff marks on tree bark. He advanced steadily toward his target.

The sniper was good. He'd probably have finished second or third in competitions. Which were not at all the same as active field conditions.

Flint located the sniper setting up a new position behind a fallen log, hyper focused on his scope adjustment.

He never heard Flint coming through the trees until it was too late. Flint had a clear sight line to his target.

The sniper whipped around, attempting to aim the rifle.

Flint shot first.

Two quick bullets.

Sniper down.

Sixth of six.

Flint hustled to secure the area. He checked each body to confirm.

No survivors. Which was more than okay.

No wounded to question or treat. Which was definitely not okay. Not even remotely.

Because Flint still had no idea who these men were, who had hired them, or why they were tracking him.

He collected the weapons and gear, confirming again that their hardware was expensive, new, and well-maintained.

With the weapons under his control now, he fruitlessly searched the bodies. None had identification or anything to indicate who hired them or why.

Their equipment cost serious money and some of it couldn't be purchased without high-level government connections. Which were easy enough to come by.

Meaning the mere existence of the equipment was not enough to supply a solid lead.

They'd driven here together. Where were their vehicles? They couldn't be far away. He gathered the weapons and ammunition and started out.

Flint didn't need to go far. He found two black SUVs parked on a logging road half a mile from the farmhouse. Texas plates. Half-full fuel tanks.

"Mystery solved," he said aloud. The second SUV must have been moved here before the firefight. There was no evidence of additional men.

A quick search of the SUV interiors revealed high-tech communications equipment stored in the center consoles.

Both vehicles were armored and equipped for surveillance operations. Bulletproof glass and run-flat tires. Highly specialized communications.

He disabled one SUV and transferred the confiscated equipment to the lead vehicle.

Then he did the same for his own gear.

He settled in behind the wheel of their SUV, which was better equipped for what might lie ahead, and left his damaged vehicle behind.

Flint tried his encrypted satellite phone. Signal restored. As he'd suspected, they'd used a signal jammer to block his calls earlier. The phone felt solid and familiar in his hands after too much of the wrong kind of silence.

He called Drake.

"I've been trying to reach you for an hour," Drake said when he picked up.

"I was busy," Flint replied. "What's your status?"

"Illinois adoption records are sealed tight, but I found a work-around. Give me a little time and I'll have the new names and addresses for all three Fisher kids."

"We don't have much time."

"What happened?"

"They sent six men to kill me. Strong team."

Drake paused. "You sure they're all down?"

"Reasonably. But they were jamming communications. They knew exactly who and where I was."

"Meaning we've got a leak," Drake said. "Assume they're monitoring everything."

"Whatever we're getting close to, they'll kill to protect it."

"I'll have the new names for the Fisher kids in a few hours. Maybe they will give us better intel. Where are you now?"

"Still on the road," Flint said as he wound his way along a dirt trail to the main drive. "Watch your back. They might come for you next."

"Copy that. And Flint?"

"Yeah?"

"Six men against one. That's some serious opposition," Drake warned solemnly.

"So don't dawdle and keep in touch," Flint agreed as he disconnected.

CHAPTER 15

March 17

Mount Warren, Texas

THE DRIVE HAD TAKEN longer than Flint expected. He'd called from the road and Sheriff Milliken had agreed to wait.

Flint arrived at the Mount Warren Sheriff's Department on the edge of town. The building was smaller than he had imagined. Single story, red brick, with a handful of patrol cars parked outside. The parking lot's asphalt had seen better decades, with weeds pushing through the edges where it met the building's foundation. A weathered American flag hung limp in the still air, and cracks spider-webbed through the concrete steps leading to the entrance. A sign by the front door read "Sheriff Ralph Milliken" in faded black letters, the paint chipped and worn by countless Mount Warren sun-drenched summers.

Inside, fluorescent lights buzzed overhead revealing every crack in the worn linoleum floors. The familiar institutional blend of coffee, old paper, and industrial cleaning solution that seemed to permeate every government building everywhere in the country. The desk sergeant looked up from her computer, her reading glasses perched on the end of her nose.

"Michael Flint to see Sheriff Milliken."

"He's expecting you. Back office, second door on the right."

Flint walked down a narrow hallway lined with public safety posters and community bulletin boards. The walls were painted an institutional beige that had yellowed with age and decades of foot traffic. Wanted posters, community event flyers, and safety notices created a patchwork of local law enforcement. He knocked once on the door marked "Sheriff" and walked inside.

Sheriff Milliken stood behind a metal desk cluttered with case files and coffee cups. The office felt cramped, with filing cabinets lining two walls and boxes of old case files stacked in corners. A single window looked out onto the parking lot. Venetian blinds were adjusted to filter the afternoon light. Milliken was younger than Flint had expected. Not yet sixty. Gray hair, solid build, wearing a crisply pressed uniform shirt with short sleeves. His hands bore the calluses of physical work and his weathered face suggested years of dealing with the harsher realities of small-town policing.

Milliken extended his hand. "Drive go okay?"

Flint shook his firm grip. "Thanks for waiting."

Milliken gave him a quick nod. "Coffee?"

"Thanks. Black, please."

Milliken poured two paper cups from a pot that looked like it had been brewing all day. The coffee smelled burnt and bitter, the kind that got stronger and more unpalatable as the hours passed. He handed one to Flint and gestured to a chair across from his desk.

"The Marilyn Baker case." Milliken settled into his chair. "Can't say I expected anyone to call about that after all these years. What's your interest?"

Flint had rehearsed this moment. He'd planned to maintain the genealogy cover story. Research for a family tree. Academic curiosity. Professional distance.

But sitting here, looking at the man who'd been first on scene thirty-two years ago, his planned approach felt wrong.

"I need to be honest with you." Flint set his coffee cup on the desk. "I recently discovered that Marilyn Baker was my mother."

"Your mother?" Milliken's eyebrows popped up as if the experience of a lifetime had flown out the window. He leaned back in his chair, the springs creaking under his weight. "I knew Marilyn Baker. She died childless. What makes you think she was your mother?"

"DNA. I was placed in foster care when I was two years old. Never knew who my mother was because she never came back for me." Flint kept his voice steady. "I learned her name only recently and that she'd been murdered. That's why she never returned."

Milliken studied him for a long moment. His expression shifted from surprise to compassion and then understanding. The lines around his eyes deepened as he processed the revelation, and Flint could see the sheriff recalibrating everything he'd assumed about this meeting.

"I'm sorry." Milliken shook his head, finally. "That explains your personal interest. How did you find out?"

"Long story." Flint didn't elaborate. "Point is, I've been avoiding this investigation for years. DNA results are impossible to ignore, I guess."

"Yeah, I can see that." Milliken stood and walked to a filing cabinet in the corner. The metal drawer protested with a screech of old tracks and worn bearings as he pulled it open. He removed a thick folder with pleated binding and returned to his desk.

"I was the young deputy first on scene back then. Twenty-two years old. It was my first homicide case." He opened the folder with the reverence of someone handling sacred relics. "I've been the sheriff here for eight years now, and I still think about the case regularly. It's always bothered me that we never solved it."

"Tell me what you remember."

"Everything." Milliken spread several photographs across the desk.

Crime scene shots. The images were stark black and white, capturing a moment frozen in time thirty-two years ago.

"We believe she died after she was last seen leaving confession at St. Michael's Church. She was found face down in the canal two days later. June twentieth." Milliken delivered the facts plainly, as if he knew Flint could take it. Which was a solid guess.

Flint examined the photographs. Her body looked small and fragile against the muddy bank of the canal. His hands remained steady as he studied the images, but something cold settled in his belly. This was his mother. The woman who had carried him, given birth to him, and then vanished from his life in the most violent way possible.

"Cause of death was suffocation. No evidence of sexual assault or beating," Milliken said, as Flint skimmed the relevant report. "Her purse, one shoe, and one glove were scattered over several hundred yards between the church and where we found her."

"Evidence trail?"

"That's what we thought at the time. Like someone grabbed her and she fought back, dropping things as she was dragged toward the water." Milliken pointed to a map marked with red X's. "Problem was, most of the physical evidence was washed away by the canal water. Made it hard to determine exactly what happened."

"What about suspects?"

"We focused on James Preston pretty early. He had a record of violence against women. No solid alibi for that night. And he was seen in the area around the time she disappeared."

"But you never charged him."

"Couldn't make it stick. Preston wasn't talking, and we didn't have enough physical evidence." Milliken closed the folder. "He died in prison. Executed. He was convicted on another murder. Different case entirely."

Flint sat back in his chair. The reports matched what he'd already discovered during his earlier research.

"Sheriff, what's your gut feeling? Do you think Preston killed Marilyn Baker?"

"Honestly? I don't know. But I always had my doubts." Milliken was quiet for a moment. He picked up his coffee cup and took a sip, maybe stalling or choosing his words. When he met Flint's eyes again, there was something else in his expression. "Don't get me wrong. Preston was a bad guy. Capable of violence, definitely."

"But?"

"But something about the Marilyn Baker case never felt right to me."

"In what way?" Flint asked.

"The scattered belongings. The location where we found her. The fact that there was no sexual assault," Milliken summarized. "Preston's offenses were crimes of opportunity. Impulsive. This felt more planned. More personal."

"You think there was another suspect," Flint said, unsure whether this was the good news or the bad.

"I know there were other suspects." Milliken stood and walked back to the filing cabinet. He knelt to the bottom drawer this time, his knees protesting audibly, and pulled out a secured evidence box. The box was gray metal with an evidence seal that had yellowed with age. "This is what I kept to myself all these years, hoping we'd be able to use it someday."

He returned to his desk and opened the box with deliberate care. The seal cracked as he broke it, releasing the musty smell. Inside were several evidence bags and a notebook filled with handwritten notes. The bags were labeled in careful block letters, each one dated and initialed.

"What am I looking at?"

"Evidence the investigators collected but couldn't use or decided wasn't important." Milliken's tone suggested cold frustration, the bitterness of a man who'd spent three decades second-guessing decisions made by others. "I was young and eager back then. Wanted to prove myself by being extra thorough. So I collected everything. Documented everything. Preserved everything."

Flint leaned forward. "What physical evidence do you still have?"

"All of it. Your mother's torn clothing. Fabric samples from the scene. Soil samples. A few other items of trace evidence, including a few blood splatters that are probably not relevant because they were diluted by the rain." Milliken picked up one of the evidence bags. Through the clear plastic, Flint could see fragments of what had once been a white blouse, now stained and torn. "You might be able to get usable DNA from what we have. Back then, we didn't have the tech for it. Nothing here will prove who murdered your mother. But something might give us a new lead, if we're lucky."

Flint stared at the bag in Milliken's hands. His mother's clothing. The fabric she'd been wearing when someone killed her. The physical connection to a woman he'd never known but whose death had shaped his entire life.

"Can we do the testing now?" Flint asked.

Milliken shook his head and gave Flint a wry grin. "You already know the answer. No town the size of Mount Warren has that kind of budget. If I had a viable suspect, maybe we could get it done. Without a good reason for the request, which we don't currently have, the budget will not be approved."

"Right. I have a lot of contacts in the best DNA testing facilities. How about I take the evidence and get it done?" Flint suggested even as Milliken was shaking his head. "Under normal circumstances, you'd have returned all of this to Baker's family at some point, right? I'm her family. You can give it to me."

Milliken sighed. "Only if you never want her killer brought to justice."

Flint stared at the evidence bag containing his mother's torn clothing. The physical proof that might finally identify her killer.

"Sheriff, I want to pursue this. I want to get that evidence tested for DNA. There may be usable trace that could lead us somewhere."

"I was hoping you'd say that." Milliken smiled for the first time since Flint had arrived. The expression transformed his weathered face, revealing a glimpse of the eager young deputy he'd once been. "I've been carrying this case around for thirty-two years. It's time to get some answers."

"What do we need to do?"

Milliken's expression shifted. He picked up the evidence bag and turned it over in his hands. The plastic crinkled softly. "That's the problem. Even if I wanted to, I can't just hand potential evidence over to you. Chain of custody rules. Any defense attorney worth his salt would get it thrown out. We'd never convict the killer."

Flint clenched his jaw. "So what are you saying?"

"I'm saying we need to do this right if we want to nail your mother's killer. Through proper channels."

The big clock on the wall had a second hand that clicked from one second to the next. The sound seemed unnaturally loud in the small office, marking time. Flint watched the clicking for ten seconds while he worked out the issues.

"Sheriff, let's be realistic here. Baker wasn't raped. There could be physical evidence on her clothing, but that won't prove who killed her." Flint swiped a palm across his face. "What are the chances we're going to find Baker's killer after thirty-two years? Even with DNA evidence?"

Milliken placed the evidence on his desk again, handling it with the reverence reserved for sacred objects. "Honestly? Not great. It's been too long, and we have too little to go on."

"So why worry about chain of custody for a case that's probably never going to trial?"

"Because I'm the Sheriff. I follow the law. It's my job to find Marilyn Baker's killer and bring them to justice, get them convicted and sentenced." Milliken met Flint's gaze steadily without equivocation. "It's precious little, but your mother deserves that much, doesn't she?"

"I admire your principles, Sheriff." Flint leaned back in his chair. "But let's be practical. The truth is that we've got a snowball's chance in a hot Texas August of finding my mother's killer with the evidence you've got. If you could have solved the case based on that evidence, you'd have done it long ago."

"Can't argue with you there. Thirty-two years of failure says you're right," Milliken admitted.

"If I take the evidence and have it tested, we might find them. I have access to resources that you can only get by following protocols. I don't have those restrictions," Flint replied patiently.

Milliken considered everything for a couple of seconds, then made his decision. "I might be able to call in a favor at the state crime lab. Rush the DNA analysis. Keep everything official and above board."

"How long would that take?"

"Few weeks, maybe a month. Depends on how busy they are."

"And I assume you'd want me to foot the bill."

"Lab fees aren't cheap. Like I said, we don't have the budget for thirty-two-year-old cold cases."

A month was a long time. But he'd waited all these years, did another month make that much difference?

Probably not. So a month was probably okay.

But the bigger issue was that once the results came back through official channels, they'd become public record. Anyone could access them. Which was definitely not okay. Flint didn't want his personal life exposed to the world in that way.

Flint said, "When word gets out that we're testing evidence in the Marilyn Baker case, the real killer could simply disappear. Or worse."

"That's a risk we'd have to take."

"You were living here when Marilyn Baker was alive. Did you know her at all?" Flint slid smoothly into discussing his mother's life instead of her death. Curiosity, he told himself. Nothing more.

"I did. She was lovely. A bit younger than me, and I was already in love with the woman who became my wife. So I wasn't looking for a relationship back then," Milliken replied. "But any man alive would have been interested in Marilyn Baker. She was definitely the marrying kind."

"I understand Felix Crane and Sebastian Shaw were living here at the time, too," Flint said. "Were they friends of yours?"

"Not hardly," Milliken snorted. "Crane and Shaw were way above my station. They were already rich and on their way to being famous. They had more money than anybody else in Mount Warren."

"Were they dating Marilyn Baker back then?"

"Possibly," Milliken said as he cocked his head and narrowed his eyes for a new perspective on old facts.

"She was Catholic and a schoolteacher. They were sons of wildcatters. Which means she was as close to a saint as women get around here while Shaw and Crane were two hellions behaving like wild cats themselves. They had very little self-control, from what I observed. We arrested them a few times for drunk and disorderly and criminal mischief and the like. They bought themselves out of every problem they ever had, for sure. But they weren't killers. Not back then, anyway."

Flint nodded, taking in the new intel. "Did you suspect either of them? For Baker's murder, I mean?"

"Tell you the truth, Flint, I always suspected Raymond Kellerman," Milliken replied.

The name meant nothing to Flint. "Who's Raymond Kellerman?"

"Marilyn's boss. He was the principal at Mount Warren Elementary where your mother taught. He'd been pursuing her for years before she was killed."

Flint frowned. "Pursuing her how?"

"Persistently. Aggressively. She wasn't interested. Rejected his advances. But he wouldn't take no for an answer. There were a couple of public skirmishes between them, even." Milliken opened one of his old notebooks. The binding was cracked and worn from years of handling. The pages were filled with his careful handwriting in blue ballpoint pen, notes taken decades ago but preserved with methodical precision. "According to several teachers I interviewed, Kellerman would find excuses to be alone with her. Made inappropriate comments. A bit of unwanted touching."

"Why didn't she report him?"

"Different time. Different attitudes about workplace harassment. And he was her boss. She not only loved the job, she needed it. Sole support of her elderly parents at the time." Milliken shrugged and turned a page. "Plus, from what I learned about your mother, she was deeply religious. Beyond devout, people say. Her parents were the same way. She believed in handling things quietly, not making waves."

"But she never changed her mind toward Kellerman? Kept rejecting him?"

"Absolutely. Three reasons. She didn't like him much, he was her boss, and he was married," Milliken said, raising one finger on his right hand for each of Marilyn's good reasons. "Beyond that, her devout parents and her own devout Catholicism meant she could never marry and have children with him, which was what she wanted out of life."

"Why not? What was wrong with him as husband and father material?" Flint asked.

"Nothing wrong with him as far as I know. He was already married and had a couple of kids. They couldn't get married in the church, even if he'd wanted to leave his wife and family. I gather, he didn't want that anyway. They're still together."

Flint processed this information. A persistent supervisor. A woman trying to maintain boundaries. Religious and moral constraints. Men had killed for less.

"What makes you suspect him?"

"Several things. Access, for one." Milliken flipped to another page in his notebook. "Kellerman had access to your mother's confession schedule at St. Michael's Church. He knew exactly when and where she'd be that night."

"How would he have that information?"

"The church kept schedules for regular parishioners who came to confession weekly. Your mother had been one of those regulars for years." Milliken met Flint's eyes. "Kellerman was on the church board. He had access to the schedules."

The pieces were starting to form a picture of a predator who knew his victim's routine. He had authority and access. He'd been pursuing Marilyn Baker, and she'd rebuffed him, but he didn't give up. Flint viewed him as a solid suspect.

"Did you investigate Kellerman at the time?"

"I tried. But the lead detective was convinced Preston was our guy. Said we didn't need to waste time on other suspects." Milliken's jaw tightened, the muscles working beneath weathered skin. "Politics. The principal was a respected member of the community. Preston was a known troublemaker. Easy choice for the department."

"What evidence do you have against Kellerman?"

"None, unless we find it here." Milliken picked up the evidence bag containing the torn clothing, holding it carefully between both hands. "Her blouse was ripped during the struggle. We have the technology to extract DNA profiles from fabric samples this degraded now."

Flint stared at the evidence bag. "You think Kellerman's DNA might be on that fabric."

"If he grabbed her. If there was a struggle. If he tore her clothing during the attack. If the rain didn't wash it away or degrade it too much." Milliken set the bag on the desk between them. "Modern technology might finally give us the answers we couldn't get before. Of course, we'd still need a confession to make it stick."

Flint considered all the angles before he asked, "So Kellerman is still alive."

"Retired about ten years ago. Still lives here in Mount Warren. Seventy-eight years old now."

For the first time since learning about his mother's murder, Flint had identified a real suspect. A motive. Physical evidence that might finally provide proof of the struggle, at least, but should definitely yield more intel than he had presently.

"What do we need to do?" Flint asked, making it clear that he'd made his decision.

"I'll contact the state crime lab. Rush the order for DNA analysis. Should have results within a month or two."

Flint's phone buzzed. A text from Drake. *Progress on the Fisher case. Need to coordinate.*

He looked at the evidence bag containing his mother's torn clothing. The physical proof that might finally identify her killer.

Then he looked at his phone. The Fisher children might still be alive. The client was paying for immediate results.

"I need to handle another case first. It's urgent. Time-sensitive."

"How long?"

"Few days. Maybe a week." Flint stood. "Marilyn Baker has waited years. She can wait a bit longer."

Milliken nodded. "Let me know when you're ready and I'll make the call."

Flint shook his hand again. "Thank you. For keeping the evidence. For caring about the case all these years."

"Marilyn Baker was well loved here. She was a kind and decent person who had a positive impact on her students and their families. She deserved better than what happened to her." Milliken walked him to the door. "And so do you."

Flint had a suspect. He had evidence. He had a path forward.

But first, he had three children to find. Drake was waiting for his call. The Fisher case couldn't wait.

But for the first time, Flint believed he might learn who killed his mother.

And why.

As Flint walked to his car, he felt eyes on him. In a town this small, strangers were noticed. Conversations were overheard. Secrets had a way of traveling faster than the people trying to keep them.

He'd come to Mount Warren hunting for his mother's killer. Was her killer hunting back?

CHAPTER 16

March 17

Ravenswood, Illinois

THE CONVENIENCE STORE WHERE Lizzy Pace had worked after the fire and before she died sat on the corner of Main and Elm as if it had been waiting for Drake to find it. Faded yellow paint peeled from aluminum siding after decades of Illinois winters. Hand-lettered signs advertised cigarettes and lottery tickets in windows streaked with grime.

An old-fashioned bell above the door chimed when he stepped inside. The sound echoed off shelves packed with quick pickup items like energy drinks and beef jerky. The store stank of burnt coffee and industrial cleaning solution.

The store's owner, Ahmad Patel, looked up from his newspaper. He was older than Drake had expected. Maybe seventy. Gray hair, thick glasses, and a cardigan that had seen better decades. Deep lines creased his face around tired eyes.

"Help you?" Patel asked.

Drake approached. The counter's scratched laminate showed decades of use, and the cash register looked older than Patel.

"Yeah, I'd like a cold bottle of water," Drake said in a friendly tone on his way to the cooler to choose one before he walked back to the register.

He placed the bottle on the counter and offered a five-dollar bill to pay for it. Patel gave him the change and Drake took a long swig.

"Wondered if you might remember someone who worked here a while ago. Young woman named Lisa Peterson."

Patel's expression shifted. Recognition mixed with caution. He set down his newspaper but didn't fold it.

"Why are you asking about Lisa after all these years? Who wants to know?"

Drake pulled out his wallet and showed his Texas private investigator's license. "My name is Alonzo Drake. I'm working for Lisa's children."

"Her kids?" Patel raised eyebrows as he continued to study the license. "They'd be grown up now."

"They're doing well." This was the tricky part, in Drake's experience. Patel wouldn't be helpful unless he felt secure. "Trying to understand what happened to their mother and piece together their early childhood. They have very few memories from before the foster system."

Patel studied the license a bit more carefully, then looked at Drake's face. "Which one hired you?"

"I can't say. Client confidentiality. But they deserve to know the truth about their mother," Drake said persuasively. "I'm sure you agree."

Patel was quiet for a long moment until, finally, his shoulders relaxed. "Lisa was a good person. She didn't deserve what happened to her."

Drake nodded. "What exactly did happen to her?"

"You don't know?"

"I know she died in a traffic accident."

"Terrible thing. She was hit by a bus. But there was more to it than that." He paused to fold his newspaper. The pages crackled in the silence. "If those kids are looking for answers, I guess they have a right to know."

"I'd appreciate anything you can tell me. I'll be sure to pass it along," Drake said.

"She was a good worker. Reliable. Always on time. Nice girl, too." Patel's voice grew warmer. "But you could see she was scared. Always worried and looking over her shoulder."

"Why?" Drake asked, but Patel didn't seem to hear.

"Those poor kids." Patel shook his head. White whiskers moved against weathered brown skin. "She was young, but she loved those kids like every child should be loved. Worked double shifts to support them. Never complained. Never once."

Drake pulled out a small notebook. He started to write. It was a technique he'd picked up from Flint. People who wanted to help were reassured when they felt that their information mattered enough to write down.

"Was she sick? The cancer?"

"Getting weaker, yes. Lost a lot of weight those last few weeks. Her hands shook sometimes when she was counting change." Patel's voice grew quiet. "I think the illness, or maybe her anxiety about it, was affecting her mind. Making her confused."

"You said she was always looking over her shoulder. Did you ever see anyone watching the store? Following her?"

"Just general anxiety, I think." Patel shook his head as he considered the question while his fingers drummed against the counter. "Lisa was one of those people who fall through the cracks, you know? She was alone in the world except for those kids. She loved them like crazy, and she worried about them constantly. She knew how ill-equipped she was to be their mother."

Drake wrote that down. "Tell me about the day she died. What happened exactly?"

Patel's face darkened as if the memory troubled him greatly.

"I saw it happen. Right out there." He pointed toward the window. "She was walking. The bus came around the corner and she stepped right into the street. I always believed she was preoccupied and simply made a mistake."

"Were you here in the store?"

"Working the register. Heard the brakes screaming, then the impact." Patel nodded slowly. "Terrible sound. You never forget something like that."

"What else do you remember?"

"Poor Tom Wilson. The bus driver. He was devastated. Kept saying she just darted right out in front of him. Like she didn't see the bus at all. He smashed the brakes, and the bus made a terrible noise, but he didn't have time to stop before hitting her. The whole town felt terrible for him."

"Would he talk to me about the accident?"

"I don't know. He quit the same day. Left town within a week. Couldn't handle it." Patel removed his glasses and cleaned them slowly. "Never came back."

Drake made notes. "What about after Lisa died? Was there a funeral service?"

Patel's face grew more somber as he shook his head again. "No family to claim the body. She couldn't afford a funeral on what I paid her. I wished I could have helped out, but back then, I was getting the store off the ground. There was no money around here, either."

"Where was she buried?" Drake asked.

Patel replied, "In the pauper's section at Hillcrest Cemetery. Just a number on a metal marker. I've never tried to find it, but there might be a record somewhere."

"What happened to the children after Lisa died?"

"The daycare called me first. Lisa had me listed as her emergency contact." Patel's voice grew quiet. "When I got there, the kids were in the office. The little girl, she was almost three at the time, I think. She was crying. The boys were five or six, maybe. They kept asking when Mama was coming back."

"How long before social services took them?"

"Maybe two hours." Patel's voice grew quiet. "The whole thing was gut wrenching. Those poor children had no idea what was happening."

"Do you remember which agency? The social worker's name?"

"County Department of Children and Family Services. The woman seemed nice enough. Said the kids would be placed with good families."

"Did you ever see them again?"

Patel shook his head. "I asked once if I could send them Christmas cards. They said it wasn't allowed. Clean break was better for everyone with young kids like that, they said."

"You said Lisa seemed overly anxious in the days before her accident." Drake leaned forward. "Was she worried about the kids?

Or was she frightened about something else?"

CHAPTER 17

March 17

Ravenswood, Illinois

PATEL WAS QUIET FOR a long moment. "Both, maybe. She was getting weaker. Lost a lot of weight. Her hands shook sometimes. Lisa was emotional, like young women are, you know?"

"I see," Drake said, to draw him out.

"That last week, she kept checking the windows. Looking over her shoulder more than usual. Twice she wanted to know if anyone had been asking about her."

"Had anyone been asking?"

"Not until you."

As the picture of young Lizzy Pace unfolded through Patel's story, Drake's sympathy increased. Too much bad luck had befallen her in her short life. Flint would feel the same.

"Do you know where Tom Wilson went? The bus driver?"

"His sister said he moved to Florida. Tampa, maybe. Changed his name back to his mother's maiden name. Thomas Murphy now, I heard."

"Changed his name? That seems unusual, doesn't it?" Drake wrote that down. Another lead to follow.

"Maybe," Patel replied. "He'd been hounded by reporters and, I'm sad to say, local residents who blamed him for Lisa's death and making three kids orphans. Even after he moved away, they kept it up. What would you have done?"

"Yeah, you're probably right." Drake nodded. "What about the kids' father? Did he show up at the funeral or try to reclaim his kids?"

"I never met the man." Patel shook his head again. "I asked Lisa about him once. She said he was evil, and she never wanted him to find those kids. She seemed really terrified, so I let it go."

Drake swallowed the rest of the water and tossed the empty bottle in the trash. "Thank you, Mr. Patel. You've been very helpful."

"Those children. Are they doing okay? The ones who hired you?"

"As far as I know, yes. Finding out about Lisa's life here will help them understand their own story. They might come to talk to you about all of this one day."

Patel nodded slowly. "If they do, I'll have nothing but good things to say about Lisa. She was young and emotional, but she tried to be a good mother."

Drake left the store and walked to his rental car. A gray Honda Accord. Anonymous and reliable. Nothing that would draw attention on Illinois highways. He'd followed Flint's advice about operational security. Boring was always better than dead.

He checked his watch. The drive to Peoria would take about two hours. Plenty of time to work his charm on the adoption records clerks before they closed for the day.

His phone buzzed. Text message from Gaspar: *Additional records attached. Foster placement details less complete than expected.*

Drake opened the encrypted files in the car. The foster care records painted a clearer picture. All three children had been initially placed with families that specialized in difficult cases. These foster families handled kids with trauma histories. Kids with false identities.

But none of the kids stayed in foster care for long. They were adopted fairly quickly.

Which meant the adoption records might be even more heavily sealed than usual.

No problem. Drake had loads of charm he could deploy to get more intel.

And if charm didn't work, he had other resources.

He merged onto the Interstate toward Peoria. Two lanes in each direction. Light afternoon traffic moved at steady speeds.

The landscape was flat and empty and still covered with snow. Farmland stretched to the horizon in all directions. Corn stubble poked through patches of dirty snow. Winter still held Illinois in its grip, although the official start of spring was only a few days ahead.

Drake spotted the tail fifteen minutes outside Ravenswood. A black SUV stayed exactly three cars back. Maintained perfect spacing through lane changes and speed variations. The driver was good.

His phone rang. Flint.

"What's your status?"

"Just finished the Patel interview." Drake checked his mirrors. The SUV was still following. "Also confirmed we've got company."

"How many?"

"One vehicle so far. Black SUV."

"Get out of there," Flint said immediately. "Abort the records search. We don't want to lead them along, just in case we do find the kids."

"Too late for that." Drake accelerated slightly. The Honda responded better than he'd expected. "I'm committed now. And we need those adoption records."

Drake cut the connection and focused on driving.

While he'd talked to Flint, the SUV had closed the gap. Only two cars back now. In the rearview mirror, Drake could see two men in the front seats. Both wore dark clothing. Straight backs. Alert positions.

Drake accelerated to eighty. The SUV matched his speed.

He slowed to sixty. The SUV slowed.

He changed lanes. The SUV followed. This was more than simple surveillance. They were in active pursuit.

Drake's military training had included convoy tactics and road ambushes where he was taught that enemies generally preferred chokepoints. Bridges. Construction zones. Anywhere the target couldn't maneuver away and escape.

Drake scanned the road ahead. The interstate crossed the Illinois River in about ten miles. Perfect ambush point.

Drake opened his go-bag and grabbed the backup pistol. Fifteen rounds of nine-millimeter ammunition. He checked the magazine. Full capacity.

The Honda wasn't armored. It was a standard civilian vehicle with thin sheet metal and glass windows. It was fast and maneuverable. Better than the heavy SUV for evasive driving.

His phone buzzed. Unknown number.

"Yeah?"

"Drake." The voice was calm. "Pull over."

"No thanks." Drake ended the call.

The SUV accelerated hard and pulled into the left lane, drawing alongside Drake's Honda. Through the side windows, he could see figures moving inside but couldn't make out details through the tinted glass.

The SUV swerved suddenly toward him. Drake yanked the wheel right as the heavy vehicle tried to ram the smaller car off the road. The Honda's tires fought for grip as he pulled onto the shoulder, gravel spraying from under his wheels.

The SUV overshot, then braked hard to match his position. Both vehicles came to a stop on the highway shoulder, engines idling in the sudden quiet.

Four SUV doors opened in unison. No wasted motion.

Four men emerged, assault rifles in hand.

When they were ten feet from the SUV, Drake floored the accelerator. The Honda shot forward.

He had maybe thirty seconds before they caught up again.

Time to improvise.

He spotted a farm road that branched off to the right. The gravel surface was worn smooth by decades of truck traffic. The road probably led to a grain elevator or farmhouse. Better terrain for what he had in mind.

Drake took the turn at sixty miles per hour. The Honda's rear end slid out. Tires fought for traction on loose gravel, but it held the road. Gravel pinged off the undercarriage like machine gun fire.

Drake glanced back in his side mirrors. The SUV made the same turn. Slower and more controlled but still coming.

The farm road led through cornfields toward a cluster of buildings. Grain silos towered against gray sky. Machinery sheds spread across muddy ground.

Nobody was around. Which meant no witnesses. Perfect.

Drake parked behind the largest shed. He rolled out of the Honda. Cold air hit his face like a slap. He left the engine running and grabbed his go-bag.

The SUV appeared thirty seconds later. It stopped fifty yards away. Tactical distance. Doors snapped open in unison again and they stepped out.

CHAPTER 18

March 17
Rural Illinois

FOUR MEN EMERGED DRESSED in full combat gear. Kevlar vests and tactical helmets. Advanced optics mounted on assault rifles. They moved in coordinated patterns with no wasted motion.

The same kind who'd tried to kill Flint in Texas.

Drake counted weapons. Four assault rifles. At least two sidearms. Probably grenades or flash-bangs.

He had one pistol with fifteen rounds.

The odds sucked.

But Drake had advantages they shouldn't expect. He knew this terrain. Farm country was his home turf. Texas farms had taught him about silos and machinery. He'd also learned a few things about asymmetric warfare in the Marines. Small unit tactics. Defensive positions. How to make superior numbers work against them.

The lead man raised a bullhorn. "Drake. We just want to talk."

Drake smiled grimly. Same lie they'd probably tried to sell Flint.

He circled behind the grain silo. The structure was concrete and steel. Reinforced to hold thousands of tons of grain. Built to last, he knew it would stop rifle rounds.

The tactical team advanced in a standard four-man formation. They covered each other's movements using textbook infantry tactics. He wondered briefly which military unit had supplied the training.

Drake let them get close to the Honda before he moved.

Close enough to commit to their approach and make retreat more difficult.

When he was satisfied with their position, Drake emerged from behind the silo and fired.

He put two rounds into the trailing man.

The target dropped without a sound, but his weapon clattered on the concrete.

The noise alerted the remaining members of his team. The three spun toward his position like a choreographed dance.

By the time muzzle flashes erupted, Drake was already moving. He rolled behind a piece of farm machinery before the bullets sparked off its metal. High-velocity rounds punched through sheet steel.

"Contact rear!" one of them shouted.

Drake counted muzzle flashes. Three weapons still in the fight. Automatic fire echoed off the farm buildings.

Drake had thirteen rounds left.

He belly-crawled under a hay baler. Cold mud soaked through his jacket. He came up on their flank.

The team had taken cover behind the Honda.

Good cover if he'd stayed behind the silo.

But it was the wrong angle for Drake's current position.

Steadily, he fired and put three rounds into the second man. The target pitched forward, landing across the Honda's hood. Blood splattered the windshield.

"Two down," Drake muttered. "Two to go."

His effort had revealed his position to the remaining shooters. They opened fire and raked the farm equipment around him.

Hydraulic fluid spurted from punctured lines. The air smelled like hot air and chemicals.

Drake stayed low. He moved toward the machinery shed. More cover. Better angles. Concrete block construction that would stop anything they fired.

His phone buzzed. Text message.

He ignored it and stayed focused on the tactical situation.

The enemy had superior firepower but an inferior position. They were pinned behind the Honda.

Drake had the entire farm complex for cover and concealment. Grain silos. Equipment sheds. Rusted machinery. Dozens of firing positions.

Basic tactics. Use the terrain. Control the engagement. Make them come to you.

Drake worked his way around the machinery shed. His boots squelched in mud mixed with old motor oil.

Finally, he could see both remaining targets. They were focused on his last known position. Scanning the wrong sector.

He smirked. Classic mistake.

Drake lined up his next shot on the team leader. He squeezed the trigger twice. Double tap. Exactly where he'd placed the bullets.

The man spun and went down hard. His weapon clattered across the gravel. Metallic ringing echoed off concrete walls.

One left.

The last shooter broke cover. He sprinted toward the grain silo. Smart move. Better concealment. Concrete walls three feet thick.

The sprint exposed him during the movement though.

Twenty yards of open ground. No cover. Nothing to conceal him.

Drake tracked him with the pistol and then fired three times. Rapid succession.

The runner stumbled. His legs tangled. He collapsed twenty feet from cover. Face down in the mud.

Drake waited a full thirty seconds. No movement from any of the targets.

Wind whistled through the farm buildings.

He approached each body carefully. He checked for life and found none.

He searched for identification. Nothing. No wallets. No phones. No unit patches or insignia. Just high-end tactical gear and expensive weapons.

Drake called Flint's number.

Flint answered immediately. "Status report."

"Four down. All threats neutralized." Drake walked back toward the Honda. Bullet holes had ventilated the rear window and both rear quarter panels. Spider web cracks spread across safety glass. The engine compartment looked intact, which meant it was still drivable.

"You sure?" Flint asked with real concern.

"Positive. But we've got the same problem. No identification. No intelligence. These guys are ghosts."

"Corporate cleanup crew?"

"Has to be. Training, serious resources, and zero accountability." Drake checked his watch.

Two-thirty in the afternoon. Plenty of time to reach Peoria before the records office closed. Government bureaucrats kept banker's hours.

"You need backup?"

"Negative. I'm mobile and mission ready. Still planning to work my charm on those adoption records."

Flint was quiet for a moment. "They knew exactly where you were going."

"Which means we're getting close to something they desperately want to protect." Drake climbed back into the damaged Honda.

Glass crunched under his boots. Cold air seeped through bullet holes, but the engine started without complaint. Japanese reliability at its finest.

"And worth killing for," Flint said flatly.

"That too." Drake put the Honda in gear. Gravel crunched under the tires as he turned toward the main road. "I'll call you when I have the names and addresses. Should be within three hours."

"Be careful."

"Copy that." Drake ended the call and drove back toward the main road.

In his rearview mirror, four bodies lay motionless beside the grain silo.

The farm looked peaceful again from this distance.

The dead men would be discovered soon enough.

With luck, Drake would be long gone before local law enforcement came looking. He glanced at the clock on the Honda's dash. Not much time to make it to Peoria. He floored the accelerator.

CHAPTER 19

March 17

Peoria, Illinois

DRAKE STARED AT THE adoption records clerk across the scarred laminated counter. She shook her head for the third time in ten minutes. Her graying hair was pulled back in a tight bun that looked like it hadn't moved since the Truman administration.

"I'm sorry, but you cannot see those records. Illinois sealed adoption records require a court order," Brenda Cruz repeated with professional sympathy but remained firm. "There are narrow exceptions for the biological parents or the adoptees, which don't apply to you. Not for private investigators, not for other family members, not for anyone without a judge's signature."

Drake had expected bureaucratic obstacles, but he'd underestimated just how ironclad the system would be. His usual charm offensive worked on records clerks from

Houston to Miami. But it was hitting a brick wall with Brenda Cruz.

"What if I told you this was a matter of life and death?" he tried.

"Then I'd tell you to get a lawyer and file a petition with the court." Cruz leaned back in her chair. "Life or death could qualify as good cause, depending on the circumstances. Good cause is a legal term. It means a legally viable reason for the judge to unseal the records and let you see them."

Drake nodded. He understood the legal requirements. He already knew good cause was a high bar in adoption cases. Judges protected sealed records unless there were compelling reasons to open them.

He had compelling reasons, but he couldn't share them with her.

"How long does the whole process usually take?" Drake asked.

"Depends on the court's schedule and how compelling your case is. Could be weeks, could be months. Most petitions get denied unless you have relevant medical emergencies or other serious circumstances."

Cruz was being helpful within the bounds of her job. After several attempts to persuade, and her absolute refusal to budge, Drake could see this avenue would take too long and might not succeed anyway.

Drake thanked her and walked back to his rental car through the echoing marble corridors. The Honda's interior still smelled. Acrid reminders of gunshots and burning upholstery clung to the fabric seats.

He snagged his encrypted satellite phone and pressed the redial.

Flint answered on the second ring. "How'd it go with the adoption records?"

"About as well as a failed root canal." Drake started the engine and pulled out of the courthouse parking lot.

"That bad, eh?" Flint said with a grin in his voice.

"Worse," Drake replied with a scowl. "Illinois doesn't mess around with sealed adoptions. Sealed means locked and buried forever. We're looking at petitions, months of legal proceedings, and no guarantee of success."

"That's what I was afraid of. Work-arounds?"

"I'm heading to the Illinois Department of Children & Family Services office now. Foster care records from before the adoptions might be less restricted. Maybe I'll find a lead," Drake said. "Where are you?"

"About an hour out. Call me when you're done at DCFS and we'll make a plan," Flint replied before he disconnected.

Drake navigated through Peoria's late afternoon traffic, following the GPS through a maze of one-way streets and construction zones.

This part of the city felt gray and tired under overcast skies. Heavy dark clouds pressed down like a wool blanket, threatening snow.

Industrial Midwest at its most uninspiring. Strip malls and fast-food restaurants stretched along the main roads. Occasional abandoned storefronts punctuated the decay with going-out-of-business signs from years past.

The DCFS office occupied the ground floor of a concrete building that looked like it had been deliberately designed to avoid sunlight. Brutalist architecture at its most depressing.

Inside, fluorescent lights buzzed like angry wasps and turned the worn linoleum floors the color of old mustard. Cracked and broken plastic chairs that had seen better decades lined the walls.

Drake approached the reception desk where a tired-looking woman was pecking at a keyboard with two fingers. She typed without enthusiasm, suggesting she'd rather be anywhere else. Her desk was cluttered with coffee-stained paperwork and a small plastic Christmas tree as decrepit as everything else.

"I'm hoping you can help me locate foster care records." He deployed his most winning smile.

"You're family?" she asked without looking up from her computer.

"Private investigator." Drake showed her his Texas license. She barely gave it a passing glance. He checked her name plate. "Ms. Stevens, we're working on an identity theft case. My client is an elderly widow whose late husband left her a small inheritance. A woman claiming to be the husband's illegitimate daughter from a previous relationship showed up and my client has been sending her money. The widow's son hired me to verify whether this woman is really who she claims to be. If she is, my client has a sister he wants to get to know. If she isn't legitimate, then she's a scammer. She says her name is Lisa Peterson. Everything I've learned so far suggests she's a scammer."

That got her attention. She stopped typing and looked at him with renewed interest.

"Identity theft from the elderly is serious business," Stevens replied. "People should go to prison for that."

"Very serious and yes, if she's a scammer she needs to go to prison," Drake said as if he were warming up. "I located several women named Lisa Peterson and ruled them out. I tracked the last one to Ravenswood, Illinois. Records and witnesses say she was killed in a bus accident. Her three children went into foster care and then were adopted. I need to interview her children before the scammer bankrupts the widow, or worse."

"What would be worse than scamming a sick old lady out of her money, leaving her alone and destitute?" Gloria asked, as if she could think of nothing more reprehensible.

Drake cleared his throat but didn't argue since Gloria seemed to be softening. "She probably has several widows and widowers involved in her scam. They often do."

"That's disgusting." Gloria studied his card more carefully until she made up her mind. She squared her shoulders. "I've got a sick, old mother and I'd do everything in my power to stop someone like that from scamming her. You got names for the kids?"

"Melvin, Dennis, and Carolyn Peterson." Drake cleared his throat and put a pleading note into his voice. "I've hit every possible dead end up until now. If I'm going to help these people, the real Lisa Peterson's children are my last chance. You'd be doing a real public service if you helped me out."

Gloria turned to her computer and typed for several minutes. Drake watched her expression shift from bureaucratic indifference to something that looked like recognition.

"Peterson kids," she said finally after she skimmed through the summary reports. "I remember that case. That poor woman and her children went through enough."

"You worked here back then?"

"Been here twenty-eight years next month." Gloria's fingers continued clicking across the keyboard. "They all had it rough. The mother was all the family those kids had. We tried to locate other family members at the time but had no luck. Sad situation. Very sad."

Drake felt his pulse quicken. "What makes you so certain about the family?"

"Well..." Gloria glanced around the office to confirm they were alone and then leaned closer. "I lived over in Ravenswood back then. Met Lisa Peterson several times at the convenience store where she worked. She was the real deal. A devoted mother who'd clearly been through hell to protect her children. And so young, too. Anyone using her identity now to scam is despicable."

"Now's your chance to help her take care of those kids," Drake said, nodding with a winsome smile as he stretched his neck to peer at her screen.

CHAPTER 20

March 17
Peoria, Illinois

THREE FILE SUMMARIES WERE displayed in a cramped font that only a government agency would love. His quick glance showed basic placement information. Names, dates, case numbers reduced to bureaucratic shorthand. He could see enough to confirm the basic intel Gaspar had found and a bit more.

She noticed him looking and gave him a glare before she gave a warning glance up at a CCTV camera in the corner and turned her monitor away from his view. But only after he'd had enough time to memorize a few things.

"The kids were separated and placed with families trained for high-trauma cases," Gloria said as she looked through the files. "We had to be careful. The kids had been through tough times even before losing their mother. Carolyn wouldn't speak for months. The boys had nightmares and separation anxiety."

"She looks really young to have three kids," Drake said with sympathy. "Are you sure Lisa Peterson was their real mother?"

"She was young. Which was part of the tragedy. No teen would take on three kids like that if she had a choice." Gloria's voice dropped to a whisper. "The way she talked about them, cared for them. The love they obviously showered on her. Ahmad Patel over at the store told us how devoted Lisa was to those kids. And the children's reaction when she didn't come back. You can't fake that kind of grief."

"Why couldn't you find her family after she died?" Drake asked as if he were genuinely puzzled.

"That's what made the case so complicated. After she died, we found that Lisa Peterson and her kids seemed to have no official history. We pulled DNA from all four of them but couldn't get a match anywhere. They weren't listed in any databases in Illinois. We even checked the public DNA sites. No luck." Gloria leaned closer and lowered her voice. "Lisa told people her ex was vicious. Violent. Drug addicted. Some say the kids resulted from sexual abuse. She didn't want him anywhere near her kids. It was pretty clear she was hiding from someone dangerous."

Drake kept his expression neutral. "So Lisa Peterson couldn't prove her own identity?"

"Well, she was deceased by the time we were looking. If Lisa had survived, she could have, I'm sure."

"But then you wouldn't have been asking," Drake agreed, nodding to encourage her.

"We've had people impersonating others before. Unlike Lisa, they usually have some fake documentation because they know they'll be asked. Lisa was trying to disappear, not commit fraud." Gloria shook her head. "When she died, we were very careful. Her kids were placed with good families. We all believed Lisa was protecting them from something terrible and we wanted to honor that."

"I need to track those kids down now, though," Drake said. "Can you help me with that?"

"It gets complicated." Gloria clicked to another screen. "Once the adoptions were finalized and sealed, our jurisdiction ended. The adoptive families are free to move, change names, do whatever they want. We have no way to maintain updated records."

"Which really does mean the only way I'm going to get some answers about this scammer is to talk to those kids," Drake said with naked appeal.

"I understand the importance, but I don't even have access to that information." Gloria shook her head sadly. "The later adoptions were sealed to protect both the parents and the kids."

"Was that unusual?"

"No. The parents requested secrecy, and the court-appointed guardian recommended it."

Drake sighed. He'd hit a dead end, but at least he'd confirmed the adoptions. "Do you remember anything that could help me find Lisa's children?"

"The judge agreed that given the circumstances and Lisa's apparent need to hide, the children would be safer with their new identities sealed." Gloria replied flatly as she gave Drake a warning look. "If someone is using their identities now, could those children be in real danger again? After all this time?"

"Yes, I think so. Scammers like this fake Lisa Peterson can be vicious when backed into a corner," Drake said.

"I wish I could help you." Gloria shook her head slowly. "But I can't."

Drake thanked her and headed out to his car through the lobby's stale air. The automatic doors wheezed open, releasing him into the late afternoon chill.

His phone rang.

"Tell me you have good news," Flint said.

"Mixed. The identity theft cover story is working well, but the legal obstacles are exactly what we expected." Drake summarized his conversations with the adoption records clerk and Gloria Stevens. "Court orders will take months, and there are multiple cases that could complicate our search."

Flint was quiet for a moment. "The identity theft angle is smart misdirection. It explains our interest without revealing what we actually know."

"Exactly. And it makes people want to help Lisa Peterson's kids."

"How long would court petitions take?"

"Six to eight weeks minimum. And that's assuming we can demonstrate good cause, which might be difficult without revealing the truth."

"We don't have that kind of time," Flint said.

"We need a different approach. The legal route is going to take too long, and we might not even get approval."

"What are you thinking?"

"Everything about this case is risky," Drake said. "But we're not going to find the Fisher children by filing paperwork and waiting for judges to maybe grant us access to records."

"I'm about thirty minutes out. We'll discuss this when I see you," Flint said and rang off.

Drake merged onto the interstate, heading toward the hotel. He checked his mirrors. No black SUVs, no obvious surveillance. But that didn't mean much. Good teams could maintain surveillance without being detected.

As he waited to turn left at a traffic light, a white pickup truck drove slowly past. The driver studied Drake with obvious interest. Nothing immediately threatening, but enough to catch his attention.

He checked his mirrors. The white pickup must have gone around the block. It was following now, maintaining a careful distance.

Drake tested the tail by varying his speed and changing lanes. The pickup matched his movements but stayed farther back than trained surveillance would have. Either they were very good at appearing amateur, or they actually were amateur.

Drake pulled into a Mobil station and watched the white pickup drive past. He caught a glimpse of the driver.

A middle-aged man in a faded Cubs baseball cap who looked more like a curious neighbor than an operative. Still, after the earlier ambush, Drake wasn't taking any chances.

He filled his gas tank, bought a coffee that tasted like it had been brewing since morning, and waited fifteen minutes before getting back on the road. No sign of the pickup truck.

His phone rang as he merged back onto the interstate. Flint again.

"Where are you?"

"Fifteen minutes out." Drake glanced in his mirrors. Clear road behind him. "Thought I had a tail for a while, but it might have been nothing. Local curiosity."

"I'll get a shower and meet you in the restaurant in the lobby," Flint said before he hung up.

As Drake drove through the fading afternoon light, he reflected on how the system had actually protected the Fisher children exactly as it was designed to do. When Lizzy died and left three traumatized children with no verifiable identity, the social workers and courts had done everything right to keep them safe. They'd placed them with good homes and sealed their records to protect them from unknown dangers.

It was effective protection.

It was also keeping them hidden from the only real family they still had. A family they would likely want to know.

The three adults were living somewhere under false names. They were unaware that their older brother was spending millions of dollars to find them.

Drake smiled grimly. Flint had advantages the court system couldn't account for. Unlimited resources, expertise, and the determination of a wealthy brother who believed his siblings were alive.

Surely, they could breach the brick wall erected around them by the State of Illinois with those resources without going through the courts.

Drake was sitting at a table in the hotel bar nursing a beer when Flint walked through the door. The bar was dimly lit with fake Tiffany lamps and decorated in an aggressive Irish pub theme that had probably seemed like a good idea at the time.

"How was Mount Warren?" Drake asked as Flint settled into the opposite chair at the corner table. He always chose a corner table so they could both sit with their backs to the wall. A precaution that had proved effective more than once.

"Productive." Flint replied and signaled the waitress for a drink. To shut down further questions, he said, "Tell me about your progress."

Drake briefed Flint more fully on his conversations.

"So do we have potential leads on any of Lizzy's children?" Flint asked.

"Not yet. Gaspar says he's close." Drake took a sip of his beer.

Flint nodded. "Jason Fisher called twice today asking for updates. He's getting impatient."

"How much do we tell him?"

"Nothing yet. Not until we have concrete information about current identities and locations." Flint leaned back in his chair. "But we need to move faster. Someone is still willing to kill to keep this all buried."

Drake raised his beer in a mock toast. "To finding needles in haystacks."

"To bringing Jason Fisher's family back together," Flint replied, "before someone makes sure they disappear forever."

"Sounds like a plan. When do we start?" Drake said, lifting his beer for a swig.

"Right after we eat and get some sleep," Flint said as he signaled the waitress.

CHAPTER 21

March 18
Peoria, Illinois

FLINT'S PHONE BUZZED ON the nightstand, cutting through the predawn silence. Cold air leaked through the window seals making the heating unit work overtime with a loud and steady mechanical hum.

He rolled over and checked the caller ID. Gaspar.

Flint cleared his throat and took the call with a husky, "You're up early."

"Never went to sleep. Got the report on those Illinois adoptions." Gaspar's wired energy was fueled by too much caffeine and too little rest. "Seven cases match the profile."

Flint sat up in bed. "Tell me."

"All from the same eighteen-month window. All children with no verifiable family history. All placed in sealed adoptions due to protective circumstances." The sound of keyboard clicks came through the phone. "Before you ask, no. The circumstances are not listed."

"Any other similarities?" Flint threw back the covers and sat on the edge of the bed, resisting the urge to go back to sleep.

"Each case involved children who entered the system with false or incomplete identities. That's as close as they all come. Mothers died in accidents. Fathers missing. Families disappeared. Kids found abandoned with no traceable relatives." Gaspar read from his notes. "Social services treated all seven cases as high-risk placements requiring extra security measures."

Flint walked to the window, bare feet cold against the hotel room's thin carpet. The parking lot spread below the window, empty except for a few scattered vehicles dusted with morning frost. Dawn was breaking over the flat Illinois farmland, painting the winter sky in shades of gray and pale gold.

"Any of the cases definitively connected to the Fisher kids?"

"That's the problem. Without access to the sealed adoption records, we can't make positive identifications. The foster care records only show the names for the initial placements." Gaspar's frustration came through clearly. "I've got families in Peoria, Springfield, Chicago, and four other Illinois cities. All adopted children in the right age range. All with sealed files."

"Sealed files that require court orders to unseal, I gather."

"Every single one. No exceptions."

Flint considered the tactical situation. Seven potential targets. Multiple jurisdictions. Months of legal proceedings to gain access to records that might not even contain the information they needed.

"There's another problem," Gaspar continued. "Even if we get court orders, some of these families might have moved out of state. Illinois only tracks adoptions within their jurisdiction. After that, the trail goes cold."

"Did you happen to look through records in Kentucky?" Flint asked.

"You think the kids could have been adopted in other states?" Gaspar replied.

"I don't know. But can you do a quick check?" Flint rubbed the stubble on his jaw. He needed a shave. There was a single-cup coffee pot in the room. He walked over to make it while his brain slowly came to life.

"This investigation has reached a critical decision point," Gaspar said. "You can spend massive resources over the next several months to years and maybe learn what you need to know."

"Meanwhile, Jason Fisher is growing more impatient and hostile forces are actively hunting those kids." Flint said as he pushed the button for the coffee and inhaled the heavenly aroma as it brewed.

"Yeah, and they won't care whether the means and methods they use are legal or not," Gaspar said matter-of-factly. "But we can't spend months looking, either."

"Okay. Right. Send me everything you have," Flint said after a sip of the marginal coffee. "Names, locations, whatever details are available. We'll figure something out."

"Already in your secure email. Drake's, too." Gaspar hesitated. "There's one more thing. I ran background checks on the adoptive families. Three of them have moved out of state in the past five years. Two changed their surnames after the adoptions."

"Making them harder to track."

"Yep," Gaspar said as he signed off.

Flint checked his encrypted email. He found Gaspar's files, which contained detailed intelligence on seven adoption cases. Each presented a potential path to Jason Fisher's siblings. But Fisher had no patience for the time and effort that would be required. Neither did Flint. He needed a better approach.

He reviewed the case summaries carefully. He needed a thread he could unravel. Social services had treated these children as high priority, requiring maximum protection. Sealed records. New identities. Careful placement with specialized families.

Flint shook his head. He had seen state and federal witness protection files with less security than these adoptions. He recognized similar standard procedures for children fleeing dangerous situations.

His phone rang. Drake.

"You done reading Gaspar's report?" Drake said without preamble. "Seven families. No definitive matches."

"Yeah. The legal barriers are even worse than what you described yesterday." Flint finished the coffee and looked around for a room service menu. "Court orders for sealed records. Family court judges who take privacy seriously. Months of proceedings, if we can succeed at all."

The hotel room felt smaller after spending the night. He found the room service menu and made his selections.

"Jason Fisher isn't going to wait months for answers," Drake said. "You know he's been calling asking for updates."

"We need a different approach." Flint opened the case files again and considered the options.

But Jason Fisher had resources they lacked. Unlimited funding. Legal teams. Political connections. Most importantly, he had standing as a family member seeking a reunion with blood relatives.

And giving Fisher something to do would keep him out of Flint's way for a while. Maybe.

"I'll call Fisher," Flint said. "Delegate the legal issues to him. Maybe he's got a contact in the governor's office or the Illinois Attorney General who can speed things up."

"Good. Calling in favors is what these billionaires do best." Drake was quiet for a moment. "What will we do while we're waiting?"

Flint reviewed Gaspar's intelligence again. Seven adoption cases. Multiple families.

But the records only told part of the story. Real people had lived through these situations. Neighbors remembered unusual circumstances. Social workers handled difficult placements. Administrative staff processed paperwork.

People talked. Especially about memorable cases involving traumatized children and mysterious backgrounds.

"Human intelligence," Flint said. "Find people who were involved in these placements. Interview them. Gather information that's not in the official files."

"The kind of intel that might help us narrow down the options," Drake replied with approval.

"Exactly. Fisher's lawyers can handle the court orders. We'll handle the fieldwork," Flint said. "Somebody will know something, say something, and we'll find the right direction."

"Solid plan," Drake said. "What's up first?"

"Breakfast. I'm planning to order breakfast sent up. Want anything?" Flint asked as he picked up the desk phone to make the call.

Drake ordered ham and eggs and a pot of coffee. "Be there in ten. I'll get a shower and come up."

"Bring your stuff. We'll leave from here." Flint hung up and then called room service and headed to the shower.

Before he got there, his laptop chimed with an incoming video call request. Jason Fisher.

For a moment, Flint considered ignoring the call. But Fisher wouldn't give up. He'd call back until Flint finally answered.

"Might as well do it now," Flint said aloud as he moved to the small table near the bed, opened the laptop, and accepted the call.

Fisher's face filled the screen, lean and intense even at this early hour. His dark eyes held the focused energy that had built a tech empire, while his slightly receding hairline caught the morning light streaming through what appeared to be floor-to-ceiling windows behind him.

The background suggested Fisher was calling from one of his penthouses, probably New York given the urban skyline visible through the glass.

"Tell me you have news." Fisher said with the impatience of a man accustomed to immediate compliance.

"Possibly," Flint said.

"What does that mean?" Fisher demanded.

"Well, you have the video of the man you believe is your brother, either Kevin or Dylan. So we're assuming at least one of them survived," Flint said calmly. "We've identified seven potential families that could have adopted him in Illinois. All involve sealed adoption records requiring court orders to access, which might take months. Maybe longer."

Fisher was quiet for several beats. His eyes narrowed as he processed the information. Behind him, the city was waking up, early morning traffic creating streams of light in the distance. "That's unacceptable."

"Which is why I'm recommending that you take over. Use your lawyers and family connection to expedite the process. Or call in a favor from the Governor. Whatever you have to do to find out whether Kevin or Dylan was adopted in Illinois," Flint suggested.

Fisher leaned forward, "While you do what?"

"We might have another lead. We're chasing it down. If it pans out, I'll let you know."

Fisher considered the suggestion. His fingertips were pressing together at the tips, in and out, a repetitive gesture that suggested his methodical thinking process. The morning light had shifted to illuminate the sharp angles of his face. "You think it will work?"

"It's our best option if you want to get the answers quickly."

"What do you need from me for your part?"

"I'll let you know when we exhaust your retainer." Flint pulled up Gaspar's list and emailed it to Fisher. "These are the potential placements we've identified as most likely. Your legal team can file petitions to open the sealed adoption records in each jurisdiction. Frame it as a family reunion case. Emphasize your desire to reconnect with your brother who survived a family tragedy."

"That's actually true." Fisher's expression softened slightly, a rare glimpse of the emotional stakes behind his business-like exterior.

"Which will make your petition more compelling to family court judges. They're more likely to unseal records for legitimate family reunification than for general investigation purposes."

"I can have my lawyers file petitions today." Fisher's tone shifted to all business. His shoulders straightened as he made the mental switch. "What's your timeline?"

"Depends on what we find. But we'll move faster than the court proceedings," Flint replied. "If you get anything sooner from your contacts, pass it along and we'll check it out."

"I'll get my team started immediately." Fisher's image flickered as he reached for something off-screen, probably making notes or sending messages to his attorneys.

Flint ended the video call and headed to the shower. He finished getting dressed and gathered his gear just as room service rapped on the door.

He was still considering resource allocation, strategic delegation, and multiple approaches working toward the same objective.

As the waiter was leaving, Drake slipped into the room, tossing his duffel onto the bed. He took a seat at the table and lifted the cover from his plate. "Fisher on board with the plan?"

"Yeah."

"You tell him that Lizzy and the kids survived the fire?" Drake had poured coffee and was shoveling eggs into his mouth.

"No. Until we have more intel, I don't want him bigfooting us or making things worse," Flint replied as he took the seat across from Drake. "We'll be heading back to Ravenswood."

"Why?" Drake asked after he swallowed the eggs.

"Lizzy Pace lived in Ravenswood for almost two years before her death. She had relationships. People who knew her. Details about her life that weren't in any official records," Flint said.

"We can ask her boss, Patel, the convenience store owner to give us some names of neighbors who might remember more details of Lizzy's life with the kids while she was there," Drake replied, finishing his food.

"I've got an SUV. Your rental is destroyed, so just leave it here. Call the rental company to pick it up." Flint packed his laptop. "You bring your bags?"

"Yeah. I'm ready when you are," Drake replied, dropping his napkin on the table and collecting his duffel. "Let's go."

Flint's phone buzzed with a message from Jason Fisher. *Legal team mobilized. Expect court filings today in all seven jurisdictions. Keep me informed of your progress.*

He read the text aloud to Drake.

"Fisher works fast when he's motivated," Drake said on his way out. "Good to know."

Flint replied: *Understood.* He dropped the phone into his pocket, checked his weapon and travel gear, and headed out behind Drake.

CHAPTER 22

March 18
Ravenswood, Illinois

THE DRIVE FROM THE hotel to Ravenswood took forty minutes through flat farmland. Drake was behind the wheel, which left Flint's attention free to wander.

Bare cornfields stretched endlessly to the horizon under a pewter sky heavy with unspilled snow. Skeletal trees lined the rural roads like sentries, branches black in the pale morning light. The SUV's tires hummed on asphalt still slick from overnight frost, and the heater worked steadily to combat the cold that seeped through the windows.

Drake kept checking his mirrors for surveillance. His gaze scanned the empty road behind them. The desolate landscape offered nowhere to hide, which worked both ways.

"No signs of pursuit yet," Flint said.

"Yeah, refreshingly boring," Drake replied with a smirk. "Only the occasional farm truck or sedan to break the monotony."

Flint set the navigation from the passenger seat. The GPS cast blue light across the cabin.

Drake said, "Patel's convenience store is three blocks ahead on the right."

The parking lot's cracked asphalt held two cars and a pickup truck with rusted wheel wells. Metal surfaces beaded with moisture from the humid morning air.

"Same place you interviewed him yesterday," Flint said as they pulled up to the curb, gravel crunching under the SUV's tires.

"Yeah. Nice guy. Remembers Lizzy well." Drake shut the engine down and unbuckled his seat belt. "I told him we were working for her children, trying to piece together their early childhood."

Flint nodded. "Let's keep the focus on Lizzy. We don't want the Fisher connection made public."

"Copy that," Drake agreed.

The brass bell above the door released a sharp chime that echoed off metal shelving packed with quick-grab items. The interior felt cramped and worn, with narrow aisles between displays. The aroma from a fresh pot of coffee reached Flint's nose, overshadowing the smell of less pleasing products.

Ahmad Patel looked up from behind the register. Recognition dawned across his weathered face like sunrise when he saw Drake. Wrinkles mapped his forehead and radiated from tired brown eyes behind thick glasses that had been repaired with tape at the bridge.

"You came back. Didn't find everything you wanted yesterday?" Patel's slight accent reflected English as a second language. His comfortable cardigan was charcoal gray and worn around the elbows and cuffs. Newspapers lay folded beside the register, headlines barely visible in the dim light.

"Getting there," Drake replied. "This is my colleague, Michael Flint. We're hoping you might remember more details about Lisa's time here, now that you've had a chance to refresh your memory overnight."

"If I can help Lisa's kids, I definitely want to do that. Be nice to see them again after all these years, too." Patel studied Flint's face with the careful attention of a man who'd spent decades reading customers, evaluating their intentions and creditworthiness with a glance. His fingers drummed silently against the scratched laminate counter, a nervous habit.

Flint approached the counter with his wallet out. The store felt smaller than it looked from outside. Inventory stacked to the ceiling seemed to compress the space. Behind Patel, cigarette cartons formed a wall of colorful packages.

"Lisa's children deserve to know the truth about their mother," Flint said in a friendly way as he put a five-dollar bill on the counter. "We'll take two coffees."

"She was a good person," Patel replied as he slipped the bill into the register. "Worked hard. Loved those kids."

"We're hoping to learn more about her personal life. Maybe talk to a few more people," Flint said as he stepped toward the coffee station. He poured two cups and handed one to Drake. "Did she have friends? People she spent time with outside of work?"

Patel removed his thick glasses. He cleaned them slowly with a small cloth he kept beside the register as if the repetitive motion helped him organize his thoughts. When he replaced the glasses, adjusting them carefully on the bridge of his nose, his expression had softened.

"Lisa kept to herself mostly. Worked here six days a week. Picked up the kids from daycare. Went home." He gestured toward the large window that faced Main Street, where pedestrians hurried past, bundling themselves in heavy coats against the morning chill. "She was young. Pretty girl. Dark eyes and long hair, usually pulled back out of her face. But she never seemed interested when men tried to talk to her."

"No boyfriend?" Drake asked, as if they were talking about mutual friends.

Patel cocked his head and seemed to think about the question. "Not for the first year or so. She'd turn down anyone who asked her out. Polite but firm. Like she had her walls up."

"How about later, once she'd settled into her new life here?" Flint asked.

Patel's expression shifted and his eyes seemed to focus on some distant memory. "Yeah, I think so. Maybe around

Christmas time, a few months before she died, a man started coming around."

Flint's pulse quickened. "What do you remember about him?"

"Nice looking young man. Around Lizzy's age. Maybe a year or two older. Dark hair, needed a haircut. Broad shoulders, like he did physical work." Patel gestured vaguely with hands marked by decades of labor. "He'd come in to buy small things. Soda from the cooler. Candy bars. Always friendly to Lisa. Respectful. Not pushy like some of the others."

"Were they dating?" Flint asked.

"Eventually, yes, I think so. I saw them walking together a few times. He'd stop by to pick her up after her shift sometimes." Patel paused, watching a car crawl past the window through the morning gloom. "Lisa seemed happier once he came on the scene. Less anxious. She'd actually smile when customers made small talk, instead of just being polite."

"Lisa's kids would love to know that she was happy." Drake leaned his hip against the scarred counter. "How so?"

"She smiled more. Started humming while she worked. The kids seemed to like him too." Patel pointed through the window toward a small park across the street, where bare swing sets and a playground sat empty in the winter cold. "I'd see them together over there sometimes. He'd push the little girl on the swings. Played catch with the boys using a tennis ball he kept in his truck."

"Do you remember his name?"

Patel shook his head. "She never introduced us. Just called him her friend when I asked."

A mysterious boyfriend who appeared three months before Lizzy's death. A man the children trusted. Who made Lizzy feel safer. Could be a fruitful lead.

"Did you ever see them after Christmas?" Flint asked.

"Oh yes. He was around quite a bit in January and February. I'd see his truck parked outside her apartment in the evenings on my way home sometimes." Patel lowered his gaze and cleared his throat, as if the memory made him sad. "Then Lisa died, and I never saw him again. He was probably as devastated as everyone else."

"He didn't stick around to help with the kids after Lisa died?" Flint asked.

Patel shook his head slowly. "I don't remember that he did."

"You said the kids liked him," Drake said. "How could you tell?"

"Children either trust someone or they don't." Patel smiled slightly. "Lisa's kids would run to him the moment they spotted him coming down the street. The boys especially. They'd climb all over him like he was their father, hanging on his arms and shoulders."

"Could he have been their father?" Flint asked.

"I don't think so," Patel replied. "Lisa never had anything positive to say about their father. She was terrified of him. So I'd say no. This guy was someone else."

Flint exchanged glances with Drake. A man who had formed a relationship with Lizzy and the Fisher children during their final months in Ravenswood should have more intel, if they could find him.

"Mr. Patel," Flint said as he drained the last of his coffee, "do you know anyone else who might remember this man? Neighbors? Other store owners?"

"The Klines might remember. They had children around the same age. Went to the same daycare back then. Sometimes the kids played together in the yard."

Drake wrote down the name. "How can we contact them?"

Patel provided directions.

"Thank you Mr. Patel. If we find Lisa's boyfriend, the kids will be pleased." Flint put a ten-dollar bill on the counter this time. "You make great coffee. Can we get two large cups to go?"

"There's one more thing about that young man. He had some kind of scar on his left hand. Small one, right here." Patel rang up the coffee and gave Flint his change. Then he pointed to the webbing between his thumb and index finger, the skin there pale against his darker complexion. "Lisa mentioned the scar once after I asked how they met. Said he'd had some kind of accident with machinery when he was a teen."

An identifying mark that might help them confirm the man's identity.

"Thank you, Mr. Patel."

"You've been very helpful," Drake said as they headed back to the SUV.

CHAPTER 23

THE TEMPERATURE HAD GROWN colder and the air more brittle. Gray clouds had thickened overhead like a heavy blanket, blocking what little sun had managed to penetrate the winter gloom. Scattered snowflakes drifted down, melting instantly when they touched the still-warm pavement.

"Think this boyfriend is significant?" Drake said as they resumed their seats inside the vehicle. He started the engine.

"Possibly. Pretty young girls tend to pick up boyfriends easily at that age. But a guy who will date a woman with three young kids? Way less common," Flint replied. "Let's talk to the neighbors."

The Kline house sat on a tree-lined street three blocks from the convenience store, its brick facade and neat landscaping reflecting middle-class stability. A modest two-story colonial with white trim and shutters painted forest green. Children's toys were scattered across the front porch while the yard was well-maintained even during the dormant season.

Flint knocked on the brightly painted front door.

A woman answered while pulling her brown hair back into a practical ponytail. Dressed in well-worn jeans and a University of Illinois sweatshirt with a coffee stain near the left shoulder, she looked like a soccer mom although she was probably a grandma by now. Behind her, Saturday morning cartoons played in a living room painted warm yellows and blues. The smell of pancakes and maple syrup wafted through the doorway.

"Mrs. Kline? I'm Michael Flint, this is Alonzo Drake. We're private investigators looking for information about Lisa Peterson. Ahmad Patel at the convenience store suggested you might remember her."

"Yes, I remember Lisa." The woman's open, friendly expression grew cautious. "She lived down the street with her three children. Tragic what happened to her."

Flint gave her a friendly smile. "We're working for her children now. They're trying to understand their mother's life here in Ravenswood."

Mrs. Kline's face softened. "Those poor children. They were so young when she died. Please, come in. Younger than my grandkids are now."

The living room reflected comfortable chaos. School papers and children's artwork covered the refrigerator in the adjacent kitchen, colorful magnets holding them in place. Toys occupied strategic corners where they'd been hastily gathered during the morning cleanup routine. The couch showed the gentle wear of constant use, with cushions that countless family movie nights and homework sessions had shaped.

"What would you like to know about Lisa?" Mrs. Kline asked after offering them a seat on the couch.

"Mr. Patel mentioned Lisa had a boyfriend during the winter before she died," Flint said. "Do you remember him?"

"Sure. He was tall, maybe six feet. Dark hair that looked like he cut it himself." She closed her eyes as if she were visualizing him. "Strong looking, with callused hands like he did physical work for a living."

"What else can you tell us about him?" Flint asked.

Mrs. Kline's face brightened as the memories returned. "My kids took to him immediately. He played basketball with them in our driveway sometimes, teaching them how to shoot free throws. Very patient with the younger ones."

Flint waited to encourage her to continue.

Her eyes seemed to be focusing on details from years past. "Always polite during our conversations. I remember thinking Lisa seemed much happier after he started coming around."

"What was his name?" Flint asked.

"Lisa just called him Frankie. But she did formally introduce us when they were walking past with the children," Mrs. Kline said. "The last name was long. Italian, I think. Might have started with a T. I can't really remember. I'm sorry."

"Do you remember anything else about him?" Drake asked.

"He drove an old pickup truck. Blue Ford, I think. Sometimes he'd help Lisa carry groceries from the store or fix things around her apartment." Mrs. Kline's gaze turned inward as she sifted through more old memories. "He was unusually good with her children. Most men that age don't have much patience for small kids, especially someone else's kids. But he seemed to genuinely enjoy spending time with them."

"How long were they together, Frankie and Lisa?" Flint asked.

"Maybe three or four months. Started around Christmas time, and then poor Lisa died the following March." Mrs. Kline's face grew sad, the happiness of remembering good times overshadowed by the tragedy that followed. "I always wondered what happened to him. He just disappeared after the accident. Never saw him anywhere else in town."

"Do you know where he lived?" Flint asked.

"It was a long time ago." She shook her head.

"Are there any photos of him?" Flint asked. "Maybe from holiday gatherings or neighborhood events?"

Mrs. Kline considered the question. "You know, Mrs. Kowalski might have some. She lived upstairs from Lisa and was always taking pictures of the children playing together. She loved documenting everything."

"We can certainly follow up on that," Flint replied.

Her face brightened. "Actually, I remember now. She invited Lisa and the kids up for Christmas morning. I think Frankie was there too. Lisa told me Mrs. Kowalski took lots of photos that day."

"Is Mrs. Kowalski still around?" Flint asked.

"She passed away last year, but her daughter Elena has all her mother's photo albums. Elena Kowalski-Martin. She lives on Maple Street, the yellow house with the brown trim." She gave him the address.

They talked for another ten minutes, gathering details about Lizzy's daily routine and her relationship with the mysterious Frankie. None of it was particularly helpful.

When they finished, Mrs. Kline walked them to the door.

"I hope those children are doing well," she said. "Lisa loved them so much. She would have done anything to protect them."

Back in the SUV, Drake started the engine and let it warm while the defroster cleared the windshield. Snow fell in fat flakes that stuck to the glass and accumulated on the grass. Cold seemed to seep through every seal and gasket.

"Mrs. Kowalski next?" Drake asked, rolling the SUV in that direction. He turned onto Main Street. The SUV's tires crunched through the thin layer of snow accumulating on the asphalt.

They found Elena Kowalski's home on the other side of town where the streets were quieter, and the houses showed more character. A ranch-style home with pale yellow siding and white trim with a tidy front yard. The dormant flower beds held only brown stalks poking through patches of snow, but Flint imagined they would be a riot of color in the spring.

Drake parked at the curb, and they walked the concrete sidewalk that led to the front door. Evergreen shrubs flanked the porch and provided the only color in the winter landscape.

Elena Kowalski-Martin answered the door after the first knock, as if she'd been expecting them. Which she probably was. Flint assumed Mrs. Kline called to say they were coming.

A woman in her fifties with prematurely graying hair pulled back in a loose bun answered the door. Intelligent brown eyes blinked behind wire-rimmed glasses that had slipped down her nose. She wore a thick cardigan over dark sweatpants, the kind of practical clothing that people who spend time caring for others choose.

"Mrs. Kowalski-Martin? Mrs. Kline gave us your name. I hope we're not bothering you," Flint said before he offered his card and the same brief introduction he'd supplied earlier. "We're looking for information about Lisa Peterson, who once lived in your mother's apartment building."

"Yes, Penelope called. Please come inside. You'll catch pneumonia out there." Elena's face lit up with recognition and sadness. "Lisa and her children. Of course I remember them. Mother loved having children in the building again.

She adored Lisa and the kids adored Mom. I'm happy to help if I can."

They followed her inside and Drake closed the door behind them.

Family photos covered every available surface, creating a visual timeline of birthdays, graduations, and holiday celebrations spanning decades. Weak sunlight filtered through sheer curtains, creating gentle shadows that danced across polished hardwood floors. Elena led them to the living room, gesturing toward a well-worn sofa that showed decades of family use.

"Mother passed away six months ago," Elena said in the manner of a daughter who had processed grief and moved into acceptance. "She talked about Lisa often, especially in her final years. She felt terrible about what happened to that poor girl."

"Your mother watched the children sometimes," Flint said to encourage more.

"When Lisa had to work late shifts or when one of the kids was sick and couldn't go to daycare. Mother enjoyed it immensely." Elena's face softened with fond memories. "She'd been widowed for years by then and the children made her feel useful again. She'd bake cookies for them and teach them Polish words. They called her Babcia, which means grandmother."

Flint leaned forward. "We understand Lisa had a boyfriend during her final months. Did your mother ever mention him?"

"Frankie Tantanella. Yes, Mother liked him very much." Elena smiled, the expression transforming her features and revealing traces of the young woman she'd once been. "She said he was respectful and wonderfully patient with the children. Mom very much approved of Lisa's choice."

"Mrs. Kline said your mother might have photos of the kids and Lisa and Frankie," Flint said.

"Actually, yes. Mother loved taking pictures all the time. She had quite a collection when she passed." Elena's eyes brightened with sudden enthusiasm. "Let me get the photo albums. I think we'll find a few photos in there."

Elena disappeared into another room and soon returned carrying two thick photo albums bound in burgundy leather. The covers were worn smooth by frequent handling. She returned to the couch and opened the first album. She flipped though carefully revealing page after page of memories preserved beneath plastic sheets until she found the group she wanted.

"Mother documented everything. She always said memories fade but photographs last forever." Elena flipped through pages of photos showing children playing in snow, neighborhood barbecues, birthday parties, and quiet moments.

Then she stopped at a page near the back, pointing to a specific photo. "Here's one. Christmas morning that last year before Lisa died."

Flint leaned forward and stared at the photographs. Clear color images showed Lizzy Pace and three small children in a living room decorated for Christmas. A small artificial tree stood in the corner, lights twinkling against reflective tinsel that caught the camera flash.

Wrapped presents covered the floor around the tree in bright paper creating a festive explosion of reds and greens. The children were laughing, faces bright with the joy that only Christmas morning could bring.

Flint stared at the photographs. Standing behind the kids with Lisa, smiling broadly with genuine warmth, was a young man in his early twenties. Dark hair fell across his forehead in a way that suggested the kids had mussed it. His flannel shirt showed wrinkles that might have come from crawling around on the floor.

His build was exactly as Mrs. Kline had described. Tall and strong, with the kind of physique that came from outdoor work.

But it was Frankie Tantanella's expression that struck Flint. He wasn't posing for the camera or trying to look good. He was completely focused on the kids with the kind of unguarded affection that couldn't be faked.

His left hand was visible in one photo, positioned on the shoulder of one of the boys, and the small scar in the webbing between his thumb and index fingers was exactly as Patel had described it.

"Is this him?" Flint asked, pointing to the photo.

Tantanella's face was clearly visible in multiple shots from different angles, creating a photographic record that any decent facial recognition system could analyze. The lighting was good, the focus sharp, and his features were unobscured.

"Yes, that's Frankie," Elena said softly with fond remembrance. "Mother took these on Christmas morning. Lisa had invited her down to watch the children open presents. Mother was so touched to be included."

Drake pulled out his phone and took high-resolution pictures of the photographs, making sure to capture every detail and angle. The phone's camera flash reflected off the plastic sleeves around the photos, but the images remained clear and distinct.

"Do you mind if we borrow this photo?" Flint asked, pointing to the group photo of Lisa, Frankie, and the kids.

"Of course. If it helps Lisa's children to know more about their mom, that's exactly what my mother would have wanted." Elena carefully removed the photo from the album as if she were handling a religious artifact. She handed the photo to Flint, who slid it into his jacket pocket.

"Any idea where Frankie is now?" Drake asked.

Elena shook her head slowly, as if she were thinking about the question carefully.

"If you recall anything more about Frankie Tantanella or Lisa and the kids, here's my card." Flint gave her a business card as they left. "Anything at all might be helpful."

Outside, snow was falling more heavily now, transforming Ravenswood into a winter postcard. The flakes grew smaller and more persistent, accumulating steadily. The temperature had dropped enough that Flint's breath formed visible clouds in the frigid air.

They sat in the SUV with the engine running and the heater working overtime, examining the Christmas photos on Drake's phone. The interior felt warm and secure against the storm building outside.

"Clear facial shots from multiple angles," Drake noted. "High quality images with good lighting. We can use these."

Flint said, "We'll get Gaspar to run the photos through facial recognition before we take them to Jason Fisher."

"You think Fisher might know Tantanella?" Drake asked. "Or that Lizzy knew him before, in Kentucky?"

"Makes sense. Tantanella shows up in Ravenswood, out of the blue, and all of a sudden Lisa has an instant boyfriend who is playing with the kids and attending Christmas celebrations. It's odd when we've been told repeatedly that Lisa kept to herself and had few friends," Flint replied as he fished out his sat phone to call Gaspar. "At the very least, we need to rule it out."

"You don't trust our client?" Drake asked, mildly surprised.

Flint shrugged. "I'm a belt and suspenders guy. You already know that about me."

"What are you worried about?"

"Not sure. With a guy like Jason Fisher, you never see his hole cards. Never really know what kind of game he's playing," Flint replied.

"So you think he's hiding something?"

"Of course, he is," Flint said flatly just before Gaspar picked up. "I'm sending you a photo of Lizzy Pace and the three Fisher kids. There's a guy with them. We think his name is Frankie Tantanella. Can you check him out?"

"Got it. What do you need to know about him?" Gaspar asked. "Criminal history, current location, things like that?"

"Give me the whole nine yards," Flint replied before he disconnected the call.

CHAPTER 24

March 18

Ravenswood, Illinois

FLINT'S ENCRYPTED PHONE RANG as they drove away. The sound cut through the steady hum of the SUV's heater and the slapping windshield wipers battling the falling snow. Ice crystals collected in the corners of the windshield despite the defroster running at full blast.

"What did you find?" Flint said, putting the call on speaker so Drake could hear the intel firsthand.

"I've identified Lizzy Pace's boyfriend," Gaspar replied. "Francis Daniel Tantanella, born in Harlan County, Kentucky. He attended the same high school as the Fisher brothers and also Lizzy Pace, but he was a year older than Jason."

Flint straightened in his seat. "What else?"

"He's got a juvenile record. Three arrests between ages fifteen and seventeen. Two for petty arson. One for theft. All charges dropped or pleaded down to community service." Gaspar paused, but his rapid keyboard clicks were audible through the phone. "Last known address was his father's place in Kentucky."

"So no records are available after the Fisher house fire?" Flint asked.

"Exactly. Kid disappeared completely. No employment records, no tax filings, no driver's license renewals. Nothing." Gaspar paused a moment. "I'll move on to records in Illinois and federal databases. But it looks like the kid fell off the grid. Probably on purpose."

"We're low on fuel and who knows when we'll find another station out here," Drake said as he pulled the SUV into a gas station. The building squatted beside the rural highway like a beacon in the gathering storm, its neon signs reflecting off the wet pavement in wavering pools of color.

Gravel crunched under the tires. Snow had accumulated on the windshield faster than the wipers could clear it. He hopped out to fill the tank and clear the windshield while Gaspar continued his summary. The bitter wind cut through Drake's jacket, and his breath formed white clouds in the frigid air.

"Send me the files." Flint wearily wiped a palm across his face.

"Already in your secure email. Photos from his high school yearbook, arrest records, family background. His father died of cancer a couple of years after the Fisher fire," Gaspar said. "Mother remarried and moved to Florida."

"Siblings?"

"Still searching."

"Copy that. Keep us updated."

"Will do," Gaspar said before he rang off.

Flint located his laptop and opened it. After a couple of seconds, it hooked up to his secure satellite. The screen cast blue light across his face in the dim interior, creating sharp shadows that made his features look carved from stone. He found the files Gaspar mentioned and opened them one at a time. Tantanella's high school yearbook photo showed a lean teenager with wary eyes, arrest records painted a picture of petty crimes and second chances, family background revealed the grinding poverty that shaped too many lives in rural Kentucky.

The juvenile files were sealed, but Gaspar had contacts, both personal and professional. Which meant Flint now had access to the sealed records as well.

Frankie Tantanella had been a local kid from a struggling family. His father worked construction when he could find jobs. His mother cleaned houses. Frankie was familiar to the local cops as a teenager but had committed no crimes serious enough for jail time.

The arrest records told the story. In mid-September, he was hit with a petty arson charge, pleaded down to community service. A month later was the last time he did odd jobs for Harry Fisher. The Fisher house fire soon followed. Tantanella's truck was found abandoned two days later in a Wal-Mart parking lot. He hadn't been seen at school or around the area again.

Meaning Tantanella had vanished completely after the Fisher house burned down. There was nothing more in any of the files. Nothing at all.

Drake finished pumping the gas and climbed in from the frigid outdoors to the warm cabin. His jacket dripped melting snow onto the floor mats, and the heater immediately began working to chase away the cold he'd brought inside. Before they got on the road again, Flint brought Drake up to speed.

"Call Jason Fisher?" Drake suggested when Flint finished his summary.

"Yeah, he might know where to look for Frankie Tantanella," Flint said as he chose one of Tantanella's mug shots from Gaspar's files and then placed the call from his laptop. "He might have reasonable intel to offer, too."

"Have you told him that Lizzy and his siblings survived the fire?" Drake asked as he pulled onto the road.

Flint shook his head. "That's the kind of intel I need to deliver in person once I can tell him what happened to the three of them with some level of certainty."

"So for now, we ask about Tantanella and nothing else," Drake replied with a nod.

The video call connected after two rings. Jason Fisher's intense face filled the screen, his dark eyes focused sharply. Behind him, floor-to-ceiling windows revealed the gray-black skyline through the icy rain. The city looked hostile and unwelcoming, a concrete jungle wrapped in winter's grip.

"What did you find?" Fisher asked when he picked up.

"I need you to look at a mug shot. Just sent it to you. Did you get it?"

"Just a second," Fisher said as he searched for the photo. "It's Frankie Tantanella. Why did you go looking for this?"

"So you do you know him?" Flint asked.

"We went to high school together. He was a year older than me."

"Tell me what you know about Tantanella."

"Not much, really. I was a kid. Frankie, too. Local guy. Did odd jobs around town for pocket money. His family didn't have much." Fisher paused, as if he were struggling with his memory. "I remember he had a thing for Lizzy Pace. She was hot. Lots of guys were besotted with her. Frankie used to follow her around like a lost puppy."

Flint nodded. "Did he ever work for your family?"

"Sometimes. Dad hired him to do yard work, fix things. Frankie needed the money and Dad liked helping local kids."

Flint said, "What happened to him after the fire?"

"Nobody knew. His truck was found abandoned on a back road a few days later. No sign of Frankie," Jason shrugged. "I guess most people assumed he'd either moved on or joined the military, like the rest of the local kids did."

"Call your brother, Bruce. Show him this photo. See what he remembers about Tantanella," Flint said.

Fisher nodded before he ended the call. "I'll get him on a call now and get back to you."

The video ended and Fisher's face disappeared from the screen.

"So Tantanella knew the Fisher family," Drake recapped. "He had access to their property, knew their routines."

"And he had a juvenile record for arson." Flint closed his laptop with a soft click. "Someone could have hired him to burn that house down."

A video call came in. Jason Fisher calling back.

"I've got Bruce on with us," Fisher said when Flint answered. "Bruce, this is Michael Flint. He wants to ask you about Frankie Tantanella."

Bruce Fisher's face appeared in a smaller window beside Jason's on the laptop screen. The family resemblance was strong. Same dark hair, same sharp jawline, same intense eyes. But where Jason radiated corporate intensity, his brother seemed calm and relaxed. The contrast was striking between the two men shaped by the same tragedy.

"Flint, show him the photo," Jason said without preamble.

Bruce leaned closer to the screen. Behind him, Flint caught glimpses of a workshop. Metal sculptures caught the light from overhead fixtures, welding equipment stood ready for use, the controlled chaos of an artist's studio that spoke of creativity born from pain.

"I can see it fine from here. That's definitely Frankie Tantanella."

"You're certain?" Flint asked.

"Dead certain. He went to school with us." Bruce's tone lacked his brother's urgency. "His dad was sick most of the time. Cancer, I think. Frankie did odd jobs around town to help pay bills."

"Jason said he also worked for your family from time to time. Do you remember that?" Flint asked.

"Sometimes. Dad hired him to help us with chores. Yard work, fix fence posts, that kind of thing." Bruce paused as the import of Flint's questions seemed to soak in. His expression grew troubled. "Frankie knew our routines. When we'd be home, when we wouldn't."

Drake shifted in the driver's seat, following the conversation even as he navigated the snowy roads. The windshield wipers maintained their steady rhythm against the falling snow. Outside, the landscape had turned into a monochrome painting of white and gray, trees bare and skeletal against the overcast sky.

"Was there anything unusual about him? Any reason to think he might be involved in what happened to your house?" Flint pressed.

"Frankie wasn't a bad guy," Bruce said slowly. "His family was struggling. He needed the work. But..."

"But what?"

"He always seemed nervous around the house after Dad started acting strange about his business. Like he knew something was wrong but didn't know what to do about it."

Jason leaned forward on his end of the call. "What do you mean Dad was acting strange?"

CHAPTER 25

March 18

Ravenswood, Illinois

BRUCE WAS QUIET FOR several seconds, probably sorting through two decades of buried memories. Before he spoke again, he cleared his throat. "You were seventeen, Jason. You were focused on school and getting into Stanford. You weren't home as much, didn't see what I saw."

"Which was?"

"Dad was scared. Really scared. He'd get phone calls and afterward he'd pace the house for hours. He started keeping a gun in his desk drawer. He'd drive different routes to town, check his mirrors constantly." Bruce rubbed his forehead with work-scarred fingers. Each callus told a story of metal shaped by fire and force. "I thought he was just stressed about the business. I had no idea about the DEA thing until years later."

Harry Fisher's fear had been visible to at least some members of his family. Flint filed that tidbit away. "When did you last see Tantanella?"

"Few days before the fire. He came by to fix a section of fence that had blown down in a storm. He seemed jumpy, kept looking over his shoulder." Bruce's eyes focused somewhere beyond his camera, seeing something from long ago. "After the fire, he just disappeared."

"Did anyone look for him?"

"Maybe. I don't know." Bruce shifted, and Flint heard the creak of a wooden chair. "Nobody thought to connect him to what happened to our house, as far as I heard."

Flint replied, "Was there anything about Tantanella's behavior in those last few days that seemed off? Anything that might suggest he knew what was coming?"

Bruce was quiet for a long moment. He'd cocked his head and closed his eyes, as if he were reliving those days in the past, before the fire, when his family was still intact. The pain of memory etched lines around his eyes that hadn't been there as a teenager.

Behind him, rain was streaking past the workshop windows. Droplets caught the light and cast moving shadows across the metal sculptures behind him. "There was one thing I noticed. The day Frankie came to fix the fence he asked me about our family's schedule. Wanted to know when we'd all be home together. Said he had something he wanted to tell Dad."

"Did he say what it was?" Flint asked.

"Dad wasn't there that day. Had driven to Lexington for some kind of meeting." Bruce shook his head and frowned. "I told Frankie we'd all be at the basketball tournament that Friday night. The whole family always came to the games."

The weight of implication settled over the conversation like a heavy blanket. The only sounds were the SUV's heater and the rhythmic sweep of windshield wipers.

Finally, Jason asked, "Are you saying Frankie Tantanella might have set the fire?"

Bruce's shoulders sagged as he shook his head. "I've spent twenty-four years trying not to think about that night. Trying not to wonder what we could have done differently. How we might have saved the others. Lizzy, too."

"Did you have a crush on Lizzy?" Flint asked.

"Every boy in town had a crush on Lizzy. She was hot. Kind, too. And sweet. Everybody loved Lizzy, including the parents and the teachers," Bruce replied. "The whole town mourned when she died."

"Including Frankie Tantanella?" Flint asked.

Bruce shrugged. "Sure. Frankie, too."

"Were they dating? Lizzy and Frankie?" Flint asked.

"It's possible. Sure, Lizzy might have dated Frankie. She would have felt sorry for him, like the rest of us did." Bruce replied.

"None of this was your fault, you know," Jason said. "We were kids. We didn't even know there was anything going on with Dad."

"I was sixteen, you were seventeen. Old enough to pay attention and ask questions. But we didn't. We'll never know whether we did the right thing." Bruce looked directly into his camera. "Jason, think carefully about what you're doing here. We believe these people killed Dad's DEA contact. What about Mom? If you keep pushing this, they might come after her. We're both here, like sitting ducks."

"Live the rest of your lives in fear? Never knowing what happened to the others?" Jason frowned. "I can't do that. If they want to find us, they will, whether we go looking for them or not. We need to expose them. Find the truth. That's the only way we'll all be able to live in peace."

"Or we could simply let sleeping dogs lie," Bruce said firmly.

The brothers stared at each other across the video connection. All these years of processing the same trauma in completely different ways had carved different paths through their lives.

Jason had escaped Kentucky and built an empire.

Bruce had stayed home, caring for their mother, channeling his pain into art. Two different responses to the same devastating loss.

"I can't stop now," Jason said quietly. "Not when we're this close."

Bruce nodded slowly, as if he'd expected that answer. "Then be careful. Both of you." His gaze shifted to Flint. "And find out what really happened to our brothers and sister. Whatever it takes. We'll have no peace until you do."

Bruce ended the call and Flint's screen went dark, leaving only the reflection of his face in the black glass. He closed his laptop and stared out at the swirling snow.

The storm had intensified while they talked. Silvery flakes danced in the headlight beams like ghostly moths.

The pieces were starting to form a picture, but it was a dark one. Tantanella had known the family's schedule. He'd asked about it specifically. He'd been nervous and jumpy in the days before the fire.

But if he'd been hired to burn the house, why had the children survived? Why had Lizzy Pace ended up in Illinois with the Fisher kids? Why had Tantanella disappeared only to reappear as her boyfriend months later? Where had he been all that time? How had he found Lizzy again?

"So Tantanella was involved," Drake said, breaking the silence. "He might have torched the house. He may have helped Lizzy disappear. Who knows what else he was involved in?"

"Looks that way," Flint replied, still mulling the new facts.

Drake navigated around a slow-moving snowplow. Orange lights flashed through the gray afternoon like a lighthouse beacon in the gathering gloom. "Maybe Frankie couldn't go through with it when he found Lizzy and the kids were still in the house."

"Or maybe there's more to the story than we know."

"Meaning what?" Drake asked.

"Sounds like Frankie and Lizzy were dating," Flint replied slowly. "Frankie thought the house would be unoccupied that night. Say he gets there to torch the place and finds Lizzy and the kids are upstairs. You think he would have killed her and the kids intentionally?"

Drake wagged his head slowly. "Doesn't sound like that to me."

"Yeah. Me neither," Flint replied. "So Frankie helps Lizzy and the kids get away. Then he torches the house."

"Makes sense," Drake said. "More sense than anything else we've come up with, anyway."

"The rest unfolds afterward. Lizzy shows up in Ravenswood. Takes care of the kids. Frankie comes later to join them."

"And then Lizzy has a run of bad luck. Gets cancer. Dies. And the kids get adopted," Drake murmured as he tried the idea. "Okay. I can buy that. But what happens to Frank Tantanella?"

Flint shrugged. "I don't know. But we do know that the bus driver involved in Lisa Peterson's death has moved to Florida. Tampa, I think Patel said. Let's start there."

"Works for me. At least it won't be snowing in mid-March," Drake replied with a smirk and headed toward the airport.

"Back to Houston, first. I've got a few things to do. We'll head to Tampa in the morning," Flint said as Drake maneuvered the SUV through the traffic.

CHAPTER 26

MICHAEL FLINT TURNED ON the background music with frequency interference to confound listening devices and stood at the front window of his cozy bungalow in Houston. The room was bathed in the blue glow from the cable box.

He imagined the morning traffic crawl along the freeway in the distance, red brake lights bleeding together in the gray dawn haze. The coffee had gone cold an hour ago, but he hadn't noticed. His mind was working through the implications of what they'd learned about the Fisher home fire and Frankie Tantanella.

Drake emerged from the kitchen with a fresh cup of java, steam rising from the dark liquid. "You've been staring out that window long enough. Something interesting happening out there?"

"Just mulling through the facts. Tantanella helped Lizzy and the kids escape the fire and found them again in Ravenswood." Flint turned away from the glass. "But how the hell does a local Kentucky teenager track down a woman and three kids who are hiding under new identities? Lizzy didn't exactly leave a forwarding address."

"Good point. That's not easy to do, even now. Back then?" Drake shook his head. "Would have taken serious resources or connections."

"Right. So either Tantanella had help we don't know about, or the reunion wasn't as coincidental as it seemed to the people who knew Lizzy." Flint reached for his laptop. "But after Lizzy died, the kids went into the Illinois foster system. That's where we lost the trail."

"Right. Which is why Jason's lawyers are working the court angle."

"Yes, but that could take months or years, if it works at all." Flint opened his secure connection. "We need a faster approach."

Drake settled into a chair across from Flint. "What are you thinking?"

"Patel said Lizzy was increasingly anxious and frightened in her final days. She was looking over her shoulder, asking if anyone had been inquiring about her." Flint started dialing. "She was scared."

"You think someone was hunting her?"

"I think someone was getting close to finding her and the kids. And if Lizzy knew she was in danger, she might have made contingency plans."

"That could have been a simple backup." Drake leaned forward, nodding with approval. "Someone she trusted to take them if something happened to her."

"And in a small town like Ravenswood, where she didn't know many people." Flint continued dialing. "Tom Wilson drove the same bus route every day. Lizzy would have been a regular passenger. Friendly woman, attractive, troubled. Wilson would have talked to her."

"You think she confided in the bus driver?" Drake asked.

"I think when you're scared and alone with three kids to protect, you talk to anyone who'll listen," Flint replied. "Even the bus driver."

Gaspar's familiar face appeared on the laptop screen surrounded by the blue glow of multiple monitors in his home office in Miami.

"Morning," Gaspar said. "What do you need?"

Drake grinned. "Is that how you always greet your callers?"

"The ones like you two who only call when they need something? You bet," Gaspar replied.

"Guilty as charged. We need intel on a guy," Flint said, unwilling to waste more time. "Thomas Murphy. Now lives in Tampa, Florida. Used to be Tom Wilson, bus driver in Ravenswood, Illinois until he retired."

"Got it." Gaspar's fingers moved across his keyboard. "What am I looking for?"

"Current address. Employment. Basic background," Flint said.

The silence stretched while Gaspar worked the keyboards. Flint could hear the soft clicking noises through the connection.

"Here we go," Gaspar said after a couple of minutes. "Thomas Murphy, age sixty-two. Lives at 4847 Davis Boulevard, Tampa."

"Current status?"

"Still confirming," Gaspar said shaking his head while he scrolled through files. "Actually, Murphy died four years ago."

Flint leaned forward. "How?"

"Skydiving accident. Equipment failure during a training jump."

Drake raised his eyebrows. "The bus driver became a skydiving instructor?"

"Looks that way. He owned Murphy's Sky Adventures for about fifteen years." Gaspar continued reading as he scanned the contents. "Routine training jump with a student. Murphy's main chute failed to deploy properly. Reserve chute also malfunctioned. Student landed safely, reported the instructor's death to authorities."

Flint said, "Name of the student?"

"Good question," Gaspar replied with a grimace. "He paid in cash. His ID was fake. He was never located for follow-up investigation."

Flint and Drake exchanged glances. Amateur students didn't pay cash or use fake names.

"Anything else unusual about Murphy's death?" Flint asked.

"Investigation was brief but thorough. Single fatality, experienced instructor, equipment failure. No obvious signs of sabotage." Gaspar scrolled through files. "Murphy was cremated three days later. Case closed within the week."

"Who inherited his business?" Flint asked.

"Wife, Helen Murphy. Still lives at the same address on Davis Boulevard."

Drake said, "So the only witness to Lizzy Pace's death also ended up dead in what looked like a murder disguised as an accident. That's how we think this went down?"

"Sounds like it. Gaspar, send us what you have on Murphy's death," Flint said. "We're heading to Tampa. We'll talk to the widow and let you know if we need more."

"Copy that." Gaspar paused. "You think Wilson was killed by a hired assassin?"

"Bus drivers don't usually end up dead in suspicious accidents years later," Flint replied. "It's a reasonably safe guess that someone wanted him silenced and had the wherewithal to make it happen."

"Why?" Drake asked. "Wilson lived about fifteen years after Lizzy's fatal accident. Why kill Wilson now?"

"My guess is that Lizzy told him people were hunting her back then and her plans for the children if something happened to her," Flint said. "Could have been more than enough to get Wilson killed, too."

Drake stood up and stretched. "So we're going to Tampa."

Flint closed the laptop. "How fast can you get the jet ready?"

"Hour and a half if I push it. Weather's good between here and Florida." Drake was already pulling out his phone to call the hangar. "Peter O. Knight Airport on Davis Island should work for landing. It's close to the residential areas."

While Drake requested the jet and coordinated the flight, Flint gathered his gear and considered what they might find in Tampa. If Wilson had been eliminated four years ago, whoever ordered his death might still be monitoring for inquiries about him.

A visit to Wilson's widow could draw attention they didn't want.

But Helen was their only lead to whatever her husband knew about Lizzy.

As his friend Kim Otto often said, when there's only one choice, it's the right choice.

CHAPTER 27

AN HOUR LATER, THEY were airborne over the Gulf Coast. Drake handled the Pilatus with his usual competence, threading between thunderstorms that dotted the route to Florida. Through the windscreen, Flint watched the Texas coastline give way to open water. To the north, were green marshlands along the coasts of Louisiana and Mississippi, although he couldn't see them from this distance.

Two hours later, Drake brought them down smoothly at the small field on Davis Islands that catered to private aircraft. Within minutes they were taxiing toward the terminal.

Florida's March warmth surrounded them like a cozy blanket when they stepped off the plane. Drake arranged for fuel and secured the aircraft while Flint located the rental SUV.

They drove through sparse afternoon traffic along Davis Boulevard. Small businesses lined the sidewalks and blurred past the windows as they navigated toward the residential neighborhood.

The Murphy residence was a modest single-story house with a well-maintained yard and a narrow slice of view of Hillsborough Bay. Pink stucco walls and a tile roof marked it as typical Florida construction from the late 1900s. A sprinkler system kept the St. Augustine grass green, and bougainvillea climbed a trellis beside the front door.

Drake parked the rental two blocks down and across the street under the shade of a massive live oak.

Flint studied the neighborhood. Quiet residential area dotted with similar stucco houses, each with its own variation of tropical landscaping. Retirement-age neighbors were tending gardens, but no children played in the yards. A few parked cars sat baking in driveways, some doorbell cameras on a few of the homes, but nothing screamed serious active surveillance in the area.

They walked up the sidewalk to the front door. Flint pressed the doorbell and heard chimes echo inside the house.

"If you're selling something, I'm not interested."

The woman was in her early sixties. Graying hair. Tired eyes. She made no move to unlock the screen door or invite them inside.

Flint gave her his most disarming smile. "Mrs. Murphy? I'm Michael Flint. This is Alonzo Drake. We'd like to ask you about your late husband."

Her expression hardened. "Tom's been dead for years. Let the man rest in peace."

"I understand," he said with compassion. "We're investigating a bus accident your husband witnessed in Ravenswood, Illinois. Before you moved to Florida."

Helen Murphy's face went pale. Her grip tightened on the door frame.

"Can we come inside?" Flint asked respectfully.

She seemed ready to refuse, but something caused her to relent. She unlocked the door and stood aside as first Flint and then Drake crossed the threshold.

The open floor plan living room was decorated with photographs of Tom Murphy's skydiving adventures. Action shots of him in freefall, arms spread against blue sky and white clouds. Images of him teaching students, both feet planted firmly on airport tarmac. More pictures of him standing beside small aircraft, grinning with abundant confidence.

The room was a shrine to a good man who'd died doing what he loved.

Or so it appeared.

From long experience, Flint knew Helen Murphy wouldn't tell him anything unless she wanted to. So he tried to warm her up a bit.

"Mrs. Murphy, any chance we could get a glass of water?" Flint asked.

She hesitated but relented. "Sure."

When she returned from the kitchen with two cold water bottles, Flint thanked her and took a big swig as if she'd offered him an elixir from the fountain of youth. Drake showed similar appreciation for her hospitality and engaged her in small talk for a few moments.

Flint waited for a lull in the conversation before he said, "We've heard that Tom owned a skydiving business."

"Murphy's Sky Adventures. He did local instruction but also took experienced jumpers on trips to other locations." Helen's pride had surpassed her grief at some point, which was helpful. "Mexico, Honduras, Belize, Cuba. Uncommon places for aerial photography and skydiving. People loved it."

Drake asked. "Can Americans travel to Cuba?"

"The regulations were tricky, but Tom knew how to handle the paperwork. He loved skydiving in Cuba and students always wanted to go." She paused, her expression growing troubled. "Actually, he'd just returned from a Cuba trip not long before he died."

"Yeah?" Flint encouraged her to continue without being too eager.

Helen nodded. "That trip was different, though."

"Different how?"

"Tom was quiet when he came home. Distracted. He kept checking his phone and looking out the windows. I asked him about it. He said it was nothing. The group had been difficult clients, that's all." Helen twisted her wedding ring. "But Tom had dealt with difficult clients many times before. This time, whatever happened there, it really bothered him."

"Is there any paperwork from that trip? I'd like to find Tom's passengers and talk to them about it," Flint said earnestly.

Helen shook her head. "I sold the business soon after Tom died. Skydiving wasn't my thing, it was his. I didn't keep anything from the business except the photos you see here. No reason to."

"What about the new owners? Would they still have the old paperwork, do you think?" Flint asked.

"Probably not. They went out of business and liquidated everything a couple of years later. Bad economy, they said," Helen replied. "It's all gone as far as I know."

"No worries." Flint gave her a friendly nod. "We're looking for information about that bus accident. What did Tom say about it at the time?"

"Tom never talked about that," Helen said, wagging her head slowly. "He'd had accidents before, but no one had ever died. He was shaken up for quite a while. Tom said that one haunted him."

"He didn't tell you what happened?" Flint pressed. He couldn't imagine Tom had said absolutely nothing to his wife about such a serious situation.

"A young woman with three children. She must have stumbled into the path of the bus. Tom tried to save her. He stopped and jumped out of the bus and stayed with her until the ambulance came. But she was dead when they arrived. Too seriously injured they said." Helen twisted her wedding ring. "He blamed himself for not being able to do more.

He said she was really messed up. Her face was horribly crushed. He said he couldn't get that mangled image out of his head."

Flint nodded as if he'd already known about the condition of the body.

"You changed your names after you moved here?" Flint asked. He paused to allow her time to compose herself.

"People blamed him. Newspapers and such said he should have done more to save her. Made those three children orphans." Helen's voice carried old pain and her eyes filled with tears. "They kept calling. Threatening him. We changed our name and moved away from the only home we'd ever known just to get some peace."

Flint noted the details and gave her a bit of time to compose herself. "Mrs. Murphy, do you think your husband's skydiving death was really an accident?"

Helen was quiet for a longer moment. When she spoke, her voice was barely above a whisper.

"Tom was the most careful instructor I ever knew. He checked and double-checked everything, every time. He'd never lost a single skydiver. Not one. In all those years." She shook her head. "Both main and reserve chutes failed? That doesn't happen by accident to someone like Tom."

Flint nodded in sympathy. "Sometimes, the most experienced people get complacent, though. Or distracted. Like when Amelia Earhart ran out of gas. No one thought that could possibly have happened to such an experienced pilot."

Tears welled in her eyes and threatened to spill over as she continued to shake her head. "Maybe so, but not Tom. He took his responsibilities as leader very, very seriously."

"I understand." Flint waited a few moments before he changed the subject. "Can you think of anyone who might have wanted to hurt him?"

"I don't know. He never mentioned anything like that to me. But he was always looking over his shoulder after we moved away."

Helen stood up and walked to the window to stare at the water. Sunlight slanted through the glass, casting shadows across the tile floor. In the distance, sailboats moved like white triangles against the water. "The day before he died, he got an upsetting phone call."

Drake shifted forward in his chair. "Who was calling?"

"He said it was reporters that had tracked us down." Helen turned to face them. "But Tom was scared. Really scared. More scared than I'd ever seen him."

"Scared of what?" Flint asked.

She shrugged. "I don't know. He wouldn't say. The more I asked, the angrier he became until I just dropped it."

Car doors slammed outside interrupting the conversation. Drake moved quickly to the window.

"Three vehicles. We need to go now," Drake said quietly.

Flint stood up. "Mrs. Murphy, is there a back exit?"

"Through the kitchen." Her voice shook, but she waved them out the back exit.

Flint and Drake hustled around the alley toward the rental. They jumped inside and Drake pulled out, traveling away from the Murphy residence.

Drake said, "Why kill the bus driver? Doesn't make sense, does it?"

"Not yet," Flint replied. "But now we know there's something off about that bus accident and his death, too. We also know where to look. Let's get back to the Pilatus."

Drake was already rolling steadily toward the airport. "Miami first?"

CHAPTER 28

March 19

Coconut Grove

"CUBA," FLINT SAID, LEANING back in Gaspar's desk chair when they arrived at his Coconut Grove home. "That's where Tom Murphy went. That's where he saw something that got him killed."

Drake paced the cramped office. Computer screens glowed from every surface, casting blue light across stacks of equipment.

Gaspar said, "And you think Frankie Tantanella not only had something to do with it, but he's also been hiding in Cuba all these years?"

"Makes perfect sense. Cuba has no extradition treaty with the US, so we can't get him back here to stand trial. Cash economy over there. Plenty of Americans living off the grid he can pal around with," Flint said, thinking through the operational challenges. "Murphy takes a group of students on a skydiving trip to Cuba. Some fluke puts him in the wrong place at the wrong time."

"Okay. I can buy that. What was wrong about it?" Drake asked.

"Dunno." Flint shook his head. "But whatever it was, he comes home scared. Gets himself killed soon afterward. That tracks for me."

"The connection is pretty thin," Drake said. "And Helen was certain Tom wouldn't have made a mistake with his equipment, but we both know that's the most likely explanation."

"I'm betting on Cuba. Unless you've got any better leads?" Flint asked.

Drake and Gaspar both shrugged.

"We know Murphy was driving the bus that killed Lisa Peterson. Two questions came up instantly. First, what happened that caused Murphy to change his name and run?" Flint said, thinking aloud.

"Something we haven't discovered yet. And once he'd found a solid hiding place, the killer didn't know where to find him," Drake said. "Simply put, the killer couldn't find Wilson earlier. If Frankie killed him and got away with it, he got lucky."

"Frankie sounds like an inordinately lucky guy, don't you think?" Flint asked sardonically.

"The second question is more difficult, though," Gaspar said as if Flint had actually voiced it. "Why did the killer wait so long to eliminate Tom Murphy?"

"He didn't," Drake nodded slowly like a dim pupil catching up on last week's math lesson. "He killed Murphy shortly after he discovered Murphy's location."

"Helen Murphy believes her husband's death was connected to Lisa Peterson's accident. We should rule that out, at the very least," Flint said firmly.

"Go to Cuba, you mean?" Drake replied.

"Cuba is our only lead to Frankie Tantanella at the moment." Dark circles under Flint's eyes betrayed his restless night and the adrenaline crash. "We could wait for him to leave Cuba, but it makes more sense to do this now."

Gaspar offered them steaming cups of Cuban coffee. The rich aroma filled the room.

"Any new insights from what Helen told us?" Drake asked as he reached into his pocket for his phone. He glanced at the screen. "This is my DEA contact. I'll be back."

The call was brief. Afterward, Drake stepped in from the balcony, phone still in hand.

"And?" Flint asked, preoccupied.

"Harry Fisher's DEA handler died in a car accident a few weeks after the Fisher house fire. Internal Affairs suspected he was killed in retaliation, but they never proved it."

"Which tells us DEA knew the handler was dirty. And protected him anyway," Flint said flatly.

"Money talks," Gaspar said.

Drake settled again into one of Gaspar's leather chairs. The worn material creaked softly under his weight. "And you think Tom Murphy recognized Tantanella from their time in Illinois?"

"That's likely. Ravenswood is a small town. Murphy was local. He might have known Tantanella by sight, but he would certainly have recognized Lisa Peterson unless her face was horribly disfigured by the impact." Flint opened his secure laptop.

The screen cast a blue glow across his face as the encrypted system hummed to life. A soft electronic whir accompanied the startup.

"Question is whether Murphy tried to confront Tantanella or blackmail him or something else," Drake said. "Either way, Murphy ended up dead."

"And we need to find out why." Flint pulled up an encrypted list of private contacts he knew he could rely upon and scrolled to find the one he wanted. "Cuba's not exactly a tourist destination for American private investigators. We'll need official permission to travel there legally."

"How are we going to manage that?" Drake asked.

Flint found the number he needed. "I have a contact at the State Department who owes me a few favors."

Drake leaned forward. "Nothing that makes you a target, I assume."

"Kept his son out of federal prison three years ago. Drug charges that would have ended the kid's career before it started." Flint found the number he needed. "Ben Hayes. Deputy Assistant Secretary. He can expedite travel authorizations for us."

The call to Hayes took fifteen minutes of careful negotiation even though Hayes remembered the favor clearly. His son was now a successful attorney in Dallas with a spotless record and a stellar reputation. Hayes had not forgotten that it was Flint who made that possible.

"We'll say you're on an academic research mission. Historical investigation of Cuban American family connections," Hayes explained over the secure line. "That's your cover story. You're investigating genealogy for American citizens with Cuban heritage."

"Perfect. How long will it take to get authorization for travel?"

"I'll arrange for the embassy to issue travel documents tomorrow morning. Cultural research gives you legitimate business there and freedom of movement on the ground. As long as you don't make any waves, you should be okay," Hayes explained bluntly. "But if you draw the wrong kind of attention you'll be arrested, and I may not be able to get you out."

"We're looking for a witness. We won't be there long enough to get into trouble," Flint assured him.

"Don't make me regret this, Flint." Hayes was accustomed to cutting through bureaucracy. "Cuba's not a place for freelance operations. You can die there, and the US government might not hear about it for decades."

Flint replied, "We'll keep our noses clean."

"You'd better. One embarrassing international incident and you'll be persona non grata for the rest of your career, even if I can extract you," Hayes said. "The Secretary is not amused by rule breakers, regardless of whether your mission succeeds or doesn't."

After Hayes disconnected, Flint began making operational assessments. Equipment they could carry. Cash they'd need. Local contacts they could trust.

The familiar ritual of mission planning settled over him like an old coat. The methodical process of risk assessment and contingency planning had kept him alive through three tours and countless private operations.

"So what's the plan?" Drake asked, leaning forward in his chair.

"We treat this like any other hostile territory operation." Flint closed the laptop. "Minimal footprint, maximum preparation. Get in, get out, nobody gets hurt or compromised."

The office door opened. Gaspar's careful gait reflected his damaged body. "I heard you talking to Hayes. Cuba's tricky territory. I've been across a few times over the years."

"What do you know about current conditions?" Flint asked.

"Travel is easy enough when it's allowed, but you'll have limitations. No weapons. Constant surveillance. Communications monitoring. Throw litter on the street and you're asking for severe sanctions." Gaspar's voice of experience came over the soft hum of cooling fans and multiple computer systems providing background noise. "What's the mission?"

"We're tracking Frankie Tantanella," Flint replied.

"Cuban authorities don't cooperate with US law enforcement, but they don't like harboring wanted criminals either. If you want to bring Tantanella back, they probably won't help you. Depends on the crime and the Cuban government's whims in the current political climate." Gaspar flipped through the screens on his tablet. "I know a guy in Havana. Former asset. Runs a private investigation firm now. He can provide local support if you need it."

"Good. What about equipment restrictions?" Flint asked.

"Forget weapons. Cuban customs will search everything. Bring cash. Lots of it. American dollars work best." Gaspar sipped what was probably his tenth cup of sweet Cuban coffee that day. "You sure this lead is worth the operational risk?"

It was a reasonable question. They'd been attacked already. Trained killers with sophisticated and pricey equipment. Helen Murphy had been targeted simply for talking to them.

The stakes had escalated rapidly for reasons that were not altogether clear.

But Tantanella was the only connection they'd located so far to any of the missing Fisher kids. After more than twenty years, Jason Fisher wanted answers and Flint agreed with him.

"Tom Murphy is dead. Operatives tracked us to his widow's house," Flint said, meeting Gaspar's gaze. "That tells me we're on the right track."

"The right track to what, though?" Gaspar asked.

"Good question." Flint made his decision. "But if Tantanella's alive, he could be the key to finding those kids.

If Tantanella's not there, we'll come back. Nothing lost but a few hours of our time, which Jason Fisher can well afford to subsidize. We're going."

"Then you may need more support." Gaspar's fingers rapid-fire clicked on his keyboard as he worked multiple databases simultaneously. "I'll need to make some calls."

Flint gestured to Drake, and they left Gaspar to his work.

On the patio, Drake said, "We'll need equipment, and Gaspar says everything we bring along will be inspected."

"And we assume they'll know our travel plans as well." Flint leaned against the garden wall with his hands resting in his pockets. "Whoever's behind the attacks on us has resources. Government connections, possibly. International reach, most likely."

"Speaking of which, how did they find Helen Murphy so fast today?" Drake asked. "That tactical team arrived pretty quickly."

Flint agreed. The timing was too precise. Either they'd been monitoring Helen continuously or they'd tracked Flint and Drake directly to her.

"Suggests they're better equipped than we initially assessed."

"Which means what?"

"It means we assume they are monitoring our coms and plan accordingly."

Drake's expression hardened. "Assume real-time surveillance. They're listening to everything."

Flint weighed the options. Abort and lose their only lead to the Fisher children. Continue and walk directly into a trap prepared with unlimited resources.

"We change everything. Different timeline, different route, different communications protocols." Flint opened a fresh satellite phone and sent encrypted messages to alternative contacts. Clean phones. Alternate travel arrangements. Counter-surveillance protocols.

Drake was planning equipment modifications. "How do we communicate once we're there?"

"We'll start with Gaspar's contact in Havana. Face-to-face meetings only." Flint powered down the fresh phone and dropped it into his pocket. "We go dark starting now."

"And if Cuba is a trap?" Drake asked.

"Then we spring it on our terms."

The afternoon sun cast long shadows across Gaspar's garden like geometric fingers reaching toward Biscayne Bay. The water sparkled beyond the palm trees in orderly patterns of blue and white.

"They've made mistakes. They tried to stop us three times already. We assume they know more about Tantanella in Cuba than we do." Flint gave Drake the first genuine smile of the day. "Tantanella's probably exactly where we think he is."

Flint imagined the streets of Havana where answers waited among the shadowy brutality of the Caribbean dictatorship. He wasn't going in blind. He'd been there before.

CHAPTER 29

March 19
Havana, Cuba

FLINT STEPPED OFF THE Aeroméxico flight onto the tarmac at José Martí International Airport. The March weather was similar to what he'd left in Miami. Warm but comfortable, with a breeze carrying the scent of jet fuel and tropical vegetation.

Drake followed close behind. Both were dressed in lightweight khakis and button-down shirts to mimic academic researchers investigating Cuban American genealogy.

The terminal buzzed with typical travel chaos at a regional airport in a communist country.

Uniformed officials scrutinized documents at every checkpoint. Once again, Flint handed over his passport and travel authorization to a stern-faced customs agent.

"Purpose of visit?" The man's English carried a heavy accent.

"Academic research. Historical investigation of Cuban American family connections," Flint replied. He maintained eye contact.

Embassy workers here routinely used commercial flights to maintain lower profiles, which was why Flint chose to enter here. The embassy was small and Cuban airspace restrictions made direct military or private jet flights complicated.

The agent studied the State Department letterhead and Hayes's authorization a moment too long for Flint's comfort. But a few moments later, he stamped the passports and waved them through.

While they waited, Cuban customs officers searched their luggage methodically. Every item examined. Every pocket explored.

"What is this?" One officer held up Flint's digital camera.

"Research documentation. We photograph historical sites and family records."

The officer turned the camera over in his hands, then handed it back. "And these?" He gestured to Drake's notebooks.

"Genealogy notes. Family trees, dates, locations."

They examined each page carefully but found nothing suspicious. Two academic researchers with cameras, notebooks, and genealogy materials. Nothing to see here.

Flint had brought ten thousand dollars in small bills, distributed throughout his gear in zippered compartments. American currency worked well in Cuba's underground economy. The customs officers' search missed most of it. What they found, they stuffed in their pockets.

"Welcome to Cuba," the lead officer ultimately said with indifference.

Outside the terminal, Drake flagged a taxi. The driver was a middle-aged man with a weathered face, and his hands were baked into deep wrinkles by the sun, but his eyes were alert and the gaze suspicious.

"Habana Vieja," Flint said when they settled into the back seat.

The driver nodded and pulled into traffic. Soviet-era vehicles were mixed with restored American classic cars from the 1950s. Like the people, Havana's infrastructure looked tired. Cracked roads. Faded buildings. Power lines strung haphazardly between poles.

"First time in Cuba?" the driver asked in English.

"Yes. We're researching family histories," Drake volunteered to put the man at ease.

He nodded and flashed a toothless grin. "Many Americans come for that now. The past is important."

While Drake kept the driver engaged in meaningless small talk, Flint studied the city through the window. He'd been here before on a mission he couldn't discuss. The once elegant but now decrepit streets seemed familiar and unchanged despite the passage of time.

The taxi dropped them at the Hotel Inglaterra in Central Havana. One of the oldest and most historic hotels in the city, Hotel Inglaterra was a colonial building with elegant columns and wrought-iron balconies.

Flint checked them into a two-bedroom suite using the academic credentials. The suite overlooked the Capitolio. The massive dome reminded Flint of the US Capitol in Washington, DC, but it was painted in tropical pastels that seemed to fade in the afternoon sun.

"First order of business," Flint said as he unpacked his bag. "Check in with the embassy."

Drake nodded. "Then Gaspar's contact."

"And we assume we're being watched from the moment we walked onto that plane."

"Hotel room's probably bugged too."

"Count on it." Flint closed his suitcase. "Remember we're academic researchers with nothing to hide. Let's go."

Drake flagged down another taxi to take them to the US Embassy, which occupied a modern building in Vedado. American flags flew alongside Cuban security checkpoints.

Flint presented their credentials to the Marine guard.

"Mr. Flint and Mr. Drake. You're expected," he said, waving them through.

A consular officer named Natalie Williams met them on the other side of the gate and led them to a secure conference room. A quick glance showed her to be mid-forties, professional demeanor, tired lines around her eyes that suggested long experience with complicated situations.

"Ben Hayes briefed me on your research mission," she said. "How can we help?"

"We need a secure base of operations. Communications support if possible."

Williams leaned back in her chair. "I can provide limited assistance. Secure phone access. Meeting space if required. But understand our position clearly. You're on your own out there. If you can make it back onto embassy grounds, we'll get you out of the country if we can. Beyond that, we have no resources to offer."

"Understood."

"Cuba's not a forgiving place for freelance operations. The government monitors everything. Neighborhood committees report suspicious activity. Prosecutors can authorize surveillance without judicial oversight." Williams handed him a card. "That's my direct number. Memorize it. Destroy the card. Use the number only in emergencies."

Flint memorized the number and handed the card to Drake who did the same before handing the card back to her. "What about American citizens living here off the grid?"

"They exist. Cuba doesn't have an extradition treaty with the United States. Some people find that appealing," Williams said flatly. "But we don't track them, and we can't do much to help them if they get into trouble."

Drake spoke up. "Any particular areas where Americans might settle?"

"Old Havana has a foreign community. Artists, writers, people who want to disappear. But it's also where the surveillance is heaviest." Williams stood. "Be careful, gentlemen. Cuba may seem relaxed, but it's still a police state. They execute people in the streets here without much fanfare."

"Copy that," Flint replied as he turned to leave. "When we come back, we could be in a hurry."

Williams nodded. "I figured."

Without conversation, Flint and Drake left the embassy and took another taxi to Gaspar's contact's address in Old Havana. The neighborhood was a maze of narrow streets and colonial architecture. Buildings showed their age. Peeling paint. Cracked walls. Iron balconies that had seen better decades.

"Look at this place," Drake said quietly. "Like a museum that's falling apart."

Flint replied, "That's exactly what it is."

The address led to a small office above a restaurant. A sign in Spanish advertised private investigation services. Flint climbed the narrow stairs and knocked.

A compact man in his fifties answered. Gray hair, alert gaze, and a firm handshake that suggested he kept himself in good physical shape.

"Luis Castro," he said in accented English. "Gaspar said you might visit."

"Michael Flint. This is Alonzo Drake."

Castro gestured them inside. The office was sparse but functional. A desk, two chairs, filing cabinets, and a window that overlooked the street below.

"Gaspar explained your interest in genealogy research," Castro said with a slight smile. "Family connections that might have brought Americans to Cuba over the years, he said."

"That's right. We're looking for someone who might have settled here about twenty years ago. An American named Frank Tantanella."

Castro's expression remained neutral. "Common enough situation. Americans who needed a fresh start. Cuba offers sanctuary for those with the right connections."

"What kind of connections?"

"Money. Patience. The ability to blend in and live a quiet life." Castro opened a desk drawer and retrieved a notepad and a stubby pencil used almost to the end of its life. "What can you tell me about the man you seek?"

Maintaining operational security, Flint provided the basics without mentioning any criminal activity or giving Tantanella's name.

Castro made notes. "I'll need to ask around carefully. Americans living off the grid here are careful about revealing themselves. But the community is small. People talk."

"How long will it take you to find him?" Flint asked.

"Your travel authorization is good for twenty-four hours. After that, you become interesting to the authorities," Castro replied.

Drake leaned forward and lowered his voice. "What about surveillance?"

CHAPTER 30

March 19
Havana, Cuba

"CUBAN INTELLIGENCE MONITORS ALL foreigners and suspicious locals. Neighborhood committees report unusual activity. Your hotel room is also monitored." Castro stood and moved to the window and whispered to Flint, "But there are ways to work around the system if you're careful."

He pointed to the street below and spoke at normal volume. "See the old man selling newspapers? He's been there fifteen years. Knows everyone who comes and goes. The woman sweeping her doorstep? She reports to the local committee. The teenagers playing dominoes? They work for various people who pay for information."

Flint studied the street. Normal neighborhood activity that masked a surveillance network. He cataloged the faces. The positions. The sight lines.

"I'll need counter-surveillance support," he said quietly.

"I can provide that. Limited resources, but effective. My people know how to move around the watchers." Castro returned to his desk. "Give me two hours to make inquiries about your guy. Meet me at the Café Taberna on Plaza Vieja at six o'clock."

"What if you can't find anything?"

"Then your genealogy research ends with disappointed academic researchers returning to Miami tomorrow." Castro smiled thinly. "But I have a feeling that family tree has interesting branches."

Flint decided to use the two hours productively. They left Castro's office and walked through Old Havana's streets. The architecture was impressive despite decades of neglect. Colonial buildings with arcades and internal courtyards. Baroque churches. Neoclassical facades reflected the island's former grandeur.

"Notice anything?" Drake asked.

"Two men in casual clothes. Been behind us since we left the embassy. Different faces from the ones at the hotel."

"How many teams you figure?"

"Cuban intelligence probably has three or four teams rotating surveillance. Question is whether anyone else is watching."

They paused at a plaza to study a colonial church. Flint used the reflection in a storefront window to spot another pattern. Non-Cuban faces had appeared at multiple locations. Too well-dressed for tourists. Too alert for casual observers.

"We've got more company," he said.

Drake followed his gaze. "Same as the Kentucky team?"

"Possible they tracked us here somehow," Flint replied. "Could be someone else."

"So much for going dark with coms."

"Tells us they're resourceful. Connections probably extend to Cuban operations."

Flint continued walking. He made mental notes of escape routes. Narrow alleys that led away from main streets. Buildings with multiple exits. The old defensive walls that surrounded parts of the colonial city.

He also studied the infrastructure. Power lines. Electrical substations. Water systems. Communications equipment.

Cuban public utilities were notoriously fragile. The entire national electrical grid had collapsed four times in the past six months. Any significant disruption could trigger widespread failures.

Good to know.

At six o'clock they entered Café Taberna, a small restaurant with exposed stone walls and low lighting. Castro waited at a corner table in the dark where he had a clear view of the entrance.

"Find anything useful?" Flint asked as he sat down.

Castro ordered Cuban coffee strong enough to power machinery for all three. "Your target has been a careful man. But he is not invisible."

He leaned forward and spoke quietly. "There's an old man who knows the American expatriate community. Raúl's been helping people settle here for twenty years. He says there's a couple that fits your description. American man with a scar on his left hand. Lives with his wife in a building near the cathedral."

Flint felt a familiar surge of anticipation. "Address?"

"Calle Mercaderes. Three blocks from here. Colonial building, blue door, second floor." Castro sipped his coffee. "Raúl says they're good people trying to live quietly. They help their neighbors. They don't cause trouble."

"We just want to talk."

"Raúl also mentioned the man sometimes has visitors. Other Americans who don't stay long. Business meetings, perhaps."

Drake raised an eyebrow. "What kind of business?"

"The kind that requires privacy."

"Recent visitors?"

"Within the past month. Raúl didn't get a close look, but he said they were well-dressed. Not tourists, for sure," Castro explained. "He said they didn't socialize with the locals."

Flint and Drake exchanged glances. Recent and regular visitors could mean many things, none of them good.

They finished their coffee and carefully discussed logistics. Castro could provide counter-surveillance. His people could watch for Cuban intelligence and any other parties showing interest.

"Face-to-face communications only. No phones, no electronic messages," Flint reminded him.

"One more thing," Castro said with a nod as they prepared to leave. "The building on Calle Mercaderes is old. Many of these colonial structures are unstable. The government lacks resources for proper maintenance. Be careful if you need to move quickly."

"How unstable?" Drake asked.

"Buildings collapse here regularly. Sometimes from hurricanes. Sometimes from age. Sometimes from nothing at all." Castro stood. "Just be aware of your surroundings."

They left the café separately. Castro went first. Drake and Flint followed five minutes later.

Old Havana at night was a different world. Streetlights provided uneven illumination. Shadows stretched between buildings. The tourist areas bustled with activity, but the residential neighborhoods grew quiet after sunset.

Flint and Drake made their way through narrow streets toward Calle Mercaderes. They paused frequently to check for surveillance. His experience with Cuban watchers caused him to describe them as competent but predictable. They maintained distance and rotated positions on schedule.

But Flint had advantages they didn't know about. He understood Cuba's infrastructure vulnerabilities. He'd studied the electrical grid again during their afternoon reconnaissance.

Calle Mercaderes was a narrow street lined with colonial buildings. Most showed signs of age and neglect. Peeling paint. Cracked masonry. Iron balconies that had seen decades of Caribbean weather.

Flint found the building with the blue door. Three stories, typical colonial construction, with a narrow staircase visible through an open entrance. Light flickered from windows on the second floor.

He settled into a doorway across the street where he had a clear view of the building. Drake had filed off a couple of streets back. He should be approaching from the opposite direction, establishing visual contact from a different angle.

Flint pulled out binoculars and focused on the second-floor windows. Movement inside. Shadows passing in front of the light.

A man appeared briefly in the window. Dark hair, visible scar on his left hand. Frank Tantanella, older but still recognizable from the photographs.

Then a woman joined him at the window.

Flint adjusted the focus and studied her profile. Something familiar about the way she moved. The set of her shoulders. The angle of her head.

She turned toward the window, and the light illuminated her face as if she were a heavenly angel.

Flint raised his eyebrows when he recognized her and murmured, "Well, well, well."

Tantanella's wife wasn't a Cuban woman. She wasn't really a stranger at all.

Lizzy Pace was alive. Living in Cuba with Frank Tantanella. After more than twenty years.

"How is that possible?" he wondered aloud and lowered the binoculars.

Lizzy hadn't died in the bus crash. She'd been hiding in Cuba all this time. Presumably with Tantanella's help.

She might know where the Fisher kids were now, too.

But who did die in that bus accident?

Flint was so focused on the revelation that he almost missed the movement in his peripheral vision.

Armed men emerged from the shadows at both ends of the street. Cuban security forces came from one direction. Private operatives from the other. He glanced up to see more security personnel appearing on rooftops and in doorways.

All converging on Calle Mercaderes.

Flint keyed his radio. "We've got multiple hostiles. Cuban authorities from the north. Unknown hostiles from the south. Unknown count on the rooftops."

"Copy that. I see them. What's the play?"

Flint assessed the situation rapidly. They were outnumbered and outgunned. Running would only delay the inevitable.

Across the street from Tantanella's building stood a neighborhood electrical substation. A collection of transformers and switching equipment that distributed power to several blocks of Old Havana. The kind of aging system that regularly failed under normal circumstances.

"I'm going to level the playing field," Flint told Drake. "When the lights go out, move fast."

Flint crossed the street quickly. He stayed low. The substation was enclosed by a chain-link fence, but the lock was old and yielded to pressure.

He slipped inside and studied the transformer configuration.

The system was exactly what he'd expected. Soviet-era equipment that had been patched and modified over decades. No modern protection systems. No redundant safeguards. No spinning reserves to compensate for sudden failures.

Perfect for creating a cascading grid collapse.

"You sure this will work?" Drake's voice crackled back.

"No. But it should." Flint pulled a small demolition charge from his gear that he'd collected at the embassy. "All it takes is the right push in the right place."

"How do you know that?" Drake asked.

"Training supplied by Uncle Sam," Flint replied as he placed the charge against the main transformer's control panel.

He set a thirty-second timer.

"Thirty seconds and counting," he radioed Drake on his way out.

"Copy that. I'll be ready to move."

Flint retreated to the street and counted down.

The explosion was smaller than he expected but perfectly targeted. The transformer sparked and died. The immediate area plunged into total darkness.

For a moment, nothing else happened.

Then the cascade began.

Flint's sabotage created exactly the kind of transmission line fault that had caused four total grid collapses in the past six months.

The blackout spread like a wave across Old Havana. Block by block, the lights went out. Within minutes, entire neighborhoods were dark.

In the confusion, all the high-tech surveillance equipment went dead. Night vision goggles, communications systems, electronic coordination tools. All technological advantages vanished.

Cuban security forces lost their command-and-control systems. Streetlights failed. Traffic signals died. The organized manhunt dissolved into chaos.

"Drake, you copy?" Flint whispered into his radio.

"Roger that. Cuban forces are scattered," Drake said, reporting what he could see in the limited moonlight. "They might have backups, but right now they can't coordinate without their electronics."

"Lost their night vision, too. They're stumbling around like the citizens," Flint said.

In Tantanella's building, the power failure seemed to have killed the structure's aging electrical systems completely. Water pumps that kept moisture from the foundation stopped working. Emergency lighting systems that provided basic safety illumination had gone dark.

The colonial building, already weakened by decades of deferred maintenance, began to shift and settle. Its minimal modern supports failed.

Flint heard the first ominous creaking sounds. He moved toward the building. Cuban security forces were shouting orders in the darkness. Operatives were trying to coordinate without their electronic systems. Civilians were pouring into the streets. They banged pots and demanded answers about the blackout.

Perfect chaos.

"What the hell did you do?" Drake's voice came through the radio.

"Gave Cuba what it gets regularly. A total grid failure."

"The building's making noise."

"Right. Castro warned us these structures are unstable."

Exactly what Flint needed.

He reached the blue door. The building's internal structure gave a major groan of distress.

Somewhere above, plaster was falling. Wood was splintering. The kind of sounds that preceded the partial or total building collapses that occurred regularly in Havana.

Flint looked up at the second-floor windows where he'd seen Lizzy Pace. The woman whose death had been faked more than twenty years ago. Twice. The one who claimed to be the mother of the missing Fisher children.

She was alive. She was thirty feet above him in a building that was about to fall down.

While armed hostiles converged from multiple directions in the blacked-out streets of Old Havana, Flint moved quickly toward Lizzy Pace, dodging bullets as he ran.

CHAPTER 31

March 19

Havana, Cuba

THE BUILDING GROANED AS its ancient timbers creaked under the strain of centuries-old construction finally giving way.

Flint reached the weathered blue door and grabbed the handle. The wood had swollen and warped in the perpetual Caribbean humidity. The frame had shifted, creating gaps where mortar had crumbled away.

He pulled hard. The door opened six inches and stuck fast against the sagging frame.

"Come on," he muttered, putting his full weight behind it.

Chunks of yellowed plaster mixed with splinters of weathered mahogany and cedar rained down from above. Dust filled the humid night air with the chalky taste of disintegrating mortar.

The colonial structure had lasted more than three hundred years, but it was failing fast. Each tremor sent more fragments cascading into the narrow street. He needed to hurry.

"Flint, where are you?" Drake's voice crackled through the radio.

"Blue door. Building's unstable."

"I'm coming to you."

"Negative. Cover the exits. Multiple hostiles converging."

"Copy that. How bad is it up there?"

"Bad enough. This whole place is coming down."

Flint put his shoulder to the swollen door, feeling the resistance of wood that had absorbed decades of Caribbean storms. The aged timber cracked sharply. He squeezed through the opening, scraping against the rough-hewn doorframe.

Inside, the narrow staircase was barely visible in the dim amber of emergency lighting that flickered from dying battery-powered units mounted on the peeling walls. Sixteen-inch-wide limestone steps, worn smooth by use, wound upward at a steep angle designed for defense. The wrought-iron handrail felt loose under his grip as the mounting brackets pulled free from crumbling masonry.

Above Flint heard voices filtering through the thick limestone and heavy timber that did little to muffle sounds. Spanish and English words mixed together in urgent tones. Tantanella's faded Kentucky accent and the woman who looked like Lizzy Pace responded with tired, fearful questions.

"We need to get out of here now," Tantanella said.

"But where can we go?"

"I don't know, but staying here isn't an option. The building is falling down around us."

The building shuddered and groaned. Old cedar and mahogany supports gave way with sharp cracks that reverberated through the limestone. The sound echoed through the hollow structure, each snap marking another step toward total collapse.

Flint took the worn limestone stairs two at a time, his boots finding purchase on stone polished smooth by three centuries of foot traffic. Each step creaked ominously under his weight. The wrought-iron handrail pulled farther away from the crumbling mortar wall with each grip. Metal brackets loosened from the limestone that had endured Spanish treasure fleets and hurricanes but could withstand no more.

Through the wide-plank hardwood over limestone joists, he heard shouting from the street below. Cuban security forces were trying to coordinate without sophisticated electronics and failing badly.

Citizens demanded answers about the blackout in rapid-fire Spanish voices rising from doorways and balconies throughout the darkened neighborhood. The chaos was exactly what he needed. More confusion to mask his approach could only be a good thing.

"What's happening?" someone shouted from a nearby balcony.

"The power's out!" came the reply from the street.

"Drake, you hearing this?" Flint whispered into his radio.

"Yep. Street's full of people wandering around in the dark. Perfect cover."

On the first landing, Flint paused to listen, pressing himself against the cool limestone wall.

"Listen to me," Tantanella was saying. "We've been through worse than this."

"Have we, Frankie? Really?" The woman's voice carried exhaustion and fear in equal measure. "Because this feels like the end. Our luck has run out."

Flint continued upward while dodging debris.

The second-floor landing had three closed doors, all made of heavy Caribbean mahogany. Warm amber light spilled from under the middle door onto the worn stone floor.

"Someone's coming up the stairs," a man with an American accent said quietly.

"How many?" Tantanella asked.

"Just one, I think. Probably armed."

"Could be Cuban law enforcement," a second American man said.

"Yeah, and I've got some swamp land I can sell you," the first American replied snidely.

The building shook again with the violence of an earthquake. Chunks of mortar and roof tile debris fell like rain.

"We need to get out of here now. The whole building's coming down," the woman said clearly despite the terror that must have gripped her as the building disintegrated around them.

"Follow me," Tantanella commanded.

Flint moved closer to the door, his boots silent on the limestone floor worn smooth.

He guessed Tantanella was near the narrow window that overlooked Calle Mercaderes because of the slight echo that indicated proximity to glass and the stone wall beyond.

The woman was between Tantanella and the door.

Which was when Flint saw the operatives spread out in a tactical formation covering the exits, suggesting years of training at specialized facilities.

"Drake," Flint whispered into his radio. "We've got a problem."

"What kind of problem?"

"Unknown operatives with our targets."

"Shit. How many?"

"At least two. Probably more."

The building gave another major groan. Somewhere above, centuries-old masonry cracked, and the sound reverberated through what remained of the old walls.

The structure couldn't hold much longer. Three hundred years had finally claimed it as a victim.

"Building's going down," Drake's voice came through Flint's radio. "You need to get out while you still can."

"Copy that. But I need the woman."

"What about the operatives?"

Flint tested the door handle, a piece of tarnished brass that had turned green by tropical oxidation. The mechanism moved freely in his grip, unlocked and falling away from the stone.

He waited for the right moment. When the structure shook again and everyone inside was distracted by the ominous creaking of failing supports, he quickly pushed the heavy door open and stepped inside.

The room was exactly what he'd expected. Small and sparsely furnished, with narrow windows that overlooked the stone streets below. Generations of occupants had scarred the walls. Emergency lighting cast everything in harsh amber shadows that flickered with each tremor of the failing structure.

Tantanella stood near the window that faced Calle Mercaderes. Older than the photographs but unmistakably the same man who had vanished twenty-five years ago.

The woman beside him was Lizzy Pace. Thinner than she'd been years ago, with graying hair but the same delicate bone structure revealing the beautiful young woman he'd seen in pictures.

Two men in dark clothing stood between them and the entrance like sentinels. Operatives. Straight backs, steady alert gaze, and hands that never strayed far from their weapons.

All four turned when Flint entered.

"Drop your weapon," one of the operatives said with an American accent. He raised his gun directly toward Flint.

"Easy there." Flint kept his weapon low but ready. "I'm a licensed private investigator. Working a missing persons case."

"Not anymore," the second American said. "This is our operation."

"In Cuba?" Flint asked. "That's interesting jurisdiction you've got there."

"Our jurisdiction is not your concern," the first operative replied.

Flint noted standard gear that could have been US government issue. Body armor, communications equipment, and weapons that came from the same manufacturers who supplied the US military.

These guys could be government operatives, private contractors, or well-funded mercenaries. But why were they here?

The building shuddered again. Chunks of yellowed plaster fell from the ceiling with loud thuds. The window glass cracked and shattered.

Mere minutes until the entire building and everything in it was reduced to a pile of rubble.

CHAPTER 32

March 19
Havana, Cuba

THE BUILDING LURCHED AND its entire frame shifted as it finally surrendered to time and neglect. The overwhelming grinding sound indicated massive structural failure.

When the limestone floor sagged toward the center of the room, Flint grabbed for support as furniture slid across the tilted surface.

"Everybody out!" an operative shouted over the cacophony. "Now!"

Flint and the others understood that hesitation meant death.

The building shook again. This time part of the ceiling collapsed near the window. Chunks of limestone and timber crashed to the floor.

Dust filled the air in a choking fog while it dimmed the amber emergency lighting to ghostly halos.

Tantanella broke away from the operatives. Obviously, he knew this building and the neighborhood. He darted toward a section of wall that looked solid but likely concealed an old service passage as if he were checking escape routes.

Flint had come too far to let Frankie and Lizzy go.

The operatives were disoriented by the collapse.

More ceiling hit the floor.

The confusion provided perfect cover for Flint to grab Lizzy's arm. "Lizzy Pace. You're coming with me."

Her eyes widened when he said her name, but she didn't move. She tried to pull away, panic rising in her voice. "I can't leave Frankie!"

"You don't have a choice," Flint said, jerking her toward the exit.

"Building's coming down," Drake's voice crackled through Flint's radio. "Cuban forces regrouping north side."

"Copy that. Coming out with witness."

"Tantanella?" Drake asked.

"Lost track of him."

Flint pulled Lizzy toward the stairs, dodging falling plaster. Limestone steps threatened to crumble under their weight.

The wrought-iron handrail had torn away from the wall completely. Carefully, they descended the steep colonial staircase. Each step creaked. Wood and stone ground against each other as the structure died around them.

"I can't breathe," Lizzy gasped, choking on the dust-filled air.

Flint lifted her arm to cover her nose and mouth as well as possible. "Keep moving."

A massive beam crashed down behind them, blocking the stairway. The others would need to find a different way out.

The old building failed in sections, the way it had been built. Exterior walls buckled outward. The roof sagged inward. Timber supports snapped like bones.

They reached the ground floor just as another section of roof caved in behind them with a thunderous crash.

Flint jerked the weathered blue door open and pushed Lizzy into the street beyond which lay in complete darkness.

"What's happening out here?" Lizzy whispered, her voice choked with fear.

"Power blackout affecting the whole island. Stay close," Flint said, nudging her along.

"What about Frankie?" she asked fearfully.

"We'll find him as soon as we can," Flint replied.

They pushed into the panic that turned total darkness into total pandemonium. Salt water, tropical vegetation, and masonry dust filled the air.

The building collapse had awakened every resident in the area.

People poured from surrounding buildings with flashlights and candles, shouting panicked questions in rapid Spanish. Piercing sirens wailed. Dogs barked. Children cried. The narrow street echoed with voices calling for missing neighbors and family members.

"Dios mío! What happened?"

"Is anyone trapped inside?"

"Where are the bomberos?"

Flint kept his grip and moved Lizzy along through the chaos.

"I can't see anything." Lizzy stumbled against him as they tried to navigate through the gathering crowd.

"That's the good news. You can't see them, and they can't see you. Move."

When they were half a block away, the old building gave a loud, final, catastrophic groan. The remaining walls buckled outward, and the structure, finally, collapsed.

The crash echoed through the narrow streets louder than thunder.

Dust rose like a small volcano, creating a choking cloud that sent people running in all directions.

"My love," Lizzy whispered, staring at the monstrous pile of rubble through streaming eyes. "Frankie was in there."

"Not likely," Flint said, giving her a rough shove to get her moving again. "He knows these buildings. He got out. We'll find him or he'll find us."

The crowd outside was growing larger and more agitated. Without emergency services to coordinate rescue efforts, citizens were trying to organize themselves. Some called out names of people who might have been inside.

Others approached the debris pile with flashlights, looking for survivors.

"Drake, we need an exit route. Too many civilians," Flint spoke into his radio.

"I count maybe fifty people around the collapse site, more coming. Operatives withdrew to vehicles two blocks east. Tantanella isn't with them. Cuban patrol moving south," Drake replied while scanning the scene. "Take the alley west of your current position, away from the crowd."

"Copy that."

The blackout was now absolute except for scattered flashlights and candles in windows. Flint had a flashlight in his pocket, but it would act like a beacon if he turned it on.

Instead, he fished his phone from his pocket, opened the night vision app, and used it to lead Lizzy through the darkened alleys and away from the destruction.

She stumbled over debris in the roadway. Her breathing was rapid and shallow, as if she'd swallowed too much dust.

Her voice shook when she asked, "Who are you and where are you taking me?"

"Somewhere we can talk."

"I'm not going anywhere with you. You don't have a clue what you're doing."

Flint didn't have time for such nonsense. "I know you faked your death twice and now you've been hiding for more than twenty years."

She tried to pull away from his grip. "You can't just kidnap me."

"You'd already be dead if not for me. Show a little gratitude, why don't you?" Flint replied.

When they rounded the corner, a police officer stood at the next intersection, waving a flashlight and trying to direct traffic around disabled vehicles. He was alone and overwhelmed. When citizens approached him he gestured helplessly, and they moved on.

"Help me!" Lizzy called toward the officer in Spanish. "This man is taking me against my will!"

The officer looked up through the darkness and waved them past the intersection. He had bigger problems at the moment than what must have appeared to be a domestic dispute.

"Come on before something worse happens," Flint said, pulling her along.

They continued through the maze of darkened streets following Drake's suggestions from the radio. Citizens with flashlights moved past them in both directions, some heading toward the collapse site to help, others fleeing the area to avoid more unstable buildings.

"Why are you doing this?" Lizzy asked, planting her feet firmly where she stood.

Flint gave her a little jerk to move her along.

"Right turn ahead," Drake's voice came through the radio. "Clear path for two blocks."

After several minutes of moving through the darkness they reached a small, abandoned building. Three stories of weathered limestone appearing to be structurally sound but definitely vacant.

Flint guided Lizzy inside and up to the second floor.

She collapsed against a wall, breathing hard and shivering despite the humid heat.

Flint took position near a window overlooking the street. Through the darkness, residents with flashlights were still moving toward the collapse site. The immediate chaos was settling into a more organized rescue effort, but without emergency services or lighting, progress would be slow.

"Drake, status?"

"Infrastructure failure citywide. Communications down. Emergency services overwhelmed. The operatives have regrouped at their vehicles but haven't approached the collapse site. No sign of Tantanella."

"Official Cuban response?"

"Minimal. Maybe three officers in the immediate area, but they can't coordinate or communicate. They're focused on crowd control around the collapse."

"Harbor status?"

"Patrol boats active but communications scrambled. Their usual coordination is disrupted."

Flint studied the darkened streets below. The searchers had no electronic surveillance or coordinated security, which meant he and Drake had the advantage. But it wouldn't last forever.

"Are you going to kill me?" Lizzy asked suddenly.

Flint looked at her. Fear had replaced the exhaustion in her eyes. Years of hiding had taught her that men with guns were rarely good news.

"What sense does that make? If I wanted you dead, I could have left you back there."

"Then what do you want?"

"To get you out of Cuba alive."

"And then?"

"Then you answer some questions, and we decide what happens next."

She stared at him in the darkness. When she spoke again, her voice was barely audible. "What kind of questions?"

"Drake, initiate movement to harbor," Flint said into his radio.

"Copy that. Moving to overwatch position."

Flint turned back to Lizzy. "Time to go."

She wiped her eyes and slowly stood up. "I hope you know what you're doing."

"So do I."

CHAPTER 33

March 19
Havana, Cuba

FLINT STOOD NEAR A window, listening. Shouts echoed from the streets outside. Distant sirens rose and fell like an urban heartbeat.

The abandoned building sported broken windows and peeled paint. Discarded furniture was scattered across stained concrete floors. Unoccupied, but not safe.

The window frame held jagged glass remnants that caught the smoke-hazed darkness. Three blocks away, flames licked at a rooftop. The sound of running footsteps clattered against pavement somewhere below.

The city was coming apart at the seams, which meant the departure window was shrinking by the minute.

Behind him, Lizzy sat on the edge of a battered metal desk. The thing had been gutted for salvage years ago.

Drawers hung open like empty mouths. She stared at the floor. Hadn't said a word since they'd arrived.

Flint assessed the room again. Two exits. The door they'd entered through and a window that led to what looked like a fire escape. He smelled rust and old water damage. Brown stains ran down the walls where rain had leaked through holes in the roof. Dust motes danced in the weak light. Everything about this place screamed decay and abandonment.

Perfect for hiding but hell to fight his way out of when things went sideways.

He crossed the room, boots scraping against concrete littered with chunks of fallen plaster. The sound echoed off bare walls.

"You've been hiding a long time," he said. "But things like this never stay buried. You had to know someone like me would come eventually."

Lizzy didn't look at him. Her shoulders hunched forward. Hands folded in her lap like she was praying. Defensive body language, trying to make herself smaller.

Flint had interrogated enough people to know she was holding back. Her stillness was self-preservation, not ignorance.

He'd have to break through her defenses first, fast and blunt.

"Jason Fisher hired me. He thinks his siblings survived the fire."

Nothing. No flicker of recognition. No denial. The silence stretched between them like a wire under tension. But her breathing changed slightly. Became more shallow.

She knew things she didn't want to reveal.

Question was whether he could persuade her to give them up willingly.

"Jason's not chasing ghosts. He found a concrete trail. He hired me to do the rest."

Still nothing from her.

But Flint caught the subtle shift in her posture. She was fighting the urge to respond. Good. Meant she wanted to talk.

"He wants answers," Flint said. "He wants the truth. He's entitled to that, surely."

Her eyes lifted to his for the first time. Hollow. Haunted. The kind of look that came from carrying secrets too heavy for one person to bear.

Flint had seen that expression before. Survivors. People who'd made impossible choices and lived with the consequences.

"You don't know what it cost to keep them safe." Lizzy's words came out barely above a whisper. Raw. Like they'd been scraped from her throat with a blade leaving years of pain underneath.

"Then tell me what happened. I can leave you here and not tell Jason where you are and you'll never see me again," Flint said calmly. "But Jason and Bruce and their mother deserve to know. The kids do too."

She didn't speak immediately. Her shoulders rose as she pulled in a breath and held it. Flint waited. Sometimes silence worked better than pressure. Give her space to fill the void herself.

"We weren't supposed to be in the house that night," she said finally. "Frankie tried to stop it."

Flint waited for more. The words had cost her something. He could see it in her white-knuckled grip on the edge of the rust-stained metal desk.

But she'd opened the door. Now he had to decide how hard to push.

She didn't continue.

Before he could ask anything else, he heard boots on concrete outside. Heavy. Deliberate. Male, based on the weight and stride pattern. Not trying to be quiet.

Then three short knocks on the door followed by two long knocks.

Recognition signal. Prearranged.

Lizzy said quietly, "It's him."

Flint drew his weapon. The Glock settled into his palm.

He moved beside the door with his finger indexed along the trigger guard.

The angles were covered. Good field of fire. They weren't trapped. Not yet anyway.

The door squealed open slowly on rusted metal hinges, a noise so loud that it cut through all noises inside and out.

Flint was ready to fire.

Frankie Tantanella stepped inside.

Shirt torn at the shoulder, the fabric dark with blood that had soaked through and dried to a rusty brown. His movements were careful. Controlled. Like a man who knew he was hurt but wasn't ready to show weakness.

Flint saw one hand hovering near the grip of a knife sheathed at Tantanella's belt.

Operational but compromised. Dangerous but bleeding.

The kind of wounded animal that could still take them down.

Tantanella scanned the room methodically. Gaze landed on Lizzy first, then shifted to Flint. Taking inventory. Calculating distances and angles. Threat assessment.

Since he left Kentucky, Frankie Tantanella had acquired some training.

No one moved.

A man accustomed to being obeyed, Tantanella said, "Give her back."

But he was wounded and exhausted, too. Running too long with too much weight on his shoulders, probably.

Flint didn't answer. Silence made people uncomfortable. Made them fill the void with information they shouldn't share.

Tantanella tilted his head slightly. "Who are you and what do you want with my wife?"

Flint watched as he waited. Tired people made mistakes.

When Flint failed to respond, Frankie nodded once as if he'd made a decision. "Devon Cole."

Devon Cole?

The name seemed to fill the entire building.

Devon Cole. Tech billionaire, one of the most powerful men in the world, worth billions, and connected to everyone who mattered. Running a wide-ranging conspiracy for decades, ordering arsons and murders and more? Not likely.

But Flint's expression didn't change. "What about Devon Cole?"

"He's the reason everything happened," Tantanella said. "Back then, he was a congressman. Cole told me to burn the Fisher place. Destroy everything in it to persuade Fisher to quiet things down."

Flint studied Tantanella's face for deception markers. Steady eye contact. Consistent body language. Either he was telling the truth, or he was a five-star liar.

Given his apparent background, could be either.

"You set that fire at the Fisher house?" Flint asked.

Tantanella didn't blink. Didn't flinch. "It was supposed to be vacant."

"But Lizzy and the younger Fisher children were there when you arrived that night."

"Unfortunately." Frankie cast a meaningful glance toward Lizzy.

CHAPTER 34

March 19
Havana, Cuba

LIZZY RETURNED HER HUSBAND'S look with shared understanding built on years of common secrets and survival, concealing what had happened that night at great personal cost.

They were certain they'd done the right thing back then. Flint could tell.

"So I changed the plan," Tantanella smirked, probably calculated to deflect Flint's attention from Lizzy.

"What did you tell Cole?"

"Nothing. He told me to torch the house and get the hell out of town. I did all of that." Tantanella's expression didn't change. "No reason to tell him anything else and he never asked."

Flint said, "So Cole still believes Lizzy and the kids actually died?"

"Who knows what he believes? He never checked. That much I can say for sure." Tantanella's words carried cold contempt. "Man gives an order and assumes it gets carried out. Never bothers to confirm. That's his problem, not mine."

Corrupt politicians and soulless billionaires were cut from the same cloth. Give the order, delegate responsibility, maintain plausible deniability, move on while ignoring the destruction. Same story every time.

But in this case, Tantanella was wrong. Cole might not have cared about the Fisher kids when he hired Tantanella to torch the house. But he was a junior congressman back then with a lot less to lose than he had now.

If the full story got out, or if Cole felt threatened in any way, he would most definitely care now.

Which made him more dangerous than a rabid tiger.

Flint took a step forward. The floorboards creaked under his weight. "And you? What have you been doing all this time?"

Tantanella didn't answer. He stood ready for whatever came next. Blood continued to seep through his shirt, but he showed no sign of weakness or surrender.

Flint said, "She's coming with me."

"She's not a prisoner." Tantanella looked at Lizzy. Something soft crept into his expression. "You want to go?"

She remained frozen between the past and whatever future Flint and her husband were offering. Trauma did that to people. Paralyzed them when they needed to make choices.

Flint said, "She has answers. The Fishers deserve to hear them directly from her."

"She's my wife. She stays," Frankie said, making the decision.

Flat. Final. No room for negotiation or compromise.

He stepped forward.

Flint raised his weapon. "That's far enough. Let her go."

No luck.

Frankie's right hand moved fast along his flank and drew a knife.

Long, slim, sharp as hell.

The blade caught what little light came through the broken windows and threw it back like a warning. The kind of deadly weapon designed for only one purpose.

Tantanella stayed balanced on both feet, ready to move in any direction. He didn't posture or waste energy on threats or intimidation. He was an experienced knife fighter.

Defend against the blade. Get inside his reach. Control the weapon. Don't get cut.

Without warning, Tantanella lunged.

The blade came in fast, slashing for Flint's side in a killing stroke aimed at his liver. Quick and quiet. And almost lethal.

Just in time, Flint twisted a hair's breadth away from the blade.

The knife whispered past his ribs, close enough to slice the fabric of his shirt.

Lightning fast, Flint thrust his hand forward and caught Tantanella's wrist.

Flint redirected the momentum and Tantanella stumbled.

They slammed into the wall with enough force to shake loose more plaster.

Tantanella staggered but didn't fall. Tough. Experienced.

He adjusted his grip and struck again. This time aiming for Flint's groin to sever the femoral artery.

Flint spotted a broken chair leg on the floor near his feet. Heavy hardwood with good weight and reach.

In one quick sweep, he bent, grabbed the makeshift club, and swung low.

The club connected with Tantanella's knife hand and knocked the blade wide and away.

The steel sparked against stone as it deflected off course.

Disarmed, Tantanella adjusted again.

But he was slower and weaker than he should have been, already bleeding from whatever had happened before.

They grappled.

Shoulders locked.

Breath coming hard.

Each man trying to control weapons and positioning.

Tantanella drove his knee into Flint's ribs.

Pain shot through Flint's torso like lightning. He grunted but didn't let go.

Couldn't allow Tantanella a chance to pick up the knife again or the space to use it effectively.

Flint turned Tantanella's arm and shoved it up behind his back. He applied pressure to the joint until the tendons creaked under the strain, but Tantanella resisted with more force than Flint expected.

Flint forced Tantanella's arm down and drove his hand into the sharp edge of the metal desk, slicing deep into Tantanella's palm.

Flint kicked the knife farther away and the blade clinked along the limestone floor, spinning until it hit the far wall and landed in a pile of debris.

Tantanella stumbled back against the wall, breathing hard. Blood ran freely from the earlier injury to his side now. A dark stain spread across his torn shirt. He pressed one palm there, applying pressure, but the blood didn't slow.

Lizzy stood frozen in horror. Her face had gone pale. She couldn't bear to look at Tantanella's injuries.

His voice was rough and strained when he spoke. "You don't know what you're starting."

Flint picked up the knife. Tested its weight and balance. It was one of the finest knives he'd ever handled. He set it on the table behind him where Frankie couldn't easily retrieve it. "If you want to stop me, you're welcome to try again."

Tantanella gave him an outraged glare.

Flint looked at Lizzy. "Let's go."

She stood still, torn between loyalty and survival. Between the past and an uncertain future.

She had been protecting secrets for decades. Hard to walk away from that kind of commitment.

Flint stepped toward her to make it clear there'd be no argument or hesitation.

She looked back at her husband once more. A final glance that carried years of shared survival. Then she allowed Flint to lead her toward the exit while he eyed Tantanella until they were out of the building.

Tantanella stayed on the floor against the wall. Hand clamped to his side. Blood seeping between his fingers. Watching the exit.

Still breathing.

Still dangerous.

And probably already planning his next move.

Flint went outside and closed the door behind them with a solid thud that echoed through the building. Drake was waiting.

"Is he done?" Drake asked as they began to hurry through the dark streets.

"We'll probably see him again," Flint replied.

Lizzy glanced back one last time.

Probably hoping that her husband would rally and come for her again like he'd done in Ravenswood all those years ago.

"This way," Drake said, leading them down into a dark alley heading toward the harbor.

Flint watched their backs. Tantanella said Devon Cole was his boss. Cole's current power, resources, and reach had been more than enough to keep Lizzy afraid and controlled. Crossing him now was terrifying her.

Lizzy was right to be afraid. A well connected billionaire like Cole and a handful of others had access to power in ways mere mortals did not. He wouldn't let Lizzy or anyone else thwart him, no matter what he had to do to stop her.

Nothing Flint could do about Lizzy's fear.

Even less he could do about Devon Cole's reactions.

Which meant he'd need to find the Fisher kids before Cole got wind of the truth.

CHAPTER 35

March 19
Havana, Cuba

THE STREETS OF HAVANA burned all around them. Smoke coiled up from rooftops and trash fires, staining the night air with the stench of melting plastic and scorched concrete. The acrid smell cut through the humidity and clung to everything.

He called to Lizzy over the noise. "Keep moving."

He stayed close to the rear of their tight formation. Glass crunched under his boots with every step. His gaze swept the skyline, jagged now with collapsed rooftops and buildings missing whole chunks of structure. Sirens wailed two blocks over, pitch rising and falling like wounded animals. Somewhere close by, a dog barked once and fell silent.

"How much farther?" Lizzy's fear squeezed her voice box and softened her tone to barely audible.

"Not far," Drake answered.

The blackout held. No streetlights pierced the darkness. No traffic signals blinked warnings. The flicker of flames dancing in windows and the sharp edge of panic bleeding through every side street threatening to grow into violence like tossing a burning match onto spilled gasoline.

Drake moved fast up ahead. He cut left across a narrow alley that skirted a boarded-up cantina. The metal security grate rattled in the wind.

"This way," he said, gesturing for them to follow.

Lizzy hurried behind him, arms pumping, breath coming short and ragged. She hadn't complained once since they had left the abandoned factory.

Flint was impressed. She was tough. Scared, yes. But steady.

"You okay back there?" Drake called.

"Fine," Lizzy replied. "Just keep going."

Flint scanned for threats behind them. This time, he noticed unusual movement in the shadows. Two men, maybe three, keeping pace but not closing. They moved too carefully for civilians running from a disaster.

Which meant they were being followed.

Drake came to a sudden halt at the mouth of a cross street.

"Crap," he muttered under his breath.

When Flint caught up he saw the checkpoint. Cuban military trucks were angled across the road, forming a wall of steel. No soldiers were visible on the ground, but the mounted guns were manned. A spotlight scanned the area, sweeping from building to building like a searchlight from an old prison movie.

They couldn't advance any closer to the harbor.

"Can we go around?" Lizzy whispered.

"No. Back," Flint said quietly, gesturing. "Same way we came."

Drake turned without another word and Lizzy followed. The smell of rotting garbage and motor oil rose from the gutters as they walked along the alley.

They emerged onto a side street slick with rain and leaked fuel.

An argument was raging half a block down. Two men shouted in Spanish on a stoop beside a tiny corner market. Between them, an old, beat-up sedan idled at the curb. The engine coughed and wheezed, but it continued to run.

The driver's side door hung wide open.

"What do you think?" Drake asked.

"Yeah," Flint replied. "Take it."

Drake didn't hesitate. He slid into the front seat and threw it into gear. The transmission whined.

"Get in," Flint told Lizzy.

Flint opened the rear door and shoved Lizzy inside, then climbed in behind her and yanked the door shut.

"This is stealing," Lizzy said. "Stealing isn't tolerated here. You'll go to prison."

"We're just borrowing the car. We'll leave it at the harbor, and he can pick it up," Flint replied. "We won't be back to face charges."

Shouts erupted behind them. A bottle shattered against the car's trunk. Glass exploded in a spray of amber fragments. Drake gunned the engine and pulled away. The tires slipped on broken pavement.

"Hang on," Drake called out as he pressed the accelerator and fled.

Flint glanced through the rear window. One of the men from the stoop was pointing at the car and yelling. A helmeted rider on a motorcycle pulled out, phone raised to catch the license plate and a glimpse of passengers.

"Drake," Flint said. "We've got a tail."

"I see him."

"What do we do?" Lizzy asked.

"We outrun them," Drake said.

The vehicle sped through the dark streets as fast as possible. The sedan was underpowered, rattling at every turn, but it ran. The smell of hot metal and burning oil seeped through the vents. For now, that was enough.

A second motorcycle appeared in the rearview mirror. Sleeker, faster than the first. Both riders gained on them, weaving through debris scattered across the asphalt.

"They're getting closer," Lizzy said.

"Hold steady," Flint said to Drake.

He rolled down the window. Hot air rushed in, thick with smoke and the smell of fear-sweat from the crowds lining the sidewalks. He leaned out, braced his elbow on the window frame, and sighted down the short barrel of his sidearm.

The lead rider was close now. Ten yards. Five. Flint could see the man's face beneath the helmet visor.

Flint fired once. The shot echoed off the buildings and debris.

The bike wobbled, veered hard left, and crashed into a pile of rubble. Chunks of concrete and a cloud of dust flew in all directions. The rider tumbled over the handlebars and landed hard. He didn't move.

The second bike peeled off and vanished into the smoke like a ghost.

"Nice," Drake muttered. "But they'll be back."

They reached the edge of the harbor minutes later. The stench here was different. Salt and diesel fuel mixed with the smell of rotting fish and tar.

"Kill the lights," Flint said.

"Copy that," Drake said as he cut the lights and coasted through a shadowed service lane behind a crumbling freight terminal.

The building's corrugated metal siding was streaked with rust and peppered with bullet holes.

"There," Drake said, pointing ahead.

A rusted crane loomed to the left. Beyond it, the docks came into view. Angled piers stretched into the dark water like broken fingers.

Derelict shipping containers were stacked in haphazard towers. Dark water stretched beyond the seawall, reflecting the orange glow of fires burning in the city.

"That's our ride?" Lizzy asked.

"Yep." Drake killed the engine. They slid out of the sedan and moved quickly across surfaces slick with fuel and condensation.

"Stay quiet from here," Flint whispered.

They hugged the metal siding of the nearest warehouse, staying in the shadows.

The boat was waiting.

It was ugly, loud, and perfect. A forty-something-foot diesel patrol craft, stripped of insignia, patched with rust, and riding low in the water. It had no name on the hull. No flags. A single bearded man stood on deck, arms crossed, watching them approach.

The boat's diesel engine was running and rumbled like a predator's growl. Exhaust fumes mixed with the salt air making it difficult to breathe.

"Is that him?" Lizzy whispered.

Drake gave a signal. The man nodded once.

"That's him," Drake confirmed quietly.

"Let's go," Flint said.

They moved fast across the open ground toward the dock. Their footsteps echoed on the concrete. Somewhere in the distance, another siren began to wail.

Then Lizzy stopped.

She grabbed Flint's sleeve. Her voice was low and urgent. "Wait."

He turned to her.

She pointed across the water to a service platform about thirty yards down the quay. A single yellow bulb flickered overhead, casting sickly light onto the deck. The bulb buzzed like an angry insect.

A man stood beneath it.

Still. Watching.

"That's Frankie," she said.

Flint stepped in front of her and raised his weapon. Tantanella didn't move. He stood like a statue, silhouetted against the weak light.

Then the single yellow bulb flickered out and he was gone.

Vanished into the dark.

"On the boat," Flint said, giving Lizzy a push. "Now."

They rushed to board as the diesel engine rumbled louder and began to move away from the dock. No spotlight. No questions.

The boat turned toward the open sea at full throttle. Spray kicked up from the bow, misting them with salt water.

And Havana burned in the pitch dark behind them.

"How long will it take to reach Key West?" Lizzy asked, looking back toward Havana and hunching down into her jacket in the cool night air.

"Too long," Flint replied, scanning the darkness for pursuers.

He saw no one following, but it was only a matter of time. After sunrise, they'd be too visible for comfort.

CHAPTER 36

March 19
North of Havana

THE BOAT HAD BEEN running for just under two hours when the first drops fell.

Flint stood near the stern. He watched the dark horizon, one hand resting lightly on the salt-crusted railing for balance. The deck vibrated beneath his boots from the steady thrum of the diesel engine pushing them northward into open water. Behind them, Cuba was long gone. Nothing remained visible but dark sea and black sky.

He checked his watch. Just past 4 a.m.

The rain started light. A few cold drops tapped against the canvas above his head. Then more. Within minutes, it was falling steadily. The wind picked up, not fierce yet, but restless. The kind that made experienced sailors secure loose gear and check safety lines.

He crossed to the wheelhouse where Drake stood beside the weathered captain studying the radar screen. The captain's beard was streaked with gray and white, matted with salt spray. Deep lines carved his face from decades of squinting into ocean glare.

"We've got a front building from the southeast," Drake said. He kept his eyes on the screen. "Pressure's dropping fast."

"How fast?"

Drake's expression said they were in serious trouble.

Flint nodded and stepped back into the weather.

Lizzy sat curled on the bench under the canopy. Her knees were drawn to her chest, soaked through from spray and rain. She didn't flinch when he approached.

"We'll be out of this soon," he said.

"Sure," she replied flatly. Lizzy Pace had come full circle. She was no longer a sixteen-year-old girl thrust into a tough situation she couldn't control.

Flint crouched beside her. Her eyes were red rimmed from exhaustion and strain, but still alert.

"You know, back at the Fisher house, you could've gone back," he said. "You got the kids out. The investigation ended. Nobody knew what happened to you and the kids. So why not lay low for a couple of years and then bring the kids back?"

She didn't answer right away. She stared out at the rain sliding off the canopy in wide silver streams.

"If I'd come back, they'd have taken the kids from me," she said finally. "I had no legal rights. No proof of anything. I crossed state lines with three children and a fake name. Best case, that's several felonies, even if I was trying to protect them."

"You didn't think you could fight that?"

"Against who?" she said. "The Fishers? The state? Cole? I didn't know who helped start the fire or who was covering it up. And if Cole ever found out we were alive, he'd have finished the job."

Her voice was flat, unemotional. She recited the facts like items from a grocery list.

Flint studied her face. That wasn't the full story. Maybe not even half. Her answers came too smoothly, like lines from a script she'd rehearsed and replayed for years.

Maybe true. Maybe not. Either way, she seemed to believe what she said.

That made her desperate. Or dangerous. Possibly both.

Before he could press further, Drake's voice cut through the rain.

"Flint!"

He stood and moved toward the bow. Drake pointed portside toward lights on the horizon. Low. Fast. Closing the gap.

"Friendlies?" Drake asked.

"Doubtful." Flint grabbed the binoculars and focused on the approaching vessel.

No running lights. No flag. Just a long, narrow hull and an engine that growled like it wasn't built for fishing. The boat rode low in the water, built for speed rather than cargo.

"They've been tailing us since we left the Cuban coast," Drake said. "Pacing just outside radar range. I clocked them twice, both times same bearing."

Flint turned and ducked into the wheelhouse. He pulled the sat phone from its waterproof pouch and dialed Gaspar's number.

"You're up early," Gaspar answered.

"Fishing trip's not going so well. Weather turned bad and we've got company."

"How bad?"

"Bad enough that we need a ride home. Soon."

Gaspar was quiet for a moment. "Where are you fishing?"

Flint checked the GPS. "About sixty miles south of Key West."

"Got it. Let me make a call. Stay on this line."

The phone went quiet for two minutes. Then Gaspar was back. "Your ride's coming. Look west. Few minutes out."

"Thanks."

"Don't mention it. Literally."

He stowed the phone and stepped back onto the deck. The captain was lashing a coil of line to the cleat near the rail. Flint crossed to him.

"You should come with us," Flint said, raising his voice over the wind. "Storm's getting worse. That other boat might not be friendly."

The captain shook his head. "This old girl's been through worse. I'm not leaving her."

"You sure?"

"I'm sure. She's mine. Besides, they'll be after you, not me. I stay off their radar."

Flint hesitated. "You get into trouble, you've got Gaspar's frequency."

"I know where to hide if I need to."

They locked eyes for a moment. The captain gave a tight nod, then turned back to securing the deck.

The wind had shifted again. It sliced sideways now with real force, carrying salt spray that stung his face. The boat climbed one wave and slapped down the other side with bone-jarring impact. Rain hammered the cabin roof like machine gun fire. Lizzy gripped the rail. Her knuckles were white.

"Hold on," Flint said. "We're not out of it yet."

Lightning split the sky. For an instant, everything was bright as noon. Drake on the bow, the boat lurching, the dark water boiling in every direction. Then darkness slammed down like putting a lid on a flame.

Thunder cracked overhead. Close and deep. The kind that punched the ground and left bystanders dead.

The helicopter materialized out of the storm almost like magic. Low, black, riding the wind currents. As it came closer, rotor wash hit the boat like a physical blow, driving salt spray across the deck in stinging sheets.

The aircraft hovered twenty feet above the deck. Pontoons skimmed the wave crests. The open bay door swung wide, revealing the red-lit interior and a co-pilot in tactical gear.

Ropes dropped. They whipped in the wind like angry snakes.

Drake moved first. He grabbed Lizzy around the waist and half-carried her toward the stern. She stumbled once and nearly went down on the slick deck. Flint caught her by the elbow and steadied her.

"Look at me," he raised his voice to be heard over the rotor noise. "We're getting on that bird."

Her eyes were wide with terror.

The pilot fought to hold position as the waves bucked below. The helicopter rose and fell with each swell, pontoons lifting clear of the water, then slamming back down.

Drake boosted Lizzy onto the skid. She scrambled up, her soaked sneakers slipping against the slick metal. Wind howled around her, whipping the rain sideways like needles.

She dropped to her knees, clutching the cold steel bar with both hands, locking her fingers as if they were glued to the steel. Terror etched deep lines across her pale face. Her hair, drenched and heavy, clung to her scalp like a dark helmet, plastered flat by the storm.

But she held on. Every muscle in her body trembled as she crouched on the narrow ledge, the black void of the sea yawning just inches below.

Flint stepped up behind her. He hooked her arm and hauled. She came up with a gasping cry, soaking wet and shaking.

Drake's boot slipped on the wet skid. He pitched sideways toward the churning water.

Flint lunged forward, caught Drake by the collar, and pulled him bodily into the helicopter.

Before he jumped into the helo, Flint glanced back at the deck. The captain stood near the wheelhouse, a hand braced against the swaying frame.

Flint shouted over the storm and the rotor noise, "You sure you won't come?"

The captain's reply was steady, shouted back through the wind: "She's my boat. I ride her out."

Flint gave him a final nod, the kind men exchanged when there was nothing more to say.

The boat dropped beneath them, disappearing into a wave trough.

Flint didn't wait for an invitation. He turned and leapt.

For half a second, there was nothing but air and motion and the deafening roar of rotors. Wind tried to tear him sideways. Then the steel slammed into his boots, and he scrambled inside the cabin.

The pilot peeled away hard, angling the aircraft westward, rotors screaming against the storm.

Below them, the boat vanished into the gray.

Flint lay flat on the cabin floor. Water dripped from his clothes onto the non-slip decking. He struggled to breathe.

Lizzy was pressed into the corner, curled tight, shaking. Her eyes were squeezed shut.

Drake leaned back against the bulkhead. Blood leaked from his knuckles where he'd scraped them on the helicopter's frame.

No one spoke.

The co-pilot handed out towels and bottled water. He checked each of them for injuries and found nothing requiring immediate medical attention.

Above them, the helicopter climbed into the dark, carrying them away from Cuba and toward whatever came next.

CHAPTER 37

March 20
Miami, Florida

THE HELICOPTER BLADES CHOPPED through rain and wind while rain hammered the windscreen in a downpour that made the world outside a gray blur. Inside the cabin, salt spray mixed with diesel fumes created a sharp, acrid odor.

"How much longer?" Lizzy's voice was barely audible over the engine noise.

The aircraft bucked and shuddered. Each gust of wind sent them sideways before the pilot corrected course. The engine strained against the storm, the whine rising and falling with each thermal they hit.

"Twenty minutes, maybe less," the co-pilot shouted back, checking his instruments.

Through the porthole, Flint watched the endless dark ocean below. Cuba was already long gone. No lights. No signs of pursuit. Just black water stretching in every direction.

Lizzy sat curled against the bulkhead. Wet hair clung to her face. She stared at nothing, tracking the cabin floor like she was reading invisible text written there.

"You okay?" Drake asked her, concerned.

She nodded without looking up. "Frankie got away. That's what matters."

Drake leaned back with his head against the cabin wall. Blood still seeped from his knuckles.

"That needs stitches," Flint said, nodding toward Drake's hand.

"I've had worse."

The co-pilot checked his watch and shouted something to the pilot. Flint couldn't make out the words, but he caught the gesture toward the fuel gauge. They were running close to the margin.

"Fuel?" Flint asked.

"We're good," the co-pilot replied. "But Miami better have a clear approach."

Soon Miami's skyline appeared through the storm like a mirage made of glass and steel. Rain still lashed the city, but the wind had calmed enough for commercial aircraft to resume operations. Jets taxied slowly across the tarmac, navigation lights blinking red and white in the pre-dawn darkness.

"There she is," the pilot called back. "Coming down hot."

"Copy that," Drake said. "Hang on, Lizzy. Rough landing ahead."

Lizzy seemed to barely register the words, but she moved into a seat and buckled herself in.

The helicopter landed at a private helipad near Miami International Airport. Wind and spray whipped across the concrete in unpredictable gusts that bent palm trees and scattered debris.

"Move fast," the pilot shouted over the rotor wash. "I've got to get back."

He kept the rotors spinning while they unloaded.

Flint climbed down first. His boots splashed in a shallow puddle that had formed beside the landing pad. The stench of fuel and vegetation permeated the air making it difficult to breathe.

"What a night," Drake muttered as he climbed out.

His wet clothes hung heavy, and his face was drawn with fatigue.

Lizzy emerged last. She wrapped her arms around herself and stood in the downpour, looking lost. Rain plastered her shirt against her thin body. She looked like someone who hadn't slept in weeks.

"This way," Flint said, guiding her toward the waiting vehicle.

A black SUV waited near the perimeter fence. No government plates. No insignia. Nothing that would draw attention or invite questions. The driver took one look at them and unlocked the doors without a word.

"Airport Jameson hotel," Flint told him, giving a silent nod to Gaspar who, as usual, thought of everything.

"Yes, sir," the driver replied. "Picked up your go-bags from your plane. They're in the back."

Gaspar again. Always reliable and a step ahead.

Fifteen minutes later, they checked into the Airport Jameson Hotel. The lobby smelled of damp and cold recycled air. Overhead lights cast everything in sharp glare and dark shadows.

"Checking in for Smith, Jones, and Gale." Names Flint had used before but would burn after tonight.

"How many rooms?" the clerk asked.

"Three. Side by side on the third floor if you have them."

"Certainly, sir," the clerk replied. "I have two rooms with a connecting door and the third on the other side, with a separate entrance. How's that?"

"Perfect." Drake paid in cash and added a bonus for the desk clerk.

The clerk slid the key cards across the counter without requesting ID or payment.

Drake accepted the keys and scanned for the elevator. "Any room service?"

"Twenty-four hours, sir."

"Good. We'll need coffee. Lots of it."

Upstairs, the hallway stretched under lights that hummed like angry insects. The air-conditioning ran too cold. The carpet smelled like chemicals that no amount of cleaning could eliminate.

Drake opened Lizzy's door first. He stepped inside and checked the bathroom, the closet, behind the curtains.

"Clear," he called out.

Then he moved to his own room and repeated the process while Flint did the same with his.

The rooms were identical. Two beds, a small table, a chair by the window. Mass-produced furniture designed to be forgettable. The kind of place where people stayed when they needed a bed for the night between flights.

Flint handed a key card to Lizzy. "You're next door to me."

She nodded slowly. Her fingers closed around the plastic card, but she didn't look at it. Didn't ask how long they'd be staying.

"All clear," Drake said once Lizzy was safely in her room. "No surveillance. No tails. Nothing suspicious downstairs."

"For now," Flint replied. "Cole's people will find us eventually. It's just a matter of when."

"What about Frankie?"

"What about him?"

"He saw us take her. You think he'll come after us?"

"Count on it." Flint nodded grimly. "But first we get what we need from her. Everything she knows about Cole's current operations. Then we figure out how to keep everyone alive."

"You think she'll cooperate?"

"She'll have to. Her survival depends on it. So does ours."

Drake studied Flint's face, noting the cold calculation there. "Understood. I'll set up perimeter monitoring from my room. Motion sensors on the stairwells, cameras on the parking lot feeds."

"Good. And Drake?"

"Yeah?"

Flint said, "If Frankie shows up, we try to take him alive. He might have information we need."

"Assuming Frankie makes that possible." Drake nodded and disappeared into his room.

The door closed with a soft click that echoed in the empty hallway. A moment later, Flint's door also closed behind him.

Flint peeled off his wet clothes and dropped them on the bathroom floor. They hit the tile with a wet slap that reminded him of helicopter rotors cutting through rain. His shirt reeked. He tossed it into the trash along with his other clothes.

He stepped into the shower and cranked the water as hot as it would go. Steam rose immediately, fogging the mirror and coating the walls with condensation. The water seemed to burn his skin as it rinsed away the salt, blood, and diesel that had clung to him since Havana.

He allowed the scalding spray to work into muscles that had been clenched too tight for too long. Luckily, he did some of his best thinking in the shower.

Lizzy Pace was the key to bringing down Devon Cole, but she was also a risk. Frankie would come for her. Cole's people would hunt her. And she'd already proven she could vanish for decades.

This might be his only shot at getting the truth out of her.

A sharp knock on his bathroom door cut through the sound of running water.

"Flint!" Drake's voice was urgent but controlled. "We've got company."

Flint shut off the water immediately. "How many?"

"Four vehicles in the parking lot. Just arrived."

Flint grabbed a towel and moved quickly. "Who is it?"

"Unknown. But they're not tourists."

CHAPTER 38

March 20
Miami, Florida

FLINT TOWELED OFF AND dressed rapidly in dry clothes from the go bag. Denim shirt, black jeans. He didn't have a spare pair of boots in the bag, so he slipped both feet into his wet boots.

As he collected his few belongings, he raced through the options. The hotel had limited exits. If they were being watched from multiple angles, escape would be difficult.

"Status on Lizzy?" Flint asked.

"Still in her room. But we need to move. Now."

Flint checked his weapon and grabbed the satellite phone. "Back exit?"

Drake replied, "Service elevator to the loading dock. I've got eyes on it through the security feeds."

"Route?"

"Clear for now. But that won't last."

Flint opened the connecting bedroom door. Lizzy sat on her bed, still wearing the oversized clothes from the hotel gift shop. She looked up when he entered.

"We're leaving," he said. "Right now."

"What's wrong?"

"Company. Get your shoes."

She didn't ask questions. Within thirty seconds, they were moving down the hallway toward the service elevator. Drake led, checking corners and sight lines. Flint stayed close to Lizzy, ready to shield her if necessary.

The service elevator was ancient and slow. As it descended, Drake monitored his phone for updates from the security feeds.

"Still clear at the loading dock," he reported. "But they're moving through the lobby now."

"How long do we have?"

"Maybe five minutes before they reach our floor."

The elevator finally opened onto a dimly lit loading area. Industrial concrete floors, overhead fluorescent lighting, the smell of garbage and cleaning supplies. A black SUV waited near the loading dock with its engine running.

"Gaspar's guy left it here for us," Drake said in response to Flint's inquiring glance.

They moved quickly across the loading area to the SUV. Flint helped Lizzy into the back while Drake took the driver's seat. He slipped behind the steering wheel, slid the transmission into drive and pulled away immediately after Flint settled into the passenger seat.

"Where to?" Drake asked.

"The Kendrick Hotel. Downtown," Flint replied. "You know it?"

"Yeah. Been there before."

As they drove through the pre-dawn Miami streets, Flint turned to face Lizzy. The urgency of their escape had stripped away any pretense of safety.

"Who is after us?" Lizzy asked from the back seat. She sounded terrified, but Flint guessed that could change depending on the answer to her question.

"Frankie's people, most likely. He saw us take you from Cuba," Drake said, checking the mirrors.

"We don't have time for careful conversation anymore, Lizzy," Flint said quietly. "Those people back there were here because of you. So we're going to talk, and you're going to tell me everything. Starting now."

Twenty minutes later, they were settled into two adjoining rooms at the Kendrick. Drake had swept both rooms and confirmed they were clear of listening devices.

Flint dropped into the chair beside the window and clicked on the television. The screen flickered to life on a cable news station.

He ran through a few channels. Local affiliates. International feeds. All carried the same story.

"Breaking news from Cuba last night," one anchor said with artificial gravity. "Massive power outages across Havana..."

Images flickered across the screen showing Havana in chaos. The blackout had affected the entire island.

Fires burned near the harbor. Orange flames licked at the colonial buildings like a lizard. Roads were closed by debris and abandoned cars.

Military vehicles moved along slowly in the streets. Armed men patrolled near the docks in the harbor.

Rumors flowed like water, which the news anchor read from the prompter while grainy cell phone footage of boats moving in the darkness displayed on the screen.

No mention of Lizzy Pace or Frankie Tantanella. No sign of who had lived or died in the chaos left behind.

Flint watched until the images blurred together, and the same footage looped endlessly with different commentary. Same fires burning in the same streets. Same boats disappearing into the same dark water.

"Nothing new," he said to the room, and muted the sound because Drake had flopped out on the second bed and was already snoring.

Flint left the Havana story running in silence. Blue light from the screen painted shadows that moved and shifted like ghosts on the walls.

Flint's thoughts wandered to the woman who had died on that sidewalk in Ravenswood all those years ago. The woman whose death had given Lizzy Pace the chance to disappear.

No name in the papers. No headlines. No obituary that anyone would remember. Just a broken body on wet pavement, another casualty of desperation and bad luck.

Maybe she'd had family somewhere. Someone must have wondered where she went. Maybe they still did, all these years later. They might be checking missing person websites and hoping for news that would never come.

The thought hit Flint harder than he expected.

He had spent years, off and on, wondering about his own biological mother. Not knowing where she'd gone or why she'd left him. Just emptiness and unanswered questions that grew faint with time.

Now he knew that Marilyn Baker was his mother, and she'd been murdered. Which was why she never came back to the orphanage for him.

This unknown woman was erased from the world so completely that even her death had been stolen. Absorbed into Lizzy Pace's escape plan like the woman had never existed at all.

A soft knock at the connecting door between the rooms interrupted his thoughts. His watch showed 5:17 a.m.

He rose slowly and opened the door. Lizzy stood there in the hotel robe, her damp hair pulled back.

"Can't sleep?"

"I keep thinking about what happens next." Her voice was steady, but her hands trembled slightly. "About what you want from me."

"Smart." Flint stepped aside, but his posture remained guarded. "Come in."

She crossed the room and sat on the edge of the bed. Her arms were folded tightly across her chest like she was trying to hold herself together through sheer force of will. The overhead light made her skin look pale and translucent.

Flint settled into the chair and studied her expression with an experienced investigator's focused attention.

"Won't we wake up Drake?" Lizzy asked, glancing toward the snoring man.

"Yeah. Let's go into your room and talk about Devon Cole," Flint said following her through the connecting door. "I need to know about his current operations. Personnel, finances, security protocols, anything that might help us."

Lizzy sat on one of the beds and allowed Flint to take the chair after he'd closed the door. "I don't know those things. Frankie kept me away from—"

"Stop," Flint sliced through her protest. "You lived with Frankie for more than twenty years. You're his wife, which means that you can't be forced to testify against him. So don't tell me you don't know how he makes the money you live on."

She flinched but held his gaze. "I'd be dead now if Cole knew I survived the fire at the Fisher house."

"I understand you were trying to protect yourself," Flint said. "But Cole's going to know you're alive now. The question is whether we can use what you know to stop him before he comes after you."

She flinched and her composure cracked slightly but didn't break.

"You want me to betray Frankie. My husband. The man who saved my life and gave me the freedom to live," Lizzy said flatly.

"I need to understand Devon Cole. You seem to think he would have been okay burning a teenager and three young children alive in their beds." Flint's tone was firm but not cruel. "The man who's spent the past twenty years building wealth and power while those children grew up orphans thinking they had no family and no one who cared for them at all."

She stared at the muted television screen where the burning Havana videos played on an endless loop. As if she'd been muted, too, she said nothing.

"Tell me about the accident in Ravenswood," Flint asked, changing the subject slightly simply to get her talking. "And the woman who died in the bus accident."

CHAPTER 39

March 20
Miami, Florida

LIZZY LOWERED HER GAZE and closed her eyes. She was quiet for a long moment. When she finally spoke, her voice was barely audible.

"We couldn't make a proper home for those kids. We were just kids ourselves. I lied about being sick because we thought it would make everyone more sympathetic toward the kids and then they'd take care of the little ones after we disappeared," Lizzy said quietly.

"And what happened with the woman?" Flint asked.

"We called her Suzie. She was drunk all the time when we saw her around the shelters. High or hammered or maybe both." Lizzy's fingers worked at the hem of her shirt, twisting the fabric into knots. "We knew her a bit. Frankie more than me. She was just always there, you know? Invisible. Part of the scenery."

"What was her real name?"

"I... I don't know. We never asked."

"Of course you didn't." Flint's tone carried no sympathy. "Tell me what happened."

She swallowed hard. The sound was loud in the quiet room.

"A couple of weeks earlier, I had offered her one of my old sweaters. I didn't realize I'd left Lisa Peterson's library card in the pocket. Frankie and I were standing on the sidewalk when Suzie came walking past us and stumbled into Frankie when the bus was coming," Lizzy said. "Frankie tried to pull her out of the way. Not shove her into the bus. But she lost her balance. Fell face first off the curb and into the moving bus."

"And then what?"

"She hit the bus, fell to the pavement. The bus wheels ran over her head and shoulders." She shuddered as if she were reliving the moment of impact. "And then it was over. Just like that. One second she was standing there swaying to close to the street, and the next she was gone."

In the brief silence, Flint noticed the sound of jet engines spooling up outside the hotel windows.

"We didn't even talk about it at first. Obviously, we couldn't stay there and give statements or anything like that. We just ran." Lizzy paused when her voice cracked on the last word to regain self-control.

"And later?" Flint asked.

"Frankie said we'd never get another chance like that. A dead woman badly mangled, Lisa Peterson's ID, no one who'd miss her. It was a perfect answer."

"Perfect for you and Frankie, maybe," Flint said. "But what about the kids? And that woman had a life too. People who might have cared about her. Now she's forgotten while you lived and loved and thrived for a very long time."

"We were desperate—"

"She was a convenient patsy. Don't try to soothe yourself with placating lies, at least." Flint stood and walked to the window. "Tom Wilson, the bus driver, never got over what he saw that day. Did you know that?"

She looked up sharply. "What do you mean?"

"I mean he quit his job because he thought he'd killed that woman. Left town. Changed his name. Spent the rest of his life haunted by what happened to her." Flint turned back to face Lizzy and gave her a cold stare. "Until someone killed him, too."

Her face went white. "Tom Wilson is dead?"

"Skydiving accident, they say. But I don't believe it. Do you?"

Lizzy's hands flew to cover her mouth as if to hold her screams inside. She wiped her face with the back of her hand, but once the tears began, they kept coming.

"We saw him in Cuba. Walking on the street. Just one of those fluke things, you know?" Lizzy explained. "He acted like he recognized me. So I pretended to be someone else. He seemed a bit skeptical, but I thought he was convinced."

"How many more people have to die to keep your secrets, Lizzy?" Flint's question hung in the air like heavy black smoke from a petroleum fire.

"You don't know what it was like." Her chin quivered and the tears kept coming as if she hadn't cried in all those years, either. "We were kids. Scared. Running for our lives."

"You've had twenty years to find another way," Flint said quietly. "To contact the authorities or reach out to the families. Instead, other people have died to protect your secrets."

"That's not fair—"

"You want to talk about fair?" Flint's voice turned dangerous. "What about the Fisher kids and that nameless woman rotting in a pauper's grave? What about Tom Wilson's wife? Was any of that fair?"

She doubled over slightly, as if his accusations hit her in the belly with the full force of his anger.

"It's long past time to get this settled," Flint continued, deadly calm. "You'll tell me everything you know about Devon Cole's operations. How he moves money, who he uses for enforcement, where he keeps his records. Everything."

Her face revealed stark terror and her voice trembled, "I can't. If he finds out—"

"He already knows you're alive. Frankie works for him, remember? You think he doesn't know who Frankie Tantanella's wife really is?" Flint's questions peppered her from all sides. "You think he won't learn that Frankie's wife was extracted from Cuba by American operatives last night?"

Flint's logic was brutal and undeniable. Lizzy stared at him with horror, wagging her head as if she might erase his words from her mind.

"I'm not here to judge what you did as a sixteen-year-old," Flint reminded her. "But I won't allow Cole to keep going. And right now, you're the best source of information I have about how he operates."

Lizzy continued to stare at him as if he'd asked her to jump into the Grand Canyon and splat onto the Colorado River.

"Help me, Lizzy," Flint said. "If you don't, Cole's people will find you anyway. At least if you work with me, you might survive this."

She studied his face which was filled with determination but not cruelty.

Flint waited to give her time to absorb his offer. He wouldn't abandon her to killers, but he did expect her to do the right thing.

"I'll tell you what I know." Her shoulders slumped as her spine rounded, all arguments finally defeated. "Her real name was Suzie, I think. The woman who fell into the bus."

"What about her last name?"

She shrugged and shook her head to indicate she didn't know. "She lived, off and on, at the Ravenswood shelter. That's where I met her initially."

Over the next hour, Lizzy told him what little she knew about Suzie, Devon Cole, and the fate of the Fisher kids.

By dawn, the storm had calmed but the sky remained a bruised gray. Rain clung to the windows in slow-moving sheets that caught the weak morning light. Outside, traffic across the wet streets was picking up.

Life had resumed its normal rhythm. But inside the hotel room, everything had changed.

Flint poured black coffee from the in-room pot. The smell was bitter and artificial, nothing like the Cuban coffee they'd left behind in Havana.

"Want some?" he asked.

Lizzy sat wrapped in the hotel blanket, her face pale but resolved. The frightened woman who'd entered his room was gone. In her place sat someone harder, more determined.

"Please," she said quietly.

He handed her the second cup. She took it with both hands to absorb the warmth through her palms.

"Frankie told me about the fire," she said finally. "The real story. Not until years later, after we were married."

"In Cuba."

She nodded. "Simple ceremony. No paperwork that would hold up anywhere outside of Cuba. Just a promise between us. That's when he told me the truth."

"That he was the arsonist."

"Yes. Cole told him to scare Harry Fisher and burn some old records. Just a warning. Me and the kids weren't supposed to be there. The house was supposed to be empty. Even the maid had the night off."

"But you stayed because one of the twins was sick."

"One of the twins had a fever. I didn't want to drag him out in the weather." Her voice grew quieter. "Our whole plan that night changed because he was sick, but no one told Frankie."

"So Frankie doused the place, lit the fire, and then realized you were all inside," Flint guessed.

Lizzy nodded and sipped the coffee. "He came inside to plant more accelerant in another wing of the house and heard me upstairs with the children. That's when he found us."

"And got you out."

"It wasn't easy. Fire was already moving through the first floor. We were all so scared. I wrapped the baby in wet towels. The kids didn't even have shoes on, and it took me a minute to find them." She paused as if she were back there, experiencing the horror again as if it were fresh. "Frankie kicked through a back door, and we made it outside, coughing and gulping fresh air. We were in the woods for hours on our own until Frankie found us again."

The image hit Flint hard despite his resolve to stay detached. A sixteen-year-old girl and three small children, fleeing through dark woods while a house burned behind them. Of course, she was terrified. Anyone would have been.

But he wasn't ready to give her a pass, either. "You could've gone to the police."

"Cole had half the county in his pocket. And Frankie was already in too deep. He thought if we surfaced, Cole would finish the job himself. We'd all die."

"What was Harry Fisher into that was worth killing his whole family?"

Lizzy was quiet for a long moment while she gathered her courage. "Opioids. Early on, we all believed they were miracle pain killers. Harry wanted to invest in the businesses. Doctors, pharmacies. He thought he was doing a good thing for the community and everyone who lived there. Including his own family."

"And later?"

"Later, we all learned how dangerous and addictive opioids were. So many people died..." Lizzy shuddered again. "And Harry wanted no part of it. He wanted out. Which Cole could not allow."

"So Cole decided to make an example of Harry."

Lizzy nodded. "A warning to others who might be getting cold feet, too. At that point, we all knew the lawsuits and criminal charges were coming."

Flint understood the scope of the problem.

The rapid increase in opioid use caused a crisis and eventually reached epidemic proportions. Hundreds of thousands of deaths were attributed to opioid overdoses around the country.

Harry Fisher, a family man and pillar of the community, must have been horrified when he learned the truth about opioids.

He also wanted his money back. Cole refused. Because a man like Devon Cole never has enough money.

"The fire was meant to be a lesson to Harry," Lizzy said wearily. On top of everything else, lack of sleep was wearing her down. "Harry made another mistake, too. Telling Cole he knew about Cole's congressional activities. Vote buying, defense contracts, campaign finance violations, corruption, self-dealing. All of it."

Devon Cole had been a corrupt congressman. He'd also been running a full-scale criminal enterprise while in office and for many years afterward. Which was how he became a billionaire, if Flint had to guess.

"What do you know about Cole's current operations?" Flint asked.

"Frankie was careful about what he told me. But I picked up things over the years." She paused. "There's money moving opioids through Central America now. Lots of it."

"Specifics?"

"I don't know specifics. But Frankie made trips. All over. Costa Rica, Panama, sometimes Colombia."

"How often?"

"Two or three times a year. He'd be gone for weeks."

"And when he came back?"

"Scared. Like he'd seen things he wished he hadn't."

This was useful intel, but Flint sensed she was still holding back.

He said, "Jason Fisher hired me because he suspected one of the twins, at least, survived the fire. Video from an ATM camera captured a man who looked like Dylan or Kevin. When Jason saw it, he started putting pieces together."

Her eyes widened. "And the others?"

Flint shrugged. "We won't know until we find them, but we believe all of the Fisher siblings are still alive. The question is what happens when they learn you and Frankie are too."

She was quiet for a long moment, drained the last of the coffee and tossed the paper cup into the trash. "What do you want me to do?"

"First, you're going to help me tell all of this to the Fisher family."

"And after that?"

"Then you're going to help me bring down Devon Cole."

She stood and walked to the window, staring into the breaking dawn. "And if Cole comes after me?"

"Then we'll deal with that when it happens," Flint replied. "Once we make that call, there's no going back. Cole will know you're alive at that point for sure. Frankie will know you've chosen sides. And the Fisher family will know you've been lying to them for twenty years."

"You said Cole already knew I survived," Lizzy said suspiciously.

"He should. He probably does. In his shoes, I would know. But I haven't asked him personally," Flint replied.

She nodded slowly. "Then we'd better make sure we're ready for what comes next."

"Right after we get some sleep," Flint said as he returned to his room.

Outside, shafts of sunlight cut through the clouds and painted the wet pavement gold. There was time for rest. The world would keep turning.

When he'd closed the connecting door, he located his satellite phone and made the call.

CHAPTER 40

March 20
Miami, Florida

FLINT PACKED HIS GO-BAG. Weapons secured. Cash counted. Fake identification hidden well enough to withstand a cursory search.

Outside the window of his room at the Kendrick Hotel, Miami's skyline caught the morning light. Glass towers reflected gold against a clear sky and traffic moved steadily along the streets below now that the city was fully awake. The distant hum of air-conditioning units and the muffled sounds of breakfast service filtered through the walls.

They needed to be gone within the hour. After Lizzy's revelations about the fire, staying in one location too long was dangerous. The smart play was to keep moving until they figured out how to use her information without getting them killed.

His satellite phone rang. Texas area code. Mount Warren. The device felt cold against his palm as he answered.

"Sheriff Milliken," Flint answered, continuing to pack.

"Flint, I've got news about your mother's case." Milliken sounded excited, which was unusual for a Texas lawman. "The state crime lab fast-tracked our request after I told them we would pay the expedited fees. DNA results came back this morning."

Flint set down the cash he'd been counting and stopped packing. The bills scattered slightly in the air-conditioned breeze across the hotel room's generic mahogany dresser. "What did they find?"

"Male DNA on Marilyn's skirt. Not the victim." Milliken paused. "Which means we've got foreign DNA that could belong to her killer."

"Matches in the databases?" Flint's words were raspy because his mouth had dried up.

"That's the thing. The lab ran the DNA through CODIS. No hits. But the sample's clean enough for comparison testing if we get a suspect," Milliken said, still obviously pleased with the results of his efforts.

Flint walked to the window and scanned the street below. Palm trees swayed gently in the morning breeze, and joggers moved along the sidewalks. His mother's case was finally moving forward, but he couldn't do much about that at the moment. "What do you need from me right now?"

"When can you get back to Mount Warren? We need to discuss next steps. Maybe look at that Kellerman angle we talked about."

"Yeah. I'm in the middle of something urgent. Take me a few days."

"This case has been cold for years. Now we've got real evidence. We should move on it," Milliken replied, obviously disappointed that Flint hadn't committed immediately.

Before Flint could answer, his phone rang on the other line. Gaspar. The buzzing vibration against his ribs felt sharp and insistent.

"Send me the report, Sheriff. I'll call you back," Flint said, switching to the incoming call.

"What's up?" he said to Gaspar.

"We've got a problem," Gaspar said urgently. "People are asking questions about what happened in Cuba. Knows what they're doing, too."

Flint swiped a palm across his face. The stubble felt rough against his skin. "What kind of inquiries?"

"Tracked down the helo. Pressuring my contacts for intel such as who hired the helicopter. Where the passengers went. What the operation was about." Gaspar paused. "These aren't cops, Flint. These are people with serious resources."

"How much do they know?"

"Everything. Flight path. Timeline. Landing location. They've reverse-engineered the entire operation." Gaspar paused. "I figure they'll be looking for you in Miami shortly. Time to get out of there. We can track this another way."

Flint walked to the window and scanned the street below. He saw nothing obviously wrong, but that meant nothing. "How long do we have?"

"If they can pressure my network, they can find you. I'd say assume you're already blown."

"Copy that. We're moving now."

"Be careful, Flint. Whoever this is, they've got reach," Gaspar warned before he hung up.

Almost immediately, Flint's phone rang again. The electronic chirping echoed in the quiet hotel room.

"I'm a popular guy all of a sudden," he murmured, looking at the caller ID.

Jason Fisher.

Flint grabbed his go-bag and moved toward the door. The carpet felt thick under his feet. "Morning, Fisher."

"I know you found a woman." Fisher's tone was flat. Cold. No preamble. "I know she's alive and with you in Miami."

Flint stopped at his door and listened. Footsteps in the hallway. Hotel staff, possibly. The sound of wheels rolling across carpet was probably a housekeeping cart. "What are you talking about?"

"Project Janus has been monitoring you since Kentucky." Fisher's tone carried absolute authority, as if he were the boss. Which, most of the time, he was. "Facial recognition flagged a possible match at the Kendrick Hotel. Age progression algorithms. Bone structure analysis."

The footsteps stopped outside his door. Flint drew his pistol and moved away from the entrance. The weapon felt familiar and reassuring in his grip. "You've been watching me."

"I've been protecting my investment. Making sure you were actually working the case instead of taking my money and disappearing." The sound of jet engines filtered through the connection and Flint realized Fisher was airborne. "Age progression isn't perfect, but combined with you disappearing to Cuba and coming back with a woman the right age? The math works."

"What do you mean?"

"There's an 87 percent probability that the woman you brought back from Cuba is Lizzy Pace," Fisher said. "Have you actually found Lizzy Pace? Is she there with you now?"

An exceptionally loud alarm pierced the air with several long blasts. The shrill sound reverberated off the hotel walls and made Flint's ears ring. Then the building's PA system crackled to life with static before more loud blasts.

"Attention, please. We have detected a gas leak in the building. Please evacuate immediately using the nearest stairwell. Do not use elevators. Hotel staff will direct you to safety."

A hard knock on the door came next. The sound echoed in the small room. "Please leave the building now."

Flint moved to the connecting door between rooms and knocked three times. The signal he'd arranged with Lizzy. The door felt solid under his knuckles.

Lizzy knocked back twice. All clear.

"We need to meet," Flint said to Fisher, keeping his voice low as the alarm continued its piercing wail.

"I'm thirty minutes from you." Fisher's tone carried an edge now. The jet engines were louder in the background. "If my brother is alive like I think he is, and you've got Lizzy Pace, then maybe they are all alive."

Another knock. Harder this time. The door frame rattled slightly. A man spoke loudly through the closed door. "Sir, it's no longer safe for you to remain in your room."

"We need to meet," Flint said to Fisher, keeping his tone low as the alarm continued to blare.

"Like I said, I'm thirty minutes out from Miami Executive Airport." Fisher's tone carried an edge now. "I need to know if this woman killed my siblings or saved them."

Heavy knocking on his door. The pounding reverberated through the room. "Sir, you need to evacuate immediately. Gas leak emergency."

"Yeah, coming," he said as he moved to the window and looked down.

Fire trucks were already arriving, red lights flashing against the skyscrapers. Hotel guests were streaming out of the building like ants from a disturbed hill. Staff directed people toward specific areas of the parking lot while wearing orange safety vests and holding clipboards.

"The woman has information about what happened that night," Flint said without confirming Lizzy's identity.

"Bring her with you. One o'clock. My home on Windsor Island. I'll send a private boat to pick you up." Fisher paused. "Twenty years, Flint. I've long wondered if my family's murderer was walking free."

"We'll be there," Flint said as he ended the call, though he wasn't sure how.

CHAPTER 41

March 20
Miami, Florida

THE KNOCKING ON HIS door became pounding. The sound was relentless now. "Sir, this is a mandatory evacuation. Open the door immediately."

Flint moved quickly to the connecting door, opened it, and stepped into Lizzy's room. The air smelled faintly of her shampoo and the cleaning supplies the hotel used. Drake was already there, armed, standing at the window, looking down at the evacuation.

"How convenient," Drake said. "Gas leak right at the moment."

"We're leaving. Right now," he said.

Lizzy nodded, grabbing the small bag they'd given her. No questions. No hesitation. She had learned to move fast when necessary.

Drake had already checked his gear. "Service elevator's probably shut down for the emergency. Stairwells will be packed with guests and staff."

"Which means we go a different way," Flint said.

The pounding on doors continued throughout the floor. Staff moving room to room, forcing everyone out. The alarm was even more deafening now, the sound bouncing off the walls and making conversation difficult.

"Window?" Lizzy asked.

Drake shook his head. "We're twelve floors up. Even if we had enough rope, they'd spot us rappelling down."

Flint visualized the hotel layout. "Maintenance access. Every floor has service corridors for housekeeping and building systems."

"Where?"

"Most likely it's next to the ice machines. Hidden behind unmarked doors."

They moved quickly to the door. Flint listened for a moment. The surface felt cool against his ear. He heard voices in the hallway as staff directed guests toward the stairwells.

Flint opened the door and stepped out, gesturing Lizzy to stay close behind. Drake came last, protecting the rear.

The hallway was chaos. Hotel guests emerging from rooms, staff in emergency vests herding people toward the exits, alarm bells echoing off the walls. The carpet was thick underfoot, muffling footsteps as they moved with the crowd.

They had joined the flow of people moving toward the stairwell, but at the last moment, Flint veered toward the ice machine alcove. Drake and Lizzy followed.

Behind the ice machine, Flint found an unmarked metal door. He tried the handle. Locked. The metal felt cold under his palm.

Drake pulled out a multi-tool and went to work on the lock mechanism while Flint kept a lookout. The scraping of metal on metal was barely audible over the alarm. A few seconds later, the door swung open.

"Service corridor," Drake said with satisfaction as Flint gestured Lizzy through and followed behind after closing the door again.

The narrow passage was dimly lit, running parallel to the guest hallway. Pipes and electrical conduits lined the walls. The air smelled of industrial cleaning supplies and machine oil, and footsteps echoed in the confined space.

They moved quickly, heading toward the far end of the building where the service elevator should be.

"There," Flint said, pointing to a service elevator at the end of the corridor.

Drake pressed the call button. Nothing. All elevators, including this one, had been shut down for the emergency.

"Stairs?" Lizzy asked.

Flint found the service door. Unlike the main stairwells, this one was not being used. No guests, no staff. Just concrete steps leading down into shadows.

They descended quickly. The alarm was muffled here, but still audible. Twelve floors down to street level. The only sound echoing in the stairwell were their footsteps.

At the eighth floor, Flint held up a hand. "Listen."

The sound of boots on concrete. Multiple sets, moving up the stairs.

"Building security," Flint said quietly. "Checking the service areas."

They backed up to the landing and found another corridor entrance. Flint tried the door. Unlocked.

The eighth-floor service corridor was identical to the twelfth. Narrow, dimly lit, running the length of the building. But this one had something more useful. A laundry chute.

"That probably goes straight to the basement laundry facilities," Drake said, looking at the opening.

"You first," Flint said to Lizzy with a grand sweep of his arm.

She looked at the narrow chute, then back at the approaching footsteps. "How do I know it's safe?"

Flint shrugged and gave her a soft push.

She climbed into the chute opening feet first and disappeared down the shaft. A few seconds later, they heard a muffled thump from below.

Drake went next, then Flint.

The laundry chute deposited them into a large canvas bin filled with dirty hotel linens. The fabric smelled of detergent and human sweat and other things Flint couldn't immediately identify.

Lizzy had already climbed out of the bin. "Which way?"

Drake climbed out next and then Flint did the same.

The basement was a maze of mechanical rooms, storage areas, and service corridors. Emergency lighting cast everything in harsh shadows.

Flint oriented himself to the building layout. "Loading dock should be on the north side."

They moved through the basement, past water heaters and electrical panels, following signs toward the service areas. The concrete floor was cold under their feet. The alarm was fainter here, but they could hear activity above. The evacuation was still in progress.

"There," Drake said, pointing to a ramp leading up to a loading dock. They trudged up the ramp as unobtrusively as possible.

The loading dock area was abandoned except for a few delivery trucks due to the alarm. Sunlight streamed in through the open bay doors, momentarily blinding them after the dimness of the basement.

Beyond the trucks, Flint saw the hotel's parking lot, where hundreds of guests were being organized into groups by emergency personnel.

"Now we just walk out like we belong out there with the rest of them," Flint said.

They climbed into the back of an empty delivery truck and waited on the cold, hard metal floor. Five minutes later, the truck started up and drove away.

Flint's satellite phone vibrated in his pocket. He looked at the screen. Jason Fisher again.

"Where are you? I just landed. My security team says the hotel was evacuated for a gas leak."

Flint said, "Still on for one o'clock?"

"Absolutely. Private boat. Don't be late."

Flint ended the call and looked at Drake and Lizzy.

"Well," Drake said. "That was interesting."

Flint replied with a quick nod. "Whoever forced that evacuation knows we escaped. They'll be looking for us."

Through the truck's rear window, they could see smoke rising from the hotel area. Not from a real gas leak, but from the chaos of the evacuation.

"So what now?" Lizzy asked.

CHAPTER 42

March 20
Windsor Island

THE DELIVERY TRUCK DROPPED them at Terminal Island Road just off the MacArthur Causeway. Flint checked his watch. They had forty minutes to make the rendezvous.

"Ferry terminal's this way," Drake said, leading them toward the water.

The area was surprisingly quiet for Miami, mostly causeway infrastructure and security checkpoints. Palm trees swayed in the warm March breeze. The weather was perfect for Miami, with gentle breezes carrying the scent of Biscayne Bay and the sweet perfume of gardenias.

Lizzy walked between them, scanning every parked car and security camera. She'd spent twenty years looking over her shoulder. Old habits die hard. Her clothes stuck to her back with nervous perspiration despite the comfortable temperature.

The private dock was straight ahead. Fisher had arranged for his boat to pick them up from the Terminal Island area. Security cameras no doubt tracked them from discreet positions.

Fisher's thirty-eight-foot Viking sport fisherman waited with its twin diesels rumbling at idle, the sound a deep bass note that vibrated through the concrete pier. The name *Meridian* was painted in gold letters across the transom. The boat's finish was so perfect it seemed to glow in the afternoon sunlight.

A crew member in pressed white shorts and a navy polo shirt stepped onto the floating concrete dock as they approached. The uniform was so crisp it could have come straight from the dry cleaner. Young face, weathered hands.

"Mr. Flint?"

"That's right."

"Mr. Fisher is expecting you. Please come aboard." His voice carried a slight accent Flint couldn't place. Caribbean, maybe.

The boat's interior was pristine white leather and polished teak that smelled of expensive conditioner and salt spray. Not ostentatious, but every detail perfect. Even the drink holders were made from brushed stainless steel.

"Nice ride," Drake commented, running his hand along the polished rail.

"Mr. Fisher appreciates quality," the crewman said with pride.

As they pulled away from the concrete floating docks, the diesel fumes from working boats gave way to the clean salt tang of open water. The Viking's powerful engines settled into a steady growl of precision engineering and unlimited maintenance budgets.

Miami's skyline stretched along the horizon to their left. Glass towers caught the afternoon sun like mirrors, throwing back sheets of golden light that made Flint squint.

"Wow, look at those yachts," Lizzy said, pointing to their right where superyachts up to two hundred feet long sat anchored in perfect rows at the island's marinas. Crews in crisp uniforms polished chrome that already gleamed. The sound of the wake slapping against the hulls echoed across the water.

The water changed from the greenish harbor color to clearer blue-green as they moved through the bay. The depth gauge showed fifteen feet, then twenty, then deeper water beyond. Seabirds wheeled overhead—pelicans, cormorants, and egrets hunting in the shallows.

"Dolphins," Drake pointed as a pair of bottlenose dolphins surfaced nearby. The dorsal fins cut through the gentle swells like black knives before disappearing again with barely a splash.

"How much farther?" Lizzy seemed absorbed by the luxury surroundings after her years in Cuba where prosperity was nonexistent.

"Eight minutes to the island," the crewman replied over the engine noise.

Windsor Island emerged ahead through the March haze like something from a travel magazine. The exclusive 216-acre island housed seven hundred residences, owned by citizens of thirty countries.

Perfectly manicured palm trees lined pristine private beaches maintained by armies of groundskeepers. Behind the beaches, massive estates were monuments to wealth, each positioned for maximum privacy and stunning water views.

"How the billionaires live," Flint muttered, catching glimpses of tennis courts, swimming pools, and helicopter pads tucked behind landscaping that cost millions.

Lizzy gripped the boat's rail as they sliced through the calm water. Her knuckles showed white against her tanned skin. The engines' steady rumble mixed with the sound of spray hitting the hull and the distant cry of seabirds. She watched the yachts drift past like floating palaces with crews in crisp uniforms preparing for evening cocktail parties.

"Money makes everything different here," she said quietly. "Clean, antiseptic, removed from the real world."

"You nervous?" Drake asked, raising his voice over the wind and engine noise.

"Wouldn't you be?" She gestured toward the approaching island with a trembling hand. "Look at this place. His world. I haven't seen him in more than twenty years and I'm about to tell him his father helped poison half of Kentucky with pills."

Flint caught the bitter edge in her voice. "Harry Fisher made his choices. You saved those children."

"Did I? Or did I just drag them into twenty years of hiding from their own family? Parents and siblings who loved them passionately." Lizzy paused to blink her tears away.

Windsor Island filled Flint's vision now. The scent of money was everywhere. In the perfectly maintained landscaping, the private beaches raked smooth as golf course sand, the estates that could house small towns, and an army of workers to attend every whim of the billionaires who lived here. The clean, antiseptic smell of wealth that insulated itself from the real world. Even the air felt different here, filtered and perfected.

The boat pulled up to a private pier that gleamed with fresh teak planking. Another crew member waited to tie them off. Beyond the dock, a golf cart sat ready with a driver wearing the same navy polo uniform. The cart itself was spotless, more like a small luxury vehicle than ordinary transportation.

"First time to Windsor Island?" the driver asked as they climbed into the cart. His tone carried the same careful neutrality as the boat crew.

"For me, yes," Drake and Lizzy replied at the same time.

Flint said nothing. He'd been to Windsor Island many times. Several residents had been his clients at one time or another. No reason to say so now.

"Mr. Fisher's residence is just up the hill," the driver continued.

The road wound through tropical landscaping that probably cost more to maintain than the purchase price of most US homes. Orchids bloomed. Koi ponds reflected the late afternoon sky. Even the pink crushed shell gravel crunched expensively under the cart tires.

"Everything's perfect," Lizzy observed. "Controlled. The kind of environment where you can forget the real world exists."

"Yep. Keep out the riffraff. That's the point," Drake said quietly.

Fisher's estate sprawled along the island's western shore like a scene from Architectural Digest. A magnificent Spanish-style mansion with arched windows and terra cotta tile roofing caught the afternoon light giving it a burnished copper glow.

The Mediterranean architecture followed the island's strict design guidelines while it conveyed understated elegance. Wealth that expressed itself through quality rather than flash.

"I count at least thirty rooms," Drake said, studying the main structure.

"Probably more," Flint replied.

Jason Fisher waited on the covered terrace overlooking the water, running his hands through his hair as if he were nervous. He looked older than when Flint had first met him a few days ago. Dark circles under his eyes suggested sleepless nights. The obsessive search for his siblings had taken its toll.

"Flint." Fisher's tone was controlled, but Flint caught the underlying tension.

His eyes went immediately to Lizzy, showing no surprise or uncertainty. He'd been expecting this moment since his phone call. Flint could see the recognition in Fisher's face, mixed with what might have been relief or dread.

"Lizzy Pace. It's been a long time, but I'd know you anywhere." His voice was steady, but his hands betrayed him with a slight shake. "Thank you for coming."

He gestured toward one of the seating areas on the terrace overlooking the ocean decorated with furniture that probably cost more than most cars.

The terrace furniture was carefully arranged. Miami sparkled in the distance like a handful of diamonds scattered on black velvet. Boats moved across the bay like toys, lights beginning to twinkle as dusk approached.

"Beautiful view," Flint observed, settling into his chair.

"It's designed to keep all the problems of the world away," Fisher said bitterly. "But some problems can't be solved by money alone."

"No, they can't," Lizzy agreed quietly.

Fisher's gaze never left Lizzy's face, studying her like she might disappear if he looked away. "I need to know what happened to my family."

Lizzy dropped her chin and gazed at the terrazzo tile on the floor.

"What happened that night?" Fisher's voice seemed to crack slightly. "The fire. The twins. Little Mo. All of it."

Lizzy glanced at Flint, who nodded encouragingly. She took a deep breath that seemed to steady her.

"I managed to get them out." The words came out like a confession.

Fisher's hands gripped the arms of his chair so hard his knuckles went white. "All three of them?"

Lizzy nodded, tears starting to track down her cheeks. "Dylan, Kevin, and Maureen."

Fisher was quiet for a long moment, his face unreadable. He stared at a fixed point on the table, processing the information in a methodical way. Due to his autism he needed time to absorb shocking news, to work through it systematically.

When he looked up, his expression was controlled, though Flint caught the slight tension around his eyes.

"Where are they now?"

"I haven't seen them in a very long time." Lizzy's eyes filled with fresh tears, and she cleared her throat before she could continue. Her voice shook with decades of suppressed emotion. "I don't know what happened to them later."

"Start from the beginning," Flint said gently. "Tell him everything."

Fisher seemed to understand that he couldn't push her too far too fast. He waited as if he were patient when Flint knew otherwise.

"I was babysitting that night. The twins had colds, so your parents decided to leave them home instead of dragging them to the basketball game." Lizzy took a shaky breath and wiped her face with trembling hands. "I was upstairs in the nursery with all three children when the fire started. I didn't notice the flames right away."

Fisher leaned forward, hanging on every word. "When did you notice the fire?"

"Not until I started to smell the smoke and Kevin began coughing." Her voice grew steadier as she continued, as if telling the story was helping her relive it clearly. "We grabbed the children and got them outside. I took them deep into the woods."

"You said 'we.' Who helped you get them out?" Jason's question was sharp, focused.

"Frankie Tantanella." Lizzy's hands trembled slightly as she spoke the name.

Fisher's face changed. "You knew you weren't allowed to have boys over when you were babysitting. What was Frankie doing there?"

Lizzy looked at Flint again. He nodded, his expression encouraging but serious.

"He needed money," she said, her voice dropping to barely above a whisper. "To get out of Kentucky. Someone had offered him enough cash to disappear if he'd torch your father's house. He would never have hurt us. Frankie didn't know we were inside."

The color drained from Fisher's face. His mouth opened slightly, but no sound came out. When he finally spoke, his voice was ice cold. "Who paid Frankie Tantanella to burn down our house?"

She glanced at Flint again for reassurance. He nodded once more, his jaw set.

Lizzy cleared her throat and wiped her tears with the back of her hand. She straightened in her chair and raised her eyes to give Jason a steady stare.

The words came out clear and final, like a judge pronouncing sentence.

"Devon Cole."

CHAPTER 43

March 20

Windsor Island

WHEN LIZZY FINISHED HER confession they all went quiet while a door opened and a staff member came outside.

"Iced tea?" A woman in her fifties with graying hair pulled back in a neat ponytail, wearing the crisp white shirt that marked her as estate staff. "It's warm out here, isn't it?"

"Thank you, Elsa," Fisher said without looking up from the table.

Elsa carried a pitcher of freshly brewed tea and filled their glasses. The ice clinking softly. "Will you and your guests be staying for dinner, Mr. Fisher? I can tell the kitchen."

"Not tonight," Fisher replied, still staring at his hands.

Elsa nodded and withdrew quietly.

Fisher sat motionless in his chair. His breathing remained steady and controlled, but his knuckles had gone white where they gripped the table edge. Something fundamental had shifted behind his dark eyes.

A yacht horn sounded somewhere in the distance. Palm fronds rustled overhead in the ocean breeze.

"Devon Cole," Fisher repeated the name as if he were opening a vault of old photographs.

His fingers began that repetitive pressing motion Flint had noticed before. Ten fingertips together pressing in and out. He seemed to be thinking through decades of information, building connections with the same systematic process that only existed inside his head and had made him billions.

"Dad's business partner," Fisher said. "Uncle Devon, we called him."

"He was close to the family, then?" Drake asked.

Fisher nodded. "He was at our house sometimes twice a week. Family barbecues, birthday parties, Christmas mornings. Especially in the early years."

The tropical air felt suddenly heavy. Even the sound of the waves seemed muted.

"What kind of relationship did you have with him?" Flint wanted to know.

"He taught me chess. Brought me computer programming books." Fisher shrugged. "As you can imagine, I was a difficult kid. But Uncle Devon said I reminded him of himself at that age."

Flint nodded but stayed silent, watching Fisher's face for any crack in the analytical armor. There was none. Just systematic processing.

A helicopter approached and landed nearby. It was not the first helo Flint had heard since they'd boarded the boat to approach the island. When the rotor noise finally quieted, conversation could resume.

"Dad tried to end their partnership once," Fisher continued, his tone as level as if he were discussing a dry quarterly earnings report. "Said Cole was getting into things that Dad didn't approve of. It wasn't until years later that I learned what those things were."

Fisher seemed to be systematically assembling the timeline in his head, each piece of data clicking into place as he pulled it from stored memories.

"They were both respectable businessmen. At least on the surface," Fisher said. "But Dad got scared about where the money was really coming from when he figured out that Cole was pushing pill mills and illegal prescriptions and people were dying."

Fisher's dark eyes held the same focused intensity that had built an empire, but now there was something colder lurking.

"Later, I found out Dad went to the DEA. Started cooperating. His handler was Agent Gerard, found dead in his car six months after the fire. Murdered, they said."

"You remember Agent Gerard?" Flint asked.

"I remember everything. Every conversation. Every meeting. Every phone call Dad thought I wasn't listening to." Fisher shrugged. "My memory is a blessing and a curse."

"The fire came soon after your father began working with the DEA," Flint replied. "It was a warning."

Fisher stood and walked to the terrace railing. The setting sun cast long shadows across the golf course below. The perfectly groomed fairways stretched out like a green carpet toward the water.

A lone golfer was finishing up on the distant eighteenth green while his caddy waited patiently beside the flag.

"Seems like the actual timing of the fire wasn't random, either," Fisher said.

"What do you mean?" Drake asked.

"Cole would have known our schedules. Hell, Dad probably told him we'd be away that night," Fisher replied. "It's not like the basketball schedule at the high school was a secret. The whole town would have known we'd be there. Both Bruce and I were on the varsity team, and everyone knew it."

He stated the insight like an engineering assessment. Problem analysis delivered in the same tone he might use to discuss server capacity or bandwidth allocation. No emotional weight at all. As if the events Fisher chose to focus on happened to total strangers.

The breeze picked up, stirring the gardenias again. The scent was almost cloying in the cool evening air.

Fisher turned to lean against the railing and faced them as the dying sunlight caught the sharp angles of his face.

"Cole came to the funeral. Held Mom while she cried. Helped her plan the memorial services for Lizzy and the kids. While knowing he'd caused it all," Fisher said as if he was reciting a bedtime horror story.

Drake shifted in his chair and the wicker creaked under his weight. "That's a cold-hearted bastard."

Fisher's expression didn't change, but he shook his head. "He feels nothing about what he did. Agent Gerard's murder, all those deaths. Just problems solved for Devon Cole."

The words were clinical. Detached. But accurate in a way that made Flint's skin crawl.

"Over the years since the fire, Cole and I have done business together. Joint ventures. Charitable causes. He's been friendly enough, but not overly familiar," Fisher said. "Like the past, when he was almost a part of my family, never happened. But also like we were colleagues and equals in the world today."

"Are you? Equals?" Drake asked.

Fisher's eyes narrowed and his tone was steely. "Not even close. I could buy and sell Cole several times over. Maybe I will."

A pelican glided past the terrace, wings barely moving as it rode the evening thermals over the golf course. The mundane normalcy of it felt obscene in the moment.

Near the terrace, a gardener in khaki work clothes tended to the flower beds, clipping and deadheading gardenias with quiet concentration, oblivious to the conversation taking place above.

Fisher paused, his fingers resuming the repetitive pressing motion. Flint could almost see him processing probabilities, calculating present dangers, and analyzing threat assessments.

"But if Cole learns there were survivors, if he discovers Lizzy is alive and talking," Drake said by way of warning. "Then we all become targets."

"Already happened," Flint replied. "Cole must know you hired me. He probably thinks Frankie's to blame. Regardless of what he's worried about, that's why he's sent armed mercenaries to stop us."

Fisher's head tilted slightly to one side, the way it did when he was working through complex problems. "Every attack, every attempt to kill you. That was Cole trying to shut us down before things led back to him."

"He's protecting old crimes," Flint said. "But he's also still running active operations. International drug trafficking, for one."

Fisher absorbed this information. His expression never changed as he grasped that Cole's involvement expanded far beyond the drugs and the cold case arson and the Fisher family.

The shadows were growing longer now across the golf course. Security lights began flickering on automatically on the estate grounds and along the cart paths, creating pools of warm light in the gathering dusk. The setting was peaceful and serene, even if the conversation was not.

"He could be monitoring my legal proceedings to unseal the adoption records." Fisher simply stated the facts. "We're threatening a criminal empire. Cole will want to stop us. Sooner rather than later."

Flint watched him carefully.

"Cole is rich, and he's got resources, sure. But he's not as rich as I am." Fisher walked back to the table. "I have advantages he doesn't know about. Technology, security, financial resources, far beyond his. If we have a battle of the billionaires, I'll win. No contest."

It was like watching a computer boot up and run diagnostics, Flint noticed. "Assuming he doesn't kill you first."

"I've solved harder problems than Devon Cole." The absolute confidence was vintage Jason Fisher. Once he'd made a decision, the matter was settled as far as he was concerned. In his world, no one thwarted him. "We need to find my siblings and protect them simultaneously. He'll try to get to my mother, too. Once they're secure, we deal with Cole."

Flint said nothing.

Fisher pressed a button on his phone. "Nancy, I need you out here please."

Within moments, a woman appeared on the terrace. She wore a tailored navy blazer and carried a leather portfolio. Her dark hair was pulled back in a bun.

"How can I help?" she asked pleasantly enough.

"I need you to coordinate a few calls for me," Fisher said. "Legal teams, security firms, surveillance vendors. Full mobilization. I'll text you the list."

Nancy pulled out a tablet and stylus, settling into a chair at the far end of the table. "Of course, Mr. Fisher. What's the priority sequence?"

Fisher gave her the specifics while she took efficient notes on her tablet. Legal teams to expedite the adoption cases. Private security firms to line up protection. Surveillance technology vendors to keep him informed.

"Start with the law firms," Fisher said. "I want judicial orders unsealing those adoption records within forty-eight hours. Whatever it takes."

Nancy nodded and moved to a quiet corner to begin. Occasionally, she'd ask questions of Fisher, but she handled things efficiently.

The yacht lights were twinkling across the water like fallen stars. Somewhere in the distance, a dinner bell chimed. Flint heard a couple of helos land and take off again.

People went about their evening routines both on the island and on the mainland, insulated from the kind of violence that had torn Jason Fisher's family apart.

"Okay. We locate my family, ensure their safety, gather evidence of Cole's current crimes, and eliminate the threat." Fisher said with the same intense focus. "What else do we need to do?"

The question was aimed at Flint. Nancy was still on the phone, speaking quietly to what sounded like a security firm. The gardener had moved closer to the terrace, working on a row of orchids directly below the railing. Elsa returned with another pitcher and a few cookies.

For Fisher, the personal stakes were clear but not emotional. He was utterly determined, exhibiting the same relentless certainty that had created his empire.

The golf course had emptied, and the final players headed back to the clubhouse.

Before he could respond to Fisher's question, Flint noticed a shadow moving across the closest green.

At first, he thought it was a late golfer, but something about the man's gait caught Flint's attention. He was walking directly toward the terrace, striding across the manicured fairway.

As he came closer, Flint could make out an expensive golf shirt, perfectly pressed khakis, and the kind of casual confidence that came with owning everything he surveyed.

Nancy looked up from her tablet at the same moment, stylus poised over the screen. She reached for her phone and immediately hit the speed dial.

Elsa didn't stray from her tasks. The gardener continued working below, unaware of the new arrival.

Fisher's eyes widened as he recognized the intruder.

CHAPTER 44

March 20

Windsor Island

FLINT HEARD A RIFLE shot across the golf course.

Nancy's head snapped back. The tablet fell off her lap and shattered on the terrace stone. Blood sprayed across the table as she toppled from her chair and landed on the patio.

Everyone else hit the deck.

When no further shots were fired, Fisher jumped to his feet and started toward Nancy's body, then stopped when he saw her lifeless eyes and the blood beginning to pool beneath her.

Flint pressed himself against the terrace's low wall while he scanned the field of fire. Drake had rolled behind a planter. Lizzy crouched near the table legs with her hands over her head. The gardener and Elsa had fled.

The intruder walked off the golf course and onto the private patio as if he'd been invited. Casual. Unruffled.

Unmistakable.

Devon Cole, one of the richest men alive, with a face more familiar than the Pope. His image had appeared everywhere, every day for more than twenty years. Only a blind man could have failed to recognize him.

What the hell was he doing here?

Flint scanned the area quickly, but the peace remained mostly undisturbed.

Fisher's security system should have been screaming by now. Motion detectors, audio sensors, perimeter cameras, and more. The estate's sophisticated security network would have registered the gunshot immediately. But the usual security protocols weren't happening.

"Seems that communications and systems are experiencing some temporary interference." Cole's smile was cold and satisfied.

"You son of a bitch," Fisher replied, shaking with impotent rage. "You killed Nancy in cold blood."

"I'm sad to lose Nancy, too. She'd been with me for years. But I could no longer trust her. She'd become way too loyal to you." Cole's expression showed genuine regret. "My security team saw her spot our positioning around the estate. She must have thought we were a threat to you because she attempted a call for assistance. We had no choice. We were forced to eliminate the threat."

Fisher fumed on the sidelines but didn't argue.

Cole pulled a satellite phone from his pocket. "Perimeter status."

As Cole was distracted listening for the report, Flint heard another helicopter approaching. Cole disconnected and gestured toward Lizzy.

Coldly, he said, "Elizabeth Pace."

Lizzy looked up, terrified. "You remember me."

Cole stepped closer and Fisher moved protectively toward Lizzy. "What do you want?"

Cole ignored him, focused entirely on Lizzy. He reached to grab her arm and Lizzy deftly stepped aside.

"Command, this is Overwatch," Cole's radio crackled. "Additional security approaching from marina. Three vehicles. Armed personnel deploying."

Cole keyed his radio: "Copy that. No engagement unless they breach perimeter."

Flint saw the tactical picture developing. Cole's security had isolated the estate, neutralized Fisher's immediate protection, and was now managing the extraction and backup response as well.

"What do you want?" Fisher demanded again.

"I want you and your hired guns to stay out of my way," Cole replied, indicating Flint and Drake with a tilt of his head. "That message was clear enough to your father until he joined up with the DEA. Unfortunate mistake. We all know how that turned out. You can avoid making the same error."

"You're not after Lizzy, then," Fisher replied.

"Elizabeth Pace has been dead a long time. She needs to stay that way," Cole replied. "I will fix that, too."

Lizzy's voice was barely a whisper. "Except I'm not dead. Never was."

Cole gave her a hard, steady glare. "I underestimated you, Lizzy. A mistake I would have corrected years ago if I'd known. I won't make the same error a second time."

The radio crackled with static. One of Cole's men stated, "Command, perimeter breach attempt. Fisher security trying to advance up the north access road."

Cole raised his hand for silence, staring at Lizzy. "That's another problem I'll solve. Immediately."

Fisher stepped between them. "Lizzy saved my family. Dylan, Kevin, and Maureen. They're alive."

"She claims she rescued them, but what else would she say?" Cole replied sardonically. "We both know the house burned to ashes. The official records reflect that nothing survived. Lizzy included."

Flint stepped forward. "What did you use? Aviation fuel? Thermite? White phosphorus? Something that burns hotter than a normal house fire to destroy all the evidence."

Cole ignored Flint's questions.

"But we didn't die. I'm standing right here. Frankie saved all of us," Lizzy nodded.

"Nice job of hiding all these years, Lizzy," Flint said. "Cole here would have killed you long before now if he'd known you were alive."

Cole continued to ignore Flint. He stared at Lizzy as if she were a ghost. "You're telling me both you and all three of those kids got out of the house?"

The radio crackled again. "Fisher security has reached the main gate. They're demanding entry."

Cole didn't respond. His carefully controlled world was collapsing around his old miscalculation.

"Sir, we need guidance on the security response," his operative pressed.

Four men rappelled down from the helicopter, weapons ready, spreading out to secure the terrace. They stood waiting for orders from a commander who was no longer thinking tactically.

Cole asked Lizzy, "The children. Where are they?"

"I don't know," she said. "We got separated years ago."

"You're done, Cole." Drake emerged from behind the planter, weapon ready. "We'll find them. And when we do, they'll remember everything."

The radio chatter became more urgent: "Situation escalating. Multiple agencies now en route. We need immediate guidance."

Cole looked around the terrace. Fisher. Lizzy. His own security team waiting for orders and running out of time to execute them.

Flint and Drake, weapons drawn.

Perhaps for the first time ever, Devon Cole didn't know what to do next.

Flint saw his moment.

Cole's shock at learning about Lizzy and the surviving children had broken his tactical focus.

Shifting his weight, Flint signaled Drake.

But Cole's lead man had been watching Flint's movements.

"Sir, subjects are preparing to engage," the man reported calmly.

Cole's head snapped back to the present situation. Shock was replaced by cold calculation.

"Secure Fisher and the woman," Cole ordered. "Minimum force."

The four guards immediately adjusted their formation. Two moved to flank Fisher and Lizzy keeping their weapons trained on Flint and Drake. Two more guards held their positions to block escape routes.

"Fisher security at the gate is demanding immediate entry," crackled one of Cole's men over the radio.

Cole keyed his radio with steady hands. "Redirect to the south gardens. Tell them Mr. Fisher needs assistance there immediately."

"You're splitting their response," Drake said.

Cole replied, "While they secure the empty gardens, we leave from the marina."

The helicopter's rotors increased pitch overhead.

"Mr. Fisher, Ms. Pace," Cole said formally. "Time to go."

Fisher stepped protectively in front of Lizzy. "We're not going anywhere with you."

The nearest guard moved closer, weapon ready but not directly threatening. "Sir, please don't make this difficult."

Flint started to raise his pistol, but two rifle muzzles immediately tracked him. Drake was similarly covered from his position behind the planter.

"Don't tempt me, Flint. Four trained militia against two civilians and two investigators," Cole observed. "Poor odds for you."

"South garden diversion successful," the radio reported. "Marina approach is clear."

Flint saw his last chance slipping away. Fisher and Lizzy were being moved toward the helicopter extraction point, surrounded by mercenaries who maintained perfect discipline.

Any aggressive move would put Fisher and Lizzy in the crossfire. Cole and his team had positioned themselves to use the civilians as shields while maintaining tactical superiority.

Cole moved toward the terrace edge where the rescue basket waited. "Thirty seconds, people."

Three armed guards pointed weapons at Flint and Drake while the guard nearest Fisher gestured with his rifle. "This way, please."

Flint calculated rapidly to confirm.

No good options left.

Only the bad options.

Which were better than nothing.

Flint lunged forward, driving his shoulder into the nearest guard's midsection. The man stumbled backward, his rifle swinging wide for a crucial second. He kept moving, scrambling toward Fisher.

But the other guards reacted instantly. The lead guard's rifle butt caught Flint in the ribs, doubling him over. A second guard grabbed Flint's gun arm, twisting it hard and high behind his back.

Drake rolled out from behind the planter with his weapon raised. Instantly, two rifle muzzles trained on him.

"Stand down!" the lead gunman commanded.

Drake scanned and evaluated the situation. Two expert marksmen less than ten feet away aiming straight for his chest. No chance. He lowered his weapon.

One of the men fired. Drake was hit. He dove to one side, landed on the ground, and rolled toward cover.

Flint struggled against the arm lock, but the guard applied pressure to his wrist until his fingers opened, and his pistol clattered to the terrace stone.

"Predictable," Cole observed calmly. "But pointless."

The guard Flint had tackled was already back in position, covering Fisher and Lizzy.

"Sir, extraction basket is in position," came the radio call from the helicopter.

Flint was forced to his knees, one guard maintaining the arm lock while another kept his rifle trained on Drake.

"Time to go," Cole announced.

Fisher gave Flint a look of helpless frustration as he was guided toward the waiting extraction basket.

Lizzy's terrified eyes met Flint's for a moment before she too was moved toward the helicopter.

Cole paused before he entered the basket. "Better luck next time, Flint."

The basket rose into the night sky, taking Cole and his prisoners with it.

There was nothing more Flint could do here. All the money in the world wouldn't stop a bullet aimed at point blank range.

CHAPTER 45

March 20

Windsor Island

FLINT AND DRAKE WERE moving before the helicopter's rotor noise faded completely.

They hustled across the terrace toward the path leading down to the marina.

No running. Nothing to attract attention from anyone who might be watching.

Drake favored his left shoulder as blood seeped through his shirt, but he kept pace without complaint.

Behind them, the estate seemed deceptively calm. From this distance everything looked normal and undisturbed.

The landscaped path wound down the hillside between perfectly maintained palm trees and flowering shrubs. Security lighting cast gentle pools of illumination offering a peaceful evening stroll.

Sirens wailed in the distance, but they seemed to be moving away from the estate rather than toward it.

"How does Cole get away with this?" Drake asked. "A stunt like that should have first responders converging on this place in droves like ants at a picnic."

"Rich people," Flint shrugged. "Helicopters come and go from these estates every day. I heard at least two helos while we were talking before Cole arrived. Business meetings. Dinner parties. Weekend trips."

Drake nodded. "So nobody thinks twice about it."

"Cole's helo probably filed a flight plan. Listed it as executive transport," Flint replied. "By the time anyone asks questions, the paperwork will show Fisher requested the pickup."

Drake winced as his shoulder protested. "And just like that, three people simply disappear."

"Happens all the time with billionaires. They fly to Monaco. The Bahamas. Private islands," Flint said. "Fisher's staff will think he's on a business trip."

"While Cole cleans up the evidence," Drake said flatly. "No charges will be filed."

"Nope. Cole owns half the politicians. The other half owe him favors," Flint said. "In other words, the wealth and power dynamics make Fisher and Cole invisible to normal oversight. No one will be looking for them officially."

Drake glanced back as they reached the path and saw the same quiet estate as before. "What about the cleanup? Nancy's blood and whatever else we left behind."

"Like I said, billionaires have unlimited resources," Flint replied. "Cole probably has a cleaning crew on standby. If we walked back there, we'd probably find zero evidence."

A few minutes later, they reached the private pier. Fisher's boat waited exactly as they'd left it. The crewman in the navy polo stood on the dock, coiling lines to prepare for the next cruise.

As if nothing unusual had occurred, he said, "Mr. Fisher told me I'd be needed to take you back to Terminal Island. Are you ready to go now?"

"Where is Mr. Fisher?" Drake asked. "We need to thank him for the hospitality."

"I'm not sure. He said he had other business to attend to this evening."

Flint studied the crewman's face. Either he was an excellent actor, or he genuinely didn't know what had happened on the terrace. Hard to tell.

"Let's go," Flint said.

They boarded the boat and the crewman cast off the dock lines. The twin diesels rumbled to life and the Viking pulled smoothly away from the pier.

As they left Windsor Island, Fisher's mansion looked exactly as it had when they'd arrived. Peaceful. Elegant. Undisturbed.

No emergency vehicles. No flashing lights. No signs of crisis.

By the time any legitimate investigation began, there would be nothing to investigate. The gardener and Elsa would report a quiet evening with no unusual visitors. Hell, they were probably on Cole's payroll, too. Just like Nancy.

Jason Fisher and Lizzy Pace would have simply vanished without a trace.

Fisher would be missed. He had a full calendar every day. He was quirky and brazen and always visible.

On the other hand, Lizzy's disappearance might fly under the radar. After all, she'd supposedly died twice before.

But Frankie Tantanella would wonder. He might try to find her. If Cole left Frankie alive.

The boat cut steadily through the calm waters of Biscayne Bay, heading back toward Terminal Island. The lights of Windsor Island faded behind them as they traveled in relative silence.

Flint used the time to follow up on Marilyn Baker. He pulled out his satellite phone and scrolled through his contacts. Sheriff Milliken's recent call was still fresh in his mind. The lab had found male DNA on Marilyn's skirt, foreign DNA that could belong to her killer. No CODIS matches, but the sample was clean enough for comparison testing if they got a suspect.

Milliken had wanted to pursue "that Kellerman angle," but Flint had access to resources beyond what a small-town sheriff could offer. Genealogy databases had solved cold cases before by finding familial DNA matches. Time to try again.

He found the contact number for his preferred DNA lab and placed the call.

"Hey, Lydia. This is Michael Flint. I need to expedite a genealogy database search on a DNA profile from a cold case. I have the lab report with the genetic markers."

"Flint. Good to hear from you," Lydia Brimley replied. "I can start with the profile and run it against the major genealogy databases. If I find anything promising, I'll need the actual sample for confirmation testing."

"Agreed. I'll send you the report now. Rush priority."

"Should have preliminary results within twenty-four hours. Maybe sooner," Lydia promised.

Flint ended the call and put the phone away. After more than thirty years, technology might finally reveal who killed his mother.

About ten minutes later, the boat slowed as it approached the private pier. Terminal Island looked different at night, Flint noticed. Fewer people. More shadows.

"Thanks for the ride," Drake said to the crewman as they stepped onto the dock.

"My pleasure. Have a good evening."

They walked quickly away from the pier, footsteps echoing off the concrete. Drake's shoulder was worse now. Blood had soaked through his shirt and started to show through his jacket.

"How's the shoulder? It's looking messy," Flint said.

"Been worse." Drake winced briefly when he tried to move it. "I'll live."

"Maybe. But you won't be much use if you pass out from blood loss," Flint teased. Drake rewarded the effort with a weak grin.

Flint pulled out his satellite phone and called Gaspar. The phone rang twice before connecting.

"Drake needs a doctor," Flint said when Gaspar answered. "One who won't ask questions."

Gaspar didn't ask for details. Plausible deniability was a skill he had long since mastered. "What kind of medical attention?"

"Gunshot wound. Through and through. Shoulder," Flint replied. "He'll be fine. Just needs some stitches."

"Dr. Ana Vega. Completely trustworthy." Gaspar gave him an address in Little Havana. "I'll call ahead. She'll be expecting you."

"Got it. Thanks." Flint ended the call and looked at Drake, who was leaning against a lamppost as if he might need the support. "Little Havana. Twenty minutes."

Flint flagged a taxi. Drake climbed in on his good side. Flint gave the driver Dr. Vega's address. If he noticed Drake was injured, he gave no indication. But he meandered through the less traveled streets like a pro.

The clinic was in a converted house on Calle Ocho. The smell of Cuban coffee drifted from neighboring buildings. A middle-aged woman with steady hands and no questions answered the door.

She took one look at them, told Flint to wait and turned to Drake. "Follow me."

After they disappeared into an exam room, Flint walked outside into the warm Miami night and pulled out his satellite phone. He needed help from an expert who could keep secrets, and he knew who to call.

FBI Special Agent Kim Otto answered on the second ring. "Flint. How can I help?"

He grinned. He'd worked with Otto before and he appreciated her straight up, no nonsense style.

"You know who Devon Cole is?" He replied.

"Who doesn't? Self-made billionaire. Owns dozens of businesses. Started out selling shoes and now he's one of the richest men in the country," Otto said. "Rumors say his is the usual story with billionaires. Where there's a fortune, there's a crime."

"I need everything the FBI has on his current operations," Flint said, straight to the point. "Any chance?"

"Why do you think we have anything at all? We're not in the habit of investigating the country's richest citizens. They have too much power." Otto said quietly, as if she might be overheard. "It's that old joke. If you shoot at the king, you'd better not miss. Agents die that way. Careers are killed that way, too."

"Yeah. In this case, I'm sure there's fire beneath all this smoke," Flint replied. "This guy is as dirty as they come. Has been for at least three or four decades. I'm betting folks inside the Bureau know all about it."

"Suppose that's true. Why do you care?" Otto asked carefully, as if she didn't want to know too many details.

Flint filled her in. The Fisher home fire. Lizzy Pace and the three Fisher kids. The Windsor Island operation. Nancy's murder. The helicopter extraction.

"Sounds like a carefully orchestrated operation," Otto said when he finished. "Military contractors, you think?"

"Likely," Flint replied.

"If we have anything going on here and if I can share it with you, when do you need to know?"

"Not long."

"Twenty-four hours?"

"Maybe less."

"Our mutual friend might be faster," Otto said. "But I'll see what I can find out. Real-time intelligence. Satellite feeds. Whatever I can get."

"We'll need it," Flint replied just before he disconnected and walked back inside. She was right to suggest Gaspar, though.

Through the examination room door, Flint could hear Dr. Vega working. The clink of medical instruments. Drake's voice, steady despite the pain. A few moments later, Drake emerged from the examination room with his arm in a sling, looking pale but alert.

Dr. Vega handed Drake a small bottle of pills.

"Two types. One for pain, but it will make you drowsy so take it before bed. Nothing stronger than Tylenol otherwise," she instructed. "And antibiotics. Keep the wound clean and dry."

Drake nodded. "Thanks, Doc."

"Be more careful," she said as they headed out. "Both of you."

Outside, Drake asked, "Now what?"

CHAPTER 46

March 21

Coconut Grove

FLINT TOLD THE TAXI driver to drop them at the end of a random tree-lined street in Coconut Grove, just in case he was ever questioned. Flint paid the man in cash and added a generous tip to ensure his memory stayed fuzzy.

They waited for the driver to turn the first corner. Then they walked several blocks through residential neighborhoods before approaching Gaspar's house.

Spanish moss hung from ancient oak trees. The air carried the scent of jasmine and faint diesel exhaust from the distant highway.

Drake favored his left shoulder. His arm still rested in the sling Dr. Vega had provided. Pain showed in the tight lines around his eyes, but he stayed alert to their surroundings.

"Company?" Flint tilted his head toward the cars lining the curbs as they rounded the last corner.

"Not likely." Drake scanned the street again. "Could be watching via satellite or local CCTV hacks. Otherwise, no identifiable watchers."

Gaspar's house sat back from the street behind a wall of bougainvillea and royal palms. The Spanish colonial architecture fit the neighborhood perfectly. Red tile roof, white stucco walls, wrought iron details. Nothing about it suggested the electronic fortress inside.

Flint pressed the doorbell. A camera hidden in the porch light fixture captured the image and the lock clicked open. They went inside. Drake closed the door firmly and the electronic lock slipped into place again.

It was late and Gaspar's family were asleep, which saved them from small talk and his wife's usual generous offers of hospitality. The house was quiet except for the soft hum of central air-conditioning and the distant tick of an antique clock.

Flint led the way through the foyer toward the back of the house. Gaspar's home office buzzed with electronic activity. Multiple monitors displayed data streams while keyboards and communication equipment occupied the workspace.

Flint got a whiff of strong Cuban coffee. He looked around for the coffee pot.

"Bad night?" Gaspar glanced up when they came through. "As you Texans would say, you two look like you've been rode hard and put up wet."

"Drake needs to sleep," Flint replied with a nod. "I could use some coffee."

"Second door on the right." Gaspar gestured Drake to head down the hallway. "Clean sheets. Fresh towels."

"I'll take a pill and grab some shut-eye, and I'll be good as new." Drake headed toward the guest room without argument. The shoulder wound and blood loss had finally caught up with him.

After he heard Drake's door close, Flint poured a coffee and settled into the chair facing Gaspar's desk. The coffee was thick as motor oil and twice as strong. "Cole's got Jason Fisher and Lizzy Pace."

"Figured it was something like that when you called." Gaspar's fingers seemed to move across multiple keyboards simultaneously.

"What do you have so far?"

"Devon Cole says he owns more businesses than Amazon, Alphabet, and Apple combined. *Tripple A Plus*, he calls it. Shipping. Logistics. Tech services. Media companies. Even a space flight program. He's got tentacles everywhere." Gaspar pulled up financial records on one of the larger monitors. "But for your purposes, here's what's interesting."

The screen displayed a complex network diagram showing money flows between dozens of companies. Lines and arrows formed a spider web of financial connections that would take an army of forensic accountants months to untangle.

"See these cash transfers?" Gaspar highlighted several transaction patterns. "Shell companies moving massive amounts through Mexico and around the world. Way more money than any of his most successful legitimate businesses generate."

Flint studied the financial web until he spotted the most important point. The numbers were staggering. "Drug money? Harry Fisher, Jason's father, was in the opioid pill mill business with Cole way back when. Nothing I've seen so far suggests Cole got out of that business after Harry Fisher did."

"Probably. Fentanyl has mostly supplanted the opioid market, but it makes sense. And look at this." Gaspar switched to satellite imagery of several other ocean platforms. "Cole's got seventeen research facilities in international waters. Most are legitimate. Oil exploration. Marine biology. Renewable energy development."

"Most?"

"One is the jewel in his crown." Gaspar zoomed in on a platform three hundred miles west of San Francisco. "This beauty."

Flint studied the image of the structure that dominated the screen. At a glance, he noticed it was seven levels above the waterline. Multiple helicopter pads and a runway suitable for Flint's Pilatus or maybe Harriers. Industrial cranes and processing equipment.

Flint had seen and even visited such platforms before. But this one was massive enough to house hundreds of people. It looked like an oil rig crossed with a small city.

"What's Cole call the place?"

"New Geneva." Gaspar grinned. "Clever name. Sounds boring and scientific to regulators, but it's ironic. Geneva's where international laws get made. New Geneva is where Cole reigns supreme and makes his own laws."

Flint's satellite phone buzzed. Kim Otto's number appeared on the screen. He could hear the tension in her voice before she even spoke.

"This is Flint." He answered on the second ring after he put the call on speaker. "I'm here with Gaspar."

"Hey, Chico. Got the intel you wanted." Otto greeted Gaspar before she delivered the bad news. "We suspect Cole's floating platform is a base for illegal activities. We believe there's a drug processing operation and possibly other crimes going on. Disguised as the corporate headquarters for several of his marine research operations and other legitimate enterprises."

Which was what Flint had suspected, but confirmation was good. "Can the Bureau breach the place?"

"Physically? Sure. We've got equipment and manpower. But practically speaking, no. International waters plus Cole's political protection makes it untouchable through normal channels." Otto lowered her voice as if she was concerned about being overheard. "Our satellite surveillance also shows increased activity over the past twenty-four hours."

"What about Cole? Did he land there with hostages?" Flint asked. "He took Jason Fisher and a woman from Fisher's estate on Windsor Island a couple of hours ago."

"Not yet. But New Geneva is all the way across the country from Miami and three hundred miles off the coast of California. Give him time," Otto replied. "You think he is eliminating witnesses? That might give us jurisdiction, if they're Americans."

"Hard to know," Flint said.

"It'll be difficult to eliminate Jason Fisher. The public outcry would land him on death row somewhere," Gaspar said. "Fisher is beloved. He might also be the only billionaire on the planet who is more powerful than Cole. Which puts Cole between a rock and a hard place."

Otto said slowly, "So he's running an active criminal empire through legitimate businesses. New Geneva is where he conducts operations too sensitive for anywhere else."

"Which means it's a place where he could kill two people and get away with it." Flint absorbed the implications. "What kind of illegal activity?"

"International drug trafficking. Money laundering. Contract murders. We're talking about a criminal enterprise worth billions," Otto said. "And he's got the resources to disappear anyone who threatens him."

"Including Jason Fisher," Gaspar said flatly.

"Especially Jason Fisher. A tech billionaire investigating Cole's operations is exactly the kind of threat Cole would want to eliminate, if he can get away with it," Otto said.

"What about timeframe?" Flint asked. "How long before Cole moves against his hostages?"

"Based on the satellite activity, he's already mobilizing. Supply ships, personnel transfers. Whatever he's planning is happening soon," Otto said. "Hours, not days."

"Any intel on New Geneva's defenses?"

"Private security force. Paramilitary contractors. The place is a floating fortress with serious firepower," Otto replied. "I can't stress this enough. You're talking about assaulting a billionaire's private army in international waters. This is way beyond normal operations."

"Understood," Flint replied. Which was not even close to the assurances she wanted.

She paused a few moments, and no one filled the silence.

Before she rang off, Otto simply said, "Don't make me regret giving you all of this."

"Copy that, Mom," Flint said with a smirk as he ended the call and looked at Gaspar. "As expected. Conventional law enforcement can't touch him. Not legally, anyway."

"Exactly. He's created his own sovereign nation out there." Gaspar switched to architectural diagrams of the New Geneva platform. "But that doesn't mean he's unreachable."

"How so?" Flint had his own ideas, but he wanted to hear Gaspar's.

"The platform has submarine docking facilities. Large enough for submarine access during supply operations." Gaspar highlighted the underwater sections. "With the right resources, you could get close without being detected."

Flint considered the logistics again because Gaspar had identified the same solution he had come to. "I'd need a submarine."

"Funny you should mention that." Gaspar's grin widened. "Remember Captain Walsh? Owes you a favor from that Baja operation a few years back."

"Yeah, I recall."

"He's got connections at Naval Base Ventura County."

The pieces started falling into place. Cole's vast resources. Domestic and foreign contacts willing to bend rules. A billionaire's floating fortress operating outside all laws.

"Drake's in no condition for this kind of operation." Gaspar seemed genuinely worried, which Flint took seriously. Gaspar rarely worried.

"Drake's tougher than he looks. And I can't do this alone," Flint replied. "You want to come along?"

"My wife would kill me. Assuming I survived the assault." Gaspar pulled up nautical charts showing approach routes to the platform. "Cole made a mistake when he grabbed Fisher. Now he's doing more than covering up old crimes, for which he might have been forgiven. One billionaire trying to destroy another? That's a recipe for a long prison term when he's caught. Which he will be. No jury will give Devon Cole any sort of sympathetic verdict."

"Normal people have jaundiced views of billionaires, for sure," Flint agreed. "Love 'em or hate 'em. No middle ground. And no one believes billionaires can be trusted."

Flint studied New Geneva's building plans on Gaspar's screens. Seven levels of criminal enterprise protected by international law and private security.

Two hostages, one of whom might already be dead. The other too visible and powerful for a quick death.

On top of that, the platform looked impregnable from every angle.

An impossible mission with no backup and no official support.

Flint smirked. "When do we leave?"

"Walsh's contact can be ready to move in six hours. It'll take you that long to get ready and get out there." Gaspar was already working his phones. "But understand what you're walking into. Cole's platform is a floating fortress. It's also his personal kingdom where he makes all the rules. Once you breach New Geneva, you'll be totally on your own."

Flint replied, "The bigger they are, the harder they fall."

"If you intend to kill yourself, please call Scarlett and tell her. Because she'll have my hide if she finds out I knew what you were doing and didn't report in," Gaspar said.

"Don't worry. She's your boss, but she's the closest thing to a sister I've got." Flint smirked again. "I'll handle Scarlett. I've been doing it my whole life."

Gaspar nodded and reached for another secure phone. Through the office window, the first hints of dawn were beginning to lighten the Miami sky. "Get some sleep. I'll make some calls."

CHAPTER 47

March 21

Coconut Grove

FLINT'S PHONE BUZZED AT 6:30 a.m., cutting through the morning silence. He saw Spanish moss hanging motionless from ancient live oak trees outside Gaspar's windows and the air carried the faint scent of jasmine through the open window. He'd managed maybe two hours of sleep on Gaspar's leather couch. His body felt stiff all over.

He glanced at the screen and picked up the call. "This is Flint."

"Walsh here. Rendezvous coordinates confirmed for this evening."

Flint's back protested from the night on the unforgiving surface coupled with fatigue and anticipation. "Timeline?"

Walsh said, "Flight to Santa Barbara. Then helicopter transfer. My submarine surfaces at 1500 hours Pacific time."

"Copy that," Flint replied.

"We can pull your gear together on the sub. Tell me what you need," Walsh said.

"Thanks." Flint considered the necessary gear for the mission. "Waterproof communications equipment sealed in protective cases. Diving equipment tested and double-checked. Weapons cleaned and loaded. Everything needs to fit into two compact black tactical bags, organized for rapid deployment in hostile waters."

"We've got everything you need," Walsh said before he disconnected the call.

Flint climbed off the couch and headed toward the kitchen for coffee. Gaspar was already there. He'd probably been there several hours already. He didn't sleep because of the pain in his leg from an old injury on the job when he was with the FBI.

Drake emerged from the guest bedroom moving like a man testing his limits. His left arm was still in the sling, but he was using it, and his right hand was steady and sure. The pain medication and sleep had restored some color to his face. His jaw remained set with determination. He refused to be sidelined.

"Walsh says he's good to go," Flint reported. "We need to be wheels-up in two hours. Refuel in Nevada. Then on to Santa Barbara."

"Walsh will have skilled personnel on board," Gaspar said while refilling his mug with the sweet, syrupy Cuban coffee he preferred. "He'll provide whatever you need. Just ask."

"Thanks." Flint drained the coffee and placed his mug in the sink. "Ready, Drake?"

"Been ready since yesterday."

Drake tested his shoulder's range of motion, rotating the joint slowly and gauging his limitations. Movement was restricted but functional enough for what they needed to do. Pain flickered across his features but was quickly suppressed.

"Walsh's pilot knows the drill," Gaspar said. "He's done submarine pickups before."

"How many times?" Flint asked. It was no job for an amateur.

"Don't worry. Navy contractor for five years before Walsh recruited him." Gaspar handed them coffee to go in paper cups with tight fitting lids. "Jimmy Restrepo. Former Coast Guard, knows the Pacific like his backyard."

Flint's encrypted phone buzzed while he was reviewing Gaspar's intelligence files on Cole's financial network. The caller ID showed his DNA lab contact, Lydia Brimley.

He held up a finger to indicate he needed to take the call and walked into the next room for privacy.

"Michael Flint."

"Hey, Flint. I have preliminary results on that genealogy search. We found several promising familial matches in the databases."

Flint set down the financial reports and gave the call his full attention. "What kind of matches?"

"Multiple partial connections that point to the same family tree. The surname keeps coming up as Kellerman. But here's the thing. I need the actual DNA sample to run confirmation testing," Lydia said. "The genetic profile you sent was sufficient for the initial search, but for definitive results, I need the physical evidence."

"How definitive are we talking?"

"With the actual sample, I can give you a 99 percent confidence level on familial relationships. Without it, this stays preliminary."

Flint considered his options. Sheriff Milliken had been cooperative so far, but asking for physical evidence was a bigger step. Destroying the chain of custody could prevent prosecution of the killer.

"How long for the confirmation testing once you have the sample?"

"Twenty-four hours. Maybe less," Lydia replied.

"I'll get you the sample."

Flint ended the call and pressed number one on the speed dial. Katie Scarlett had occupied that position on his phone since forever. She was the closest thing to a sister he'd ever had.

"Don't even think about telling me you're gonna bail on taking Maddy to Disney World, Flint," Scarlett said when she picked up the call. Maddy was her seven-year-old daughter. Flint adored the kid and the feeling was mutual.

"Wouldn't dream of it," Flint replied with a grin in his voice. "But I need a favor. Can you drive to Mount Warren, Texas? Small town, about seven hours from Houston."

"I know where it is. And I know why you're aware of the place," Scarlett said, cutting his explanations short. "When do you need me to go?"

"Today if possible. Tomorrow at the latest."

Scarlett gave an exasperated sigh that traveled across the miles. "You're finally looking at your mother's case. Good. What's the job you need me to do?"

"Pick up evidence from the local sheriff. A new DNA sample from Baker's case," Flint explained. "Play it by ear, but you may need to pose as my forensic consultant."

"Hostilities?"

"None. The sheriff's cooperative. He's expecting someone from my team." Flint paused. "This one's important, Scarlett. If we can identify this guy, we might be able to solve Marilyn Baker's murder."

"I'll leave within the hour. Text me the sheriff's contact information and what exactly I'm picking up."

"Copy that. And Scarlett? Handle this one personally. Don't delegate," Flint said. "And it should be obvious, but don't discuss this with anyone else."

"Understood," she replied before she disconnected.

Gaspar and Drake gave Flint an inquisitive look when he returned, but he didn't explain. They knew nothing about Marilyn Baker and, for now, Flint intended to keep it that way.

"Eighteen hours maximum before this becomes an international incident," Flint replied as if there had been no interruption in the conversation.

Gaspar nodded. "Fisher's disappearance is already generating media attention. Questions are being asked."

Flint nodded. "We need to move."

"Car's waiting outside," Gaspar said, gesturing toward the front door. "Cuban kid who doesn't speak English and won't remember your faces."

They headed for the door through Gaspar's hallway, past framed photographs of old Havana and vintage maps of Miami. No time for lengthy goodbyes, even if they'd been prone to offer them.

The drive back to the Pilatus took twenty-two minutes through early morning traffic. The Pilatus waited on the sun-baked tarmac like a sleek metal bird.

Drake performed the preflight inspection methodically despite his injured shoulder, while Flint dealt with the paperwork. The morning sun beat down mercilessly on the concrete and sweat beaded on their foreheads as they worked.

"Fuel stop in Nevada," Drake said, settling carefully into the co-pilot seat and adjusting his sling. "Then straight through to California."

Flint started the engines, contacted the tower for permission to take off, and then taxied onto the runway.

The Pilatus lifted off smoothly into the pale dawn sky, banking west as Miami's sprawl fell away beneath them. The city's concrete and steel gave way to the endless green expanse of the Everglades and then the sparkling waters of the Gulf.

The flight to Nevada was scheduled for four hours. Flint kept the aircraft at thirty thousand feet and speed steady.

They touched down at a private Nevada airfield Flint had used before. Twenty minutes on the ground for refueling and a chance to grab sandwiches and coffee from the weathered FBO building that looked like it had been baking in the sun for decades. Which it probably had. But it provided basic services, fuel desk, restrooms, vending machines, and gallons of coffee.

Flint checked the news on his phone, scrolling through financial websites and business channels, while he waited for the fuel to fill.

"Fisher's people are starting to ask questions," he told Drake. "Stock price is down three percent on 'uncertainty about CEO whereabouts.'"

"How long before authorities get involved?" Drake asked.

"Not long." Flint finished the fueling and replaced the hose. "We've got a few hours to find Fisher before this becomes too big to contain."

They were airborne again quickly. The Pacific Ocean eventually appeared on the horizon like a blue promise. Soon enough they began their descent into Santa Barbara.

The private airfield near Santa Barbara nestled between rolling hills covered in chaparral and eucalyptus trees, a single runway surrounded by hangars and palm trees that swayed in the ocean breeze.

The Bell 412 helicopter wouldn't arrive for a while yet. The operational delay gave them time to have a decent meal and make a few calls before they headed out to meet Walsh.

When they returned, the Bell sat waiting on the tarmac, painted in civilian research colors. White with blue stripes that suggested legitimate scientific operations.

The pilot, Jimmy Restrepo, stood beside the aircraft checking his flight gear with the methodical attention of a man whose life depended on details. Mid-forties, weathered face lined by years of coastal flying, steady hands suggested countless successful missions over hostile waters.

"Flint and Drake? Jimmy Restrepo. Captain Walsh says to give you guys whatever you need." His firm handshake and careful once-over was the quick assessment of an operator evaluating a new team. "Ready to launch? There's a storm out there. We should be okay but get a wiggle on."

They climbed into the Bell. Restrepo ran through his preflight checklist, checking instruments and controls with the kind of attention that kept helicopters in the air and passengers alive.

"Walsh is moving into position for an on-time connection," Restrepo said, adjusting his headset as he coordinated with Walsh via encrypted radio. "Weather's good. Seas are calm so far. Here we go."

The Bell lifted off. Restrepo banked west toward the Pacific, leaving California's golden coastline behind as they flew. Below them, the ocean stretched endlessly toward the horizon. Mist shrouded the Pacific as they flew west toward open ocean.

CHAPTER 48

March 21
Pacific Ocean

"SUBMARINE RENDEZVOUS IN ABOUT ninety minutes," Restrepo's voice came through their headsets.

The Bell broke into clear air above the cloud layer. Two hundred miles of ocean stretched below, empty except for the occasional whitecap. No ships visible on the horizon. No visible aircraft nearby in the vast Pacific sky.

"There," Restrepo pointed ahead through the cockpit windscreen. "Right on schedule."

A dark shape broke the surface a thousand yards away. Water cascaded in white torrents from its black hull as the USS Monterey emerged like a surfacing whale. The submarine stabilized in the gentle Pacific swells, its conning tower plainly visible.

"Beautiful sight," Restrepo said approvingly. "Walsh runs a tight operation."

He positioned the helicopter in a steady hover fifty feet above the submarine's wet deck, the downdraft created circles of disturbed water around the vessel.

"Standard personnel transfer," Restrepo said through the headset, his voice focused as he adjusted for the conditions. "Both of you can go down together, but we've got a front moving in faster than forecast."

"Seems like you've done this before," Drake teased as he watched the rescue basket moving into position.

"Twelve times. Piece of cake once you know the drill," Restrepo said with a grin. "You?"

Drake nodded. "Marines."

Restrepo replied. "Semper Fi."

Flint said, "Anything else we need to know right now?"

"Headwinds cost us extra fuel getting here. We've got enough to get back, but no margin for delays. Weather's getting worse and I don't want to be flying this route in an hour," Restrepo replied, turning his full attention to the task at hand.

Below them, the USS Monterey rolled in moderate swells under an overcast sky that had darkened considerably in the past hour. Light rain spattered the submarine's deck, and the wind had picked up enough to make the hull slick but still manageable.

"How's the shoulder?" Flint asked Drake as they watched the rescue basket sway in the freshening breeze.

"Functional," Drake replied, eyeing the deteriorating conditions. "Let's make this quick before the weather gets worse."

"I'll handle the basket," Flint said. "You focus on not reopening that wound."

On the submarine's deck, four crew members in foul-weather gear hustled. They had a narrow window before the submarine would have to dive.

"Sub's rolling about ten degrees and the wind's gusting to twenty knots," Restrepo reported. "Conditions are marginal but doable. Walsh wants you aboard now."

Flint climbed into the basket first, then helped Drake settle beside him, keeping the injured shoulder protected as well as conditions allowed.

"Quick and steady," Flint said as the basket began its descent through the gray, gusty downdraft and light rain.

The basket swayed as they dropped through the variable winds, but the crew below had good control of the guidelines. The submarine's moderate rolling was predictable, and the deck crew timed their movements accordingly.

"Coming down on the next level roll," the crew chief called out, his voice clear despite the wind. "Steady... steady... now!"

Salt spray stung their faces as the submarine's crew guided them safely onto the deck within challenging conditions.

The basket touched down firmly as the submarine crested a swell. Flint absorbed the landing and quickly helped Drake out. They moved fast toward the hatch.

An urgent call from the submarine's radio: "We need to dive now."

Tall, lean, gray-haired with the bearing of a man who'd commanded vessels in hostile waters around the world. Career Navy officer obvious every confident movement.

"Flint," Walsh said with a slight nod of acknowledgment. "Been a long time since Kandahar. Welcome aboard," Walsh said as they stepped out of the basket onto the submarine's deck. His voice carried over the sound of waves against the hull. "Welcome to the most unofficial operation in Naval history. We need to move fast. Let's get below."

Above them, Restrepo was already reeling in the empty basket and preparing to depart, the first half of his mission accomplished without leaving a trace of evidence.

"Anyone watching just saw a routine personnel transfer," Walsh said as they descended into the submarine's cramped interior through the narrow hatch.

Above them, the metal cover sealed with a resonant clang that echoed through the vessel like the closing of a vault.

"Captain," the officer of the deck called from below. "We need to dive now."

The submarine slipped beneath the surface with barely a ripple, leaving only disturbed water where moments before a nuclear vessel had floated under the sky. The hull creaked softly as they descended, the weight of the Pacific pressing against the steel that separated them from the crushing depths.

"Welcome aboard the Monterey," Walsh said, leading them through corridors lined with pipes and instruments humming efficiently. "We've got two hours to New Geneva. Time to get you ready for the impossible."

The submarine's sonar painted a picture of empty ocean ahead, its electronic pulses revealing no surface contacts, no underwater threats. The steady rhythm of the engines along with the crew's quiet professionalism and calm competence kept submarines operational in the world's most dangerous waters.

The submarine ran silent through Pacific depths, carrying them toward their rendezvous with Devon Cole's kingdom.

"Next time we see daylight," he told Drake, "this will all be over."

"And with any luck, we'll still be alive to see it," Drake replied flatly.

The submarine ran silent through Pacific depths. Two hours to New Geneva. Flint had checked his gear twice and reviewed the platform schematics until he could navigate them blindfolded.

His encrypted phone showed a new message. The DNA lab.

Flint moved to a quiet corner of the submarine's cramped communications area and opened the secure email.

"Confirmation complete. Definitive familial match to Kellerman family DNA. 99.3% confidence level. The subject shares genetic markers consistent with being a close blood relative. Brother, father, or son of Raymond Kellerman.

Full genetic analysis attached. Dr. Lydia Brimley, Houston Forensics Laboratory."

Flint stared at the screen. After all these years, they had the killer's family name. But Raymond Kellerman was the principal who'd been pursuing his mother. The obvious suspect Milliken had already identified.

He opened his laptop and connected to the submarine's satellite internet. Public records searches. Genealogy databases. Social Security Death Index.

Raymond Kellerman. Principal at Mount Warren Elementary for thirty years. Married to Helen Kellerman. Two children. Clean record except for a drunk driving arrest.

But there was more.

A brother. Thomas "Tommy" Kellerman. Five years younger than Raymond.

Flint pulled up more records. Tommy's trail was messier. Multiple addresses. Spotty employment history. Arrested twice for public intoxication. No marriage license on record.

The timeline fit. Tommy would have been the right age when Marilyn Baker was murdered. The right family connection.

Flint cross-referenced the addresses. Tommy had lived in Mount Warren during the time period when the murder happened.

More searches revealed fragments of a troubled life. Emergency room visits. A brief stint in county jail for disorderly conduct. Then, about a year after Marilyn Baker's murder, Thomas Kellerman disappeared from public records entirely.

Flint leaned back in his chair. The original investigation had focused on Father Preston and briefly considered Raymond Kellerman. But nobody had looked at the principal's troubled younger brother. The man whose DNA was on his mother's clothing.

Something he'd need to follow up on after he finished.

He closed the laptop. The submarine's sonar pinged steadily in the background. New Geneva was getting closer. Cole's fortress waited ahead in the darkness.

CHAPTER 43

March 21
Pacific Ocean

TWO HOURS UNDERWATER. THE submarine had glided through black Pacific depths in complete silence. Flint felt the subtle vibration of the electric motors through the deck plating beneath his boots. The quiet hum of machinery keeping them alive two hundred feet below the surface.

"Approaching target," Captain Walsh announced. "Coming to periscope depth. Target bearing two-seven-zero. Range, four thousand yards."

Flint moved to the periscope housing. The USS Monterey's attack periscope was smaller than he'd expected. No wasted space or weight.

"Take a look," Walsh said. "Tell me what you think."

Flint pressed his eye to the scope and adjusted the focus. Pacific swells filled the eyepiece. Gray water under an overcast sky. He rotated the periscope slowly, scanning the horizon.

Then he saw it.

New Geneva rose from the Pacific like a steel mountain. The massive structure dominated the seascape, dwarfing everything around it. Seven levels above the waterline. Multiple towers and platforms connected by bridges and walkways. Industrial cranes and communication arrays bristled from every surface.

It looked like an oil rig crossed with a small city.

"Wow," Drake said quietly. He was watching over Flint's shoulder through the secondary scope. "That thing's huge."

Flint studied the fortress methodically. The lower levels showed oil-rig architecture. Massive support columns. Steel grating. Industrial equipment. Functional and weathered by salt spray and Pacific storms.

The middle levels were different. Glass-walled sections. Modern corporate architecture. Clean lines and reflective surfaces that suggested executive offices and conference rooms.

The upper levels were pure luxury. Glass penthouse structures that caught and reflected the gray Pacific light. Multiple helicopter landing pads. Observation decks with panoramic views. Everything a billionaire would want in his floating palace.

"How many people you figure?" Flint asked.

"Satellite intel suggests two to three hundred," Walsh replied. "Crew quarters on levels two and three. Security barracks on level four. Executive housing above that."

Flint tracked the periscope down to study the waterline. The platform's base disappeared into the dark Pacific. Massive. Semi-submersible. Built to survive anything the ocean could throw at it.

"Submarine access?"

"Lower level. Underwater docking bay." Walsh pointed to his sonar display. "We can't see it from here, but satellite imagery shows an opening on the north side. Pressurized airlock system. Large enough for our submarines."

Drake studied the defensive positions. "Security?"

"Private contractors. Maybe two hundred personnel. Small arms, crew-served weapons, possibly surface-to-air missiles." Walsh's expression was grim. "This place is a fortress."

Flint continued his visual reconnaissance. The platform bristled with communication equipment. Radar arrays. Satellite dishes. Electronic capabilities that could jam communications and disable guidance systems.

"Cole's operating like a guy who calls all the shots," Walsh observed.

"Which is exactly who he is. International waters," Flint agreed. "No jurisdiction. No oversight. He can do whatever he wants out here."

The structure looked impregnable. A billionaire's kingdom floating three hundred miles from the nearest coastline. Protected by an army of contractors and the Pacific Ocean itself. Not quite as difficult as Cole's space exploration company, but tough enough.

A lesser man with a lesser fortune and fewer political connections could never have pulled this off.

Walsh checked his navigation display. "Approach complete. We're in position."

Flint stepped back from the periscope considering entry points, defensive positions, and escape routes. It would take an armed assault to breach Cole's floating empire. Even then, force would be met with deadly force.

Stealth was a better option.

Flint studied the structure through the periscope one more time. "Seven levels above water, three below."

"We believe the service elevator runs from the submarine level straight up to level six," Drake confirmed while watching through the secondary scope.

Walsh nodded. "Looks like your intel was solid."

"We had several sources. One is a former employee," Flint explained. "Worked there for eight months before Cole fired him. Disgruntled enough to talk, for the right price."

"The intel could be outdated but given the difficulty of making structural adjustments out here, it should still be good." Drake tracked the periscope across the patrol boats. "Security rotations every four hours. Guard change at the docking bay in eighteen minutes."

"Same schedule the supply boat captain described," Flint agreed. "Cole runs this place like a corporate operation. Everything's documented, everything's routine. He's hosted politicians and business contacts here to show the place off. Those people talk too much."

Walsh checked his tactical display. "What about internal security?"

"All the high-tech security you'd expect from Cole. Some of the low-tech stuff like motion sensors in the main stairwells and key cards for elevator access are easily bypassed," Flint said. "The service areas use electronic locks. Maintenance staff wants quick access during emergencies."

"Hostage location?" Walsh asked.

"Executive guest quarters, level five or six," Drake replied. "The helicopter pilot who flew them out there confirmed they went to the luxury levels. Cole's treating them like VIP prisoners. At least, for now."

Flint stepped back from the periscope. "Extraction route's up to the helicopter pad on level seven. Restrepo will be standing by for rooftop pick up."

"Assuming everything goes according to plan," Drake said.

"When does it ever?" Flint replied. "Cole will do everything he can to keep us from reaching the helipad. If we make it to the helo with the hostages and take off, he won't shoot us down. No way he'd kill Jason Fisher in front of all those government satellites watching his fortress twenty-four-seven."

Drake lowered the secondary periscope. His expression was thoughtful. "It's a hard target. But not impossible."

"How so?" Walsh asked.

"Size works against them. Too big to defend completely. They'll have strong points and weak points. The underwater approach gives us the advantage of surprise." Drake paused. "Question is, can we get in and get out before they know we're there?"

Walsh checked his sonar display. "Current sets us up for a perfect approach. Weather's holding. No surface traffic. We'll launch you in the Swimmer Delivery Vehicle. We use them in naval operations regularly. Direct underwater approach to the docking bay."

"I'm familiar with the SDV. We've used them before," Flint said.

"SDV prepped and ready," Walsh confirmed. "Two-person cockpit, battery power, silent running. You'll stay dry and invisible all the way to the target."

"Range?" Flint asked.

"More than enough. Launches from here, takes you directly to Cole's submarine bay. No surface signature, no radar contact."

Drake nodded approvingly. "A lot easier on the shoulder than swimming."

"Should work," Flint nodded. "We'll be exposed and vulnerable once we reach the docking bay, but it's our best option given Drake's bum shoulder."

Flint studied the tactical situation. Two men against a fortress. Cole's private army against whatever weapons they could carry. Jason Fisher and Lizzy Pace somewhere inside that steel mountain, probably running out of time.

"How long to reach the docking bay?"

"Twenty minutes underwater in the SDV," Walsh replied. "We'll stay submerged until you're clear and then we'll head out. Your helo will handle extraction. Restrepo's got enough fuel for the round trip?"

"Bell 412 can make it to California and back with fuel to spare," Flint confirmed.

The submarine continued its final approach toward New Geneva. Above them, Cole's fortress waited. Somewhere inside those steel walls, two hostages were praying for rescue that might never come.

Flint checked his gear one final time. Weapons. Explosives. Communication equipment. Would it be enough to assault an impossible target?

The periscope revealed New Geneva getting closer. More details became visible. Guard towers. Patrol boats. Armed security personnel moving along the upper platforms.

"Fifteen minutes to SDV launch," Walsh announced.

Flint and Drake moved to the submarine's deployment bay. The Swimmer Delivery Vehicle waited in its launch cradle. Sleek, torpedo-shaped, just large enough for two operators in the enclosed cockpit.

"Final equipment check," Walsh said. They had already strapped their gear into waterproof compartments. Weapons. Explosives. Communication equipment.

"SDV systems are green," the submarine's engineer reported. "Battery at full charge, navigation programmed, silent running mode engaged."

Flint climbed into the pilot position. Drake settled into the co-pilot seat despite his shoulder. The cockpit sealed with a soft hiss of pressurized air.

"Comms check," Walsh's voice came through their headsets.

"Copy," Flint replied. "We're ready."

"Launching SDV in three... two... one..."

The cradle released. The mini-submarine dropped away from the USS Monterey into black Pacific water.

Flint engaged the electric motor. No sound. No vibration. Just silent forward motion through the depths.

Above them, Cole's fortress waited. Somewhere inside, two hostages were running out of time.

The SDV's navigation display showed their target bearing. Twenty minutes to the most dangerous infiltration of Flint's career.

CHAPTER 50

March 22
New Geneva

THE SDV BROKE THE surface inside New Geneva's underwater docking bay. Emergency lighting cast harsh shadows across concrete walls. The facility was as Flint had expected. Three submarine berths. Massive pumps cycling water in and out of pressurized chambers.

Flint opened the cockpit. Cold air rushed in. The smell of diesel fuel and machine oil. He climbed out onto the metal dock and helped Drake from the co-pilot seat.

"Shoulder okay?"

"Good enough." Drake moved normally. The pain medication was holding.

They secured their gear and moved toward the service elevator. Two security cameras covered the docking area. Red lights indicated active monitoring. But Flint's intelligence had been accurate. The former employee who'd worked here for eight months had described the security protocols. Night shift reduced monitoring staff, and they prioritized the upper levels over the submarine bay.

Which meant they had ninety seconds before someone noticed the SDV.

The service elevator required a key card. Flint used the electronic bypass device and the lock disengaged with a soft click.

They rode the elevator up in silence. The doors opened onto level six. Here was Cole's boutique hotel providing all the comforts of palatial homes to his important visitors. Plush carpeting and mahogany walls. Everything a billionaire's guests would expect.

Flint checked the hallway. Unoccupied. Two security cameras at opposite ends, but they were positioned to watch the main elevator bank, not the service area.

"Guest suites should be this way."

He led Drake down the corridor past the instantly recognizable art on the walls. Monet's water lilies. A Picasso that belonged in the Museum of Modern Art. Van Gogh's swirling brushstrokes that Flint had only seen in textbooks. Cole hoarded masterpieces like trophies. More wealth hanging on these walls than the annual budget of several countries Flint could name.

Crystal chandeliers cast prismatic light across hand-carved mahogany paneling. Thick Persian carpet absorbed every footfall, creating an eerie silence that made the place feel like a floating mausoleum.

The first three suites they checked were empty. Flint entered each one quickly, looking for signs of recent occupancy and found none.

The fourth suite was different. Rumpled bedding. Personal items on the nightstand. Flint wondered briefly who and where the occupant was.

"Next floor?" Drake whispered.

"Try the end of the hall first."

The corner suite was larger than the others. Two bedrooms connected by a sitting area.

Flint heard Jason Fisher's voice through the door. Low but unmistakable.

He tried the door handle. Locked. He pulled out the electronic bypass device. Seconds later, the mechanism disengaged with a soft click. He opened the door slowly.

Jason Fisher sat in a leather chair by the window, still dressed in the clothes he was wearing when he was abducted. He looked up as Flint entered.

Relief flooded his face. "How did you find me?"

"Long story." Flint checked the windows. Bulletproof glass. "We're getting you out of here."

Lizzy Pace stood in the connecting doorway. She was pale and disheveled but unharmed.

"Let's go." Drake was already moving toward the door. "We need to move fast."

"Wait." Frankie Tantanella stepped into the room from the hallway.

Drake's hand moved to draw his weapon. He aimed it directly at Frankie.

"Easy." Frankie raised both hands, palms out. "I'm not here to fight."

"Why are you here?" Flint kept his voice level.

"Cole tried to kill Lizzy. She's my wife." Frankie's eyes found Lizzy's across the room. The look that passed between them was difficult to watch. Naked emotions always were.

"Why should we trust you?" Flint gave him a level stare.

Frankie closed the door. "I know every square inch of this platform. Every guard rotation. Every blind spot. You'll never get out of here alive without my help."

Flint studied him for a moment. He had a point and there was no time to argue. "What's the play?"

"Service stairs to level eight. Helicopter pad is on the north side," Frankie said. "I can get you there, but Cole will figure out what's happening soon enough."

"What's on level seven?" Flint asked, although he already knew.

"Cole's penthouse. He occupies the entire floor. You go there, you'll never get out," Frankie said flatly.

A loud alarm began sounding throughout New Geneva. Red lights flashed in the hallway.

"Looks like Cole has been alerted." Drake checked his weapon. "How many security personnel?"

"Two hundred contractors. But most are on levels one through four. The upper levels are lightly patrolled during night shift because Cole's guests generally have no desire to sneak out in the middle of the night. Nor do they appreciate being watched." Frankie moved to the window and looked down at the dark Pacific. "Cole's in his penthouse. He'll mobilize everything he has once he realizes what's happening."

Flint gestured toward the door. "Lead the way."

They left the luxury of level six behind and entered a stairwell that belonged to New Geneva's working areas. Concrete walls. Metal stairs. Industrial lighting humming with electrical current.

Frankie took the lead up the stairs toward the helipad while holding Lizzy's hand. Years of working on New Geneva had given him knowledge that no blueprint could provide. He knew which stairs were monitored and which were ignored by the security systems, among other useful intel.

"Level eight access is through the maintenance area," Frankie said over his shoulder. "Once we're on the helipad, you'll be exposed."

"Pilot arrives shortly," Flint replied.

Voices echoed from below. Security teams were mobilizing.

They climbed faster.

Drake's breathing became labored as each step sent fresh pain through his wounded shoulder. Sweat beaded on his forehead despite the cool air. But he kept pace without complaint.

Frankie stayed close to Lizzy, guiding her up the metal stairs.

The level eight door was reinforced steel. Frankie produced a key card and swiped it through the reader. Red light. No access.

"Cole's already locked down the system." Frankie tried the card again. Still red.

"Step aside." Flint pulled a shaped charge from his pack and pressed it against the reinforced hinges.

The adhesive backing held it in place while he armed the detonator.

"Ten seconds. Get back around the corner. Cover your head."

They moved into the adjacent corridor as Flint counted down and triggered the charge.

The explosion was sharp and focused, designed to shear metal without bringing down walls.

The blast hit them like a physical blow. Smoke billowed through the corridor, acrid and sharp. But the explosion did the job it was designed to do.

CHAPTER 51

March 22
New Geneva

THE MASSIVE DOOR TILTED inward and crashed to the concrete floor with a sound like thunder. The impact sent vibrations through New Geneva's superstructure. Metal fragments scattered across the floor, some pieces still glowing red-hot from the explosive force.

"So much for stealth," Drake muttered without humor while checking his weapon.

Alarms that had been distant background noise suddenly became urgent. Security teams would converge on their location within minutes.

They hurried to the helicopter pad access. Industrial metal stairs led up to level eight, the platform's roof. Service area with fuel lines, equipment storage, emergency gear. No windows, but heavy exterior doors leading to the landing pad.

Through the reinforced glass in the exit door, Flint saw landing lights marking the helicopter pad boundaries.

A circle of lights on New Geneva's north side. Empty now, but Restrepo would be monitoring the radio frequency. He'd arrive shortly.

"There." Frankie pointed. "Once you're on the pad, you're completely exposed until your pilot arrives."

Footsteps thundered up the stairwell behind them. Cole's security.

"Go." Frankie turned back toward the stairs. "I'll buy you as much time as I can."

"Frankie." Lizzy grabbed his arm, tears streaming down her face. "Come with us."

He looked at her with the same expression Flint had seen in Havana. A man who'd made peace with his choices.

"I've got unfinished business with Cole," he told her gently, giving her a sweet kiss. "I'll see you back at home in a few days."

A moment later, the first security guard appeared at the broken doorway. He raised his weapon.

Frankie's shots caught him in the chest, spinning him backward into the stairwell. Blood splattered against the concrete wall. Frankie dove behind a concrete pillar as return fire chipped fragments around his position.

More gunfire erupted from the stairwell.

Flint keyed his radio. "Restrepo, we need immediate pickup. Level eight, north pad."

"Copy. Sixty seconds out."

Might as well be an hour. Frankie was holding the stairwell, but more security teams were coming from other access points.

Flint pushed Jason and Lizzy forward while Drake provided covering fire.

They reached the exterior door and shoved it open. Cold Pacific wind hit them like a wall, carrying the salt spray and the deep rumble of the ocean far below.

The helicopter pad stretched ahead. A circle of harsh white landing lights turned the night into artificial day. Navigation lights stretched in every direction, marking the edges of Cole's floating empire. From this height, New Geneva felt like a city built on the edge of the world.

Rotor noise approached from the east. Restrepo's helicopter materialized out of the darkness. Navigation lights strobed in the night sky.

Gunfire erupted once more from the access door behind them.

Drake returned fire, grimacing as each shot sent pain through his wounded shoulder. But his aim stayed true.

The helicopter touched down with a thud that Flint felt through his boots. Rotor wash hit them like a hurricane, whipping debris and salt spray across the landing pad. The downdraft was so powerful it forced them to lean into the wind just to stay upright. The cabin door slid open, revealing the red-lit interior.

Flint rushed Jason and Lizzy toward the aircraft. Drake followed behind them, his shoulder bleeding again but functional.

While they hustled to the helo, Frankie took position at the access door, using the doorframe for cover. Automatic weapons fire erupted from the stairwell below. Cole's security teams were advancing up multiple levels. Frankie returned fire, forcing them back down the stairs.

More gunmen appeared from another stairwell. They had Frankie in the crossfire.

Muzzle flashes erupted from several directions. Frankie spun as a round tore through his shoulder, throwing him against the doorframe. Blood spread across his shirt, but he stayed on his feet.

He raised his weapon with his good arm and fired methodically at both stairwells, forcing Cole's people to take cover.

"Go!" he shouted over the gunfire.

Each shot must have sent agony through his wounded shoulder, but he kept firing. Buying seconds. Buying time for Lizzy to escape.

Muzzle flashes came from positions around the pad. Cole's security surrounded them.

Frankie fired at the nearest shooter. Then another. Drawing their attention away from Lizzy's escape.

A bullet hit him in the chest. He staggered but didn't fall.

Flint shoved Jason and Lizzy toward the helo. "Go! Get in!"

They ran across the landing pad, bent double against the rotor wash that threatened to knock them sideways. Jason's suit jacket flapped wildly in the artificial hurricane.

He reached the helicopter first and hauled himself up, then turned to help Lizzy. Her hair whipped around her face as she climbed into the cabin while Jason's hands steadied her against the buffeting wind.

Drake followed, his wounded shoulder screaming with each jarring step across the concrete. He dove through the cabin door as more gunfire erupted from the access door.

Flint was the last one aboard, throwing himself in as bullets sparked off the landing pad around them.

More shots came and Frankie went down. This time he didn't get up.

"Frankie!" Lizzy's scream cut through the rotor noise. She unbuckled and jumped toward the open helicopter door.

Flint blocked her and shoved her back into her seat.

Restrepo lifted off immediately, banking hard toward the east.

Below them, New Geneva lit up the sky with spotlights and muzzle flashes. Cole's fortress blazed with activity as security teams searched for threats that were already gone.

But Lizzy stared out where Frankie Tantanella's body lay motionless on the concrete.

Twenty-four years of loyalty to Devon Cole ended in thirty seconds of gunfire.

He'd died protecting the woman he'd loved since she was a sixteen-year-old girl. The life with Lizzy Pace that began when he led her away from a burning house in Kentucky all those years ago was finished.

Lizzy pressed her face against the helicopter's window, watching New Geneva disappear as they flew into the Pacific darkness.

"He saved us again," she whispered, tears streaming down her face.

Flint checked his watch. Three hours to California. Cole would be making calls, spinning the story attempting to contain the damage.

But it was too late. Jason Fisher was alive. Lizzy Pace was alive.

Flint had all the evidence he needed.

CHAPTER 52

Two nights later
Houston

FLINT HEARD THE CAR door slam in his driveway the night after he returned from New Geneva. He didn't look out the window. No reason to. No one came by at this time of night except Scarlett.

His home was a modest two-story structure in a quiet residential neighborhood. Clean lines, well-maintained but unremarkable. The living room where he waited was sparsely furnished. A couch, coffee table, and reading chair arranged around a small television. No personal photographs or decorative items cluttered the surfaces.

She opened the door without knocking and walked inside as if she belonged there. Which, he supposed, she did.

"You were supposed to pick up a DNA sample and get it to the lab," he said. "Nothing more."

Scarlett walked past him, poured two fingers of his best scotch into one of his heavy crystal glasses, and joined him in the living room without being invited. Wild black hair pulled back in a practical ponytail, sharp green eyes that missed nothing, athletic build suggesting she could handle herself in trouble. Which, of course, she could, courtesy of her years working for Uncle Sam. She wore jeans, boots, and a leather jacket that had seen plenty of use.

"Good to see you too," she said, raising her glass in a mock salute. "Glad you survived whatever the hell you were doing in the Pacific."

"Scarlett," he said, by way of warning.

"I got the sample, and hand carried it to the lab like you asked." She set the folder on his coffee table. "But I also spent time in Mount Warren asking questions."

Flint tightened his jaw. "I didn't authorize that."

"You didn't forbid it either. And since when do I take orders from you?" Scarlett opened the folder she had carried under her arm and spread documents across the coffee table. "And you were unreachable, not taking my calls, all for good reasons, I'm sure."

Flint stared at the papers. Church records. Interview notes. Photocopied newspaper clippings. "What did you find?"

"Tommy Kellerman had access to the church's confession schedules." Scarlett pulled out a handwritten list. "St. Michael's used volunteers for building maintenance. Tommy worked there for five years. Fixed broken windows, painted classrooms, cleaned the sanctuary."

Flint's ears perked up. "He had access to the church office?"

"Every Tuesday night. The secretary went home early and left him keys to lock up after he finished." Scarlett tapped another document. "Church board meeting minutes show complaints about Tommy. Drinking. Showing up late. Making inappropriate comments to female parishioners."

Flint scanned the meeting minutes. The complaints were dated six months before Marilyn Baker's murder.

"Raymond tried to protect his brother," Scarlett continued. "Used his position on the church board to keep Tommy from being fired. But people remember the tension between them."

"What kind of tension?"

"Raymond was embarrassed by Tommy's behavior. Tommy resented Raymond's success and respectability." Scarlett pulled out her interview notes. "I talked to five people who knew both brothers. Same story from all of them. Tommy was jealous of everything Raymond had."

Flint studied the timeline. Tommy's drinking got worse. His behavior more erratic. The complaints increased. Tommy got fired, over his brother's objections.

Then Marilyn Baker was murdered.

"Where's Tommy now?"

"That's the problem." Scarlett frowned and swigged her scotch. "He disappeared right after the murder. Left Mount Warren. Never came back."

"Any leads on where he went?" Flint asked.

"Working on it. But here's what I think happened." Scarlett arranged the documents in chronological order. "Tommy had been watching Marilyn. By all accounts, she was a beauty. You look a lot like her, by the way."

"Why is all of this relevant?"

"Tommy Kellerman used his church access to learn her schedule. Her routine. When she'd be alone."

"He was stalking her." Flint could see the pattern emerging. "And he used Raymond's reputation to cover his actions."

"Exactly. If anyone saw him at the church, he belonged there. Raymond's little brother, doing maintenance work." Scarlett paused. "The night she died, Tommy knew exactly where she'd be and when."

Flint looked at the evidence spread across his table. Scarlett had advanced the case more in three days than the original investigation had in years. She'd managed to find a lot more than he had. But to be fair, he hadn't been looking.

He shuffled through her notes. He was still annoyed that she'd gone ahead without permission. But she'd been right to do it.

"Good work," he said finally.

"Damn straight," Scarlett replied, finishing her drink and setting the glass down hard on the table to punctuate.

"Of course, none of this proves anything. Tommy Kellerman's DNA on her skirt doesn't mean he killed her. Unless we can get a confession," Flint said, thinking things through.

"Which means now you find Tommy Kellerman. Give him a chance to do the right thing after all these years," Scarlett said with a smirk. "You need to do it quick. Maddy's already packed for Disney. Spring break starts next week while I get back to my real job."

"I'll go over to Mount Warren tomorrow." Flint gave her a stern frown, which didn't phase her at all. She stood and walked out the same way she came in.

CHAPTER 53

One week later
Mount Warren, Texas

SHERIFF MILLIKEN'S OFFICE HADN'T changed since Flint's last visit. Same cluttered desk, same faded photographs on the walls, same coffee mug with a chip in the handle. Milliken looked up when Flint knocked on the doorframe.

"Well, I'll be damned. Didn't expect to see you back so soon." Milliken gestured to the chair across from his desk. "Please tell me you've got good news about that DNA."

Flint sat down and placed a folder on Milliken's desk. "Better than good. We found a match."

Milliken's eyes widened. "No kidding? Who?"

"Kellerman family male. They can't be any more specific without someone to match it to." Flint opened the folder and spread out Scarlett's research. "But Raymond had a younger brother. Thomas Kellerman. Tommy. Five years younger, lived in Mount Warren during the time of the murder."

Milliken leaned forward, studying the documents. "Son of a bitch. We never looked at the brother."

"Tommy had access to the church confession schedules through volunteer maintenance work. He knew exactly when Marilyn would be there alone." Flint pointed to the church records. "Multiple complaints about his behavior toward female parishioners. Drinking problem. Disappeared right after the murder."

"This is it." Milliken's voice held the excitement of a man who'd been working an unsolved case for decades. "This is what we missed."

"Possibly. Tommy might have an alibi. We'll need to find that out. It could also be DNA from Raymond's father or, less likely, an uncle or maybe even a cousin," Flint said. "But I want to interview Raymond. See what he knows about Tommy's behavior that night. Maybe find out where Tommy is now."

Milliken nodded. "Raymond's still the principal at the elementary school."

"Will you come with me? This needs to be official."

"Damn right I'll come." Milliken stood and reached for his hat. "I've been waiting thirty years to solve this case."

Five minutes later, they pulled into the parking lot of Mount Warren Elementary School. The brick building looked exactly like what it was. A small-town school, built decades ago and maintained on a tight budget ever since.

The hallways smelled of old-style floor wax on the polished linoleum as they moved relentlessly to the principal's office.

Raymond Kellerman was what Flint had expected. Mid-seventies, gray hair neatly combed, wearing a cardigan sweater despite the Texas heat. He looked up from his paperwork when they entered.

"Hello, Raymond," Milliken said. "This is Michael Flint. Private investigator. We need to talk to you about Marilyn Baker."

The color drained from Raymond's face.

"I don't understand," Raymond said carefully while looking Sheriff Milliken in the eye without blinking. "We discussed this years ago. I told you everything I knew about that poor girl."

"Did you?" Flint asked. "What about your brother?"

Raymond's hands began to shake. "Tommy? What does Tommy have to do with anything?"

"DNA techniques have vastly improved in the past thirty years. Using new techniques, the lab found DNA on the clothing Marilyn Baker was wearing when she died," Flint said. "The DNA was from one of your close male relatives."

Raymond's mouth opened but no words came out.

"Where is he, Raymond?" Milliken leaned forward. "Where's your brother?"

"I don't know what you're talking about." Raymond's voice was barely a whisper. "We lost touch when Tommy left town. I haven't seen him in years."

"The church records show Tommy had access to confession schedules," Flint continued. "He knew when Marilyn would be alone. He'd been watching her."

"That's not true."

"Isn't it? Because at least five people in this town remember Tommy's drinking problem. His inappropriate behavior around women. And they all remember how you protected him."

Raymond stood abruptly. "You need to leave."

Milliken said, "Not until you tell us where Tommy is."

"I want a lawyer." Raymond's voice was stronger now. Determined. "I'm not saying another word without a lawyer present."

Flint and Milliken exchanged glances. They'd pushed too hard too fast.

Raymond walked to his office door and opened it. "Please leave. Now."

"We'll go. But we'll be back after we've found your brother," Flint said on his way out.

Back at Milliken's office, the sheriff typed Tommy Kellerman's name into several database searches. After twenty minutes of searching, he shook his head.

"Nothing. No Social Security death record, no prison records, nothing after he left Mount Warren," Milliken said. "But it was a long time ago. Not everything was computerized back then. I'll make some calls."

Flint stared at the computer screen. Another dead end in a case that had defined his entire life without him even knowing it. He'd never known who his mother was while she was alive. Now, he might never know for certain who killed her.

He pulled out his phone and scrolled through his contacts until he found Rodney Rich, a criminal defense attorney he'd worked with on a few difficult cases. Rich owed him several favors.

"Rodney, it's Michael Flint. I'm looking for information. Guy's name is Thomas Kellerman."

"You think he's in state prison in Texas?" Rich asked.

"He left Mount Warren more than thirty years ago and hasn't been seen around there since. Could be several explanations for that, but prison makes sense with this guy. He was not a law-abiding citizen, by all accounts." Flint said.

"Prison records from that era are still in file boxes," Rich said. "But I've got connections with retired guards. Some of those guys remember everything. I can ask around. What's this about?"

"Personal matter. It's important."

"Give me a few days."

Flint spent those days unable to concentrate on anything else. He'd waited thirty-four years to learn his mother's name. Now he might finally know who killed her. He was surprised how important that information seemed all of a sudden.

He had lived his life in the moment. Never worrying about what tomorrow might bring or how yesterday might have been different. He liked it that way.

Marilyn Baker had turned his life upside down and he didn't like it.

Rich called while Flint was sitting in his living room, staring at the DNA report and reviewing Scarlett's interviews again.

"Found your man," Rich said. "Tommy Kellerman died at Eastham Unit. The guy who killed him was named Poe. Died of cancer about ten years ago."

Flint felt something cold settle in his chest. "How exactly did Kellerman die?"

"Guard I talked to remembered it clearly. Said Kellerman got caught stealing another inmate's chocolate bar from the commissary. Poe strangled him with his bare hands right there in the yard."

Strangled. The same way Marilyn Baker had died.

"You still there, Flint?"

"Yeah. Thanks, Rich."

Flint ended the call and sat in the silence of his empty house.

Tommy Kellerman had most likely murdered Marilyn Baker when she rejected him, and escaped justice for decades. But in the end, he'd died the same violent death he'd given her. Strangled by someone stronger, someone angrier, someone who decided Tommy's life was worth less than a chocolate bar.

Flint closed his eyes and tried to picture his mother's face from the photographs he'd found. She'd been twenty-three when she died. Beautiful. Devoted to her faith. Trying to raise a child alone in a world that wouldn't forgive her for being a single mother.

She'd never seen him grow up. Never knew what kind of man he'd become. Never learned that he'd spent his life finding people who couldn't be found.

Now he'd most likely found her killer. Dead fifteen years. Justice served by a lifer named Poe over something as meaningless as a candy bar.

It wasn't the ending Flint expected. But it was the only ending there would ever be.

CHAPTER 54

Three Months Later
Kentucky

FLINT STEPPED OUT OF his rental and stood for a moment in the gravel driveway, listening to the sound of laughter coming from inside the Fisher house. Real laughter. The kind that comes from relief and joy mixed together.

The rebuilt Georgian colonial looked exactly as it had the first time he'd visited, but everything felt different now. The afternoon sun painted the red brick walls gold, and the rolling Kentucky hills stretched away in all directions under a sky so blue he squinted.

He walked up the front steps to the porch. Through the tall windows, he could see the Fishers sitting around the dining room table. Five adults who looked nothing alike and everything alike at the same time. Jason's sharp angles and dark hair. Bruce's quieter presence and artist's hands.

Dylan's softer features and nervous energy. Kevin's height and easy smile. Maureen's delicate bone structure and expressive hands.

The front door opened before he could knock.

"Michael." Jason stepped onto the porch, closing the door behind him. He looked ten years younger than he had three months ago. "Thanks for coming."

"How are they adjusting?"

Jason ran a hand through his hair which meant he was processing something complicated. "Dylan cried for two hours yesterday. Not sad crying. Happy crying. He kept saying he remembered the sound of my voice reading him stories."

Through the window, Flint watched as one of the twins gestured animatedly while telling some story that had the other twin, Maureen, and Bruce doubled over with laughter.

"That's Kevin doing all the talking. He's been asking about everything. What Dad was like. What happened to our old toys. Whether I remember him trying to climb the oak tree behind the house." Jason's voice caught slightly. "I do remember. I remember all of it."

Maureen got up from the table and disappeared into the kitchen. A moment later she returned with a fresh pot of coffee, pouring refills for her brothers. Bruce said something that made Dylan laugh so hard he nearly spilled his coffee.

"And Maureen?"

"She's the caretaker. Always has been, apparently. Keeps trying to mother all of us." Jason smiled. "Yesterday she made me eat lunch because she said I looked thin."

Flint's phone buzzed. He glanced at the screen. A news alert about Devon Cole's death in federal custody. He'd died under suspicious circumstances three weeks after he was arrested. An investigation into his death finished up today, but the official story remained unchanged. Suicide. No foul play suspected.

"You see the news?" Jason asked, noticing Flint's expression.

"Yeah." Flint pocketed the phone. "You surprised?"

"No. Men like Cole don't live long enough to face trial. Too many secrets. Too many people who need those secrets buried." Jason leaned against the porch railing. "I've been buying up his businesses. Every legitimate company he owned. By next month, I'll own his entire empire."

"What's your plan? Keep the profitable, legitimate businesses and liquidate the others?" Flint asked.

"Probably. I'll need to get an army of forensic accountants to analyze it all. Then I'll decide what to do." Jason paused. "Strange thing is, I don't feel as satisfied as I thought I would."

"Justice isn't always satisfying," Flint said with a shrug as he glanced inside again.

Dylan was showing Kevin something on his phone. Probably photos of his life in Portland. Kevin nodded enthusiastically, pointing at the screen and asking questions Flint couldn't hear. Brothers catching up on more than twenty years of separation in a few hours of conversation.

"What about Lizzy?" Jason asked.

"Federal marshals delivered her yesterday. New identity, new life somewhere safe. She'll testify when they need her, but mostly she just wants to disappear."

"She saved our lives."

"She did. More than once."

"What about the woman who died in the bus accident?" Jason asked. "Were you able to identify her and notify her family?"

Flint shook his head. "Not yet. We exhumed the body and collected DNA. No match so far. We moved her to a private cemetery. When we find her family, they'll be able to visit her grave, at least."

For a few moments they stood in comfortable silence, watching the afternoon shadows lengthen across the hills. Inside, Maureen was cutting slices from what looked like a homemade apple pie, distributing them with the same careful attention she'd given the coffee.

"Your mother around?" Flint asked.

"Resting. This has been overwhelming for her. Good overwhelming, but still..." Jason shrugged. "She keeps touching their faces, like she can't believe they're real."

Flint understood. After years of grief, joy could be just as difficult to process as sorrow.

"What about Drake? Is he okay?" Jason asked.

Flint grinned. "Drake's as tough as woodpecker lips, as my friend Kim Otto would say."

"And you?" Jason asked.

Flint arched his eyebrows. "What about me?"

"You could retire, you know. The fee I paid you could buy a small country. And I'd happily pay more, if you'll take it," Jason said.

Flint looked through the window one more time. Dylan was showing Kevin how to use an app on his phone. Maureen was laughing at something one of them had said. Bruce seemed to bask in the glow of it all. Jason was about to rejoin the family he'd thought was lost forever.

"This is what I do," Flint said simply. "I wouldn't know how to live without my work."

Jason nodded, understanding. "Thank you, Michael. For all of it."

"Take care of yourselves."

"We will."

Flint walked back to his car, listening to the sound of family voices growing fainter behind him. By the time he reached the gravel driveway, he was already thinking about his next case. Which he couldn't begin until he took Maddy and Whiskers to Disney World again. Scarlett had refused, and Maddy was a typically persistent seven-year-old.

The work never ended. But sometimes, like today, it ended well.

ABOUT THE AUTHOR

Diane Capri is an award-winning *New York Times*, *USA Today*, and worldwide bestselling author. She's a recovering lawyer and snowbird who divides her time between Florida and Michigan. An active member of Mystery Writers of America, Author's Guild, International Thriller Writers, Alliance of Independent Authors, Novelists, Inc., and Sisters in Crime, she loves to hear from readers. She is hard at work on her next novel.

Please connect with her online:
http://www.DianeCapri.com
X: https://x.com/DianeCapri
Facebook: http://www.facebook.com/Diane.Capri1
http://www.facebook.com/DianeCapriBooks
Instagram: https://www.Instagram.com/dianecapri/

www.ingramcontent.com/pod-product-compliance
Lightning Source LLC
Chambersburg PA
CBHW031242310726